LISTEN CLOSELY . . .

At this hour, trains were scarce, and the platform was crowded with late-night carousers. The heat and the rumbling of the traffic aboveground made him think of purgatory. Lane pressed his temple to the cold column to relieve the nascent headache. And he heard the chanting.

It was the same black beggar, right behind him, winking and murmuring Tune Ra's chorus.

Is he stalking me? Lane tried to move away, but there was no room . . . Suddenly the beggar's voice changed.

As he pressed forward, breathing down Lane's neck, he did not sound postmodern ironic like Tune Ra—no, he sounded more like a Buddhist monk, his voice rising menacingly from the pit of his stomach.

Feverishly, Lane began chanting *pkhat*—anything to block his mind from this voice.

The beggar's whispering went faster, his voice getting lower, now penetrating beyond Lane's ears—it seemed to be getting through the marrow of his bone. His vision blurred, objects swam; the only things he could look at were the rails below. They were a cool silvery stream, the only relief from the sticky, stinky cocoon that was enveloping him.

THE
MANTRA

DMITRY RADYSHEVSKY

Translated by DAVID GUREVICH

JOVE BOOKS, NEW YORK

THE MANTRA

A Jove Book / published by arrangement with the author

PRINTING HISTORY
Jove edition / December 2002

Copyright © 2002 by Dmitry Radyshevsky
The poems on pages 100 and 102 appear courtesy of their author, Elena Po.
Cover art by The Complete Artworks Ltd.
Cover design by Jill Boltin
Book design by Julie Rogers

Visit our website at
www.penguinputnam.com

ISBN: 0-515-13433-3

A JOVE BOOK®
Jove Books are published
by The Berkley Publishing Group,
a division of Penguin Putnam Inc.,
375 Hudson Street, New York, New York 10014.
JOVE and the "J" design
are trademarks belonging to Penguin Putnam Inc.

PRINTED IN THE UNITED STATES OF AMERICA

10 9 8 7 6 5 4 3 2 1

Book One

NEW YORK

1

RUDI Paxton was trying to achieve the impossible: concentrate amid the chaos of DeoMorte, Manhattan's trendiest nightclub. Fidgeting uncomfortably on the floor, he took out a diary he had bought earlier that day in a Tibetan store on lower Broadway and caressed the grayish rice paper. He hesitated before making the first entry. To have black ink spurt out of a Japanese-made pen, like venom out of a snake. Is that what the words of the mantra were—venom?

The book had 108 pages, one for Buddha's every sutra, for every level of wisdom. Then what? Once you reach the back cover, there will be a pause, when you forget everything you have ever learned. Then what—do you start all over again?

As a graduate student at Columbia University's School of Religion, he thought a rock'n'roll mass at a former church would make a good opening for his thesis: the sweet pot smoke for incense, rave music for a hymn. The clergy was clad in traditional black, and a nude Madonna danced onstage. In fact, these priests were relatively ascetic, confining themselves to beer and cigarettes—a modern communion. What mattered was the quest for something superior, something hidden, among the regulars. The method of the quest might change, but its essence remained the same. . . .

Downstairs, the crowd was a bubbling black cauldron of tightly packed bodies; the primordial muck, waiting obediently for Creation to begin. His ears made out a low-pitched humming sound that was going up in volume and stridency by the second. At the farther end of the room, where an altar had once stood, a white point of light flashed and began to expand into a purple beam, then into a blue one. The humming grew in sync, turning into a roar, just as the beam flickered green—yellow—orange. Suddenly, the entire cathedral was enveloped in raspberry-tinted light. The DJ climbed to the altar and hollered into the mike. His words—the Word, Rudi thought—were indistinct and meaningless, but the crowd recognized them instantly and echoed them in a joyous roar, rocking to the beat.

The party was on. The DJ was spinning house-music CDs, one faster than the other, interspersing them with standard club patter; but no remark evoked the crowd reaction as much as the Word did, and somehow he sneaked it into every phrase.

A black man in rags was dancing nearby, wielding his artificial leg adroitly, crying out the Word, drooling with anticipation. He leaned over: "Whatcha writin'? You a writer? From the *Voice*?"

Rudi shook his head. Was he the only one who knew that the gibberish spouted by the DJ was actually full of meaning? But to him, too, its exact meaning was still a mystery.

2

THE party was to go on till dawn. He still had time to reflect on what had brought him to DeoMorte. Where it all had started. The point of departure was the Word.

IT was still warm in mid-October. Seated next to an open window in class, Rudi could inhale the breeze coming in from the Hudson, which made him think of Columbia as the Island of Contemplation in the Sea of Action. If Manhattan could be thought of as the sea.

"Technology and human psyche develop in opposite directions," Professor Schechter said. "If you have a telephone, what do you need telepathy for?"

Schechter was immensely popular at the school, and his lectures on Tibetan mantras were standing room only.

"Literally, *mantra* means 'mind liberation,' " the professor went on, "but it started out as a simple incantation. Mantras go back to Rigveda, 3000 B.C. Ancient Aryans believed that a sacrifice accompanied by a proper hymn has magic powers. Actually, they were not far off: a sound is a vibration, and a human body—like any other object—can be represented as an electric circuit. Certain sounds will make the circuit vibrate with a frequency that will, in turn, produce certain physical reactions. Besides, if repeated often, these sound waves will deposit themselves in the human unconscious and create a certain behavioral pattern—"

Professor Schechter's round, meaty face, framed with a few clumps of gray hair upswept on his bald top, suggested an aging opera singer, though his abundant freckles gave him a patina of youth. Sometimes his barrage of paradoxes and references to mathematics and philosophy made one think of the Greeks; at other times, implicit verities delivered with a patient smile evoked a Chinese Buddha; and a touch of self-irony reminded one of a shtetl rebbe. In fact, that was what they called him, "the Tibetan Rabbi." Lately, he was not his ebullient self; though still spouting erudite jokes, he fatigued easily and had to sit down more often.

"We are dealing with mantras every day," he went on. "Identical words uttered by a group of people united towards a single objective are considered a mantra, and it does not have to be in Sanskrit. *'Liberté, Égalité, Fraternité'*—isn't that a political mantra? How about 'Four More Years'? What do you think brought down the walls of Jericho? A battle mantra, cried out in perfect sync by thousands of voices! Give me an example of another famous historical mantra. Rudi!"

Rudi thought for a moment. "The mantra of confession: Our Lord Jesus—"

In the audience, someone snickered. Schechter raised his eyebrows. "I thought you'd give us an example from your theory."

Rudi lowered his eyes, avoiding the students' looks of surprise. His heart fell: yes, the professor had taken a look at his proposal—and now he seemed to be making fun of it.

But Schechter was already racing ahead, on to the lecture's main subject: the Bon mantras.

"The Bon school brought together the local tribes' shamanism and the psychic practices of Tantric Buddhism. In the hands of a lama who knows how to enunciate it correctly, a Bon Po mantra can become a murder tool. Once uttered, an invocation causes an internal hemorrhage in a victim, who dies without any outward signs."

Even now Rudi remembered the aah's and ooh's in the auditorium. The professor was generous with his thespian talents, turning an esoteric subject into a campfire ghost story. His favorite trick was luring his students with a specific example and then roasting them on a slow fire of theory.

"Many travelers report that in certain remote Bon areas, mantras are used as a method of execution. Shaman lamas—*nagpa*s in Bon Po—tie the accused to a pole, then take seats in a circle around him and begin chanting the mantra in a chorus. After a certain time, the man goes into convulsions; gradually, he loses his mind and dies."

Rudi's mind wandered. What about the tie between the habit and the inexplicable guilt—the tie that kept him in a personal relationship—the tie that was gradually driving him crazy with never-ending babbling and convulsions of quarrels? Could it work the other way? Could the mantras—his theory—be the tool to cut him loose?

3

AFTER the lecture, while other students peppered Schechter with questions, Rudi, as a teaching assistant, took his time collecting the handouts from the desks. He was looking forward to walking Schechter to the professor's apartment on West 79th Street—a small perk that went with being a pet student.

In fact, he owed Schechter for both getting into the school and obtaining a study grant. Somehow, among many graduate-school applications, the professor had managed to notice an essay written by a Rudi Paxton, an obscure poet–guitar player who tried to prove that many rock'n'roll compositions are based on the principles of *pujah*, the Tibetan Buddhist service.

WHERE did *that* come from? Like any fourteen-year-old in the Bay Area, Rudi Paxton wanted to be the Greatest Living Rock Poet in the tradition of John Lennon and Jim Morrison. High school, followed by community college, was incidental; most of his time was spent on Holy Grail, his rock band. Perhaps it was a scientific bent he inherited from his father, a research chemist, that turned his mind elsewhere. Onstage, whenever certain solo guitar riffs were being played, Rudi, helped by a tab of acid, felt his body vibrate. His fingernails, his teeth, his knees were humming; he felt a tickling in his chest, a pulsing in his throat. He knew that his audience sensed it, too; they plunged into a trance when he was playing the chorus, when he relied on the raw power of combinations of sounds rather than on the meaning of the lyrics.

It was when they opened at Joey's GoGo, the rock'n'roll Mecca of the future Silicon Valley, that Rudi first felt he was dealing with real power—the power of music wedded to words.

Anybody who ever stood next to a giant speaker at a rock concert knows the feeling: like a SWAT team, the pulsating beat knocks down the eardrums and bursts into your bloodstream. Within seconds, it turns your blood into a searing red wave and drives it down your body. Resisting is futile: the simultaneous rush to death and joy overtakes every cell of your body—your eyes, swelling with madness; your brain screaming; your fingers itching; your chest humming; your arms shooting up mechanically. The beat stays with you long after you leave the arena, just as a fear of touching your primeval self flashes through your heart. Your body has learned the joy and the horror of serving a different master; instead of obeying your mind, it was controlled solely by the beat and the sound.

Soon, it was not enough. Yes, Rudi could put the audience in a trance sufficient to make their legs jerk and their arms shoot up; but he could never tug at the string in their hearts—to awaken a state of endless love, of burning out and giving themselves away. The problem was with the lyrics, he thought; or, more precisely, with the chorus. "Meaningful" poetry did not fit into the Procrustean bed of rock'n'roll; in fact, it distracted the audience by making them think and thus broke the spell of instant ecstasy.

You could not come up with a "killer chorus" by mere contemplation. It had to be lured out of its secret lair. You had to pretend you were not looking for it. You had to shut off your logical side, to relax your strained brain muscles.

Acid helped, of course. And then there was access to his father's lab. Soon the Grailers branched out into mixing their own hallucinogens. That did not work out too well: their drummer Greg tried to ride his bike, à la Evel Knievel, onto the back of a flatbed truck and ended up in a hospital with a few limbs smashed. Rudi got off with doing community service with Hmong refugees.

And this was the seemingly uncomplicated path that led him to a concert of Tibetan music.

A well-meaning social worker wangled a few freebie tickets for refugees, "to ease the pangs of separation" and blah-blah-blah, as Rudi recalled. Well, he was the one with the driver's license; would he mind driving his wards to the Broken Valley Community College. Hey, no sweat. Driving is what a California boy does best.

THE choir consisted of four lamas: squat middle-aged men in identical purple togas, their skin dried to the light brown of ginseng root. They carried four long copper horns onstage, erected them on wooden frames, donned yellow toques, pumped their cheeks, and pressed their lips to their instruments. Instinctively, Rudi closed his eyes, hoping it would be like sitting in a dark movie theater, listening to the soundtrack, free to see your own film.

The very first sound seemed to come not from the horns,

but, rather, from the throat of the horizon that suddenly opened above the ocean. Rudi saw the sky being born over the night sea: a reddish purple streak of sunrise—the blood of the dark giving birth to the light. Pushing the dark aside, the light burst into a primordial scream of birth, long and resounding.

His skin broke into goose bumps; ripples skipped along the water's surface. Somewhere at the deepest bottom, in the very Adam's apple of the horns, a sound was ripening. The note grew, like the black eye of the tsunami; it swelled as it ascended from the darkness into the light—until it exploded onto the surface in a gigantic triumphant storm wave—the heaving funnel of the Horn through which the monks blew their souls into the sky!

Like a squall, the Horn loomed on the horizon; like a nuclear mushroom, it expanded. Its sound spread through Rudi's stomach and chest; its vibrating light suffocated him, filling every cavity of his body. Finally, he blew up like an overpumped ball, soared into the space above the ocean, and throbbed against the firmament, swelling and pushing the firmament higher and higher. Rudi's whole essence was screaming out in this impossible ascent.

Suddenly, another horn, sharp and vicious, broke in; for a moment, Rudi froze on the edge with surprise, and then tumbled down, back inside the Horn. It was as if, awakened by the invasion of the sound, the forces of heaven and hell joined in an effort to squash him. A new strident, penetrating sound led these avenging forces; unlike the previous one, it pushed you down, it made the mountains collapse on top of you. Your fall gathered momentum as you sped into the black maw of the funnel expanding below. Stage by stage, terrace by terrace, the solemn menacing sound pressed you down, squeezing the life out of your every limb. Finally it zeroed down on the last spark of life in your body. It gasped for the last time and put the spark out.

The horns fell silent. Rudi was in a daze. In the silence, his head was spinning. His body was electrified and weightless. The myriad tingling sounds were still roaming through his body.

He knew he had found what he had been looking for in

rock'n'roll. These sounds tugged at the string in his heart and made it pop. In just a few moments he visited the acme of bliss and the impenetrable chasm of fear. Without a single toke or the tiniest stereo speaker. "Girl, we couldn't get much higher. . . ." Jim, what did you know?

Rudi could barely open his eyes as the monks set their horns aside and started chanting.

HIS first sensation was this: he did not understand the language, but he knew right away that this was what they spoke at his real homeland. This is what they speak in the sky where no language is needed. This is what the clouds say, and so do the rocks, and his late grandfather, who had passed away a month earlier. The incomprehensible words contained an ascent to the Himalayas—not the physical ones, but the Himalayas of the spirit, with their peaks and valleys. Unlike an ascent in a piece by Bach—a mournful procession of a widow in the wake of the funeral—this one was voiced by the sherpas who helped her along: it was solitary and surefooted, unhurried and focused, deliberate and monklike silent, leading to a new vista after every turn.

Tibetan mantras were perfect rock'n'roll. They needed no guitar solos, no drums, no synthesizers. They had a beat and a tonality; their syllables, though uttered in an unfamiliar language, were selected in a mysterious way that ensured they would be imprinted in your memory. You needed no ear for music to reproduce them; but the moment they sounded in your head, you returned into the unknown throbbing element provided by the given mantra.

Rudi needed to know the sacred symbols that underlay the monks' wondrous choruses; he needed to merge them into his music. He bought a manual, and a Tibetan dictionary in order to decode the mantras.

The deeper he immersed himself, the less he felt like going back to jam with Greg and Alex. Rudi was officially, and somewhat immodestly, renamed Rudra, one of the appellations of the future Buddha, the King of Shambala. Drugs were gone, too, replaced by meditation. He discovered that spirit needed no artificial "uplift." You needed no pills or weed; mere desire for knowledge and the will to focus could get you into the world that no acid ever could.

The old Rudi was dead, but the new one was not born yet. He was in Bardo, as Tibetans call the transitional state of consciousness. His mother's death made transition even harder. Trying to make a break with his old life, he sent an application to Columbia. Although expository writing had never been his forte, he hunkered down to put together an essay, which was subsequently singled out by Schechter.

Led by the professor's gentle hand, he moved through the alluring, mysterious labyrinth of Buddhist teaching that branched out like the corridors of Potala, the Dalai Lama's thousand-room mansion. Its air was thick with incense, exotic sounds, frightening demons, the seductive expectation of miracles, and the blissful rest of enlightenment. Like in the Himalayas, the further you climbed, the more dazzling the vistas you saw ahead.

He was expected to graduate with a master's next spring. He planned to enter the Ph.D. program, which would allow him to stay with Schechter for another five years. For Rudi, the professor was not a mere educator, but a guide in the maze, where the end promised a final confluence of theory and practice he had been searching for since childhood.

A week earlier he had handed in the topic of his doctorate: "The Nonsense That Liberates the Mind: The Mantric Principle in Rock Music Choruses."

Through the years of Rudi's studies, the idea of the mantras, the energy compressed into words, evolved from mere fascination with their effects (just as in the professor's little anecdote for his audience) to a search for their creative mechanisms. A person does not organize his innermost desires into coherent speech, Rudi argued; rather, voiced in the most heartbreaking moments of love or grief, they come out in mumbling, muttering interjections, or plain nonsense. However, certain people become the mouthpieces of common secret desires of their social, ethnic, or age groups. In the past, this function was performed by priests or shamans; nowadays, it is the rock musicians who fill the need. Like their predecessors, they do not convey the most profound aspirations of their flock in a coherent language; rather, these take the form of shouting and nonsensical song choruses. They are the new mantras, born, Rudi wrote, in the same way the old ones were: like bubbles of disjointed syllables rising to the top of a brewing cauldron.

Now, as he walked with the professor in Riverside Park, he waited nervously for Schechter's verdict. He sought approval, but he sought the money even more: could he get a grant, as large as possible? The reason was personal, and he would rather die of shame than reveal it to the professor.

The professor took his time, listing the proposal's pluses in a pedantic fashion. Yes, it was interesting that, according to the author, the best of the '60s and '70s rock was based on the tonalities of sacred Tibetan music; that talented musicians subconsciously employed sacred vibrations to awaken centers of human energy; that the link between rock'n'roll and Tibetan theology is akin to the one between classical music and Christianity. But the main idea, the unconscious mantra-making in pop culture, was perhaps too vague. . . .

Rudi froze in his tracks.

"Don't get me wrong," Schechter said. "In principle, I approve. What worries me is your ferocity: it is as if you made this some kind of a stake in a bet. Some kind of all-or-nothing deal."

Not for nothing did Rudi consider Schechter his guru: the professor saw right through him. He needed a grant, he confessed. A big one. To go to Tibet for a year. "To learn the language," he lied.

Schechter paused, looking upset. "But it's easier to stay here and learn it with me. What's the rush? You have a whole semester ahead of you."

"I need to know now. If I don't get it, I'll have to get the money in some other way."

Schechter sighed. "I could probably help you with at least a part of it. I am on the board of a new fund, Pop Culture Theories. I could push your project, but first it needs to be fleshed out. You must get more specific. For example, the genesis of a chorus in a rock song. This might be a grain of sand around which you can cultivate your pearl. Then again, it might not."

4

RUDI roamed through New York's record stores, from Tower to Disc-o-mat, listening to new rock hits. He could not recognize "the scene": so much junk had come out while he was lost in his mantras. His ears were hurting from the weight of the headsets; but nothing fit the bill. Finally, he got lucky—or so he thought then.

It was Halloween night, and Columbia celebrated the old pagan rite with a vengeance. Rudi had just left the library and was watching from the top of the stairs. Amid the motley crowd that gathered in the center of the campus, the theology postgraduates stood out, costumed with a dash of their chosen field: Franciscans, Hasids, Jesuses, lamas, dervishes, and assorted ghost monks.

At the bottom of the stairs, a rock band swayed robotlike to a primal beat, seducing the crowd to jerk and twist in sync. Their red-and-black Satanic outfits stood out against the yellow bricks of the pavement, the multicolored crowd, and the golden autumn foliage, accented by the floodlights. Reinforced by the speakers next to him, the syllables of the lyrics hit him straight in the solar plexus.

He pricked up his ears. He could never make out the rap lyrics, but one word stood out, striking in its nonsensicality. He tensed, sensing he was on to something, when suddenly someone's arms came around him from the back and a mouth planted a kiss on his neck. It was her smell—her lips! They had just had a fight; and there she was, making the move to make up—something she had never done before.

This was how the mantra came to him: in a thrill of discovery, in a mix of joy and despair, for none of their reconciliations lasted. Now he turned around, grabbed her in his arms, and danced with her. All the good times came back to him; yes, they had their problems, but they could, they should work them out.

They drew attention; a good-looking couple woven into a seamless yin-and-yang entity: Rudi, with his long blond mane, in a bright orange shirt, and Gwen, alluring in a black turtleneck, cowboy boots, and tight black jeans. Above it all, like a white fret on a violin's black body, was her finely chiseled head with tiny black curls and the huge black eyes, solemn and grave, that he loved getting lost in.

Finally, gasping, Rudi yelled out the inane chorus for the last time and headed towards the stage. "I need to know who wrote this."

"You don't know?" Gwen grinned. "You never heard of Tune Ra? This is his latest."

Of course: a journalism major, Gwen was on top of every musical novelty. Tune Ra, a brand-new MTV personality, a white rapper-cum-DJ and the host of *Tune Ra's Tuneup*, the show that systematically slew the competition in the ratings.

"What was the word, the chorus?"

She shrugged. "He puts it into every song and public appearance. It's like Beavis's *heh-heh*. It's like a new mantra for teenagers."

"Mantra, huh." Rudi gave her a deep kiss. "Thanks."

Inwardly, he shuddered: Thanks for what? For helping me shake myself free of you?

Immediately, he chased the thought away. As they walked home to West 100th, he babbled on about taking this sand grain of a chorus and growing it into a pearl of wisdom. His thoughts danced, and Broadway seemed like an endless flute; the wind from the river blew through the streets, and he, the musician, was wielding it to produce the first notes of a solemn and somewhat menacing hymn to the universe, and to his faith in himself. For he, a bass guitar in a garage band and a mere postgraduate student, was going to do something that no one had ever done before. He was going to bring together theology and rock'n'roll!

Halfway home, his fervor began to fade: Gwen was not adding to the fire. Like most of his enthusiasms, the theory went nowhere with her; the physical dance was over, and the dance of ideas was something she had always eyed warily. He fell silent, angry at their recurring failure to connect; then he was angry at himself for being critical of her. It's not me, it's my mind, he thought, but it did not help. She sensed his resentment and grew silent, too. They came home the way they always did after parties—exhausted by each other's company.

5

RUDI and Gwen met when they were teenagers. They had a tumultuous relationship, abundant with breakups and reconciliations. When he was accepted by Columbia, he hesitated before inviting her to come along. A part of him wanted her to; but another part was daunted by the logistics of the move—after all, her ambition was to become a reporter, something that might not happen right away in the pressure cooker of New York media—and how much support, both financial and emotional, could she get from a graduate student? Sensing his hesitation, she burst out in tears and slammed the door on him.

Gwen stayed in the Bay Area, taking classes and writing short pieces for small papers. But her affection for him lingered; she missed him badly—and then she wrote him.

Her timing was good. For a few weeks, Rudi's spirits had sagged. Buddhist teaching seemed like a lot of vacuous intellectualizing. Nothing could keep the ghost of loneliness at bay. Once again, he came to think he could not live without her. He did not merely respond; he began bombarding her with letters and phone calls, he made friends with people at Columbia's School of Journalism, he persuaded her to send in an application. It seemed to him that by sheer will-power he forced the Fates to have Gwen accepted at Columbia.

In order to set the two of them up in an apartment, he

took a part-time job in the library and talked Schechter into
hiring him as an assistant. He wrote his school papers at
night and subsisted on macaroni and cheese.

Finally, she arrived. At first, they were in a world of their
own, blissful together in an exciting city. Rudi was bursting
with enthusiasm as he played the guide, from the Cloisters
to the Staten Island Ferry—long, exhausting tours that
ended at East Village clubs and heated, fierce lovemaking.
Yet the bliss did not last. Within days, they were fighting
again.

As a former musician, he found it easier to conceptualize
their discord by comparing them to musical instruments.
Gwen was a violin: nervous, tender, sensitive, full of compassion, one who had an uncanny feeling for the taut string
of the truth in every given issue.

He was a horn: the power of its sound, sometimes weeping, sometimes furious, depended on what flowed into it
plus a superb control over the purity of this flow.

Their life together was a duet, abounding in counterpoints
of misunderstanding, exaggerated claims, and disaffection—
but also tenderness, passion, and jealousy. Gwen was often
resentful of Rudi's female classmates, susceptible to his
good looks and charm, and the most innocent bit of flirtation
on his part would set her off. In these fits, she accused him
of being "no more Buddhist than the rockers" he disdained,
that he was a mere follower of "Tibetan shtick and Hollywood Buddhism: mantras'n'models."

Wounded by her words, Rudi shut himself in and threw
himself into his studies, trying to be more ascetic than a
medieval monk. Then Gwen came to understand that the
true object of her jealousy was his mysticism—what Buddhism refers to as "the vision of Emptiness." With her perfect female intuition, she realized that Rudi was no monk,
that he had academic vanity, to say nothing of physical joys,
including their bed. Yet there were moments, especially
when he was sticking to his meditation schedule or got carried away with another crackpot idea, like this rap mantra,
when Gwen saw him as being truly close to his ideals. At
these times, he seemed to lose his physical shell, becoming
a pure spirit, pale in appearance. As such, he needed no

woman; he seemed to put up with her out of habit, or because he was afraid of breaking up and causing her pain. At moments like these he seemed to see her as a sister and a comrade-in-arms, but certainly not as a lover or—down the road—a wife.

Once, as they were lying in bed, she asked, "If you had a choice between being deaf and impotent, which would you choose?"

"Impotence, of course," he said seriously. "Then you can still be a great mystic and listen to the divine sounds."

Gwen took it in stride, but she was still jealous of Rudi's knowledge and fearful that he would leave her all-too-real love for the ethereal, hyper-real one. He was aware of her fears, which she shared with perfectly pitched violinlike sincerity. Their year together was filled with love and intimacy—but also disharmony.

How can a true Buddhist be a family man? he tormented himself. How is it compatible with being a mystic—a yogi—an Enlightened One? If one considers that the quarrels, reconciliations, and mutual torment took place in a tiny studio, in a postage stamp–sized space between their cluttered desks and the bed . . . it was hard for Rudi not to see his existence as a trap. But he found it difficult to discuss all of this with her, afraid of losing her.

But should he break free?

The simplest and noblest thing he could think of was getting hold of a lot of money. He would give the whole sum to Gwen, so that she could stay at school—but he would leave for Tibet. He would escape to the Roof of the World.

But it would take money to make this simple and noble escape a reality. This was where the grant came in. The mantra was a gift from the Buddhas and Boddhisattvas. All that was left to do was to include it in the thesis and hope that Schechter could persuade the committee to approve it.

6

EVERY Tune Ra song included the mysterious chorus refrain. Promoted incessantly by MTV, the chorus became a brand product, a popular mantra for youth. It seemed as though, in the absence of a good voice and any degree of originality in the music or the lyrics, this nonsense alone accounted for his success. The more Rudi listened, the more he doubted his theory: the chorus was gibberish, a nonsensical combination of syllables. But how could millions of young people who were echoing it be saying, in effect, nothing? The mantras of classic rock contained a call for freedom, revolution, nonconformity. . . . Was Tune Ra a pure nothing—a PR-aided expression of Generation X's mindlessness?

Judging by the pictures hourly beamed at the audiences, Tune Ra was a typical MTV "personality," which in itself was a perfect oxymoron. He could be twenty-five or thirty-five; he could be a man or a woman. His numerous rings, his long colorless hair, his clothes, his features revealed no clues to his age or gender.

"A good DJ must sense the audience's emotional field and turn it around," Tune Ra orated on a late-night show. "You have to harvest the energy from the dance floor and toss it back. I love playing with energy: the bigger the crowd, the higher the adrenaline level, the higher I get. Rave culture is the highest union of the DJ and his crowd."

His every phrase was accompanied by the Word. But what he or his fans invested in it was still a mystery to Rudi. To him it meant nothing but the embodied chaos of the video-clip culture; he, too, was a child of it, but the more he watched, the more irritated he became.

Buddhism taught that a given negative emotion is a habit of the mind, but that did not help. A glance at Tune Ra's and others' clips, unburdened with any evidence of rational thought, produced a picture of a culture polluted by video clips. Rudi felt like a biologist who watches the dance of myriad bacteria in the microscope in a cold, uninvolved fashion; then he would wash this liquid off the glass, having distilled the drop needed for his experiment.

The trouble was that he could not distill the drop.

He tried to meditate while listening on his headset. According to his theory, the chorus of rock mantras had to contain a subliminal suggestion; perhaps his consciousness prevented him from understanding it. He squatted on the floor and rubbed a gray sweet-smelling powder between his eyes. The powder was a gift from Schechter—the ashes of a famous Rinpoche, or a Venerable Lama, who had initiated Schechter into Buddhism. After the Rinpoche was executed and his body was burned by the Chinese, his ashes were smuggled to the West and, according to the Rinpoche's will, delivered to Schechter.

Schechter told Rudi that, if a follower rubs the remnants of his late teacher in the area of his "third eye" and then concentrates on this organ of clairvoyance in the course of meditation, he will see his late guru and hear his advice and predictions. It's like marking a target, Rudi thought, so the holy spirit does not miss.

Yet, whenever he immersed himself in a meditative calm, then turned on a Tune Ra song and focused on the chorus, its sound caused him nothing but further irritation, like a turbid wave ripping through a mirror-perfect surface. Most jarringly, the wave lingered after he turned off the sound, as if it were prodding him to take his irritation out on someone or something.

It was during one of his listening sessions that he got into an argument with a neighbor, a young computer programmer; Rudi knocked on his door and asked him to turn down his TV. In turn, he was told to buzz off. . . .

But the primary target of his irritation was Gwen. As never before, Rudi was tormented by the size of their apartment. The amount of money is in inverse ratio to the decibels around you, he thought in despair; the richer a person, the quieter his environment. Everything irritated him: the

TV that Gwen watched with her headset on (the sound
seeped through anyway); the radio, her chatting on the
phone. These sounds of civilization collided with the chorus
on which he was trying to focus and added to his irritation.
He felt like tossing these "journalistic implements" out of
the window. But he knew she needed them for her courses,
as well as for her job, writing pieces against workfare for
free downtown papers. "At least I'm doing something for
the people," she would say, "instead of working on this
mystic hype."

Mystic hype? They had two desks; he took the one at the
mirror, ceding her the better one, at the window. In the
evening, he would stare at his reflection, and, instead of
focusing on Tune Ra's chorus or his thesis, he thought of
one thing only: *Escape.* As he listened to the tape, he stared
at the computer screen with his unseeing eyes: he could not
figure out how to talk to her. They needed to go their separate ways. He wanted to make her happy; instead, he
brought her nothing but bickering and pain. He loved her
so much, yet he had to cut himself out of her life, like a
tumor, and flee this cell. Close quarters and the inevitable
noise exist only up to a certain poverty level. Beyond it
comes the absolute silence of savages and monks. The lux-
urious quiet of the rich was beyond his reach. But the
blessed silence of poverty was another thing. Like the one
in Tibet . . .

Can one be happy among this cacophony? As he listened
to Tune Ra's wailing, he wondered if it held true for all
urban couples, even with both partners financially indepen-
dent of each other. Their relations were so far removed from
freedom, from free will, that the only way to stay in them
was to bend, to adapt to this complicated construction. Escape seemed the only way to clear the boards.

*One thing is notable: the emotional energy I have in-
vested in acquiring Gwen's company equals the energy I
am expending now trying to get rid of her,* he wrote in his
diary. *It seems like a case of Newton's Third,* Action Equals
Counteraction, *that applies to all areas: nature, history, human relations. First comes the acquisition effort; then, the
disquisition. This is, then, the precious drop of Knowledge:
Thou Shalt Not Wish.*

7

THAT was it. He was done with this nonsense. Disgusted, Rudi had to concede that his theory was built on sand. It was kind of Schechter to go along, but the chorus was no new mantra. Of course he could dress up this gibberish as "a socioanalysis of music among urban youth subculture." He knew the lingo, and there was more than one foundation that went out of its way trying to be trendy and showering money on hustlers posing as scientists. But he would not stoop to that.

Yet the more clearly he realized it, the more irritated he was at the whole system that encouraged this nonsense, and the more tempted he was to take full advantage of it: to cook up a thesis, to give Gwen the money, and to escape to Tibet. Away from fake theories and complicated relationships—on to genuine nature and true faith.

And so he went on tinkering with the mantra.

He broke it into syllables, as far as he could make them out. Suddenly he noticed that the first one, which he had originally taken to be simply Tune Ra's panting, sounded close to *hum*. A mystic battle cry in Tibetan Buddhism . . . but what was the battle?

Perhaps he could introduce "mantric classification of the chorus based on the breathing rhythm"? Tune Ra had a broken, raplike breathing rhythm. On the other hand, different emotional and mental conditions correspond to different breathing rhythms, which are combined in mantras. He could start by proposing that in Buddhism certain sounds corresponded to certain psychic and mechanical energies, and there are so-called root sounds capable of putting a person in contact with these energies. These sounds are passed in secret from teacher to student; they can be of various kinds and used to different ends. On lower levels of consciousness, one can use a combination of certain sounds to contact certain forces in order to achieve extraordinary effects. Some mantras can kill within minutes, with death accompanied by horrible vomiting; other mantras are used for curing, for causing a fire, for placing a curse, or protecting against one.

When he realized that another syllable in Tune Ra's chorus was *ram,* an odd thought flashed through his mind: the chorus was calling him into battle. How could he have missed that!

In Tibetan Buddhism, *ram* was a root syllable of fire. These mystical syllables were considered not a mere combination of letters, but a verbalized expression of the essence of things, of their concentrated energy. It took a Tibetan wizard a correct combination of breathing, rhythm, and tonality to evoke the hidden power of these syllables. And, above all, a correct visualization. For example, a lama who knew how to create a mental image of *ram*—not the fire, but the syllable itself—could ignite any object or simply cause a fire from thin air, without any fuel.

Yet even if the chorus contained *hum* and *ram,* it was not vibrating any roots. Tune Ra is a pure theological charlatan, Rudi thought in despair. Vibration is essential to mantras. Each mantra induces in the listener, and especially in the chanter, a certain humming that in turn causes a certain mood.

For comparison, Rudi listened again to his favorite Tibetan mantras. Here was one, where a student offers his ego to the teacher. The sensation: something heavy is lifted out of your system, producing a cleansing effect. Here's another, aimed to evoke kindness through the sound: the sensation of warm honey spreading through your chest. Here's yet another, an offer of peace: fields of flowers bloom in your head. How silly it was of Gwen to call it "a choir singing in prenatal language." Western music, even angelic church choirs, was the music of high spheres; Tibetan, the music of depths. Western music, with its sadness and joy, was one of the conscious; Buddhist was the rumbling of the subconscious, things one could not even name: the rush of blood, the noise of protoplasm. This was not the sound of music, but, rather, the sound of the world—the sound of the mountains, the trees, of every human organ: legs, arms, spleen. The sound was natural, untamed: the brewing of the cells, the humming of the blood, the din of the genes. It contained the vibrations of every object, normally inaudible, but magnified a million times by the lamas. Western music evoked emotions; Tibetan, the energies of which the emotions were made.

But Tune Ra's idiotic chorus caused nothing but irritation and resentment. Yet when Rudi decided to ditch the damn thing, it was too late. He could not shake it off. He caught himself not merely living with it, but even eating in sync with it as well: one chew, two chews, one chew again. He tried to think of other things, but whatever he did, the chorus took hold. The damn thing attached itself to the inside of his skull; it was a mote in his eye, and no matter how much he winked, it stayed there and, however microscopic, was poisoning his day-to-day existence.

It bespoke no spiritual content; rather, it compelled one thing only: an impatient desire to get rid of obstructions, to purify one's consciousness—and lead a clean life.

8

A few days later Rudi attended Schechter's Tibetan language class. As the students hunkered down at their desks with mantras to be translated, the professor carefully unwrapped a package of frayed red taffeta. He produced a thick bundle of his own tablets, yellowed with age, and started reading them to himself, silently moving his lips. After reading a mantra, he stayed immobile for a few moments with his eyes shut.

Rudi came up to check a large dictionary on the professor's desk, and, as he pored over it, he thought he heard something familiar. Had Schechter just now chanted Tune

Ra's mantra? But the professor had already turned to the next tablet.

Rudi wanted to ask, but another student was waiting for his turn. Back at his desk, he could no longer focus on the assignment. Had he actually heard it or was he losing his mind?

He could barely wait for the end of class.

YES indeed! One of the mantras Schechter had chanted sounded the same as Tune Ra's chorus. The professor's eyebrows went up in an expression of magisterial surprise.

"I borrowed these tablets from the Museum of Natural History. As an exception, mind you: they are not supposed to leave the stacks. They are not even translated. It's a unique collection, Rudi: the only copy existing in this country, if not the world. Eighteenth-century, Bon shamans of western Tibet. . . . There's a mantra I'm trying to find here. See, you repeat a mantra and listen to yourself, while I select a mantra that would fit my feelings and try to resound along with them." He waved. "Shooting fish in a barrel is what it is. A mantra cannot be effective unless you know the right tone. Your case seems interesting. So this mantra is popular among the young people?"

He read it once again, syllable by syllable.

"I see a *hum,* a *ram,* a *tu,* and a *ri. Tu* is the occult force of Bon Po magicians. *Ri* is the Tibetan word for a mountain. But"—he shrugged—"a mountain cannot have a *tu.* It is pointless to use *hum* in order to invoke a nonexistent mountain force. From the morphological viewpoint, it is a mess as well: *hum* and *ram* are from Sanskrit, *tu* and *ri* are Tibetan. It doesn't make sense, yet in a way it does: many Bon mantras precede Buddhism, and the lamas don't know the translation, either. When Tibetans developed an alphabet, the lamas wrote down what they had heard from their teachers, who did not know some of the meanings. All they used was their hearing, and, frankly, they were not a terribly literate bunch. This particular mantra comes not from Yundrun Bon, which is more or less researched, but shamanic Bon, which never had an alphabet to begin with. The only way it could have been written down was by a visitor, which means another distortion: think of how words must sound to an outsider. Distortion upon distortion . . . but, a lucky break for your thesis. Congratulations!"

The professor was grinning, yet Rudi could not help feeling that he was holding something back. "Is it possible that Tune Ra read these tablets? Could he have seen them in the museum? Or with you?"

"I don't think so." Schechter resolutely shook his head and zipped up his briefcase. "Sorry, I have to be going."

"But he may have read it someplace? Can it be a coincidence that he just stumbled upon this Bon mantra?"

"Miracles happen. This is your wish coming true: an open-and-shut thesis." He put on his coat. "See you tomorrow."

"What were the feelings you were looking for a mantra for?" Rudi called out.

Already at the door, the professor paused. He bit his lip and, with a vague gesture, left.

RUDI shrugged: he did not mean to intrude. Besides, he could not hold back his excitement: if there was no way Tune Ra could have found the chorus in Bon manuscripts, he had to have come up with it on his own. The musician had instinctively picked verbal gibberish that coincided with sacred syllables. And it worked! It stuck to you the way a piece of gum sticks to your shoe. The sacred combination made the song a hit because it struck the right energy centers. A synthesis of Eastern theology and modern music. That was good for more than an itsy-bitsy doctoral. That was . . . why, *Sacred Cadences of the East in Western Pop Music* by Dr. Rudra Paxton.

He stacked the tablets up, again and again. If millions got hooked on the chorus, it could not be all nonsense, as Schechter said. It had to mean something.

As he deposited the tablets in the desk, he felt an odd unpleasant sensation. He felt infected. A mantra had to contain a command, a suggestion. But everyone repeated it—how could everyone be infected?

He spent a few moments in a suspended state. Then, as his eyes focused, he noticed a scrap of paper on the floor.

It was a flyer from DeoMorte, a club where Tune Ra was taping a special.

So: all his questions were resolved easily. All he had to do was take a downtown train to the club.

He stared outside, where the streetlamps were going on. He could not move. His body was caught in a stupor. An inexplicable fear deposited itself in his stomach, preventing him from standing up.

Don't do it. The grim black silhouettes of the buildings spoke to him. The white columns of the library, like beacons of light in the night, spoke to him calmingly: *You're safe here, with your books, with your knowledge.* His legs, which by now had merged with the floor, whispered to him, *Let us be.*

In Sanskrit, it is called *gavakha,* he thought. The sabotage of the body, the paralysis of the will.

He clenched his teeth and struggled to his feet. The action of the will had to be answered with a counteraction.

9

THOUGHTS of Gwen and their tortured relationship would not leave him even in the middle of the disco. The imperatives lined themselves up smoothly: to stop the torment, he needed money; to get the grant, he needed to find out the truth about the mantra—to confront the DJ. Hence, he needed to stay till closing.

Onstage, Tune Ra was dancing away, the beat accelerating. The drums were hammering at the bottom of Rudi's stomach; the floor was trembling, and the colored light beams ran across it like cracks in the ground during an earthquake.

This was his dream: to inject mantras in rock'n'roll, to turn both art and life into sacred items. Then people would become one big rock band, one ashram, one disco. Could

Tune Ra's disco be it? But this reminded one rather of a triumphant dance at the bonfire after the mammoth had been slain. Tune Ra was a shaman who used the beat to manipulate the tribe, to send them into ecstasy and convulsions. Every yell of the chorus went like a cannon shot through Rudi's brain; every drumbeat pumped up the vein in his temple, forcing him to press it down. If a person has to grab his head in the same way as a glutton grabs his stomach, he is trying to hold together the shell of a nut that has already split—it's too late.

The black guy in rags reemerged at Rudi's side. "Got smoke?"

Rudi shook his head.

"Whatcha writin'?"

This was the second time he was being asked the question. Writing at the disco looked bizarre indeed. He rose and made his way through the crowd towards the stage.

Close to the stage, the madness reached its apogee when Tune Ra descended from his throne to dispense some autographs. Like a communion, Rudi thought, fighting to get near the idol.

At close quarters, Tune Ra looked short, with mousy features. His pale forehead was covered with droplets of sweat and smudged with gray. There was something androgynous about him: properly clad, he could pass for a young nun.

To stand out, Rudi pushed forth a marker pen decorated with a Tibetan motif. Tune Ra's eyebrows went up as he held it.

"Did you make up the chorus yourself or borrow it from Bon Po?"

"Bon who?" Tune Ra sized up his erudite fan and grinned condescendingly. "Bon Jovi? He was cool, dude—long time ago. . . ."

"Did you come across it while meditating?"

"Yeah, dude—hey, we've got a Bon Jovi fan!" To the crowd's sarcastic howling, the idol dried his forehead with a paper napkin and then signed it.

Rudi felt pulled away by a thousand hands. *Who else do you listen to, dude? Axl Rose?*

What a waste, Rudi thought, walking across the emptying

dance floor. The combined heat and smoke were taking their toll. He was about to dry his forehead with Tune Ra's napkin, when a familiar smell reached his nostrils.

He inspected the napkin, smudged with the gray that had come off Tune Ra's forehead. It smelled like Schechter's Tibetan ashes. That had to be the smudge on TuneRa's "third eye."

Rudi turned back to look, and for a moment his eyes met Tune Ra's. Instantly, the star looked away and went back to signing autographs.

IO

IN the subway, Rudi kept his eyes away from others—not to avoid panhandlers or inadvertently "dissing" someone, as most New Yorkers did—but to keep up his mental discipline. Prior to Gwen's arrival, he was all eyes, both up on the ground and down in the subway. He was constantly looking for Her, for the only one—not mentally undressing her, like a proverbial Romeo, but trying her on "for size": *was she someone he could share his life with?* Once Gwen arrived and their conflict flared up once again, he grew afraid: what if he did connect, even if for an instant? One casual glance at another woman could create ripples that would grow into a storm and bury this poor observer.

He caught himself murmuring Tune Ra's chorus under his breath. What were mantras anyway? Messages of superior forces? But wasn't each of us a mantra, too, to be decoded through our lives by ourselves and those close to us?

Someone touched his elbow. A panhandler shoved forward a paper cup: "Change, brother?"

It was the black guy with a leg prosthesis from the disco. In the glaring subway lights, he looked even more despondent.

He recognized Rudi, too: "Hey, brother, you went to the

club! You dig Tune Ra?" He went rocking and murmuring the chorus.

"No, I don't." Rudi dropped a quarter in the cup and hurried away. How did this junkie make it into DeoMorte? Will a poor man really get through the eye of the needle . . . ? No: for this one, the needle itself is enough.

ON the train, he went back to his diary.

Was Tune Ra trying to fool me? Now he did, now he didn't. The conscious is like this car; the thoughts get in and out like passengers. If I am each of them, I will go crazy, getting on and off incessantly. But if I am the car, I will preserve my emptiness and state of motion.

He picked up a downtown paper off the floor, hoping to see a piece by Gwen. There was none; instead, he read an interview with a youth who had been sentenced for a misdemeanor; in jail, he was raped and infected with AIDS. The thought made him shudder: could happen to anyone.

He got off at Columbus Circle to change trains. At this hour, trains were scarce, and the platform was crowded with late-night carousers. The heat and the rumbling of the traffic aboveground made him think of purgatory.

The people kept arriving. He found himself pushed against a column by a fat man in a raspberry baseball jacket, swaying in beery stupor. Rudi pressed his temple to the cold column to relieve the nascent headache. And he heard the chanting.

It was the same black beggar, right behind him, winking and murmuring Tune Ra's chorus.

Is he stalking me? Rudi tried to move away, but there was no room. I should be patient, he told himself; every stranger teaches us perfect patience, Buddha teaches, and the resentment of the beggar must be transformed into joyous peace. He looked down, where the tips of his shoes were already over the yellow line at the edge of the platform . . . Suddenly, the beggar's voice changed.

As he pressed forward, breathing down Rudi's neck, he did not sound postmodern ironic like Tune Ra—no, he sounded more like a Buddhist monk, his voice rising menacingly from the pit of his stomach. Again, Rudi tried to shift to the side, but now he felt faint, nauseous; he held on to the column. Rivulets of sweat ran down his face. An overpowering stink of urine filled his nostrils. A lump of vomit rose to his throat. His whole body was wet and sticky, like a piece of meat being defrosted. Feverishly, he began chanting *pkhat*—anything to block his mind from this voice.

The beggar's whispering went faster, his voice getting lower, now penetrating beyond Rudi's ears—it seemed to be getting through the marrow of his bone. His vision blurred, objects swam; the only things he could look at were the rails below. They were a cool silvery stream, the only relief from the sticky, stinky cocoon that was enveloping him.

The train rumbled in the tunnel. Without stopping his chanting, the beggar lightly rested his hands on Rudi's back, as if preparing to push him.

"Shut up!" In a last-ditch effort to resist, Rudi swung around, grabbed the beggar by the shoulders, and turned him around, in effect switching places with him.

The train roared into the station. The beggar pushed Rudi away indignantly; but his artificial limb slid on the floor, his arms flailed helplessly as his body leaned over the tracks—

The first car caught him straight on the torso. Rudi caught sight of his legs tumbling down.

Gasping, the crowd ebbed. Exhausted, Rudi collapsed at the column. The screaming of the train driver filled his ears.

II

STEPPING back, the passengers formed an empty space around Rudi. He heard whistles and cries.

"Call 911!"

"Step back, everybody!"

"He pushed him!" The fat man in the baseball jacket pointed at Rudi. "I saw it!"

A policeman helped him up. The icy steel of the handcuffs locked around his wrists.

UPSTAIRS at Manhattan Homicide North, Detective Martin Rivers, a black man with a linebacker build and a shiny clean-shaven skull, went over the report in gloomy silence. Then he dropped the file on the desk of his colleague, a swarthy man with a thick black mustache and a bright bandanna on a big ruddy neck. "All yours."

"What's with the other guy?"

"No papers found on the body."

"Whatsa matter, Marty, you don't want to do a brother killer?"

"I got no brothers." Rivers went back to his desk, which was strewn with papers.

The Mustache went through the preliminaries. "What's with the name Rudra?"

"It's Tibetan." Rudi tried to sound calm and friendly, the way an innocent man would. "Your name, Baz"—he read the nameplate on the detective's desk—"probably comes from Basil, that's Greek, like your last name, Tarakis, meaning 'dragon.'"

"You sure know about that stuff. Columbia, huh?" Tarakis went over Rudi's things. "Catholic?"

"Buddhist."

"How come you got long hair? Don't you guys shave your heads?"

"Shaving one's head is a ritual, not a religion," Rudi said.

"Oh yeah? Hey, Marty, you Buddhist, too? Or is it one of dem Kwanza things?"

The black detective ignored him.

"All right." Tarakis slapped down the file on the desk. "Now tell me what happened."

Rudi tried to be logical and coherent, but as he went on about his thesis, the mantras, his question, and Tune Ra's response, he could not help feeling that his narrative was not only going into a space behind the detective's head, where the street map of Manhattan was strewn with multicolored pins, but its effect could be just the opposite of the one he intended. By the time he came to the scene in the subway, he could barely finish a phrase. "So then he, you know—and I, you see—he was chanting this mantra, a Bon Po mantra, I am quite sure."

Tarakis's pen slid down the page. "How do you spell *Bon?* That's like French for 'good,' right? What's *Po?*"

"No, no," Rudi exclaimed. "This comes from the verb *bon pa,* which means to pronounce magic formulas,' or mantras. Their vibrations filled Tibetan shamans with occult forces that control life itself. Ancient Bons could do anything with their mantras—they could revive people or have them killed!"

The detective called out with a grin, "Sound like the Mason case, Marty?"

Rivers raised his head from the paperwork and gave Rudi a long, steady look. "If it's so powerful," he said slowly, "how come it's him and not you who got killed."

"I chanted *pkhat,*" Rudi murmured. "It's the kind of mantra that stops your thinking briefly. If only for a few seconds, it bars anything from entering your mind."

Tarakis howled with laughter. "Maybe we should gag you. Maybe you're a real Terminator with them mantras-shmantras. I'll be right back." He scooped up the papers and left.

The portable radio was playing a rock station—Tune Ra, naturally. Rudi's head began throbbing again. "Can you turn it off, please?"

Rivers silently turned down the volume. Finally, Tarakis came back, carrying a printout.

"So you guys have shamans, huh?" His tone indicated clearly what he made of Rudi and his story. "I heard you can't even kill a roach! But you—they tried to kill you with a word!"

Rudi groaned. "Please—this is very serious. You can look it up in an encyclopedia. In Africa, they execute people with vibrations. They tie a person up and then start beating their tom-toms. But he is tied up so tightly he cannot move to the beat—so he goes crazy and dies!"

"No shit!" Tarakis broke up. "I got it, Marty—forget

about the chair, forget about the injection! What they should do is force them to listen to rap—white cons, that is! And classical music for black cons!"

The black detective did not change his expression. Tarakis reached to raise the volume on the radio. "I like Tune Ra myself. How come no one else in the whole country falls on the tracks or pushes someone else because of this mantra of yours?"

That's it. Rudi gripped his temples. That was the question!

"I really love that bandanna you got," he murmured in a pseudoflirtatious tone.

Tarakis was taken aback. Then his neck grew red. "You trying to be cute or something?"

"See?" Rudi exclaimed. "You're about to hit me! But I said a most innocent thing—but in an insulting tone. It's all about the intonation—like the mantra! It has to be enunciated correctly!"

"Hey, Marty—we've got a live one here!"

The black detective, engrossed in the interrogation, had forgotten all about his papers.

Tarakis cracked his knuckles loudly. "Rudi, do you mind giving a blood sample?"

"What for?"

"Maybe you're on something. Now, how would a black bum know Tibetan tones? Is this, like, *X-Files*? Or maybe it's just a regular file going back to . . ." He read from the printout. "Rudolph Paxton, arrested for possession of hallucinogens. Check this out, Marty: Paxton Senior is a chemist at Berkeley, while his son is cooking up some kind of superacid at his lab! Did you use a mantra then, too? Now— what kind of acid were you cooking up with this crackhead? Marty, call the DA's for a house search warrant, will ya? So, Mr. Paxton, why did you kick your partner under the train? He didn't pay? Or you didn't want to pay? Start talking, boy. Now. You can still go to sleep in your own apartment—you live nearby, right?"

"I want a lawyer," said Rudi.

"What do you need a lawyer for? You're just an innocent student, right? Or do you supply junk to DeoMorte? Maybe to the DJ himself?" He turned up the volume, and Tune Ra's chorus shook the walls.

Sweating bullets, Rudi reached for the napkin in his pocket. "Here—this is Tune Ra's napkin! With Tibetan ashes on it!"

"What's that?"

"I don't know! But something's not right with it!"

The detective gathered the papers in his large maw of a hand. "I'd say so. You're looking at murder, boy. Second degree. I'll give you time to think—maybe you should tell me about your experiments with LSD, instead of giving me this mantra-shmantra bullshit."

"I have a right to make a phone call."

Tarakis made a face. "You can't call Tibet from here. Not with the taxpayers' money."

Rudi tensed up to stay calm. "It's a local call."

"I know!" Tarakis guffawed. "Whatsa matter, don't you guys have a sense of humor?"

12

AFTER the bail hearing, Rudi and Gwen headed for the subway. At the entrance he panicked.

"Let's take a cab," she said.

In the car, he collapsed with exhaustion. But he was wound up too tightly to go to sleep. He sat up, watching the snow that turned to slush the moment it touched the ground.

Gwen held his fingers in her hand.

"Bite me." He raised his hand to her lips.

It was their private joke. Whenever he sensed her anger—without her having to show it—he let her bite into the flesh on the side of his palm. Biting released the steam and calmed her down.

"Bite me before I go to sleep."

She shook her head and put his hand back.

WHEN he saw her in court, bags under dead eyes, he was frightened. He believed in her intuition; her expression meant he was in more trouble than he had realized. His heart jumped out of him and his throat tightened: her worrying alone told him how much she loved and cared for him. At her side was Schechter, his complexion an unhealthy purple: his blood pressure must have been way up.

My parents, Rudi thought, watching from the dock. Gwen standing in for my late mother; Schechter, for my father, with whom I have not talked in years. Why am I causing such grief to my family? Like a rebellious teenager, I tried to flee her, but when trouble struck, I was right back, clinging to her skirt.

Gwen had phoned the professor in the middle of the night, after Rudi's call from the precinct. She knew there was no one else to post bail.

THE bespectacled girl from Legal Aid who met Rudi half an hour before the hearing took down the information with no more curiosity than Tarakis had had. "So—what are we going to do here? If you want to cop a plea, I could get you down to Man Two."

"What do you mean?" However close to fainting and ignorant of law Rudi was, this did not smell good.

"Involuntary manslaughter, three to five, out after eighteen months for good behavior—"

"What? Jail?" He held to the table for balance. *What about the grant? Tibet?*

"There's plenty of witnesses to show you did push him," she continued, unperturbed.

"I did not push him. I—I was defending myself."

"Against an evil mantra."

Her tone said it all. He did not even have to nod.

"If you want to plead insanity—"

"I—am—not—crazy."

She shrugged. "All right, fine. I guess what you need is an expert witness. Someone to persuade the jury that your fears were well founded. Can you think of one?"

Her tone suggested that the expert would have to come up with a couple of really, really good mantras. Because this was a New York jury, and they had really, really heard it all.

THE prosecution demanded that he be held without bail. Yet something about his appearance—or was it Gwen's and Schechter's at his side—touched the judge's heart. And so, to the tune of a quarter million, Mr. Rudi Paxton was released pending trial.

Outside, he began thanking the professor effusively— Schechter had mortgaged his co-op to put up bail—but the savior waved him off: "Nonsense, nonsense! Who do you think is the leading mantra expert in this town? Professor Schechter, who else! Go home and get some sleep. I'll see you tomorrow after classes."

The professor's tone could not conceal his anxiety. At least, he seemed to Rudi more anxious than the leading mantra expert should have been.

OUT of the cab's window, Rudi saw the mantra—a comic-book bubble blown out of Tune Ra's mouth—on city buses. The polished grin stared at Rudi everywhere: buses, newspaper stands, wall posters. . . .

Could it indeed be plain gibberish? Could Rudi's theories be the product of his own frustrations, which had reached their peak in the subway? Could this nonsense simply sound like the mantra that—that was just as nonsensical? And the poor unidentified homeless man was just a victim of his mania? In that case he should take the insanity plea and stop wasting everybody's time.

He fidgeted in the seat, dodging these questions, and immediately collapsed into the black abyss, where the only thing he could see were the subway tracks. They sank under his feet, and out of black holes emerged the Legal Aid girl, Tarakis, and other faces, familiar and strange, but all humming Tune Ra's chorus.

"We're home," Gwen said. "There's a surprise for you."

The place had been wrecked. The floor was strewn with

books, dishes, CDs. The wind blew through the open window, scattering the brown dust of Indian incense.

"The cops came at dawn." Gwen spoke with deliberate calmness. Only her pallor and dilated black pupils betrayed her inner state. "They said you were arrested for murder. They looked for drugs. They threatened to bust me as a coconspirator."

She picked up the shards of her talisman, a miniature ceramic scorpio. "They thought you could be keeping drugs in it." She started weeping.

He picked up a tiny leftover incense twig and lit it up. "You must dissociate. Tell yourself: This is not happening to me. This is happening to my body—my thoughts—my feelings—but not me."

She tried to fit the pieces together, but her fingers were trembling badly. "I never wanted you to deal with this mantra! I knew it—I hated it right away. I had a premonition. But you, you don't feel anything—you're too busy *dissociating!*"

She looked so vulnerable as she hunched over, trembling, on the floor. Pale, shrunken, with reddened eyes: she was a tiny beetle herself, a tiny scared beetle.

He sat her in his lap. "There, there . . . Let's be reasonable: what premonition? What fear? They come from your mind. But your mind is like a newspaper: everybody writes into it. You think it's your so-called common sense that decides what should go in? No, it's your internal editor, with its own complexes and hang-ups—just like your editor, Dorfman—and it uses its dubious judgment to decide whether given information should be under the heading of 'Fears' or 'Humor.' "

The reference to her editor, a homespun petty tyrant, made her smile. Encouraged, he went on: "Take out your myopic editor, and then information is just information— nothing positive or negative."

The color was returning to her cheeks. He reached to kiss her.

She pressed her hands into his chest. "Take a shower. You stink of jail. Then come back to me."

* * *

GRADUALLY, the hot steam of his consciousness condensed into cold drops of fear, which deposited themselves inside his skull. I lied to her, he thought; she sensed the menace with her gut, not with her mind. Me, too: I submitted myself to this piece I had read on the floor of the subway car. Which is meaningless—how can I prove the beggar's intention if his voice was not recorded? Lord—not Buddha, but our own, jealous Old Testament Lord—I promise: If I am found not guilty, I'll stop raiding Your turf. The words, the sounds—they are Yours, and I promise I'll never play with them again. Also, the one about impotence and deafness? This was a joke. I don't need all these sounds. We'll get married, we'll have a baby, I'll learn how to be a good father. That's where I'm going, to her protective warm body. . . .

BUT he did not even have a chance to embrace her. The moment his head touched the pillow, he fell into a black hollow. He woke up in a sweat in the middle of the night: he had dreamed that the hollow was a black subway track, that he was lying on the rails, unable to get up or make a sound. There was a crowd on the platform, but nobody— Gwen, Schechter, the mustachioed detective—no one saw him. And the ice-cold rails were holding him tight.

The window was still open. A cold draft blew through the room. The night was melting outside, like gray smashed ice, to the crowing of the birds in the park. He lay for a long time, listening to Gwen breathing next to him. For the first time, he realized it was a miracle. It could have turned out differently. It could have been him lying on the rails. Or the judge might have refused to grant him bail. And he still might have to go to jail and be separated from her. Isn't that what he used to want? Wasn't his cleaving to her now simply his terror at what had happened? Or was the pendulum swinging again—to her, from her?

She stopped breathing for a second, as if startled. He remembered the search. He was miserable, putting her into so much trouble. But the absence of love would be the worst. Didn't he love her? He moved closer . . . the main trouble was doubting his love.

But his body was on its way, ignoring any doubts he might have. With the tip of his tongue, he searched the mazes of her ear. She uttered a small moan and caressed herself. He breathed sweet nothings into her ear. She awoke, clinging to him, purring with pleasure. His whisper was getting more heated. He realized he sounded almost like the bum in the subway—and Gwen was feeling the heat almost in the same way as he had on the edge of the platform. He went on, secretly wanting her to feel what he had felt in the subway—to partake of this insane tension.

Her forehead was covered with sweat, her breasts heaved, her stomach pulled itself in—as he kept whispering. He had always found endearing her ability to get excited from words alone. He kept going, forgetting himself or what he was uttering, till finally she arched her back, groaned, and plunged her nails into his sides. In a moment, she was limp, dead, insensate.

"What was it you were singing?" she asked later.

"You don't remember?"

"Some gibberish. But it was really exciting."

"In what way?" He rose on his elbow.

"I don't know," she drawled sweetly. "In a nervous way. It was so sweet . . . almost painful. What was it?"

He eyed her suspiciously. She did not seem to be joking. Perhaps she was truly out of it.

"I was just improvising," he said. "Can you reproduce it from memory? I'm curious, too."

If she uses her emotional memory to pick the same mantra, he thought, this could help with expert testimony.

"Mmm . . . I can't, really. But the beat was really strange. Modus Diaboli. It's a tonality, not a nice one, I remember from music school. A tone, a half-tone, a half-tone, a tone . . ."

"I should write this down." He reached for a pencil on the floor.

Suddenly the phone rang. Who would call them at four in the morning? The caller ID was blank. He pushed the speakerphone—"Hello?"—and shrank away. The caller chanted the mantra.

*   *   *

IT was not Tune Ra's voice. This voice was low and grim, almost as if it belonged to a ventriloquist. Nor was he chanting it like Tune Ra—more like the bum in the subway. Exactly like that!

"Who are you?" Rudi grabbed the phone.

The voice did not miss a beat. Perhaps it was a recording—no, it was a live person. As if spurred by the victim's fear, the voice changed the tone: now he sounded like an airplane gaining altitude—like an ultrasound that makes windowpanes tremble and eardrums burst.

"STOP IT!" Gwen hollered and pulled the cord out of the wall.

For a moment, all grew quiet, as if someone stopped the tape. They could even hear the TV next door.

"I'm scared, Rudi." Arms around her knees, Gwen was trembling in the corner of the bed. "Who was it? How do they know our number?"

"I don't know, baby. Don't worry. It's just someone's idea of humor."

Rudi caressed her and whispered till she calmed down and fell asleep in his arms. He held her for a long time, terrified: he was sure it was no joke. Instead of love and happiness, he brought her nothing but torment and fear.

Yet he was not insane! Her reaction was similar to his!

Still, the only way to deliver her from this misery was to stick to the original escape plan. But now he could not: he could not jump bail, he could not betray Schechter . . . he was trapped.

He eyed the red light of the answering machine, waiting for it to start flashing. But gradually, the darkness enveloped all the sounds. . . .

WHEN they woke up, the autumn sun had already disappeared behind the roofs of Broadway and lit up their studio with a dull gray light. At breakfast, he held a briefing session.

First, the sound on the answering machine must always be off. Do not pick up the phone unless there is a familiar number on the caller ID. Everybody—relatives, close friends, and the two of them—will use a code. Two rings three rings, two rings. Rudi will listen to messages himself: he could handle it in the subway, he can handle it again. If Gwen picks up the phone by accident and hears either the mantra or a strange voice or something suspicious—drop the phone. Do not speak, do not yell, do not listen.

Second, do not open the door. Keep it double-locked. We'll open it for each other only after voice recognition or a predetermined signal.

Third—

"I'm sick and tired of this cloak-and-dagger game." Gwen grabbed her backpack. "I want to stop by St. John's before the lecture. Come with me. Say a little prayer. Like in the Bible. Not a mantra."

He frowned. Yesterday's weakness, the vow in the shower, was forgotten. "Don't be like those dumb cops. Mantras *are* prayers. Their objective is the same: enlightened consciousness."

"For some of them," she said before she left. "Not for all of them." She kissed him tenderly.

ALONE in the apartment, he lowered the curtains and turned off the lights. Then he mixed the aromatic debris of the incense and lit it up. He turned on the stereo, sat down with his legs crossed, closed his eyes, and started breathing. His body filled with warm golden air; he felt the dark flow of the last days' troubles and frustrations leaving his body.

He ascended to the sun, and it rushed towards him, singeing all the obstacles erected by his ego, his thoughts, and anxieties, melting the armor that suffocated him. Layer after layer, his defenses popped—when suddenly there was a click, right in his brain. He shuddered as a painful spasm gripped his body.

He opened his eyes.

The click came from the answering machine. It was the third message. None of the numbers was identified.

It was like a bomb with a live wire, he thought, softly turning on the sound and pressing Play. But no messages had been left.

Exhausted, he lay down on the bed. All he could do was pray—the good old prayers of the Book—and wait for the

evening, for the meeting with the professor . . . and another
call.

What sort of signal was his fate trying to send with this
mantra? Was it something important or more abracadabra?
Would fate express itself in an abracadabra? This was the
word cabalists used for *God*.

He tried not to think; he tried to put himself at rest, as
calm as the air in the apartment, with dust wafting through
the air. But calm arrived replete with sounds: the faint
crackling of the furniture, the swishing of tires, the car
horns, the raindrops plopping on the sidewalk. Each of these
sounds was a mantra. The world spoke to man in a myriad
of words. But man did not know their meaning.

13

BRIEF but feisty, a stormy wind whistled up the Hudson
and, en route to the valley of 116th Street, snatched hats
and umbrellas atop the stairs to Riverside Park. Watery dust
descended in gusts, a shapeless drizzle that had an equal
chance of turning into a shower or vanishing into clear
skies. The gusts brought tears to Rudi's eyes. He pressed
against the cold marble of the monument, turning away
from the wind.

When Schechter showed up around the corner, Rudi,
shrunken by the cold, tried to hail a cab—the professor
lived at 79th and Riverside—but Schechter waved in protest
and, pointing to the park below, headed down the stairs.
Rudi shrugged—he could not possibly outshout the wind—
and followed suit.

The park was windless, which never failed to surprise
Rudi; even the drizzle picked up its bags and returned to
the sky. The professor and his student dried their eyes,
caught their breaths, and smiled at each other. Oddly, Rudi
noted, Schechter's smile was as guilty as his own.

"Let's walk," Schechter said. "You never know when we can do it again."

The remark filled Rudi's mouth with bitterness. So the professor allowed that he, Rudi, might end up in jail, and this might be their last walk together?

At four-thirty in the afternoon the park was deserted. The nannies had already wheeled their wards back home, while the joggers and the dog walkers were still at their desks at work. In the ashen mist along the alleys, the yellow street-lamps lit up, turning the raindrops on naked twigs into precious glass beads.

Rudi started apologizing and thanking the professor for putting up the bail, but Schechter interrupted, putting his hand on his shoulder.

"What do you think it is worth to an old professor, to take a walk in the park with his favorite student? Perhaps love is the true bail. We save up the gold of attraction to others, and then find ourselves in situations when we want to flee our fate. But the gold has been deposited in fate's account. To flee is to lose your deposit. One must stay and wait for the decision."

Rudi stopped abruptly. "I had no intention of fleeing. I am not going to fail you."

"That's not what I mean." Schechter paused, too, and with visible pleasure took a long breath: raw, fish-ranking wind from the Hudson mixed in with the smell of wet soil and rotting leaves. "You know, this place reminds me of Italy: perhaps a Tiber embankment. In the shape of solid substance that flows into the boundless, shapeless water, perfection reaches its limit. Ancient Rome was like America, spreading the same things through their empire: the power of law, new technologies, a single currency, and schlock culture. Which brings us to statues of emperors, Coliseums, bathhouses, and their own mantras. In that case, Tibetans are the Jews of the modern world. Dispersed by another empire, China, who spreads even worse schlock, the Tibetans are spreading Buddhism the way Jews did the Bible. The world resists, it thinks it can use a pill against the virus, a prison against crime, but you can't fight the immaterial with the material. You must give yourself to the immaterial. By compressing the gas, we create an explosive situation."

Rudi frowned. Generally, he enjoyed the professor's abstractions, but today he needed something more practical. "I'm sorry, I didn't have enough sleep to follow your thoughts. What do you mean? That I shouldn't resist the immaterial mantra? Or that I should give myself up to jail?"

"You stayed up all night?" Schechter said tenderly, putting his hands on Rudi's shoulders and looking him in the eye.

The sudden surge of tenderness made Rudi uneasy. "I was afraid, Professor. I was waiting for the phone to ring. . . ."

He told Schechter about the call. "Who could it be? Who needs me? Now he calls without leaving a message. It's as if he's making sure he doesn't leave traces for evidence."

"I don't know." Schechter shook his head. "But he must be an old hand in his business. He must want direct contact with your ear, with your conscious. This will make the mantra effective. But don't worry. We'll have a bite, a drink— we need to do some thinking here."

For a while, they walked in silence.

"Remember you were looking for a mantra among those tablets?" Rudi asked. "Did you find one to match your sensations?"

Schechter did not answer. Then, unnoticed by Rudi, he concealed the answer in his question. "Magic . . . do you know what kind of sin it is?"

"Paganism?" Rudi mused. "Heresy?"

"It's a primal sin. The Fall is an attempt to acquire divine powers without uniting with Him—and this is magic. This is like peeking at answers at the end of your exercise book. And it is punished severely. On the other hand, without the Fall there would have been no Ascension. In fact, there would have been nothing, including God, because Edenic innocence is synonymous to ignorance, including ignorance of God. As for your mantra, it is not enough to find the tonality used in the subway. You also need the translation— its meaning."

"You said it is senseless," Rudi reminded him.

"Perhaps it was—until the subway accident. Fate interferes and changes the meaning of everything: life, history. Why can't it change the meaning of just one word?"

Puzzled, Rudi stared away.

"Wait!" The professor held his arm. "You've just stepped on an oak acorn, without thinking of it as a separate universe. It's dead now; you've caused an apocalypse. It contained billions of creatures—cells—both happy and miserable. They, too, wondered about their Judgment Day. And it arrived, in the form of your careless foot."

Schechter resumed walking, carefully avoiding acorns. "It was no accident: the infinite connectedness of Creation brought you at this very moment to this very acorn. However, if one of the acorn's atoms tried to understand the connection between you and it and everything else around, it would fail. Or, if it succeeded, it would then lose its mind and turn into a person. In other words, it would commit a leap in evolution and cease being a part of an acorn. A human being in the universe is the same thing. Why did you pay attention to the mantra—why did the bum fall under the train—why were you the one to be charged? Why is the foot of fate coming down at this very moment—and on us? Perhaps this is a chance for us to gain understanding and transform ourselves into angels!"

Beaming, Schechter stared at his student, but in his face he saw nothing but despair.

"So where do we get the translation?"

Schechter sighed. His student had not learned the main thing: the art of staying apart from one's consciousness.

"Even if the decoding exists, I doubt it is written down anywhere. Bon's most secret instructions, like Tibetan tantras, were passed along verbally, by a teacher whispering them through a reed into his student's ear. Remember, in medieval paintings Satan penetrates Eve's ear. On the other hand, the Holy Spirit used the same entrance for the purpose of conception. Mary conceives from the divine Word, because God is born in the human soul of the Word, just like the Devil is. . . ."

Rudi eyed the professor anxiously. Schechter had changed lately, and it was not merely his increasing inability to focus. The change was hard to grasp. At times, he thought he knew the state the professor was in: that of a man who has taken a crucial decision, a man who has ditched the ballast of a particularly burdensome thought and was now floating upward, like a balloon, with a mix of fear and joy.

"A decision is born of brain calm, not brainstorming," Schechter said suddenly, as if reading his student's mind. "You must calm your waters, so that they could reflect the answer."

A tennis ball landed at their feet. A chocolate puppy spaniel ran up, whimpering, afraid to approach the strangers.

"Easy, easy . . ." Schechter picked up the ball. "We don't want your toy. We love you. . . ." He tossed the ball away and grinned at the dog running away.

"Remember the koan, Is there Buddha in the dog? It can be viewed through the crazy wisdom of Zen, but Western metaphysics applies as well. Look: a man walks his dog, tosses the ball; the dog runs to fetch the ball. So do we: a certain Master tosses us a life, we rush off, we roll in the mud to retrieve it, we lose it, we grit our teeth when we miss it, and we run back. What is obvious to the master and incomprehensible to the dog is that the ball has no value. The value lies in the dog's return to the master and their joyous embrace. Again and again, the master tosses the ball. What does he want to teach the dog? Perhaps not to run, but to walk with dignity? Once the master sees that the dog has acquired human features, he will no longer tempt it with a toy. They will become equals. A man-God will be born."

"Perhaps he is training the dog to serve and to serve again. To obey his call?" Rudi was forcing himself to give in to the flow of Schechter's speech, hoping it would take him to the mantra. "Or perhaps he is simply having fun."

"*Fun* is not *simple!*" The professor snapped his fingers. "Perhaps the man-dog needs to learn one thing: that his effort to fetch is his master's amusement, and then he should share it with a light heart, so as to please them both. Do not bark—do not snarl at the ball rolling into a hole—do not drag it out of a pile of muck and thus soil your master's hand—but just give yourself to the game? Aha!" He clapped his hands. "The point is, the dog must learn to hold the ball in its teeth—but without making the possession a condition of its canine happiness! The dog should feel the ball in its mouth, yet should see around itself, too. Its world must not be reduced to the ball, the way it is with this spaniel—but expanded to a global view. Oh, God." He stopped. His voice was shaking now. "Why can't the dog both hold the ball and see the Big Picture? Why does it force the master to tear the ball out of its mouth?"

"Perhaps the dog needs to leap after the ball to see the Big Picture from the air," Rudi murmured, relieved that the professor's flow of metaphor had finally brought them to 79th Street.

SCHECHTER'S apartment, complete with a terrace and a view of the park and the river, took up two floors in a three-floor building with a turret on top. Like any newcomer to New York with an unresolved apartment problem, Rudi used to eye these European-looking mini-mansions enviously on his walks in the park. He wondered if they were as wonderful from the inside as they appeared from the outside. He imagined creaky parquet floors, bookshelves ascending to the ceiling with laurel-leaf and lion-face moldings, fireplaces crackling comfortably, lecterns for writing standing up, aromas of old leather bindings, and an old servant who serves pipe, coffee, and port in the library.

Schechter's apartment was the fantasy made real, with a fireplace, plenty of oak paneling, walls lined with bookshelves rising to the cracked ceiling; there was even a servant—rather, a maid—a squat elderly Mexican woman called Milagros, with the flat-nosed ceramic-looking face of an Aztec deity. She cooked, she washed, she waxed the floors: she had run Schechter's household for many years. She even put up with his noisy students, however much she disapproved of their shoes they would not take off, their wild haircuts, and their noisy behavior.

As usual, Rudi settled in the library. *It's not just real estate, it's a den of knowledge,* he thought; *and he has risked all of this splendor on me.* A gnawing fear took hold: the bail imposed obligations not on the professor alone, but on him as well—he had to meet Schechter's requirements.

He had wondered on occasion why the professor had picked him as a favorite student, but now the wondering was tinged with anxiety.

Every inch of wall space was covered with books. The shelves circled the fireplace, flanked the window that overlooked the park, and hung over the door. The library doubled as drawing room, though it had no sofas or settees: only the rug where students would recline, a couple of armchairs with an end table near the fireplace, and a ladder to reach the top shelves. There was not a trace of high tech: no computer, no TV, not even an answering machine—only an ancient turntable and an equally old rotary phone next to the fireplace.

The sea was Rudi's first love; one of the first books he had ever read was Stevenson's *Treasure Island*. In his mind's eye, he could imagine that the creaking of the library furniture and old book spines was that of shipmasts. Scaling these shelves was not unlike climbing masts, too; disguised as a bookworm, Schechter was really an old salt, soaring above the water in his lectures, wielding these books like so many ropes. Rudi felt a pang of envy: why couldn't he, too, spend his life in this pursuit of knowledge, in learning the sea lanes, the routes, and the gales of theology?

RUDI'S eyes slid to the shelves over the fireplace and he paused in surprise. Had the professor taken the books out for restoration? The shelves used to hold Schechter's collection of Tibetan writing, unique for a private owner, were empty. Rudi loved leafing through the diminutive rectangles of multicolored cloth with lamaist canons written on wooden and paper tablets, or simply inhaling their wondrous mixture of sour milk, incense, and dung smoke—the smells of Tibetan mysteries. Now they were gone, save for a few on the top shelf. Instinctively, Rudi stepped on the ladder to investigate. Behind the yellow and blue flax wrappings, he spotted a flash of red taffeta. He reached to the back and saw what the professor was hiding: the Bon tablets he had gone over during the seminar. The ones that contained Tune Ra's mantra.

It seemed rather naive to be hiding it from thieves in this

fashion. Unless, Rudi thought, replacing the package, he was hiding it from someone else.

He heard a door being shut and quickly shinnied down the mast—the ladder, that is.

HAVING changed into a rough-woven Tibetan sweater, Schechter looked transformed, his eyes shining, a welcoming smile on his face.

"We'll start a fire, have a glass of Montecillo—my Spanish students sent me a case—it's excellent therapy for heart attacks and should go well with salmon, too.

"There is no higher enjoyment than conversation with friends on a favorite subject, with the accompaniment of good food and wine, heh-heh." The professor talked as he placed kindling in the fireplace. "Perhaps life is nothing more than God talking. But to whom? What if it's just a monologue devoid of sense—*gibberish?* The word, by the way, may have come from Jabbar, a Sufi mystic. He spoke nothing but gibberish—but he had thousands of disciples. He liberated the mind from conceptual thinking and expressed its essence, while avoiding the traps of logic and verbal imprecision. That is, gibberish is a mantra of sorts, too. And vice versa. But!"—he exclaimed dramatically and held up his finger—"Ladies and gentlemen of the jury, I'd like to draw your attention to the following: just like the mantras, gibberish is not without sense. Both express the innermost essence, hiding it from ignoramuses and the censorship of one's own mind. Would you like to see an example of this meditation? With pleasure. . . ."

Schechter squeezed his eyes shut and leaned to one side. *"La-tra-ta-ta-suribo-muriya-kribadu-furimu-klaboda . . ."*

Rudi stared in amazement. Schechter was kneeling at the fireplace, his hands clasped on his stomach—like an opera hero at the bed of his dying beloved—and ranting nonsense!

As the tempo quickened, he rose to his feet and spread his arms. His face scowled in a grimace that could have been of joy or pain; he spoke yet faster, more excitedly; he began weeping, grimacing, pressing his hands to his chest, tweaking his fingers.

Rudi sank deeper into the chair.

The professor pulled off his sweater and began pushing away an invisible presence, tearing invisible pieces off his sides, crumpling his shirt over his stomach. Then he grabbed his face, as if trying to tear off an invisible mask—groaning, drooling, and hatefully spitting out incoherent syllables.

Milagros's frightened face flashed in the doorway and disappeared.

Rudi was horrified. What a nut! The jury is supposed to buy *this?*

Finally, Schechter tore off the invisible mask. His arms shot upward, his hands groped the air, his wrists turned outward like those of a belly dancer; then he threw back his head and, still sputtering gibberish and scowling, stretched his arms in front of him and upward, as if trying to take off. Suddenly, he dropped on his knees and, rolling his eyes, changed his patter to a basso profundo growling chant.

Rudi leapt to his feet and stepped to the door. It was exactly the voice of the bum in the subway. It was also the voice on his answering machine.

HE had barely realized it because the professor's voice had changed again. Now he was weeping; rather, it was a man's dry wailing that in a few seconds burst into full-fledged crying. Sniffling, he smeared the tears across his fat, veinous cheeks in large expansive movements. His patter was losing every semblance of speech; syllables seemed to be disintegrating into letters, sounds—for a split second, Rudi thought that Schechter was actually trying to say something!

There was a message, a load that weighed on Schechter's heart and fought to get out through his wailing. The struggle was apparent in his face, which changed every instant, reflecting red and dark shadows from the fire: Rudi saw a crying child, then a passionate youth, then an angry red-faced man, now an inconsolate elder, then a roaring, wrathful deity in the Tibetan pantheon.

Finally, the patter stopped. The professor raised his eyes, still squeezed shut, upward, clenched his fists—and collapsed, banging his fists on the floor.

*   *   *

FOR a second, the only sounds were the crackling of the logs and distant sirens on Broadway. Then Schechter straightened up and opened his eyes. Never had Rudi seen his professor looking so clear and relaxed.

"Now, that's how you meditate the Jabbar way, ladies and gentlemen," he drawled contentedly. Only then did he notice Rudi's expression. "Scared? Don't worry, my boy. In court, I'll be civic respectability itself. Old Schechter wouldn't fail a student of his."

"You spoke in the tone of—this basso a capella—what was that?"

"Hm. I didn't even notice. That's *kargiraa,* Tibetan throat singing, the way my Rinpoche taught me. You need to be in a trance of sorts. This is singing like a man and a woman at the same time."

"But, Professor, it's the same voice used by the bum in the subway." Rudi's throat was dry. "And the same as the voice in the anonymous phone calls."

"Really?" A shade of anxiety or, perhaps, frustration, showed in Schechter's face. "Well, that makes sense. Tibetan monks chant in a very low voice: it doesn't soar, like in the West; rather, it recedes into the deep, where everybody has the same tone, male or female. That's why everyone who chants this way sounds identical."

"If it sounds identical," Rudi murmured, "then it could have been Tune Ra himself who called me."

"I doubt it," said the professor. "*Kargiraa* takes years to learn. I don't think there are many people in the U.S. capable of doing that. And Tune Ra sounds like he's your age, right?"

"But he did have Tibetan ashes on his forehead, the same kind as you gave me! Then he must have a guru—who may have provided him with a mantra and perhaps even called me. Who would he be? And what can the mantra mean if they sent this bum after me? A bum who would know this *kar—kar . . . ?*" Rudi gripped his temples. "Am I paranoid, Professor? Is this all my nightmare?"

"You can still plead insanity," said Schechter.

Rudi could not tell if his host was serious. Schechter always had the same kindly, ironic expression.

"I'm not crazy, Professor," he said stubbornly. "But if you chant this again, we can tape it and have a doctor examine my condition as I listen to it. Or Gwen's, or anyone's—I'm sure the effect will be the same!"

"What do you mean by 'the same'?" The grin did not leave Schechter's face.

"It's not easy to describe," Rudi said uncertainly. "It's as if my innards resonate to these sounds. Everything shifts. . . . I get incredibly irritated and impatient for it to be over. Very disturbing."

"Kind of vague," Schechter noted.

"No—I just have a hard time describing it. I'm sure the test will reveal the changes, both physical and emotional. Let's tape you singing it!"

"I'm sorry"—Schechter opened his hands—"I don't have a tape recorder. I'm too old-fashioned for that. All I have is a stereo."

"Let me get mine. I'll be right back! Five minutes by cab!"

"Wait." Schechter stopped him. "Don't rush it. I'm a little tired now. This is a very taxing exercise. I need to take a rest. And have a bite to eat. After a good dinner I'll sing even better. Sit down, the food will be here any minute."

He paced across the room, lost in thought.

"Perhaps we won't need the tests. You see, mantras are like great poetry: they bypass logic to impact your mind—they go straight for the unconscious. You must listen to yourself to understand which string in your soul is affected. . . . Did you say you were irritated? But that's natural: in Manhattan, I often feel irritation and fear, too. As if the city will collapse any moment and bury me, and I'm the only one who sees that it's about to happen. But I cannot flee—not until others can see it as well."

He stopped by the window, where the New Jersey highrises, spaced wide apart, were set ablaze by the setting sun; he picked up a wet maple leaf tossed in by the wind and sniffed it with pleasure.

"For me, maple leaves smell of childhood, when I was walking with my nanny around Borough Park. A smell of rot, a sweet smell of our own decay." The professor held up the leaf. "Doesn't it remind you of an old man's brown parchment skin? The black-and-blue spots on the edges are like those on corpses. The cancer of the fall has already drilled holes in it, you can see the web of the bones, but it is still clinging to life. See how the stem is bent: as if it had been trying to hold on to the branch, just like a patient grabs on to the bed in his last agony. A silly leaf can't love death; it can't realize that it was not the wind that tore it away, that it had reached a stage in its development. That it's not murder—it is suicide. If it was torn away, it was done by God. But if a leaf is a part of God, then God tore off its own part; that's how He evolves, He's like a climber in training: He falls down in order to begin scrambling up. Rudi!" he shouted sharply.

"What?" Rudi sat up, still lost in the maze of the professor's thought.

"You're falling asleep! This is the answer: I told you it would come up. This is exactly your case! The bum who was whispering the Word—or, in a sense, handing you the fruit from the Tree of Knowledge—wanted it to sound inside you, to push you to suicide. Instead, he let the Word enter himself—and killed himself as a result. We find the defendant not guilty."

"Do you mean the mantra is decoded as a subliminal suggestion to commit suicide?" Words had a hard time sliding off Rudi's tongue. "So you have decoded it?"

"I'm trying to say, Your Honor," Schechter said slowly, with a sad smile, "that the mantra, when intoned correctly, undoubtedly generates a suicidal impulse. Let us examine the sequence of the events. Why did the defendant not find himself on the tracks? Because he chanted the *pkhat* mantra, which barred the Bon Po mantra from entering his mind. Thus the mantra bounced off, boomeranged into the consciousness of its chanter, and killed him. I'd like to draw your attention to the listed symptoms. Experts will confirm the existence of mantras that cause nausea—and this is clearly what happened to the defendant while at the precinct. It's in the police report, isn't it?"

"True," Rudi muttered. "I feel nauseous every time I hear it."

The professor's eyes were laughing.

"Furthermore, certain Bon Po mantras cause convulsions. This, and not the shove by the defendant, is what caused the victim's loss of balance and his subsequent fall."

"Wait—are you saying that Tune Ra is a leader of a suicide cult or something?"

"That's a fine suspicion to plant in the minds of the jury!" Schechter winked. "One way to establish that is to find the original source that would clearly state the meaning of the mantra. Since we are dealing with shamanic Bon that precedes the alphabet, we won't find it. Two is to find a living *nagpa,* a lama who practices Bon magic. But most of them were killed by the Chinese."

"They'll make fun of us in court!" Paxton exclaimed. "That's just another conspiracy theory! No one has ever killed himself from hearing Tune Ra's chorus!"

"Some mantras can have a delayed, latent effect," Schechter parried. "Some mantras need to be repeated for years for the vibrations to accumulate, the way snow amasses on the top before collapsing in an avalanche. If it is chanted correctly by a master, a guru, a highly dedicated yogi, it will have an instant effect. But it's a great art and takes a long time to learn. A mantra syllable is like a musician's finger: flawlessly, it picks the string intended by the composer. In the same way, the chosen syllables compose a melody, a song that would make us laugh or cry or something else. Whether it will have the desired effect or not depends on the performer's skill. If it is chanted by a layman, the effect may be cumulative."

"Wait, wait!" Rudi's head was bursting. "Something's missing in this theory of yours . . . suggestion to commit suicide? No—that's not what I felt. I don't know how to explain it. Let me get the tape recorder. I'll record you, and tomorrow I'll test it on myself with a psychiatrist present."

"Aha!" cried Schechter as Milagros wheeled in the tray with the dishes. "Dinner is served! We can sing later!"

14

"THE food chain," Schechter mused, "is another Buddhist concept accepted by modern society. Plants devour minerals, animals eat plants, humans animals . . . but who feeds on humans?"

He smacked his lips at a particularly juicy piece of fish and solemnly declared "*God.* A man lives off what he creates, and so does God. Pagans interpreted this literally and practiced human sacrifice. But God doesn't need it; bodies belong in the soil. God is a gourmet: He grows and consumes only the most delicate part—the spirit. He digests only clear thought and goodwill created by men. Whatever is not digestible is ejected into the cosmic dark and becomes fertilizer for new human reincarnations. The life of the universe is a divine feast. Careful!"

Carried away by the monologue, Rudi choked on a bone. Red with embarrassment—how did he manage to find a bone in salmon?—he waved: *I'm okay.*

"With fish, you have to watch out." Schechter patted Rudi on the back, just to make sure. "Heavenly forces in Bardo chew carefully, and so must we—slowly and thoughtfully, the way fate chews our lives. It grinds us with its teeth of troubles, it separates us from our loved ones with incisors of loss, and it moistens us with the saliva of grief. And it washes up with the wine of compassion. So—drink up. . . . We are hard lumps, Rudi. For God to digest us, we must be liquified by our fate first."

While lecturing, the professor did not neglect his duties as a host, pouring wine and placing the juiciest bits on Rudi's plate.

"To experience the taste fully, Rudi, you must caress the food and shift it around your mouth with the sensitive tongue of your heart. One must live and eat the way one makes love, smacking one's lips and moaning—one must voice one's thanks and enjoyment. Only after you have turned the lumps of life in your mouth to ambrosia can you swallow and deliver your soul to Bardo, over which you have no control. Then devourment—death—will become a refined act, rather than a lump in your throat; then life will be one long feast, rather than a fast-food lunch or a takeout dinner you stuff in your mouth over the evening news."

Slightly tipsy, Rudi wandered off and picked up only on the last word. "Nine! I have to call Gwen!"

He called the way they had agreed, dialing and hanging up.

"Aha, a code!" Schechter grinned. "I hope it's numerologically consistent?"

"That's right." Rudi grinned back. "The total must be seven: three rings—one—three again . . . Gwen?"

After a few words, he hung up and drank a whole glass of wine. "Odd," he said thoughtfully. "He stopped calling."

"Stop being paranoid, Rudi. It was someone's joke, and he got sick and tired of it. While you, on the other hand, got used to it—to the spice of doom. Without it, life would be bland. Here, have some eggplant. One of Milagros's top dishes."

"Why did you call it 'spice of doom'?" Rudi asked warily. "You consider my case to be hopeless? Am I going to jail? Is that what you think? Level with me!"

"Don't pick on my words." Schechter waved him off. "On the other hand, what is there but words?"

The professor was quite smashed, Rudi noted.

"Level-shmevel." Schechter bit into an apple, and the juice spurted on his glasses, prompting him to guffaw: "The apple got run over by the train, and the blood spurted on the windshield."

Rudi choked on his wine.

"Will you forget about your goddamn bum!" Schechter yelled suddenly. "You won't go to jail! You are not guilty! That was his karma—and you were its tool, you simply helped his transition, for which he was ready. One crack, and he dropped into God's basket. Now he's sitting on His right hand, blows his sax, and laughs at you wasting away in jail! You have already locked yourself into the cell of fear! Tell yourself: *I am free! I am full of joy! It's my life—and I'm the one free to choose between freedom and joy—and slavery and fear!*"

Milagros stuck her head in the door: *Anything else?*

"Bring us the coffee and then you can go home," Schechter ordered.

Rudi rose. "I'll go get the tape recorder."

"No! A dinner is a dinner! First we'll have cigars al fresco. Get the bottle and the glasses. Milagros! We'll be on the roof!"

THE damp night air took the edge off the wine buzz. The roof was small but had the essentials: patio furniture and a lamp. The professor would not light it, though; he sank heavily into a chair and lit a cigar instead, silently releasing smoke up into the starry sky.

Then he said, without looking at Rudi, "My son is a scientist—a geologist—did I tell you? He told me there are empty spaces between the galaxies, four hundred million light-years in diameter! Amazingly, these spaces—infinite in number and placed between infinite galaxies—are of equal size. Together, galaxies and empty spaces form an ideal geometric figure that the Tibetans call *apal-beh,* an infinite knot, or a beehive. Christians call it the Rose of the World; Muslims, Allah's Carpet; Jews, the Scroll of Heaven. How could this precision emerge by chance at such distances? According to the physicists, in the beginning this orderly structure emerged in a compact form, and then certain waves expanded this mini mockup to infinity while preserving its proportions. Do you understand what mini mockup they are talking about?"

He rose and solemnly pointed into the distance.

"The Word! In the beginning, there was the Word, the phrase, the incantation—the Mantra! It is the model of Creation: a letter becomes a star; a syllable, a constellation; a word, a galaxy; a phrase, a galactic cluster. And the spaces in between are identical!"

Schechter caught his breath. His eyes were shining, his

wrinkles were gone, there was color in his cheeks; like a woman in love, he looked half his age.

"The Book of Creation is being written as we speak! Stars are the scattered divine alphabet that we forgot how to read. But how do you find the letters of the ur-mantra that God used to create the world if they are scattered through galaxies, with trillions of light-years separating them? You must hear the Word that brought you to life. You must listen to yourself: all divine words, both creating and destroying, are right inside you. Including your mantra, Rudi. . . ."

"But what d-does it m-mean?"

Rudi had lit a cigar as well. After a couple of puffs, he realized it was a bad idea. He had already been tottering on the edge of drunkenness, and the cigar smoke was the breeze that pushed him over. His mind was still clear, but his movements were treacherously slow. He had to summon every effort to flick the ashes into the ashtray without dropping them into the glass.

Schechter refilled his glass. "Wine is a meditation tool for the lazy ones like you and me. The first few glasses shrink your world to a room, then to the table, until, sooner or later, you find yourself in a tiny black cell—in your brain! Where you can laugh your heart out, drop ashes on your pants, drink from the bottle, soar with angels, or simply bliss out in the splendid darkness! Yogi call it *samadhi*, junkies call it a superhigh, and society at large—drunken stupor or clinical death! Here comes the coffee!"

Yes, the superhigh *samadhi* stupor was doing a bang-up job washing away the boundaries of the objects and merging them together, Rudi thought. He caught himself seeing the cosmic logic in this newly created chaos.

"You must do everything as if it were your last time." Smacking his lips, Schechter sipped his coffee.

"Maybe it *is* my last time." Coffee was returning edges to objects. "I haven't heard about wine, coffee, and cigars in jail."

"Don't be silly. You'll drink cases of wine yet. In general, the purpose of this meditation is not focusing on objects, but expanding them to the infinity of Creation. Take this candle"—he pointed at a transparent green lamp with a candle inside—"a man is like a particle in the flame: he struggles, he eats up oxygen, he changes shape, he burns out. All along, he believes the universe is limited to the glass.

"Look at the cup, whose walls and shape are similar to a human body. Someone superior, unknown to both the cup and the liquid in it, poured in the liquid and warmed it up. The liquid evaporates and dissolves in the air. Look at the wineglass, where the liquid fights the glass and the air to get out. The light tries to melt the glass to get out; the alcohol, to erode the glass and pour itself into a free state. Everything wants to transcend its borders and merge with everything else. Each arena thinks that it comprises a universe. Together, they are on the table that in turns fights the floor and the walls. But beyond the walls there are millions of other creations, similar to the ones on this table. They are the true dimensions of the Creation that a man cannot realize, because he is nothing more than a particle in the flame in the glass, yet thinks that his struggle, his dance constitutes the main conflict of life. On the other hand, the Creation outside this room is no more than a dance of a tiny candle in the glass eyed by Someone with His own worlds."

Rudi nodded agreement. He had lost the train of thought long ago; he could only focus on his teacher's eyes, shiny with wine and inspiration. As the latter orated, his various embodiments flashed in front of the student's eyes—from a togaed Roman philosopher to an elderly *tsadik* to a laughing Buddha. Rudi could only grip the arms of the chair and try to keep up as he changed, too: from a young patrician heeding Seneca to an Essene at the feet of the Rebbe to the shaven-headed monk Mahakashyapa, smiling at the Nirvana that revealed itself in the form of a flower handed to him by the Blessed One.

"I had a similar experience recently," Rudi murmured. "I just got back from the court and I was standing under the shower and staring at the tiled wall covered with water drops. And I thought of myself as one of these drops. And other drops were the people around me. Whereas I, the man, off whose shoulders the drops were bouncing, was God of whom these drops could not conceive. It's sort of like what you said before: I thought that this dew on the tiles, with every drop representing a person, cannot comprehend the mechanism of the Bathroom Universe."

"Bravo!" Schechter clapped his hands. "Give me your glass."

"No, wait—I got upset then!" Rudi pressed the cold glass to his hot forehead. "I thought: someone created this gadget that brings joy to people. But at twenty-six, what can I create that would bring joy to people? I study theology. So what? If I were a teacher like you, or a preacher; if I could use words to create this cleansing flow of water, the way a shower does . . . But I can't do anything, Professor. I don't know what I am doing in life or what is the use of me. Perhaps this is the reason that fate is packing me off to jail: because I am a parasite and an idler who meditates and pores over Buddhist writings for his own enjoyment and is of absolutely no use outside."

Schechter nodded as he listened to his student's outpouring. Then, after a pause, he spoke in a suddenly weary and sober voice:

"I'll tell you something important, Rudi. I'll try to be brief." He closed his eyes and, frowning, rubbed his temples. "Thinking is the most important job in the world. Why do you think there are wars, disease, loneliness, unhappiness—first of all, our own? Because we are not thinking correctly. The energy of our evil thoughts accumulates and discharges periodically in the form of these ills. Maintaining ecology of thought is more important than Greenpeace. It means not just refraining from ill thoughts, but chucking the vanity of the conscious altogether. Our patter of reason amasses in the universe till it reaches the critical point, and then . . . We worry about our careers and families, we envy, fear, condemn, gloat, become frustrated, and pat ourselves on the back for not planning murders or terrorist acts. But all it means is that, instead of dumping a tanker of oil into the ocean, we keep sprinkling it with our lighters.

"Every time you meditate, you're doing important work: you refrain from polluting the sphere of thought. But that's merely avoidance of evil. If you want to do good, you must focus on good thoughts. By doing so, you burn the ill thoughts of others. It's hard work, concentrating on the lofty, the impersonal; it's so much easier to do material things. People who can save the world with their thoughts are as few as guides to Shambala. I failed to become one. Perhaps you can make it. Or perhaps you'll meet one of them. You must be ready: every day you must contend with your mind, with the trivial patter of reason. Every day you must fall and rise again. The longer you live, the more you realize that everything in the world is a product of your own thoughts. An atomic reactor that has spread radiation—there, it's in your hands. . . ."

By now Schechter was gripping his head and rocking, like a religious Jew. The combined effect of his words and his appearance made Rudi almost sober. He felt sadness and fear, like a child who has finally realized that his father, so brave and strong, is actually frightened. And Schechter was definitely afraid of something.

"You'll be afraid," the professor went on. "You'll want to stop your brain, to get inside it, to scrub it clean. But it will be too late. One has to start doing this in one's youth, day after day, hour after hour. Otherwise, shame will settle in. You will realize how much evil your thoughts have wrought. Not only in your own life, but in those of others as well. Then your main work will start: correcting by thought the misdeeds created by thought, too. This is more important than the comforts of the bathroom. But you won't have any time left."

Speaking of time, Rudi thought, it was already past ten, and they still had not recorded Schechter's chanting.

"Professor, you've had your nourishment!" he begged. "Let me go get the tape recorder!"

"Yes, you should go." Schechter poured himself another glass. "You must be sleepy."

"I'm not." And immediately yawned.

"Good sign, Rudi." Schechter chuckled. "You are not in danger. If a person really has little time left, sleep is the last thing on his mind."

*   *   *

BACK downstairs, the professor, grunting, lay down on the floor next to the fireplace, facing the fire.

"Of all the elements, fire is my favorite. Whatever is not burned in time ages, rots, decays, and poisons. This is how Indians meditate: they stare at the fire to see their fate in it.

"When I first met my Rinpoche in Tibet, he would not let me settle down with books in his library. Instead, he sent me to a village, three days' travel from the lamasery—a savage muddy place that just happened to have a typhoid epidemic. He told me to go there every day to watch them burn the corpses. Just sit there and watch. . . .

"At first I sat at a distance from the pyre, squeamish about the smell and the black oily smoke. It was pretty cold—springs are freezing there—so I moved closer to the fire, almost like this"—he reached for the grating; "I overcame my squeamishness, my fear: I just sat there, trying to keep warm. Then I started looking at corpses. How they catch the flame, turn red, then black, how they turn into mummies; how their bones are ground and turned into gray ashes carried by the wind all over the Himalayas. Then one day I felt I was one of these corpses. I felt it was me on the pyre. I felt I was dead."

He edged even closer to the fire, lay on his back, and, his eyes closed, crossed his arms on his chest, assuming the pose of a corpse.

"I felt the flames roar and crackle all around me"—Schechter beamed—"they were hot and loving. I did not fear them. The fire devoured my feet, turning them into ashes and blowing them away. Next, it rose up my legs, coming up to my groin. I was scared for a moment: we are so used to the primacy of this spot. But it burned out, it vanished, and I felt light and joyous. The fire roared further up, to my stomach. Once again, I felt fear—we're obsessed with our stomachs—but it turned to ashes, too. My chest, my heart were going up in blazes, but the joy was burning in my head. The fire coated my face and singed my skull. I loved it: it was so vibrant and hungry. Fire was Time itself, feeding on all in me that was temporal. I knew bliss, Rudi."

Schechter's eyes shone insanely. Rudi wondered if it was the reflection of the fire or something else.

"I felt the gray matter hiss, crackle, and turn into ashes; with every crackle, my memory, my anxieties, my desires, my whole persona, all that I knew or remembered or wanted—all of them were gone. The only thing left was a bright, free Light that has no name or form or past, present, or future; yet it illuminates and dances everywhere at the same time—in the fire, in the onlookers, in the world, the universe! I had never known such happiness. . . .

"When I came to—or, rather, died into my flesh—I realized I was smiling. I knew it was the same black smile I had observed in the faces of corpses. These depersonalized smiles had no features—no eyes, no skin; these smiles of the ashes were pure. The pure joy of the Void."

He fell silent.

"And then what?" For a moment, the professor's story made Rudi forget his own woes.

"For some time I lived like the ashes: light, shapeless, blown by life. Then I grew some flesh back."

Without getting up, Schechter pulled the grating aside and adjusted a log with his bare hand, oblivious of the fire.

"But this growth has to be burned. Our life is the path of return to this fire, whether of our free will or by force. I'll never forget the black smile of the corpse. It's so beauti—"

The phone rang so unexpectedly that Paxton felt thrown by its sound.

Schechter calmly picked up. "You can't? That's a shame. Call me back in half an hour. I have a student here; he will leave soon."

"This was my son," he explained after he hung up. "He was supposed to stay overnight, but he can't. Do you want to stay, Rudi? We can pretend we're in Tibet, in the big yurt. . . ."

He was slurring his words. Time to go, Rudi thought, rising.

Suddenly, the professor grabbed him and pulled him down hard. "Let me give you something." He rolled up his sweater and removed the beads wound in rings above his watch.

He was never without them. They were always visible in

his coat sleeve during the lectures, and Rudi liked the clatter they made whenever the professor gestured. One hundred and eight yellowed pieces of bone, each one for a sutra, divided into three groups by slightly larger red balls and forming a little mortar-shaped figure around the knot— seven beads sticking out away from the center. In Schechter's beads, the fourth one, which symbolized heart, was replaced by an oblong pebble: the eye of the tiger. They were simple Buddhist beads—old, worn, and so *cool.*

"I couldn't accept this—" he stammered, but Schechter gripped his wrist.

"I want you to wear them as a memory of your old professor." Schechter wound the beads around Rudi's hand; then he hugged Rudi and kissed his cheek. His mouth was wet and unsteady and reeked of wine and some kind of old folks' medicine. "Sorry," he moaned. "I'm so sorry. . . ."

Behind them, Milagros coughed to remind them of her presence. She glared at Rudi, who had barely squirmed out of the professor's embrace.

"You can go," said Schechter, without releasing Rudi's hand.

After the front door slammed shut, Schechter, beaming a drunken smile, stroked his guest's hand. Rudi glanced at him, irritated—but did not pull it back. He felt that this warm, heavy, sweaty body, the yellow freckles on the white skin, the boulder of a skull that sheltered so much learning, the clumps of hoary gray hair and sweat drops on the shiny pate, the teary blue eyes with red veins—this mass of flesh and thought was actually he, Rudi. It was a version of him, from past or future; now it was an old *him* stroking the hand of the younger *him*—his own hand. Unexpectedly, he bent to kiss Schechter's hand—the raw-skinned, brown-spotted hand of an old man.

"Don't go," Schechter pleaded; "stay—"

Rudi rose decisively. "Sorry. I'll come back tomorrow, with the tape recorder. Good night, and thanks for the dinner."

Schechter seemed loath to see his guest leave. Still prone on the floor, he kept wailing: "Rudi, Rudi . . ."

The old man was hopelessly drunk. The clock showed

midnight; but something held Rudi back. He glanced around: the shelves, the table, the fireplace, the glasses on the rug, the telephone—

As if on cue, the phone rang.

"Hello?" Schechter's voice was suddenly all business. "No—no one here by that name." He hung up. "Wait!" he called Rudi, already at the door. "Turn on the music. *Madama Butterfly* with Tibaldi, it's on the turntable."

The library filled with sweet, weepy sounds of the opera.

"Louder," Schechter whispered. "Close your eyes. One listens to music in the dark. No wonder the flesh responds to sounds like these. So much flesh . . ." He rubbed his stomach. "Go, my boy. Come tomorrow morning, about ten. And keep ringing the bell: I may still be asleep." He turned on his side and put slippers under his head.

"Professor—perhaps I should move you to the bedroom."

"No, I'll sleep by the fire—the Tibetan way." Schechter clumsily rolled up a corner of the rug to cover his feet. "I remember my first expedition on Lake Namtso. I spent the night in a yurt next to the stove. By morning, the glass on my watch had melted, heh-heh. . . ."

THE click of the massive front door cut off everything: the weepy aria, the drunken laughter, the crackling logs. The staircase was quiet. As if behind a wall of water, Rudi heard the faint chorus of police sirens.

15

RIVERSIDE Drive was deserted and quiet, save for the faraway sirens and the whistling of the wind. Swayed by the wind, the shadows of the maples stepped off the curb, as if to hail a cab, and timidly drew back. It was the borderline between the stone structures of Gotham and the island's original owners, the black trees of the park and the steel-gray river.

Rudi buttoned himself up to keep warm. As he put on his gloves, he heard the quiet clatter of the beads. The evening left him with an uneasy sense of uncertainty. The professor had clearly dragged on the meal; did he deliberately avoid taping his chanting?

Frustration seemed to fill Rudi's chest with carbon dioxide; he had to exhale deeply and hold his breath. Why did Schechter insist that the mantra contained a suicide suggestion? True, he almost fell under the train; but at the time he felt something else. . . . What was it?

The fresh cold from the river, the decay of the leaves, the film of frost on the ground—all of them were invigorating after the cigar smoke, dusty bindings, and slurred speeches. They seemed so natural in contrast to the fears that were choking him that his frustration turned into roaring joy.

It's my mind that's afraid of the mantra, he decided. And the mind can always be changed!

Thus, armed with newfound decisiveness, he headed for the park: raw and dark, it welcomed him, like a hand of nature extended for a greeting.

This could be fodder for the professor's constructs, he thought lightly as he descended the slope. Air, my dear students, essentially is the same as God: it gives life by containing an antioxidant in the form of death. It is absolutely bland and immaterial. Life brings aromas and takes them away, but the air remains the same.

As if in response, a gust of wind brought a whiff of roasted peanuts and gasoline—and cleared again. My problems will be carried off, too, but clarity and joy will remain.

Instead of marching down the main promenade, paved and well lit, he followed a narrow parallel mud path hidden in the trees. He was not bothered by the absence of people. The cold ocean air brought low black clouds that hid the stars, faintly flickering in the city, and the moon. Even the path, which a moment ago glittered with tiny puddles, disappeared underfoot.

He was never afraid of the dark. The night was his kingdom. For him, it was a place where the primeval fears bubbled in sweet horror—and where he shook free of them. Somehow he was sure that nothing bad could happen to him at night outdoors. Perhaps because his mother used to call him "my lion cub." And the night is the time for a lion to hunt.

It was on night walks like this that memories of his mother came to him. (Schechter would not let it go without bringing up Freud—the hell with him.)

She was nineteen when he was born: a sweet fresh-faced girl with long shiny hair who played her recorder on the Berkeley campus and marched against the war. Her pregnancy was well under way when she discovered that his father, a doctoral candidate in chemistry, considered napalm a useful product. She packed up and returned to live with her parents, though not for long.

He grew up in a commune in northern California, among "free artists" like his mother. Deprived of age peers, he wandered the woods and the beaches, intoxicated by their mystical power—not quite the traditional all-American respect of nature that James Fenimore Cooper's pathfinders had (though later he would draw a semantic parallel between Natty Bumppo and Bon Po).

At seven his mother started giving him banjo lessons, and he realized that real music came from the sounds of nature. Unafraid of the dark, he would often slip out of the house and stand on the beach, facing the fearsome vistas of moonlit ocean and listening to the night concerto: the cicadas' violins, the seagulls' sharp altos, the wind's horns, and the applause of the surf. Melodies were everywhere: the highway traffic, the noises of the city where they had moved to, the chatting of his friends, the strained silence of his father, whom his mother came back to and left again a number of times . . . the communication with each of them, including silences, had a tune of its own.

What was Schechter's tune? he wondered as he strode further into the dark. It struck Rudi as sickly and depressed: as if Schechter were being forced to play an entire symphony on the horn. Emotion was the only thing he could offer to make up for this instrumental deficit, so he pumped up his cheeks as he tried to fit his entire existence into the horn; yet nothing came out but wheezing and chaos. No: Schechter was not concerned with my mantra. My problem was just a small horn into which he tried to squeeze his own symphony.

The thought made him slow down. He climbed a bench and rose on his tiptoes. He could see Schechter's house, where only one window was lit, with a shaky reddish light—perhaps the fire was still going. A strong nagging impulse pulled Rudi back.

I should go back, hug him, find out what he is afraid of. This might help my fears, too. No: that's dumb.

He resolutely continued along the path. Yet soon he realized he was slowing down again. Someone was following him.

He turned around abruptly. The dark was impenetrable.

He heard the steps and a creaking sound that stopped the moment he stopped. Rudi's heart dropped in the ice-cold lake of his stomach, and the splashed water spread throughout like goose bumps. Someone was breathing a few feet away.

"Who's there?" he called.

No one answered. But someone was watching. Rudi clenched his jaws to stop the trembling and keep himself from breaking into a run. He walked towards the exit at an unhurried pace. Now he was listening with his back, too. Something creaked behind him. He paused again. No: just the wind and the distant sirens of Broadway.

I hear things, he thought; it was a stray dog or something. He stepped slowly, trying to distinguish the sounds behind. He should have stayed at the professor's house, he should have taken a cab. . . .

"Grrr."

He trembled as if hit with an electric charge. The sound— a guffaw? a roar?—was right behind him!

"Who's there?"

His heart beat three times loudly. And the answer came. In the dark, a hoarse voice chanted Tune Ra's chorus.

Sheer terror lifted Rudi off the ground and spun him around. Hollering, he leapt off the path, hopped through the slurping clay, and ran smack into a hard object that caught him in his stomach and his knees. He tumbled over it, hurt his head, and, grabbing cold dirty soil, stretched on his back. A huge formless silhouette was advancing towards him. He hollered again, he kicked up his legs; they slid in the dirt, and he ended up with his head against a scrubby tree.

The light of a flashlight shot him in the face.

"Yo—you pick garbage, too?"

The speaker was an elderly black man with a scraggly gray beard, wearing a torn ski jacket over a long overcoat and a ski hat topped with a soiled shawl. Atop the shawl was a professional-looking headset, its wire reaching into the shopping cart—the source of the creaking—where the man's possessions were crowned by a large portable radio.

"Who are you?"

"Wha'?" The man kept his headset on as he swayed to the music. "You find anything in that garbage?"

In one hand he held a large police-issue flashlight; in the other, a brown bag with what clearly was a bottle. In the light, Rudi saw that the obstacle he had stumbled into was a large garbage can. The detritus, wet from the rain, clung to his pants.

"It ain't safe runnin' here after dark, brother," the homeless man went on, never pausing in his dance. "You got nothin' here but dogshit and garbage cans. You gotta walk slo-o-wly, like you slow-dancin' with your lady—like I walk with my here cart." He put his arm around the cart's handles and danced a few steps, echoing Tune Ra's chorus.

Rudi sat up. "Is that what you're listening to?"

"Wha'?" The bum leaned over, reeking of an unwashed body and cheap wine.

"Tune Ra?" Rudi pointed at the headset. He could not bring himself to believe it was a coincidence.

"Yeah! You like it?" He pulled the wire out.

The mantra roared through the park. The invisible birds fluttered in the trees.

"Git up, man, 'fore you freeze yo' balls off!" The man offered Rudi his hand. "Even I don't sleep on the ground no more at this time."

His hand felt rough and hot. As it pulled Rudi up, the momentum carried him straight into the man's chest. The

touch made him shudder. It was familiar! The touch of a
strange warm body, a black face approaching, blue pupils
in huge black eyes—it was just like the subway!

Grinning, the man intoned the mantra again.

"Who are you?" Rudi exclaimed. "What do you want?"

"I'm just a po' black man, bro'. Just asking for some
change for a cup of coffee."

"Who sent you?"

"I'm poor, man. Ain't no crime." Dancing and smiling,
the man advanced. "Spare some change for a cup o' cof
fee?" He extended his hand.

Rudi gazed at his face, ravaged by booze and God knew
what else. Could he be the brother of the subway victim?
His father? Was there a whole family after him?

Tune Ra kept screaming through the abandoned park.
Keeping his eyes on the man's face, Rudi felt a bill in his
pocket and shoved it into the man's hand.

"God bless you, brother!" The flashlight revealed a five
dollar bill. "You thought I was gon' buy me some more of
that wine, didn't you? I'll tell you: I'm gon' go to Korean
man on the corner and get me some real nice fried chicken!"

He reinserted the cable into his headset. Once again, the
wind was the only sound.

"God bless you, brother." He bowed. "And don't run after
dark. Walk slow, like this. . . ." And he danced away with
his cart. In another minute, even the creaking sound was
gone.

AFTER the fall, Rudi's head was aching and spinning. He
wiped the dirt off his face and felt the bump on his head.
Fear, nothing but fear. . . . He uttered a small laugh. Life
wanted to help him shake the wrong thoughts out of his
head and smacked him into a garbage can, so that his
thoughts would become its contents. In a way, that proved
his obsession with Tune Ra's chorus. If he could have this
accident on record, it would help his case. He should drag
the bum in as a witness!

"Hey!" He rushed into the dark and immediately stopped.
Was he indeed going nuts? What did he need the bum for?
He would tape the professor in the morning. Yet the ques

tion would not go away. No, the mantra was not causing panic; it was something else. . . .

Maybe he had a concussion. He leaned against a tree. "I don't want to know what this mantra means! I don't want to think about it! Lord, free my mind from this nonsense! These thoughts are obsessing me. I need to destroy the invader—but how?"

He kicked the garbage can as hard as he could. He stomped the leftover garbage: empty beer cans, pizza boxes, crumpled papers—all the while grinding his teeth and screaming gibberish.

The professor was right: it had a liberating effect. At one A.M., in the middle of Riverside Park, Rudi Paxton, a graduate student of theology at Columbia University, was screaming—rather, barking—unintelligible combinations of sounds. He was elated. The barking changed to laughter.

"I'm not afraid!" he yelled. "I'm not afraid of the bums! I'm not afraid of the phone! I'm not afraid of the mantra!"

A blinding light hit him in the face.

"FREEZE!"

"You scared me." Rudi exhaled. "That's the second time tonight. How can I help you, Officer?"

"Turn around! Put your hands on the tree!"

There were two patrolmen. The younger one stood to the side, his hand on his holster; the other frisked Rudi with quick efficiency. Then he pointed his flashlight down at the ground.

"Who were you kicking here?"

"What?"

"You were kicking someone here!"

Paxton gave out a small laugh. "It was my mind, Officer. I was kicking my own mind."

"You have an ID?"

The policeman took his driver's license to the patrol car and, after an inordinate amount of time, came back. "You live on One Hundredth? Where are you coming from?"

"Professor Michael Schechter's place. He is my teacher at Columbia. We had dinner at his place, and then I decided to take in some air."

The sergeant took notes. "We'll give you a lift, sir. This is not a safe place to be at night."

IN the elevator, he studied himself in the mirror. The encounter with the garbage can had left him covered with mud, yet neither the bump on his forehead nor the dried clay on his cheeks put a wrinkle on his happy smile. The second bum turned out to be harmless. Perhaps the mantra was a joke, too.

He quietly turned the key—

"Who is it?" Gwen's voice slashed him like a whip.

He recoiled. "It's me. . . ."

The door opened a crack, revealing a glint of knife in the dark, and Gwen's eyes: the velvety black shells with a tiny pearl of a stye in one of them. In second grade, a classmate accidentally stuck a pencil in her eye; whenever she got excited, the spot turned shiny. Now it was dazzling, like a diamond.

"It's me," he repeated.

Inside, she dropped on the floor and broke into tears.

"He called again!" She grabbed the telephone, already disconnected, and slammed it on the floor. "The voice! Half an hour ago—and he used our code! I was already asleep, I didn't want to look for the receiver, so I pressed the speakerphone—and he started singing that mantra of yours! I kept trying to turn it off and kept missing in the dark. And he kept going louder, with his voice getting lower . . . I just tore it off."

"Calm down, calm down . . ."

As he stroked her sweet-smelling hair, he stared numbly at the telephone. Who would know the code?

"Did you give it to anybody?" Gwen asked.

"Nobody." He got up to remove his mud-covered coat.

"What happened to you? What have you been doing all this time at Schechter's?"

"Nothing—I went home through the park—I tripped over something. . . . Yes, I did tell. I told Schechter about the code."

Her eyes grew narrow.

I shouldn't have told her, he thought. She never liked the

professor. Either she was jealous, or her instinct cautioned her.

"What time did you leave?"

"Midnight—"

"So he called later, while you were on the way. But no one called while you were there."

"It's just a coincidence!" he cried out. "He must have been dialing at random! Three-one-three, some code! Schechter has nothing to do with it."

"What did he say about the voice?"

"He called it throat singing. He meditated and used the same voice in a trance. It couldn't be him!" he exclaimed, irritated at her expression. "He's my teacher, for God's sake! Why would he?"

She changed the subject. "I did a search on Tune Ra on the Web. He's into exotic drugs and eclectic religions, or vice versa. Though he told you he never heard of Bon Po. Rumored to be gay, with scandalous affairs with Hollywood's velvet mafia. What did Schechter say about him?"

"He told me I was being paranoid." Rudi lay down and massaged his temples. "I have to trust him if only because he trusts me! He is not afraid I'll run away and have him forfeit bail."

"What if he runs away himself?"

"What are you talking about? Tomorrow morning I'll go to his place to tape his trance. Which will be used for expert testimony."

"Unless he has already used his expertise for someone else," she said.

STANDING in the shower, he thought that Gwen had succeeded where his mind had failed: planting vague suspicions about the professor. Whom else did he provide with advice? And why would he run away? On the other hand . . . all those books missing from his shelves. The beads had all the makings of a farewell gift. And he had begged forgiveness. But he was drunk. He sounded oddly indifferent to Rudi's problem, to the upcoming trial. How did all of this square with putting up the bail?

Gwen was right: this could not have been a coincidence.

The code could not have come from anyone else.

"I've got myself a guru," Rudi whispered, "and he is totally nuts."

SUDDENLY it dawned on him! *Nyingma-pa!*

The discovery struck him so hard he had to turn off the water and sit on the edge of the tub. *Nyingma-pa* was a Tibetan school of mad wisdom. This definitely looked like one of their methods. Schechter had called in order to scare his student further and plunge him into a nervous breakdown.

He wants me to dissociate from my fear, Rudi thought, amazed at the crooked ways of his professor's wisdom. That's why he told me how his Rinpoche had sent him to look at the corpses. He wants to scare me into a catharsis, into the loss of my "I," beyond which lies Nirvana. He keeps training me, while I keep nurturing my idiotic suspicions. He's like any other guru: he doesn't give a fig about my problems. The only thing he wants is for me to achieve a state of enlightenment.

He vigorously rubbed himself dry. He was back in the realm of clarity and freedom. He could not wait to tell Gwen about his latest deduction.

But she was already asleep. He watched her from the edge of the bed: her eyelashes trembled ever so slightly and the skin of her eyelids rippled from her pupils' movement. She was so beautiful and vulnerable, it made his heart ache. He entered his observations in his diary and climbed under the blanket. Still asleep, she pressed herself against him and placed his hand on her stomach.

He closed his eyes, hugged her tightly, and felt serenity descend upon him. Within a moment he sank into a warm dark abyss. Outside, the sky was turning gray, and the garbage trucks groaned unpleasantly. It had been a long day but the garbage was done with, and cleanliness and emptiness ruled the city.

16

THE cab had to stop a block away from the professor's house.

"Police line, sir," the turbaned driver informed him.

Rudi stepped out into the drizzle and stood petrified, unable to strap on his backpack with the tape recorder. Past the yellow tape were the fire trucks and blue-and-whites with rotating lights. Cops were scampering all over the place, their black jackets coal-shiny with morning hoarfrost. He looked up at Schechter's apartment. The windows gaped, blind and paneless.

Rudi's legs melted and vanished in the sidewalk. He looked back. The Sikh was still counting the money. Should he go back? But his legs, or what was left of them, dragged him to the building.

This was just like his first day at a new school. He wanted to run away, but his father was holding his hand tightly. Rudi clenched his hand in a fist. The palm was empty and wet, either from sweat or from rain.

He spotted Milagros near the entrance, talking to Tarakis and his black partner. Run! Before they saw him!

"There he is!" Milagros pointed at him. Her eyes were red, her mouth crooked, her face crumpled and very, very old.

"AH, Mr. Paxton. Can I call you *Rudra*? We were expecting you. Please get in the car."

A mean grin danced on Tarakis's face, as though he could hear Rudi's heartbeat.

"What's wrong?" Rudi tried to speak calmly. "I've come to see Professor Schechter."

"Just a few questions. Get into the car, will ya? We don't want to get wet."

Tarakis plunged his talonlike hand into Rudi's elbow and led him to the car. His black partner, silent as always, followed.

"Is him, Señor Detective!" cried out Milagros.

The car reeked of sweat and cologne. Tarakis stuck Rudi in the backseat between himself and Rivers.

"Schechter's apartment burned down last night," Tarakis announced. "With the professor in it."

Rudi's face started sliding down. "Burned down?"

"Yep." Tarakis showed him pictures of a black mummy with gaping holes for eyes, nose, and mouth, with the familiar fireplace in the background.

Rudi knew the mummy's scowl: it was Schechter's smile when he saw him last. A wave of nausea rolled up: as if he were in an express elevator going down.

"Did you see the professor last night?"

"Yes."

"Did you leave before the fire or after?"

"After—I mean, before! I left around midnight—he was still alive!"

"So, which one is it—before or after?"

"I left him falling asleep next to the fireplace! It had to be an accident. Perhaps a corner of the rug caught fire. He was drunk. . . ."

"He was smashed, Marty! Sound familiar?" Tarakis winked at Rivers. "A smashed victim is not a victim, right? So was he drunk or was he high? How much did you take together—a gram? Or more?"

"We did not take drugs."

"Oh, but we did find the disposable needles. He didn't have diabetes, did he? And the maid said you were excited in a certain way."

"That's just her opinion."

"The police report says you were disorderly in the park. Is it their opinion, too?"

"In the park?" He tried to remember the time. "But they can tell you they met me before the fire. Riverside Drive was quiet—otherwise we would have heard the firetrucks!"

"Not necessarily." Tarakis kept grinning. "According to Forensics, the victim fell next to the fireplace and probably passed out. Then his body began getting roasted, on a slow flame. As if he had been rubbed with some kind of chemical. Isn't your father a research chemist, Mr. Paxton?"

"What does this have to do with my father?" Rudi began sweating again. "I haven't spoken to him in a hundred years. What are you charging me with?"

"I'm just talking to you for now. So, the fire started at his feet and then went up. He got well done, I'll say that. Only then the furniture caught fire. And the neighbors did not call 911 until the windows got blown out, which was about two-thirty. . . . You look pale, Mr. Paxton—something wrong?"

"Can we step outside? It's really hot in here."

"Let's go for a walk," Rivers suggested, opening an umbrella for himself and Rudi.

As they went down the steps to the park, Tarakis clenched Rudi's elbow again.

"One more time: Are you sure that, when you were leaving, the professor was alive? What if he dropped dead from all that booze? You got scared—and took off?"

"He was alive. In fact"—Rudi bit his lip—"he called me at twelve-thirty, right after I left!"

"He did?" Tarakis took a printout out of his briefcase. "Nothing's here. The last time he called you was at nine"—he traced the entry—"when you were still at his place."

"That's the call I made. I was calling my girlfriend. Wait—" Rudi rubbed his temples. "Wait—then it *was* an anonymous caller, after all! He used our code that only Schechter knew! Which means the professor knew him!"

"One thing at a time," Rivers said calmly.

Once again, barely staying coherent as he confused his own doubts with Gwen's, Rudi went over the events of the night before.

"I don't know who that person is, but he must have learned the code from the professor—there was no one else!"

Tarakis kept nodding, his face maintaining an ironic expression. "According to the maid, the professor shouted, 'Forget about the money!' You know something about that?"

"She heard wrong. The professor was my guru; he was dealing with my *mind,* not money."

"Just your mind?" Tarakis's eyebrows went up. "You sure your body wasn't involved? The maid saw you hugging and kissing. You're his favorite student, right?"

Rudi glared at him. "Schechter was not gay."

"No kidding." Another file came out. "Busted for possession during a raid in a gay club, another one in a bathhouse. Another arrest, with a male hooker in a motel . . ."

Rudi's legs were shaking badly. He dropped on the bench, disregarding the wet boards.

"What's wrong?" Tarakis placed his foot on the bench, baring a gun in an ankle strap. "You didn't know any of that? We talked to his son this morning, that's the first thing he said: 'Must be one of his lovers.' "

"We were not lovers! I was his student! A disciple!"

Rudi's pants, heavy with water, were weighing him down. Cold, wet pants: an irreplaceable element of childhood, classes, and death.

"I want to see my lawyer." He tried to inject steel into his voice.

"What for?" Tarakis faked surprise. "You haven't been charged yet. Actually, we're talking off the record. Don't you want to help us find whoever murdered your favorite professor?"

He took out a folded newspaper, placed it on the bench, and sat next to Rudi.

"There's nothing to be afraid of, Mr. Paxton." He patted Rudi on the knee. "This is not a premeditated murder. The prof was shooting up, made a pass at you, you pushed him back—he fell and dropped dead. You got scared, poured some junk on him, staged a fire, and took off. Right?"

"Wrong. We were supposed to work on my defense this morning. He gave me these beads as a gift." Rudi's mouth went dry; his tongue could barely move. "I need something to drink."

"Nervous, kid?" A glint of triumph came into Tarakis's eyes. "Want a cigarette? Don't smoke? Good boy. Sarge," he said into his walkie-talkie, "get me my thermos and three cups. We're on a bench by the river."

Rivers offered Rudi a stick of gum. Rudi accepted, but his fingers were shaking so badly he could not unwrap it.

"It happens, kid." Tarakis put his arm around Rudi's back. "An accident like this can happen to anyone."

His arm was cold and heavy, like a block of cement. Second day in a row, people kept touching his shoulders and knees. Rudi hated it, but he had no strength left to fight back.

"Let me see," Tarakis went on. "It was like in the subway: Schechter started chanting the same mantra, and you got scared—am I right?"

"I want my lawyer," Rudi repeated.

Tarakis took a metal container out of his breast pocket, took out a half-smoked cigar, and lit it slowly. "We can call your lawyer. She's probably bailing out some drug dealers downtown, so it'll be a while. Meantime, you're off to Central Booking. Because we'll bring up the charges. We've got every reason to do that. Then you'll wait on Riker's for your trial. No bail for the second murder. Even if the judge feels sorry for you once again, there's no one to put it up. You think your Legal Aid chick is going to hustle you up another expert? Or witnesses for the second murder? All we are trying to do here is figure it out: are we dealing with a serial killer, or is there something else involved? That's why we're just talking to you, off the record. Ah, coffee . . ."

He accepted a paper bag from the patrolman.

"My wife makes me a thermos of real Greek coffee every morning." He poured the thick steaming liquid into three paper cups, took a sip, and smacked his lips. "Not bad, huh? I shouldn't, with my ulcers, but a coffee and a cigar are the only things to get me going. You know, they got me out of bed at three A.M. for this one. You should see the inside of his apartment: black and muddy, like the bottom of the coffeepot. The walls still smoking, black ceiling, soot everywhere, water up to your knees. And smells of a fried corpse. They say nothing smells sweeter than your enemy's corpse. Right, Marty?" Tarakis winked at Rivers.

Rudi's hands kept shaking, spilling coffee. This just keeps happening to me, he thought in disgust: every time I feel sick like this, people around me start cracking little jokes with hints and winks. Perhaps life was an intimate joke between the spirit and the flesh that a suspect like himself was unable to perceive. Then he should try to share this joke, rather than get hot and bothered.

"Enough, Baz," Rivers said grimly. "The kid's about to freak out."

Tarakis puffed on his cigar vigorously. "See, Mr. Paxton, it's like TV, right? Good cop–bad cop. And you're weaving between us like a black line in this yin-and-yang thing. Yeah, my wife's into that stuff. I even tried to do it with her like the Chinks do, without coming. Black people can do it like, no sweat, eh, Marty? But for us . . . maybe you can teach me, uh, Buddhist whaddaya call it, 'prolongation without ejaculation'? Marty wouldn't teach me; not for money, not for nothing."

Rivers addressed Rudi: "Please disregard the detective's words. It's his sense of humor."

"Yeah, I better shut up, before Mr. Paxton runs off to tell his girlfriend they got nothing but racists and sexists at our precinct. We don't want her to write another shit piece for her shitty little paper."

Rudi shot him a look: What else do they know?

"Are you getting pissed off?" Tarakis rose and brought his face close to Rudi's. "Are you thinking of pushing me into the Hudson? Or are you about to swim across to Jersey? Screw the bail: the professor's got his real estate elsewhere."

"What are you talking about? Why would I be here if I wanted to run away?"

"To make it look good. To sneak a last look at the object of your affection. In my experience, a person is most often killed by whatever he loved too much. Maybe it's not good for him"—he winced as he took another sip—"yet that's what keeps him going. The things we love or hate too much—they are the ones that kill us."

Rivers coughed, perhaps bothered by the free interpretation of Oscar Wilde.

"Whatever we get high on, am I right, Marty?"

"He wasn't getting high on me," Rudi muttered stubbornly. "Wait—it was the Word! He was getting high on words—he must have been killed by the Word!" It was as if a tornado had picked him up, and he surrendered to it, sensing it was taking him in the right direction. "Check who called him! I bet it was the same guy who called me! It makes sense: the chanting makes you dizzy, nauseous, feverish . . . the mantra contains the *ram* syllable!" he exclaimed. "It's the seed of fire. If you read it properly, you can set a man on fire. Schechter should have put down the phone, but he was drunk, he kept listening—"

"If, according to him, the mantra contains a suggestion to commit suicide, then he listened to it and climbed into the fireplace?"

"It's not suicide! It's something else—"

"Quiet!" Tarakis's cellular phone rang. He listened intently, then barked, "Be right over.

"Schechter Junior is here," he explained. "Wants to talk to me."

He took the handcuffs off his belt. "Can you answer one simple question, Mr. Paxton? Can you prove you were not in Schechter's place at the moment of his death? You see, even if this anonymous call took place, you can't use it for an alibi."

Rudi's eyes ran in circles with despair: from the handcuffs in Tarakis's hand to the phone's antenna he was using to scratch his mustache.

"His son," Rudi said. "He called the professor when I was there. He was supposed to call back after I was gone. Schechter had to have told him he was alone. Ask him!"

Oddly, the newly found hope made him blush. *They'll think I'm lying.* He turned away.

"Do you mind getting him?" Tarakis asked Rivers. "While Mr. Paxton and I finish our coffee here."

FOR a moment, they were silent as Tarakis flicked cigar ashes into the jetsam in the water. The ocean kept sending powerful winds, trying in vain to chase away the clouds. The day was gray, anonymous, hopeless. The river itself felt suspect and tried to bypass the city and slide into the ocean.

Rudi sneaked a look at the detective. Tarakis was closing in on fifty. From way he stroked his mustache, it was clear he still cultivated his macho persona, but at the end of the day he was besieged by illness. The bags under his eyes alone; his beer gut, his shortness of breath, his grimace as he was sipping his coffee. He had to be counting the days to his retirement; he wanted to wrap up every case. He had the same fears as everybody: not enough love, money, health. Now he rubbed his hands, as if trying to stay warm. He needed someone to hold his hand, to stroke the birthmark on his thumb.

"So you write songs, Paxton?" the detective asked unexpectedly.

"Used to," Rudi said, suppressing surprise. "At school. How do you know?"

"I'm a detective, it's my job. You're not writing anymore?"

"Poetry, once in a while."

"Your girlfriend likes that? The nice way you put words together?"

"Once in a while." Rudi grew tense.

"She liked you being a musician—a cool guy, good-looking, into exotic stuff. While she was rotting away in a one-horse town."

"What do you want with that stuff?"

"I'm curious about you, Paxton." Tarakis held up his cup, as if saluting New Jersey. "Like, how far can you go. Or how far can someone else go for you. Or your words. Your mantras. Your expert witness has burned to death."

"How is any of this relevant?" Rudi exclaimed.

Tarakis crumpled the cup and tossed it in the water.

"It is directly relevant to our investigation, *Mr.* Paxton."

He looked at Rudi directly, too. In his eyes, Rudi could see nothing but hate.

"BAZ!" Rivers called.

After listening to his partner, Tarakis paused and then said, without looking at Rudi, "You can go. The son has saved your ass."

"I suggest you talk to him," Rivers added.

Rudi nodded and headed back to the house.

"Mr. Paxton!" Tarakis called to his back. "If you find another expert witness, you better take good care of him!"

17

RUDI could easily pick out Schechter Junior in the crowd of anxious tenants and sleepy cops. The odd appearance alone was enough—a forty-year-old in a shirt and tie, with an unzipped yellow windbreaker on top, formal gray trousers, and high-top sneakers—but in addition were his receding hairline and, most strikingly, the sky-blue Schechter eyes.

Junior emerged from the front door with a bundle of soiled rags and stood in the rain, clumsily balancing his trophy with his chin. At close quarters, Rudi saw that he was holding a stack of papers with singed edges: notebooks, Tibetan tablets, and shreds of red taffeta.

"Excuse me—are you the professor's son?"

"I was." With a nervous laugh, the man looked away and peered in the distance, looking for something down the block.

"I'm sorry, what's your name?"

"Larry. Listen, what's it to you?" He turned to face Rudi. His voice was shaking. "Will you stop this nonsense! Whom he met, who came, who went . . . I told your colleague— the black guy—whatever you're doing doesn't matter! Where the hell is my car?"

"I'm not a cop!" Rudi exclaimed. "I'm Rudi Paxton. I'm your father's student. I was at his place last night."

"So what? Aah . . ." Larry drawled. "Right, the teacher's pet. Inadvertently, I have provided you with an alibi. You're welcome!" He headed out of the crowd.

"But I need to talk to you! Wait—I think I know who killed your father!"

"Who?" Larry kept walking.

"It's a stranger who keeps calling me. I think they know—knew—each other. I want to explain this to you!"

"Why?"

Startled by the question, Rudi almost got run over by a bus. He ran up to block Larry's way as the latter was about to get into his Oldsmobile. "Maybe you know something."

"I don't have time." Larry shoved Rudi aside. "I have to stop by my office. And then I'll go see my mother."

"If you don't care who killed him, maybe she does!"

Larry paused, then opened the door for Rudi to get in.

THE inside of the car was sheer chaos: toy balls, oranges decorated by a marker pen, and pieces of Play-Doh that left smudges on the crushed velvet seats.

"He gave you his favorite beads." Larry nodded at Rudi's wrist. "Or you appropriated them yourself? Stop staring at me—I'm not suspecting you! So, what is it?"

By the time they passed the George Washington Bridge, Rudi had finished the story.

"So"—Larry coolly lit a cigarette—"it is your contention that my father was killed with a mantra. And what can I do for you?"

"You can help me find out who chanted it."

"*He* did."

"By himself?"

"Why are you surprised? He told you it urged people to commit suicide."

"But why would he kill himself? Did you know he was going to?"

"He was. He had AIDS—you didn't know?"

ACCORDING to Larry, who spoke in broken phrases, looking straight ahead, his father had been diagnosed with AIDS as recently as six months ago. The disease advanced unusually fast, with stomach infections and diarrhea. To dull the pain, Schechter injected morphine (hence the needles, Rudi thought) and used "other unorthodox treatment," as Larry put it.

Rudi closed his eyes, evoking the memory of Schechter's wet lips on his cheek—Schechter's breath, filled with wine and medication. Larry must be thinking I'm his father's lover and have AIDS, too. But the professor invited me to sleep over—*"No, he couldn't,"* he whispered.

"You don't believe me?" Larry pressed the Play button on the tape deck.

"Wisdom can be taken from a person," Schechter's voice said. *"As pain blurs their senses, people's consciousness often loses clarity."*

The voice was so unexpectedly alive it made Rudi gasp.

"Whenever I have spasms, only one thought serves as salvation: God is squeezing my soul out of my body like toothpaste out of the tube. When He's done, I will dissolve on His tongue . . . ," the professor continued in an ironic tone.

"At God's whim, a vessel can break in a man's head, and the wisest among us will slobber like a baby and put salt in his coffee. But no matter how much pain blurs his senses, he will feel love. God will never take it away. When my grandfather lost his mind after a stroke, he called for his late wife and kissed everybody who came to his bedside, thinking it was her. . . ."

The voice paused.

"I taped it a week ago," Larry said; "when we went to the hospital."

Rudi was shattered: ostensibly, he ought to be ashamed— his teacher had been dying, and he had not known it. What kind of courage did it take for Schechter to go on about his duties, including his court appearance, without letting anybody know? All he could see in front of him was Schechter's raw, sweaty flesh of last night, now a burnt black mummy in the police photo.

"I'm not dying so much of the virus," Schechter's voice came back, *"as of the fear it aroused in me. The fear that I'm not protected from myriad viruses. When I got the tests, it occurred to me that my brain—not my immune system— had lowered the bridge and the enemy rode inside the fortress. Now I'm trying to raise it again, but it doesn't work. Which is for the best, perhaps. Finally, I opened myself to the world's ills, to all the fecal matter that brews in it. AIDS opens a person for the Creation that also suffers, ails, and dies. It helps you be at one with the world, with the animals that generated the virus, with the jungles where it was nur-*

tured; they are as vulnerable to man as, it turns out, man is vulnerable to them."

The tape stopped.

"I don't believe he planned to kill himself," Rudi said. "I saw him an hour before it happened."

"Look outside." Larry pointed at the sky, turning a dazzling white. "Was *this* around an hour ago? Stress amasses in matter from the moment of its formation. Until the critical point, everything looks calm. What brings it about, I don't know: drugs, a fight with a lover, or, as you believe, an anonymous phone call from one of his associates."

"Tell me about his associates," Rudi asked tentatively. "Is there perhaps someone suspicious among them?"

"No more suspicious than you are."

After a pause, Rudi asked, "Can I see the papers that survived the fire?"

"I can't give them to you. You can look at them at the lab when we get there."

Momentarily, it grew dark, and a roll of thunder struck overhead. Sprinkled dust whirled on the road. Another blow of thunder, a flash of lightning, and everything blurred in a wall of rain. The tape came to life again, as if awakened by the storm.

"By definition, AIDS is a deficient defense," the professor's voice said gleefully, savoring the wordplay. *"It's a Buddhist or Christian way of not resisting evil. Perhaps, Larry, the dying phase is the happiest time of my life. Finally, I have surrendered the armor of my interests—AIDS has maimed it, turned it into a strainer. What horrifies me is that there's so little time left to love—and teach love to others. Only now have I started to teach students not theology but the practice of Buddhism: love and sacrifice. But it's not easy. Why do people need to become desperate to learn happiness? Why is a time bomb in your body needed to feel eternity? Why—"*

The tape stopped.

"And yet," Rudi said slowly, "what makes you think it was a suicide?"

"Because it would be fair! Look," Larry said angrily, "I

don't have time for this. I have a mother, and she's on the verge of suicide, too!"

Rudi fell silent. He did not feel like pushing: Larry could refuse to let him see the papers.

THEY drove through a gate, past a sign that said, LAMONT-DOHERTY EARTH OBSERVATORY OF COLUMBIA UNIVERSITY, and stopped outside a small bluish structure with narrow windows.

Schechter Junior's office was as messy as his car. The same Play-Doh, toy balls, orange peel, sneakers under the desk, graphs and charts strewn on the floor, unwashed ashtrays, and an unmade daybed in the corner. On the walls, world maps with continents distorted as if held against a funhouse mirror.

"You bring your children here?"

"I'm not married."

The moment they were inside, Larry's irritation changed to nervous excitement.

"Sit down, I'll make coffee. I wish I could sleep all day—and work. Both at the same time."

He hastily served coffee in a small cup, using a soup plate for a saucer. "Read away. Bury your dead. Sorry, I've got work to do."

He kicked off his sneakers and lit a cigarette, then turned on the computer in a gentle yet businesslike way, cracking his fingers like a pianist opening a piano lid.

Weirdo, Rudi thought. *His father's still warm, and he's working like nothing happened.*

He was struck by the thought that he resented Larry because they shared the indifference towards everything that lay outside the scope of their studies. Ashamed, he immersed himself in the charred tablets.

His instincts had been right: there was no mantra translation. Not a single mark on the margin. The professor respected manuscripts too much to soil them even by a pencil mark. Rudi leafed through the notebooks. Here, too, his initial enthusiasm was cooling off, just like the bland instant coffee Larry had given him. The notes contained only quotes from books and Schechter's comments. It was the

diary of a person who lived through his thoughts, rather than
through his deeds, and it was of interest more to a student
than to an investigator.

Yet the notes evoked the memories of the professor's
rhetoric the night before. In their posthumous form, Schechter's words sounded quite different:

 ... *The world resists, it thinks it can use a pill against
the virus, a prison against crime, but you can't fight the
immaterial with the material. You must give yourself to the
immaterial and transform it with love from within.* ...

Schechter knew he was doomed, yet he would not show his
pain; while Paxton (*shame, shame!*) only kept whining. ...
But Schechter's love for him, Rudi, was a deed, rather than
just a feeling, and he could not leave his student in trouble.
His dinnertime rhetoric was a way of leaving his philosophical testament. In the morning—now Rudi had no
doubt—he would have definitely taped his chanting. Didn't
he tell Rudi to keep ringing the doorbell to wake him up?

Yet he insisted, over Rudi's protests, that the mantra contained a suggestion to commit suicide. Of course: Schechter
was in pain all the time; subconsciously, he wanted to escape it and kept looking for signs that would allow him to
do it. He transferred his suicidal thoughts to the mantra. But
what about the beads? In Tibet, a ritual object is passed to
a student after the teacher's death or immediately before it.

So he had a premonition he would be killed! The final
sign was the call—allegedly a wrong number! It was after
that call that he began to bid farewell and asked Rudi to
turn on the music. ...

RUDI barely had time to reflect on his latest hypothesis,
when Larry's phone rang. His host leapt to another computer in the corner and punched a few keys. The ringing
stopped.

"Just a report," Larry explained. "A ripple of an earthquake in Alaska. Three on the Richter scale."

"I'm still convinced your father was killed. But"—Rudi
swallowed—"I can't find any proof in his papers. He received a phone call—"

"What's the difference!" Larry snapped, fiercely punching the keys. "Stop bugging me!"

For a moment, Rudi was lost. The guy was clearly deranged. But Rudi could not afford to irritate him further. "What's this apple on the screen?"

"That," Larry said with a chuckle, "is what you'd call Eve's apple. And I'm trying to map out the trajectory of the worm boring through it to tempt her."

"Seriously—I'm trying to understand what you're doing here."

"Seriously?" Larry turned abruptly and looked him in the eye. "Let me tell you a story. I learned about death when I was about five. I asked my mother as she was putting me to bed . . . no, it was in the bathtub, *Mommy, will I die, too? No, darling,* she said, *you'll never die. By the time you grow up the doctors will discover a way to make people immortal.* For some reason, I remembered it word for word. I believed her then. Now all I can think about is—who will tell *her* this, so she could believe it and stop worrying?"

"So you're worried about your mother's condition?" Rudi slowly asked. *He said it before, didn't he?* "Is she unwell?"

"Who's well? Are you?"

Patience is a cardinal virtue. With a sigh, Rudi turned his eyes to the wall, at the Himalaya-like peaks on the tectonic stress chart.

"I am, physically," he said. "But emotionally, no."

"Well, neither is she. They split up a long time ago. She suffers, but no one sees it and no one hears it."

"Does she . . . condemn him?"

"My mother never condemns anyone. Nor justifies anyone's actions."

Rudi took a deep breath. "I'd like to speak to her. Perhaps she knows something. The murderer may be one of your father's . . . associates. Your mother must be an extraordinary woman. What does she do?"

"She—" He paused. "She's a doctor. Kind of an immunologist," he squeezed out of himself.

Why did it pain him so much to admit it, Rudi wondered. Jeez, the whole family was nuts.

"Unfortunately," Larry went on, "my father preferred his

own methods of treatment. He thought that ideally these mantras of yours should be able to cure every disease, AIDS included. He claimed he felt the virus inside him and tried out all the mantras to see which one would 'scare it away.' He agonized before he started taking morphine, which interfered with the experiment."

Rudi lowered his eyes. *I thought he was having fun chanting.* "How come these tablets were hidden in the back of the bookshelves?"

"I think he hid them from himself after he tried them all out. He said he'd go crazy before he could try all the tones, and it wasn't too safe for other people that were around, either. If he asked me to ship all his remaining papers and tablets, he must have known it was the end. Look—a rainbow!" Larry nodded towards the window. His expression seemed to be clearing, too.

"Ship where?" Rudi perked up with hope. "To whom?"

"Different places: university libraries, research institutes . . ."

"And these"—he indicated the Bon Po mantras on the desk—"where are they going?"

"Some goddamn lama. I had his address someplace." Larry rifled through the papers.

Once again, Rudi's heart sank. The professor had lied to him: the tablets were not from the Museum of Natural History. "Are you sure about that?"

"There." Larry read from a scrap of paper. "Lama Ayushi, P.O. box in Colorado."

Some goddamn lama. Did they belong to this Ayushi or was it, as with the beads, Schechter's last will?

"Who is he?" Rudi grabbed the paper like a hawk. "You ever heard of him?

Larry said nothing.

"Doesn't it surprise you that your father has asked you to ship his diaries and the most valuable manuscript in his possession—one that may be worth hundreds of thousands of dollars—to some guy—"

"I can ship it straight to hell if I want to!" Larry yelled. "You'd better go. I have already spent more time on you than I should. I have to go see my mother now."

"I'm sorry." Rudi swallowed, trying to calm down. "I'll be going. You have no idea how much you have helped me. Can I please—please—deliver these papers myself? I promise you: I'll get on the plane right away!"

"You can do with them whatever you want." Larry turned away, his voice falling, his shoulders slackening. "I really don't care."

Rudi scooped up the papers and headed for the door. "Just one more thing." He cursed his inability to hold back. "Your father was truly enlightened. You should be proud of him!"

OUTSIDE, he ran down the long alley, suddenly afraid Larry would change his mind once again and demand the papers back. Soon, he was out of breath. I don't care, he thought; I have memorized Ayushi's address in Colorado. But what will I say to the lama? *Did you call the professor?* He will deny it—and that's it, another dead end. Suddenly he noted something stir near the path. He peered closer and saw a rabbit.

The animal was only a few steps away, its drenched hide invisible against the brown grass of the lawn. It must have been on its way to the woods, and, when it heard Rudi approach, it froze to merge with the background.

Good thinking, Rudi thought. While you zig and zag, you are prey. When you freeze, you merge into the landscape. Suddenly, he let out a powerful sneeze. His nose was running; his head was splitting. He took out a tissue to blow his nose; a sudden spasm ran through his body. Whether it was the reaction to fresh air after the stale smoke of Larry's office; or not having eaten all day; or that he was coming down with the flu—something strange was happening. He had a ringing sensation of absolute, crystal clarity in his head.

For the first time in perhaps twenty years he smelled the earth. The odor of rotting leaves and rich raw soil took him back to childhood, when he needed no computer to play; his best, his only playmate was the grass in the meadow; an endless variety of its forms and shapes, its blades frozen in the positions of soldiers of an infinite army. Its mysteri-

ous silence exuded the sweetly stirring, feminine smell of
the earth.

If I end up in jail, he thought, walking to the bus stop,
I'll see this quiet beauty of life all the time; if I'm deprived
of outward freedom, I'll enjoy the inward kind. The rabbit,
the smell of grass have not come from the meadow; they
have always been inside me. But they would run and hide
at every alarm signal sent by my mind.

By the time the bus arrived, it had grown dark, and he
was out of tissues. Exhausted, he reclined in the seat and
closed his eyes. Once again, he was a little boy in a dark
bus, kneading his Play-Doh into balls, guided by his touch
alone—just as he was crumpling his tissues now. The boy
has dropped his ball on the floor; he must find it in the dark,
before an adult steps on it. He has to wake them up. . . .

"Sir!" The driver, an elderly black woman, was shaking
him. "Manhattan. Last stop. And please pick up after yourself."

18

THE downpour stopped just long enough for the passengers
to board the Denver flight. Then it started again, coating the
plane window in a gray mist. Sitting on the ground was bad
enough, but wondering if your pilot had been listening to
Tune Ra's mantra all along was unbearable. Trying to distract himself, Rudi covered page after page of his diary describing the latest events.

Lama Ayushi, Schechter's colleague, rented a P.O. box
in a tiny town called Yampa, about two hundred miles
northwest of Denver. The name itself was the worst omen
imaginable: Yampa was a Tibetan death god—what was it
doing in Colorado? Rudi kept this information to himself.
Gwen was still in shock after the professor's death and
begged him not to go.

"What good will an Eastern freak do you in a New York courtroom? And if he is the anonymous caller . . . this could be a really bad meeting."

Superstitiously, she avoided using the word "fatal." In any event, she was afraid of staying alone; they had to come up with a new phone code. Couldn't he at least wait for a few days, so that they could spend some time together before he left? At least he could nurse his cold. . . .

Instinctively distrustful of pills, Rudi forced himself to take Nyquil, but the relief was ephemeral. When the plane finally left the ground, the phlegm in his sinuses started moving up, too, splitting his skull in two. Wincing, he swallowed again and again, trying to force down the pressure in his ears.

In the darkness below, the city was a giant body opened up for surgery: the flesh of the residential blocks, the sinews of the warehouses, the cells of the houses, the capillaries of the streets, the veins of the avenues. The yellow and red vehicles were like blood cells flowing through it. The real blood cells, too, he thought feverishly, must be thinking they are moving of their own accord. But the Physician of whom they could not conceive knows that their motion is determined by the laws of science. And so it must be with our motions, too, aimed at generating some kind of substance needed by the Body.

Most of the passengers in the cabin were peacefully asleep, protected by the curtains from the orangey rising sun. Against the background of their contented snoring and the hum of the air-conditioning, a woman's melodic chuckle behind him was like a solo in a concerto—

Rudi shifted in his seat to sneak a look.

The woman was immersed in a leather-bound book. She was anywhere between twenty-five and thirty-five, and her tan, rough and deep, did not seem to come from St. Bart's or sunlamps. Her green eyes, slightly Oriental in shape, and raven-black eyebrows were in contrast with her straw-colored hair, cut short, giving her a quasi-androgynous look.

For an instant, Rudi's eyes paused on the woman's hand holding the book. Her fingers were long and tanned, with nails trimmed neatly; but one finger was missing two joints, and he had a sudden impulse to press his lips against this pink stub.

Suddenly their eyes met, and he immediately shrank away, ashamed at the immodesty of his thoughts.

With a small laugh, the woman went back to her book.

Laughing at me? Rudi wondered. It did not matter: her laughter was so mellifluous, so carefree—it was as if she were skipping barefoot in a mountain stream, he thought. He wished Gwen had a laugh like that. Perhaps she did, when he was not around driving her insane.

Back to square one, he thought; to his anxieties about Gwen.

19

AS his rented Jeep climbed into the Rockies, his mood was dropping. What if Ayushi had an unlisted number? Attempts to find a person on the basis of his P.O. box would arouse suspicion. The local police, wary of big-city strangers, would call New York and learn he was out on bail. Even Gwen was not at home when he called from the airport at the prearranged time.

At the nadir of his mood Rudi realized that the blacktop had changed to a dirt road, the drizzle had stopped—and then the Rockies came into view, blue with pearly crests, like a petrified tsunami. And the final touch: a weightless rainbow soared like a sail—the Shambala Gate, the Tibetans called it.

Instantly, his mood soared with the rainbow. Once again, he was breathing the air of his childhood, when he was discovering the mountain lakes of northern California. It was as if his troubles were over, as if he had received his grant and was climbing the Himalayas.

As the road swerved uphill, the temperature fell and the traffic and roadside amenities grew scarce. The vistas of

wooded mountain slopes compensated for the lost civilization more than adequately. Yet he could not shake off his
bitterness: what if he was seeing it all for the last time?
State penitentiary: the bars on the windows, the shared cell,
sex . . . the thought made him shudder.

His fears were getting the better of him. At a particularly
sharp curve, he pulled over to the shoulder at the edge of
the cliff, set the handbrake, and stepped out. Over the ledge,
the grass was covered by a sheet of snow, lying peacefully
like a herd of grazing sheep.

Rudi dropped onto his knees in exhaltation. The view was
boundless. He closed his eyes and took a deep breath. He
wanted to fill up on this air, this view, this purity. This was
the antidote to his troubles.

He picked red berries off the bushes. Touched by frost,
they tasted bitter, but he ate them anyway, chasing them
with handfuls of snow. He wished he could hug the beauty
around him, rub it into his skin, put it in a plastic bag, pull
it over his head—he wished he could suffocate in it. This
is how people should live, he thought, racing uphill, re-
charged with energy: as if the next day were the first day
of their imprisonment. He cried, he sang, he stuck his head
out of the car window, letting the icy wind burn his eyes
and freeze his tears. He was happy as never before.

By the time he reached Yampa, his euphoria had settled
into a calmness, steady and cool, like the afternoon sun in
the mountains. Ultimately, as Schechter used to say, I'm
merely imagining that there is an "I" to whom all of this is
happening.

JUST as he had expected, there was nothing Tibetan about
Yampa, a typical mining ghost town—a one-street Western
stage set that lived off scarce tourists passing through on
the way to ski resorts. As he climbed out of his car at a
Mobil station, he was struck by the chirping of the birds.
The sun, the quiet, the birds, and the breath visible when
one spoke: it was odd to experience this bliss at a gas station, of all places. I could settle here with Gwen, he thought;
bring up children, rear horses. . . .

The two mechanics—father and son, judging by their

looks—were busy fixing a tractor. Both were unshaven and even slightly tipsy, which Rudi found an endearing change after the always sober New York.

While paying for the gas, he asked, with fake casualness, if they knew of a Lama Ayushi.

The son made an incoherent groan, which presumably meant *No*. The father glanced at Rudi's city-slicker tweed jacket disapprovingly. "Is it like one of them raw fish restaurants? We don't care for them Nips here."

The response left Rudi with a bitter aftertaste. Definitely a bad omen, he thought.

The only customers at the country store were a few local women having a lively discussion over the flower-seed catalogue. In response to Rudi's inquiry, they pursed their lips. "A Buddhist priest? We certainly don't have nothing like that."

"Well," the saleswoman in granny glasses said tentatively, "there is a synagogue in Copperfield, if you're interested. That's about fifty miles from here."

AS he had expected, the town's phone directory, which he located at the post office, had no listing for an "Ayushi" nor for a "Lama." The cheerful elderly postmistress claimed no knowledge of lamas or what they did.

"Purple robes? With shaved heads? Sorry, sir; we got nothing but plain folks here. All-American." She displayed her brand-new dentures with a smile. "I really can't tell you who rents the box. But if you have a letter, I could drop it in."

She didn't know or, like the housewives at the store, didn't *want* to know? he wondered.

HE walked with deliberate slowness, squinting at the last of the sunshine. Warm, slanted, faintly purple light turned the town into a photography darkroom, whose owner, while developing film, became a part of the picture. The polished facades of Main Street were followed by wooden sheds, piles of bricks, weeds, rusty car parts: the old and the dirty, the jetsam and flotsam of the shiny brand-new America.

*   *   *

THE investigation would be incomplete, he thought, without stopping by the local saloon. As long as he phrased his questions carefully, he would not end up flying outside with the doors swinging.

The heavily made-up plump woman who tended the bar was talkative—where was he from? business or pleasure?—but did not have any answers.

"Buddhist? Mister, we don't even have a Chinese restaurant here. Local folks don't go for that kind of stuff. We have some tacos for a special, if you're interested."

"I see." Did she tense up or was it his New York paranoia flaring up again?

Was he staying overnight? Yampa Star was the only motel around, they just got cable TV last month—

Rudi forced a smile. "Looks like I'll have to."

There was no point in driving down the winding roads in the dark, with an unlikely chance of making it to the New York flight. Should he go back at all? His quest had been in vain: no expert witness, no anonymous caller. It made more sense to flee: in a couple of days he could cross over to Mexico, sell the Jeep, buy a forged passport, fly to Tibet, find a lamasery—

"You wouldn't have a road map here, by any chance?"

But I'm not a criminal! Why should I flee?

"Try the library," she replied, unhappy with his failure to keep up the conversation. "The white house across the street."

20

THE library was a spacious two-floor structure, a refurbished horse stable. Books, magazines, carefully dried mountain flowers with homemade doilies, and a bulletin board: a chili cook-off, a knitting group, a karate class, a poetry reading. It also served as a local museum: rusty pick-axes and miners' lamps in glass display cases, yellowed pictures in metal frames, amateur landscapes. A slender fortyish woman, with thinning blond hair, in an arty-looking sweater with fringe, was behind the checkout desk, intent on painting a bunch of flowers in a crystal vase.

Must be the librarian, Rudi thought indifferently, and asked for a road atlas.

"That's a nice bracelet," she said with a nod toward his wrist as she handed him the atlas.

"Thank you. Actually, they are prayer beads."

"I know," she said cheerfully.

She had the air of a tomboy: a tiny ponytail, a sharp little chin, freckles . . . But his hands opened the atlas to the page for New Mexico. "Do you have a Xerox? I need to make a copy."

"Sure, if you don't mind waiting." She smiled again. "I keep it upstairs, in my apartment. I live here, too. This is my private business." She picked up a thin paperback. "Here—so you don't get bored. A collection of our local poets. Maybe you'd like to buy a copy? Judging by your bracelet—I mean, beads—you must like poetry."

And she was off, the sound of her cowboy boots going up the stairs.

Nothing but weirdos here, Rudi thought, opening the book absently—

His glance froze on the page. "Ma'am! Aw shit!"

As he turned abruptly, his elbow caught the vase. It shattered on the floor with the sound of an artillery missile.

"Coming!" she shouted from upstairs.

He raised his eyes to the stairs. Suddenly, there was a click behind him.

"Freeze! Put your hands up!"

Startled, he obeyed and turned slowly to see the mild librarian pointing at him what appeared to be a hefty handgun. Behind her was a door, camouflaged as a bookcase, which concealed another staircase.

At the sight of the broken vase, she sighed relief. "I'm sorry. I thought something happened." She tucked the gun under her sweater and reached to pick up the shards.

"I'm really sorry." The gift of speech was returning

slowly, though Rudi's eyes were still fixed on her sweater. "I'll pay—"

"Don't worry about it."

His hands trembling, he opened the poetry book. "Do you know who this poem is about?"

On top of a six-line sonnet, bold block letters said LAMA AYUSHI.

"I sure do." She grinned, revealing slightly yellowed large teeth. "I wrote the poem. See: Abigail Swanson. That's my name."

She straightened up and wiped her hand on her sweater. "But you can call me Abby."

Within seconds, they were seated face-to-face behind the desk, their knees touching.

"What do you need with the lama?" Abby peered in Rudi's face. "Are you a seeker?"

"Yes, I am." Rudi sighed as he recognized the lingo. "I really need to see him. I've got to give him this"—he patted his backpack with Schechter's papers—"the last will and testament of my teacher."

"He's dead?" Abby's eyebrows rose dramatically.

"Actually, he was killed." Anticipating another splash of drama, he added, "I don't know how or by whom."

"A mystery! Terrifying and romantic!" Abby offered her hands for the backpack. "I'll make sure it gets to him."

"I have to do it in person." Rudi put his hand on the backpack proprietorially. "I have an oral message from my teacher."

"Aha! A messenger with a message!" She grew serious. "But the teacher does not see strangers. You have to go through a trial period."

"But he called me—"

"He could not! On the other hand, they have cellular phones there. . . ."

"Where's that?"

"In Shambala." Abby pointed at the print of a landscape behind her.

Rudi peered closer. How could he not recognize the famous pink-mountain landscape by Nicholas Roerich, a Russian painter and Tibetologist! The Roerich Museum on

107th Street was a stone's throw away from his house!

"So, what did the teacher say to you?" Abby persisted.

"That's what I am trying to figure out."

"More mystery! All right: I'll go ask him tomorrow. You will wait, as a seeker must."

"You'll go where?"

"It's coded"—she winked slyly—"in the poem that you have just read."

Her eyes closed, she recited blissfully:

> *"My teacher is wrapped in the name of the crag*
> *That lies between us and the road*
> *He sings, wrapped in the flowing rill*
> *That is our threshold*
> *He sings atop the rippling mountain*
> *Looking down on the milky creek."*

Rudi barely suppressed a groan. Abby was not your garden-variety romantic New Age spinster; she was a mystical poetess with a personal guru and a .38. Or even a .45—he did not know much about handguns, but suspected the worst.

Yet here she was, staring at him like any creative-writing student, waiting for approval. . . .

"The poetry of the dedicated," he said pensively. "You've got more?"

"Yes." She beamed a grateful smile. "Upstairs."

BEFORE showing her guest upstairs, Abby shut the front door, then the steel door behind it, and turned on the security alarm.

This is more New York than New York, Rudi marveled, climbing the stairs in the dark. He stumbled and reached for the light switch.

"Don't do that!" she whispered as she shuttered the windows. "We don't want to be seen from the street. Someone might take a shot."

"Who?"

"A small town has mysteries, too." She lit up a candle. "Isn't it more romantic this way?"

In the flickering light, Rudi saw a bed with crystals gleaming above it, easels, bookshelves, and a table with dried mountain flowers. He sniffed suspiciously.

"There's a small gas leak," she admitted. "Don't worry: I air it often. Let me make some coffee. . . ."

She chattered on, setting the table: "Did you know that natural gas comes from the compost of ancient plants? Isn't it romantic, smelling ancient plants at your own house? I don't even feel like calling the gas repairman anymore. Can you imagine: we, too, will turn into fuel for someone? Do you like grappa?"

Rudi didn't find it romantic. Scent was added to natural gas so that people could detect a leak. But he didn't have to worry if Abby caught his skeptical expression, for she went on chattering.

After a couple of shots, Abby's eyes grew shiny as she opened a notebook in a silk flowery binding. "Let me read you one of my own, okay? This one is called 'Yampa Rhapsody.'

> *"I held my lamp on the top of the mountain*
> *Who knows how I got there?*
> *Perhaps I arose from the sea*
> *Or fell off the moon*
> *Then I noticed a valley*
> *And a plateau where once was a boulder*
> *A trace of a man*

"You see," she explained, "I consider myself a pagan Christian."

Big deal, Rudi thought. The Columbia program was chock-full of Anglican Amazons and Catholic Druids. He smiled encouragingly as he poured another round. Welcome to the world of intrigue, where you get a woman drunk not to seduce her, but to get information. "Is there more?"

Outside, the rain began beating down on the tin roof.

She nodded, flustered. "You have no idea how privileged I feel to be reading these to someone who truly understands. This one's just for you. From when I went to New York. It's called 'Hypnosis.'

> *"Driving rain washed away*
> *Silhouettes of people in misty windows.*
> *I'm standing underground,*
> *Where faces search for lines and numbers.*
> *Subway."*

He felt blushing. Subway? What the hell did the Gehenna of the subway have to do with the vestigial beauty around them?

> *"Somehow,*
> *Instead of piles of glass and steel,*
> *A train emerges from the tunnel—"*

"Stop." He swallowed. "Please. It's very powerful. For me. Personally."

"Really?" Anxiety receded, and she was ready to receive praise.

"Very evocative," he confirmed.

Unsteadily, she rose. "You're not just saying it, are you?"

Before he could dispel her doubts, she was in his lap. "May I kiss you—as one poet to another?"

A full-fledged kiss filled his mouth with the tastes of grappa, lipstick, and some kind of apple vinegar.

"That's nice." She exhaled. "Your appreciation of the finer things in life clears you for meeting the teacher. You're no seeker; you're a *chela,* a disciple."

She reached for another kiss, pressing her feverish skinny body to his. He winced as her gun jammed into his solar plexus.

"Where would we find him?" He moved away gently, refilling her glass.

"You'll see: the ripple of the mountain over the font of milk!" She threw her head back, but her arms were firmly wrapped around his torso.

He picked her up lightly and carried her to the bed. "What time are we leaving?"

"At dawn." She pulled him closer.

Disengaging himself, he carefully placed her slender hand

as far away as possible from her belt. "You need rest," he whispered. "We have an Ascent tomorrow."

"Ascent," she echoed dreamily.

The candle was almost out. The crystals gleamed, unperturbed. As he tiptoed to the door, he felt his face tickled with shame—like a sniff of gas.

HE sat in his dark motel room, wet after the dash through the rain, dialing his number in New York. Gwen did not pick up. What did it mean? It was late night in New York. Between the calls, he glanced at the raindrops racing down the windowpanes, only to disappear at its bottom. He had just wangled a clearance—for what?

21

DESPITE her pagan Christian appellation, the poetess called with American punctuality—right at dawn. "Ready for the Ascent? We can leave in half an hour."

Rudi opened the window wide. The air, fresh after the rain, burst into the room, bringing in the smell of wet leaves, tinged with the smoke from the fireplace at the saloon downstairs.

Whoever the lama turns out to be, whatever the day brings—Rudi resolved that he would be as calm and undisturbed as the Rockies, whose presence filled the room. Be it night, rain, or fog, the mountains were the same in their divine solidity. He would not be swayed by weather, or new information.

Half an hour later, his resolve softened. Abby was already made up, clad in tight jeans and a chic leather jacket. Her blonde ponytail rose flirtatiously from under her velvet jockey hat. It's for me, he thought, once again feeling a little ashamed. In the heat of argument Gwen used to accuse him of being a "Buddhist playboy." Was he really?

Abby shook his hand firmly. "About last night—I'm sorry if I . . ." She shrugged, a little smile dancing in her face.

"Nothing to be sorry about," he assured her. "You look great, by the way."

She squinted coquettishly, trying not to show her pleasure. "Let's go!"

AT the top of the hill, he glanced at Yampa behind them. The town, still asleep, was like a necklace embracing the slender blue neck of the lake, with the white library building standing out like a clasp among the brick-red beads. Half the lake, milky white, mirrored the sky, while the other half, adjoining the mountains, was a richly embroidered silk robe that reflected the wild fall colors of the wooded slopes. The colors, unseasonably bright, were just a blanket covering the lap of the mountain; beyond, it was enveloped in the fog, the dull white of cotton balls merging with the sky.

"This is our destination," Abby said, intercepting his look. "The Gate of Shambala."

This was the name of Lama Ayushi's Buddhist retreat, she explained, her voice ringing with exalted piety. "I'm blessed by his very existence here. You must understand my being cautious yesterday: all sorts of vain, greedy people are trying to intrude. But his time is precious, because he writes poetry and songs in Tibetan. My poetry is worthless in comparison. His devoted disciples try to protect him—of course, some try to monopolize him. I'm not like that." She meaningfully patted Rudi's hand. "I make a distinction. If you need to do more than just pass along the testament—to clear up a personal problem as well"—her eyebrows went up—"he can do it for you."

"I hope so." He pulled his hand away, ostensibly to adjust the rearview mirror. "How far is the retreat?"

"About a hundred miles. Remember the 'rippling mountain' in my poem? It's called Repper Pass. This is where I encoded a reference to Ayushi," she added with pride.

He stared incomprehendingly.

"Rippling . . . Repper . . ." she said slowly.

"I got it." Rudi nodded. "Milarepa, right?"

Milarepa was a Tibetan mystic, a *mila.* According to the legend, he composed his poetry atop the snowy mountain, wearing nothing but a *repa,* an obsolete Tibetan word for loincloth.

"Right! How do you know Milarepa?"

"I learned my Buddhism from the late friend of Ayushi's." And he quickly added in anticipation of another enthusiastic outburst from Abby, "How long has he been here?"

"The retreat was founded about five years ago," Abby said, "but the lama does not exactly advertise his presence among the locals."

"I gathered as much." Rudi told her about his investigative failure.

"Oh yes. Like they said, 'traditional folks.' Aren't you lucky you met me? Do you know why one feels blessed in the mountains?" she prattled on. "Because the mountains are the earth's breasts and buttocks, and He caresses them more than He does the plains, or the earth's backside."

"I thought you were a pagan Christian," Rudi said, trying to steer the conversation away from sex. "This sounds like a Mother Earth cult."

"That's what my late husband believed," she said sadly. "Aw shit!"

A police car, flashing its lights, filled the rearview mirror. Rudi swallowed. Had they found out that he had violated the bail conditions?

"My friend the sheriff." Abby reached inside her jacket.

Rudi heard a sound uncomfortably resembling that of a gun safety. His hands on the wheel turned damp.

"Good morning, Miz Swanson." A burly middle-aged cop approached the car, his thick reddish mustache twitching with displeasure. "Taking an early trip?"

"I'm going to the retreat." Abby forced a smile, her hands on her coat.

"Is this your friend? Can I see your driver's license, sir? Thank you." He went to his car.

Once they were out of the cop's earshot, Rudi nodded at the gun: "Are you crazy?"

"I'll explain later," she said.

The cop returned the license. "Something bothering you, Miz Swanson?"

"I'm fine." Her knuckles looked especially white against the black leather of her coat.

"Just making sure no one was kidnapping you." The sheriff's blue eyes were ice-cold. "Like one of those notorious Colorado militiamen?"

"WHAT was that all about?" Rudi asked.

She drew a deep breath. "It's a long story."

Over ten years earlier, George and Abby Swanson, a geologist and a poet, moved to Colorado from Chicago, seeking to start a small pagan Christian commune, an ashram of sorts. However, buying the land turned out to be a problem. The very word *commune* branded the outsiders as part of the Red Menace—not a popular image among the gun-toting "traditional folks" at Yampa and other places like it.

"They're in militias now," Abby said bitterly. "Did you see the bullet holes in the road signs? This is both target practice and turf marking. No one ever got arrested. . . . What do you expect, our sheriff's best friends are the militia activists, the Jacksons, the father and son who own the gas station."

George Swanson contacted the county sheriff about the drunken shooting. A week later, he was dead. According to the Rangers, he fell off a cliff during rock-climbing practice.

"I saw that drop," Abby said. "A sixty percent grade at best. To an experienced climber like George, it was child's play. But those guys all have optical gunsights; they could hit a rope or a binding from a mile away."

Abby did not take her husband's death lying down. She contacted the FBI, but their investigation came up empty.

"Maybe they didn't want to find anything. But ever since, the locals hate me with a vengeance—and the retreat, too. Ayushi's disciples had to pay through the nose: the locals overcharged them for every square foot of land. My husband did a survey for the retreat—he was the only one who did not cheat Ayushi. And you wonder why they wouldn't tell you about it! They don't want outsiders, period. In the retreat, they're trying to get by without Yampa, too: the P.O.

box is the only contact. If it wasn't for Ayushi, I would have left long ago." She sniffled.

Something about her reminded Rudi of his own mother: an aging relic of the flower generation. To distract Abby and himself from painful memories, he nodded at Yampa, which had by now become a tiny spot below.

"I wonder why they settled so low," he said. "They could have had such a great view. And they could have electricity and running water here, too."

"A man tries to fall down." Her eyes were still red but dry. "Falling down from the valley is less frightening."

"I thought the higher up one settled, the closer one came to heaven."

Her chuckle sounded bitter. "You put a couple of egoists in the mountains, they can turn even Shambala into hell. People bring heaven and hell with them wherever they go. You'll see for yourself in the retreat."

22

"WELL, Rudra: here's your kingdom!"

The car passed under a banner that proclaimed THE GATE OF SHAMBALA and entered the retreat. The kingdom looked more like a summer camp: a number of plain white cottages scattered on the picturesque slope.

"Doesn't look like much." Abby seemed to read his mind. "But those willing to take a break from civilization pay a premium. The water comes from the creek. The light comes from oil lamps. The menu is tofu and honey from their own hives. Cellular phones only. If you want to keep up with your stock options, better stock up on batteries for on-line access."

She could be practical, he thought. "What's that?" he pointed at a massive stone structure rising in the middle of the pasture.

"The Rinpoche's temple, paid for by his foreign sponsors." And she added proudly: "I'm painting indoor murals. There's Cliff, the manager. Pull over there."

I don't like this, Rudi thought. If the Rinpoche is the caller, and somehow I got in the way of his cult and his rich sponsors, what am I doing playing a private dick? I should be calling the FBI.

But it was too late for second thoughts. He was already shaking hands with Cliff, a tall, slender man with a squinting Buddha-like grin on a plain Anglo-Saxon face. Abby took him aside, leaving Rudi to study the announcements posted on the board on the cottage wall.

These were about dollars and cents: guests were offered residence in cottages and caves, complete with participation in rituals and spiritual training, with meditation led by the Rinpoche in person. Judging by the posted rates, Rudi saw seekers had to be exceptionally well heeled indeed.

The California commune where Rudi had spent his childhood had no rates, yet, looking back, he did not feel compelled to idealize it. As time went by, he discovered plenty of communal and personal conflicts: factions, quarrels, discontent, envy, and even suicide.

Rudi's experience made him skeptical about the idea of an Eastern ashram populated by Westerners. The communes he had seen looked tempting to outsiders interested in spirituality, but on the inside even the most advanced ones were rent by communal conflicts. The Colorado one seemed to have adopted a pragmatic approach: if you wanted spirituality, you had to pay.

"THE Rinpoche would be at his place." Cliff nodded at the white cottage farther up the slope.

As they approached the cottage, Abby folded her hands on her stomach, with the manager following suit, and cried out, "Rinpoche!"

The door creaked. Rudi involuntarily stepped back and caught his breath.

The door opened, and a tall barefoot woman in a yellow shirt and red harem pants came out.

*   *   *

HE recognized his fellow passenger right away: the straw blonde with raven-black eyebrows from the plane!

She glanced at them indifferently, not recognizing him.

"The Rinpoche went to the mountains." Her voice had a trace of an accent. She turned around, about to leave.

"Wait, Margi!" Cliff climbed the steps and spoke to her in a muted voice, nodding at Rudi.

"She is supposed to be his favorite disciple," Abby whispered, looking away, lest Margi notice her hostile expression. "They say she paid most of the bills, so she feels she can monopolize him. Whenever she comes here, he leaves for the mountains, and stays there for a long time."

"Who is she? Where is she from?" Something prompted him not to tell Abby he had seen Margi before.

"I don't know. Ethnographer, photographer, mountain climber—damned if I know. She has been coming here for a long time, but she keeps to herself."

Finally, the subject of their conversation decided to join them. As Rudi shook her hot, dry hand, he felt where the finger was missing.

"Rudi?" She had a direct way of looking you in the eye he found disconcerting. "I'll take you to the Rinpoche."

Abby thanked the manager. "He's so sweet with me," she whispered to Rudi. "Almost an Enlightened One!" Protectively, she took Rudi's hand and looked up. "Shall we go?"

"I'm sorry, Abby," Margi said. "I think tonight the Rinpoche is expecting one guest only. Rudi, that is."

Abby bit her lip. "Why? How does he know about him?"

Margi slightly arched her eyebrows. "Just had a flash . . . a vibration."

She turned around and walked up the path. Rudi glanced at Abby. Her jaws were clenched as she watched the yellow robe moving away quickly. Suddenly he found the presence of an armed librarian comforting. But . . . He pulled up his backpack and ran to catch up with the favorite acolyte.

Keeping up with Margi was no easy task, Rudi realized. Her body, big and strong under the shapeless garment, moved with natural grace and at a good clip, despite her bare feet and a toe missing from each of them. But she was not limping—quite the contrary, she was gliding easily up the path, ignoring rocks and thorns. Were it not for the slight tinkle of the golden bracelet on her slim tanned ankle, her steps would not be heard at all.

He could not take his eyes off her. An oread, a mountain siren, about to lure me to the edge of the cliff—and I would not mind following.

She paused at a turn in the path. "Need a breather?"

He shook his head. "I was on the plane, too," he said, unable to hold back. "Sitting right in front of you. You were reading from a book and laughing. What was that?"

"Milarepa." She resumed walking, though at a slower pace. Her voice was low, coming from somewhere below her diaphragm. *"The yellow leaves on the path, touched with early frost, are like the spoor of the beast. The predator—the autumn wind. You can't catch him, but if you follow it noiselessly, you can become free like it."*

Her voice was like an electric arc, sending out sparks that filled Rudy with strange joy. "Is it from Milarepa, too?"

"I'm just describing what's in front of me. Why don't you try it." She smiled suddenly, and something about her narrowed eyes made him want to groan with pleasure.

"Somewhere far off flew a butterfly," he started tentatively, anxious to impress her; *"flapping her wings towards the sun. The day burst into the sunshine, mirroring the colors of her wings."*

He peered at her, gauging her reaction. But her serious green eyes contained no approval or indifference. All she did was look and see.

"Something you worked on before?"

He nodded, flushing. God knew what she would think of him now.

"Let's go!" she declared abruptly.

The wind had cleared away the clouds, and the rays of sunshine were streaking through the trees and the shrubs.

"You come to the retreat often?" he said to her back.

"Depends on your perception of time," she said playfully.

"Does the lama have many students?"

"Depends on your perception of numbers."

"Is this a German accent you have?"

"Depends on how you define the space formed by the interaction of time and numbers. Actually, I'm Swiss."

He froze as he peered into the slits of her eyes—unblinking, and transparent like a glacier lake. Looking at her, he had a strange sensation of looking at himself in the mirror, but, startled, saw someone else, though someone like him: either himself in a dream or himself in the future.

"I noticed on the board that the retreat provides Tantric dedications," he said. "What is your degree?"

"I don't know. I avoid names. And unnecessary words." She looked at him directly, without expression. "Words are dangerous, aren't they?"

Suddenly, a phone rang, and the sound was so jarring in the mountain quietude, so reminiscent of everything that had happened to him recently, that he shuddered involuntarily.

With a chuckle, Margi produced a cellular phone from under her robe, glanced at the caller ID, and turned it off.

"You can go on by yourself. See a black silhouette on the left, below the snowline? That's where he is. But hurry: in the mountains, it grows dark early."

23

THE top of the mountain, snow-capped with gray patches, resembled a head wrapped in a soiled turban. A hooked broken nose protruded from under the turban, sniffing the frosty air: this was the granite ledge, covered with the reddish blood of the moss, that Margi had pointed out. A tall rock stuck out on the edge like a warp; atop the rock, a gray bush quivered in the wind. For a few minutes, Rudi peered up from the foot of the ledge, till he finally realized that the bush was in fact a human figure, clad in gray rags that billowed in the air.

It took Rudi a good half hour to climb to within fifty feet

of the man, who remained motionless with his back to the visitor.

"Hello?"

The wind tossed the greeting back, straight to his gasping mouth.

Rudi cursed. To get any closer, he had to climb an almost vertical slope. Grabbing at scarce twigs, his body trembling with tension, he reached the foot of the "warp": a ten-foot boulder at the very edge of the cliff. In order to see the man, he had to press himself to the rock and approach the edge in small, careful steps. The back of the man was only ten feet above him. There was no way that the boulder denizen could have failed to hear Rudi's heavy breathing and the sounds of the falling rocks. Yet he would not turn.

He has to be the caller, luring me in. . . .

The stranger's back was wrapped sheetlike in gray woolen cloth, with thin gray wisps of hair flowing on top. Looking into the sun, Rudi saw a black silhouette inked against the blue sky. He could not see the face: the old man was sitting on the very edge of the rock over the abyss.

Rudi filled his lungs with air and yelled: "Excu-u-use me!"

The man turned slowly.

INDEED, he was an elderly Oriental. For a few seconds, the two studied each other. The thin white hairs flanked Ayushi's tanned bald spot like the tail of a comet. His high forehead and oval face were dappled with brown spots. His thin nose was slightly curved, like a predator's beak, while his lower lip extended a bit forward. He would look arrogant, were it not for his tiny eyes and large ears, which gave him the appearance of an old stuffed monkey.

Could he indeed be the caller? Rudi peered intently into the man's teary eye-slits.

Suddenly the man smiled. As if someone slowly turned on a switch inside: the whole face lit up. Without showing his teeth, the man stretched his chapped purplish lips amid the hoary stubble, sending tiny wrinkles across his face.

"I brought you a package from Schechter!"

The old man smiled sympathetically and cupped his ear.

"From Schechter!" But the echo snatched *"echter"* and dropped it into the abyss.

With a grimace, the stranger waved, inviting Rudi to come closer. Rudi made a couple of steps, reducing the distance between them to half a dozen feet, and, his voice shaking, repeated his words.

The old man's smile grew wider. "Is known."

His voice was unexpectedly young, ringing, and—like that of a deaf person—incongruously loud.

"How do you know?" Rudi shouted. "Did Larry call you?"

The old man shook his head. "Message on wind."

He fell silent again, still smiling and slightly rocking back and forth, as if bowing to his guest.

Message on wind was a standard Tibetan expression for telepathic communication. His accent was Tibetan, and so was his grammar. Yet what kind of lama was he? No shaven head, no red-and-yellow robe . . . But his smile, his barely perceptible bowing were full of natural ease, just like a lama's should be.

Rudi held up the bundle with the tablets and the letter. With a nod, the lama acknowledged him and placed the bundle in his lap.

More silence. Only the wind groaning in his ears. Why wouldn't he ask about Schechter? Did he have anything to do with the killing?

"Climb here," the lama said slowly. "Hear not well."

Rudi hesitated.

The lama extended his hand, brown and calloused, like an old tree branch.

"Be afraid not. Is dangerous stand there. There lynx live behind you."

Rudi glanced back, startled. A few feet below was a hole in the ground, with tiny lumps of feces next to it. He grabbed the man's hand.

The lama laughed. "Be afraid not. He come out not in day. Maybe roar. Sometime. You wait, he roar, you afraid, you fall."

Rudi silently spread himself on the rock, like a lizard. Afraid to move, he pretended he was catching his breath.

The old man turned out to be sitting on the ledge with a good mile of nothing but thin air underneath. From the ledge, he could see the tiny yellow strip of the valley, the widening white thread of Milk Creek, the green slopes of the pass, the snowcaps of nearby mountains rising like wave crests and merging with the sky . . . sitting on the ledge was not unlike sitting on the wing of an airplane.

Rudi's face was almost touching the lama's soiled robe, which had the sour smell of an unwashed body. A dirt-black bare sole stuck out, with brownish nails, hard as shells, which were almost touching Rudi's shoulder. If we were on the subway, I would move to another car, he could not help thinking.

The lama was sitting on bare rock without anything to protect his behind and kept swaying and smiling, impervious to the freezing cold that had completely permeated Rudi's body.

"What you name yourself?" The lama revealed tiny teeth, far apart.

"Rudi Paxton. I'm Schechter's student."

"Best student!" The lama nodded at the beads on Rudi's wrist. "Guru gave him. Beads from hundred eight different skulls. Very rare!" The lama scowled.

The value of his beads was the last thing on Rudi's mind. "Did you share the same Rinpoche?"

"Yes. Tsendin Namdak. Michael, he came adult. I grow up with Nagpa. Since children."

"Your guru was a *nagpa*—a shaman?" For a second, Rudi forgot his fears and rose from the rock. "The professor never told me about it!"

The old man chuckled. "For his West students, teacher was just Rinpoche. He does not tell Michael he is Nagpa. *Nagpa* means shaman, Nagpa does magic! West fear magic.

"Rinpoche get message on wind, Chinese look for him," Ayushi went on. "But Rinpoche does not want leave Tibet. Gives Michael beads. Me he gives tablets." He patted the bundle.

So the tablets with mantras were his. But how did he know the contents of the bundle?

Rudi glanced down. The abyss—the free flight . . . Fighting nausea, he forced himself to sit down and, trying to sound confident, asked the Question: "Sir, did you ever call me on the phone?"

The old man gently shook his head.

"You never read . . . a mantra—over the phone?"

"No!" He teasingly imitated Rudi's shaking hands as he brought his hand to his ear. "I do not speak phone!"

Rudi smiled mechanically in response. Inside, a wave of joy was rolling up. Suddenly the old man no longer smelled like a subway bum; instead, he exuded clear, ringing joy— he could not have been the caller!

As Rudi continued to peer into the moist reddish whites of Ayushi's eyes, he was getting dizzy. It was as if his body were slowly freezing up with Freon, its capillaries turning into tiny porcelain tubes. With an effort, he shook it off. Why wouldn't the old man unwrap the package? Ask about Schechter? Was it Eastern etiquette, or did he already know? Or was he expecting something from him, Rudi? Of course—a *pun'ya*!

It was a part of Tibetan *pun'ya* ritual: you had to give your teacher your most precious possession—not for nothing had Ayushi mentioned the Rinpoche's gifts! In order to receive advice—and Ayushi seemed assured that that was the purpose of the visit—you must give "what your heart reflects." A symbol of your heart. . . .

He rifled through his backpack—damn, if only he had thought of it before—and came up with a miniature voice recorder. He pressed it to his forehead and handed it to the lama with a bow. "Please."

Ayushi waved it away. "No, no!"

But Rudi persisted, and Auyshi, pulling in his lower lip, accepted and pressed the gadget to his forehead. Then he carefully put it in a soiled gray bag at his side. "Now I tape my songs on your gift! Milarepa was great yogi: he did not write down, but people remember. Ayushi is small yogi: forget right away."

My teacher is wrapped in the name of the crag, Abby wrote. Indeed, Ayushi's wrinkled gray robe resembled a series of mountain passes.

"Who sent you a message on the wind about me coming?"

"From you!" The old man giggled. "You wanted badly to come here! People sometime so anxious about things, their clocks go fast. Yesterday, I hear knock-knock in my head. Who's there? Someone comes from Schechter—needs your help!"

"I do need your help. Schechter is dead."

"Huh?" The lama turned his hand funnel-like to his ear. Just like Milarepa on icons, Rudi thought.

"Come close!"

Rudi hesitated. One wrong move . . . He forced himelf to focus on the lama's eyes; this kept him from looking into the abyss. Perhaps this is where Oriental self-control comes from, he thought. One wrong gesture, and you're flying. A frozen smile is the only option. You must constantly feel you're above an abyss.

"Schechter is dead," he whispered slowly, so as not to be swayed by his own voice.

The lama nodded. "I know. He knew he die soon."

"He came to see you?"

"No. He write letter. He took these tablets to look for mantra to cure AIDS. Ayushi, he knows no such mantra. He did not find one, either."

"That's what I was going to ask you about. Have you heard about a singer called Tune Ra?"

"Toonra?"

"No, it's like a *tune* and the Egyptian god *Ra*. He fashioned himself after a famous singer called Sun Ra."

"Aha." Ayushi nodded. "To me it sounds like *thunrwa*. Is horn made of human bone. Bon magic men use it to fire mantra at enemy."

Holy shit. Rudi swallowed. "You see, Teacher, this Tune Ra—or maybe *Thunrwa*—sings one of these mantras." He nodded at the package. "I don't know how it is spelled but it sounds a bit like this—" Rudi repeated the chorus.

"Aha." The lama nodded again and repeated the mantra with his eyes closed.

Rudi remembered Schechter telling him that any throat singer could do it, but when he actually heard the lama intone in the same voice as the one he had heard at Schechter's, he had to hold on to his rock.

"What does this mantra mean?" he cried out.

The lama folded his robe under his behind and, leaning towards Rudi, rolled up his owlish yellow eyes and started blinking, as if mimicking his new adept. Then he burst out laughing, throwing his head back, as if he were drinking the air out of a huge bottle.

"I don't know!" Ayushi said finally, holding up his fingers comically. "In Bon Po, many thousand mantras! Most in Zhang Zhung, old language."

Rudi remembered Schechter telling him about the forgotten language of the old Bon kingdom.

"This mantra, too. Nobody remember what these mantras mean. Maybe Rinpoche remember."

"Remember*ed*," Rudi corrected mechanically. "The Chinese executed him, right?"

"Oh no, Nagpa alive. I got message on wind. I get better message than Michael. He needs them not, with his phone. I got only wind!"

Rudi's mouth went dry. Nagpa, the only great shaman of Bon, could still be alive! "But the professor gave me Nagpa's ashes! I was told that Nagpa had been executed and cremated, and his ashes were smuggled outside."

Ayushi chuckled. "Chinese lie about ashes. All ashes the same."

"But how does one get in touch with him?"

"Only wind. He's in Rating, big jail in Lhasa. There it matter not, dead or alive. Nobody leave."

Rudi rubbed his forehead. "Lama, this mantra was used to kill the professor," he said slowly. "We must find out who did it. We must find out what kind of command the mantra sends."

His eyes closed, the lama was turning his head in the sun, like a sunflower.

"Ayushi sit six more days, he can remember much. Ayushi wants not, but remember much. His mind fast as it was."

"Six days . . ." Rudi drawled, disappointed.

"Ayushi sit week like this. Every time his mind restless. Rinpoche told him to do. Ayushi was bad student, lazy.

Ayushi ask all the time: explain this, explain that. Rinpoche wait that Ayushi hear without words. Then, Rinpoche send Ayushi to mountain. He say, Go to highest mountain and sit on dangerousest rock seven day. But rock must not sway, or you don't concentrate. Aaaah!" Ayushi slapped himself on the knee, giggling. "Rinpoche want so Ayushi can hear without words!"

"And you did?"

"Seven day, seven night. Almost fall many time. Asleep! Here, no master's stick necessary: you fall asleep, you fall down." He demonstrated by dropping his head on his chest and keeling over.

Rudi gasped, but, before he could reach for him, the lama was straight again.

"Ayushi was like this. I don't know if I learned. But Rinpoche took me for his student. Maybe felt pity for so stupid boy. Now Ayushi's mind starts to run, he goes to mountain: sometime seven days, sometime ten. Every three month."

"What do you hear in this mantra?"

Rudi's pleading expression must have touched the old man. He stopped smiling, closed his eyes, straightened up, noisily inhaled through his nose—and froze. Seconds were ticking away. The wind's howling grew loud and menacing. The rock under Rudi was sheer ice now; he was dying to take a leak.

Suddenly the lama's mouth opened a crack, and a bellowing sound came out, making the rock tremble and vibrate. Rudi could swear that mountains, too, stirred, their masses resembling huge grayish elephants swaying in motion. The mantra was not flowing out of the lama's mouth; rather, it was sinking in it, syllable by syllable. Ayushi himself was turning into an elephant, his gray trunk erect as it made a bellowing sound.

Rudi shook his head; the vision dissipated. Ayushi was silent, his body tilted, his hand cupping his ear (that was what his new student mistook for an elephant trunk! Rudi realized). Squinting and pursing his lip, he was listening to the echo. Finally, his eyes still shut, he reached for a handful of snow and squeezed it tight into his other hand.

"You can pour water into pot quick." He washed his face with the melted snow. "Or you can drip-drop it." His smile bright and clear, he added, "Mantra drip-drop his poison."

TRYING to make sense of Ayushi's words was like crossing a mountain river, hopping from one rock of a disjointed word to another and struggling not to drown in the stream of his giggling and chuckling. He agreed with the late professor: the mantra's effect was cumulative, rather than an instant one. But, Ayushi added, in order to be effective, Zhang Zhung secret mantras needed to be read beginning on a "power date" of the lunar calendar, and continue to be read for a fixed number of days and nights. But each mantra had its own date, and Ayushi was at a loss about this one.

"Teacher, I need a witness . . . I'll take you to the airport," Rudi pleaded, his hands folded in a praying posture; "I'll pay all your expenses." (*For everything else, there's Visa;* he recalled the slogan bitterly.) "The jury must hear this."

Lord, I'll accept any answer as an expression of Your will, as an exercise in viewing the Void, he intoned to himself as he peered into the lama's face. But his heart beat so hard he could barely contain it with his folded hands.

The lama pursed his lower lip pensively, then suddenly slapped Rudi's hand. "When you want to go?"

"Now!" Rudi exclaimed, dizzy with joy. "No—today too late. Tomorrow!"

"Good!" The lama laughed, sharing in his new adept's joy. "You come tomorrow morning, we go. It's time I go to New York. See my students, see Larry. He is unhappy now. He is orphan."

"He still has his mother—"

"His mother died long ago."

DEBRA, Schechter's wife and Larry's mother, was indeed a doctor, a cancer specialist, who came from a well-to-do New York Jewish family, long established in the medical profession. Yet, with all the humanist values they espoused, both she and her family had a hard time accepting the practical side of the young Tibetologist's beliefs. Their spotless Upper East Side apartment, a gift from her father, was overrun by foul-smelling, utterly unhygienic emigre lamas, ragged prophets, and their pot-smoking followers. "This is worse than a Crown Heights Shabbas," her mother would say with a sigh, in reference to the Saturday mantra-chanting ritual.

By the time Larry was fifteen, the marriage was in shambles. As a last resort, Schechter talked his wife into joining him, with Larry, on a trip to the Himalayas.

"He think, wife see Tibet, wife love Tibet," Ayushi said, smiling quietly. "Michael love wife. He want not divorce."

But things got worse en route. The independent-minded Debra had seen the trip as a fun jaunt and bridled at the hardships imposed by the treks through the mountains. Days went by without talking.

Their destination was a remote Bon Po cave lamasery in western Tibet, where Nagpa and Ayushi lived. Schechter spent whole days in the Rinpoche's cave and tried to pass his love of meditation and mantras to his wife and son. While Larry was just a restless teenager who would rather be riding the lamasery's horses, Debra put up her Western skeptical defenses and rejected the "magic" a priori.

"She fall asleep all time." Ayushi chuckled.

While Schechter was practicing meditation with Ayushi and the Rinpoche, Debra went to play with local children at a poor village nearby. Schechter disapproved: she could be hurt by falling rocks, or wild animals, or simply contract a disease. Sure enough, when she came back from the village, she was unable to stop scratching herself. She ran a fever; her whole body was covered with boils. Three days later, she could not get up.

As if to illustrate, Ayushi reached under his robe and scratched himself with fierce pleasure, groaning. Rudi shuddered at the quasiorgasmic sound of his groans; so this was what it was like for Debra.

Schechter deemed that she was too sick to make it to a relatively modern hospital in Lhasa—a three-week trek on horseback and a stretcher. He chose to stay at the lamasery and have Debra treated with mantras and herbs. The lamas tried their best, but a week later she was dead.

The thought of his old teacher's agony made Rudi wince with pain. Imagine being crucified on the horns of the dilemma: to drag your wife to Lhasa or put your trust in Bon mantras. It was not just the wine that had sent Schechter into the torment of begging forgiveness at their Last Supper.

Had Schechter been in the closet all along or was his wife's death the event that turned him gay? Rudi felt ashamed: he had no right to open that door. It did seem as though Schechter's decision to resort to mantras as AIDS treatment was related to Debra's death in Tibet; having denied her conventional remedies, he may have felt he had no moral right to take advantage of them for himself.

"Rinpoche did not let Michael lose his mind. But Larry had young mind. He think, If father not take mother to Tibet, or if father take mother to Lhasa, she still alive. . . ."

Ayushi's eyes grew teary, either from the memories or from the nonstop giggling. Or, perhaps, from the rays of late-afternoon sunlight: wide and swaying, like silk prayer flags on Tibetan lamaseries.

"They burned her body," Ayushi said. "Tibet custom. Especially if you die from bad disease."

So it was not an anonymous typhoid patient Schechter had been telling Rudi about; no, he was talking about his own wife's immolation. *A bed of rock for the bonfire that went above the village huts . . . the corpse's blissful smile.*

"Larry is very, very unhappy. Rinpoche and I, we explain: it is his mother's karma. She take new body or become free. But he forgive not father. He think, medicine could save mother. They never talk twenty years. Only last year begin talk again. Michael, he suffer, too. But he still Buddhist."

What was it like for Larry: seven days and nights of listening to lamas' ominous incantations, of being unable to help his mother. And then watching her body turn into a black mummy on the bonfire. Next to him, his father, numbed to pain by mantras . . . No wonder that twenty-odd years later, his whole face went into a spasm at the very mention of Buddhism. Could he have accused his father of speeding up his mother's death by using mantras? In retrospect, his neurotic, irritating laughter at his father's death seemed to have contained a tinge of gloating, of revenge. But now that they were even, it was time to bury the hatchet; when all of a sudden Rudi shows up on the scene—an extra irritant. Surprising how much Larry put up with him, after all. . . .

But Schechter did not just die; he was murdered. Rudi glanced at the lama, expecting an answer.

AYUSHI was silent. The sun had already touched the top of the opposite mountain; sunlight enveloped the vista in silken red and cast an uneven, quivering reflection on the lama's face, as if he were seated next to that funeral pyre. The sight of his face calmed Rudi's anxieties. No longer did he feel like interrogating; all he wanted was to see the master's smiling face.

It was time to leave, but he did not feel like leaving.

"What do you eat here, on the cliff?"

"Nothing. Ayushi bring food, but lynx come, too, to take it. Ayushi stopped: human food no good for lynx. But stupid lynx made hole here and sits waiting!" Giggling, the lama tweaked his finger at the animal's lair. "Man is like this lynx. Karma chase him away from bad food, but he still sit here, his mouth open. Karma take away bad food. Man, he cries: boo-hoo. . . ."

Rudi could not help smiling at his imitation of human wailing. He had always found it relaxing to talk to old people, however unimportant the subject. They were in no hurry, never mind that they had little time left. It was like sitting next to a fire, warming and comforting.

"How come you're not afraid of the lynx?" Unwilling to let the fire die, he tossed in another twig.

"Nagpa trained me. He sent me all night in mountains. Imagine yourself dead log, animals not touch you. Is useful. Also, lynx not touch Ayushi because Ayushi smell like log. Ayushi shit right here down the cliff."

He laughed some more and added, more seriously, "Nagpa for me like father. He want that I become a *nagpa*, too, but I was silly. I wanted see world, run away to India. Chinese come, I'm still in Nepal. Then—here!" Ayushi patted the rock. "Rinpoche teach another kid. I hear Chinese got him, too."

As a favorite disciple of the Nagpa's, Ayushi grew up in Rinpoche's cave. While the boy was asleep, the Rinpoche would often intone mantras. Sometimes the boy would wake up and listen to his teacher. He did not fully understand the meaning yet: rather, he was excited by peeking at the giant shadow of Nagpa, cast by the bonfire, in a conical dunce cap with a *thunrwa* horn in the one hand and a *purba* ritual dagger in the other. Nagpa swayed as he intoned mysterious incantations in a muted voice, and his magic apron made of encrusted human bones, the remnants of past lamas, made a scary knocking sound. Sometimes the wind outside would howl loud enough to drown out the intoning; for a moment, its gusts would sweep open the black yak hide that covered the entrance to the cave, and the boy could see the huge stars and the yellow blade of the moon over the silvery saddle of the mountains across the pass, a view that filled his heart with a mix of awe and admiration.

Each ancient mantra had an accompanying poetic "in-struction" that described metaphorically the meaning of the mantra, its duration—when the chanting should begin and how long it should go on—and even emergency instructions on how the mantra could be stopped. While some of these mantras were included in the tablets that were now in Ayu-shi's lap, the instructions had never been written down: Nagpa would whisper them to the recipient through a reed inserted in his ear.

"Children have good memory—Ayushi remember verse like echo!"

Once, out of mischief, Ayushi read a mantra, along with the instruction poem. Nagpa gave him a good thrashing and would no longer let him sleep in the cave.

"IF you afraid I slap you, too!" Ayushi broke out laughing. "You not afraid to sit with Ayushi—why you afraid of jail?"

Taken aback by having his thoughts read, Rudi muttered: "I'm afraid of pain, separation from loved ones—I'm afraid I would not be able to become what I wanted to become."

"He who understand what is here and now"—the lama

roughly shook him by the nape of his neck—"he already become what he wanted—must not afraid nothing! Not lynx, not jail! He Buddha!"

He waved Rudi off. "Go, it will dark now! Tomorrow come, we go court!"

AT the foot of the granite ledge, Rudi paused to glance back. The sun was already down, and the mountaintop basked in soft golden light. Ayushi had not changed his position: his head turned up, his hand cupping his ear. Although Rudi could not see the old man's face, he knew the lama was smiling a blissful, vigilant smile, as if he were pricking his ear to listen to the sounds of vanishing sunlight. Across the valley, the mountains rose on their tiptoes to peek at his smile over one another's shoulders.

24

RUDI proceeded downhill at a brisk, bouncy pace, as if he had not spent hours cringing on a piece of ice-cold rock. It was as if the lama had vacuumed him clean, the way he would blow through a dusty horn, and life bellowed in him anew. Hope was back. How could the jury not be swayed by the sage's explanation?

Below, bonfires were being started at the retreat. The bright moon was reflected in the frosty autumn grass. Rudi stopped on one of these silvery mirrors, and it cracked as it turned into a puddle. Suddenly it occurred to him: if Larry had stood next to his father while his mother's body was turning into a black mummy, he could well have wished a similar death upon his father. According to Detective Tarakis, an unknown chemical may have been involved. And there was a chemical lab next door to Larry's—

"Did he help?"

Rudi turned, startled. He had not heard Margi approach.

"There's hope. The lama has agreed to fly with me to New York."

"Lucky you." She walked next to him. "Four hours aboard the plane next to the Rinpoche is a great blessing."

"I know." He smiled happily, looking at her face, white as a fresco in the moonlight.

"Careful!"

She stopped him at a steep turn in the path. She jumped first and offered him her hand. He took it, but lost balance on landing and clumsily bumped into her.

He took his hand away instantly, but even an instant of holding her body, warm and fluid, like a wave confined in skin, was enough to quicken his breath. Margi could not help noticing it; her eyes widened, but she turned away and kept walking towards the clearing—cheerfully, he thought.

"Can I try again?" he asked. "To describe what I see? *Evening in a mountain retreat / Snow on tops turns a dark blue / Smoke of fires. Quiet. A dog barking. / A passing resident smiles at you / but his smile is actually for his cherubs / a pebble rolled from a bare foot on the path / echo rustles downward to the stream / I held my guide but almost fell into the abyss / though was far from the edge.*"

"Better." She nodded approval. "But you keep bringing up the experience of the others: how would you know about their cherubs?"

At a loss for words, he was saved from embarrassment by Abby.

"Did you get to pass along your inheritance?" She would not look at Margi as she approached. "How do you like the Rinpoche?"

"Oh, he's a saint."

"Exactly! You're so lucky—it is a blessing to be with him."

"Margi thinks so, too—" He turned but his guide was gone. "Vanished," he murmured. "No 'good night.' "

"Yeah, she does things quietly," Abby said with disapproval.

He did not react, but she felt that her tone was not appreciated and changed the subject to make fun of the group fireside meditation, led by the retreat manager. "He orders special logs from Oregon, can you believe it?"

OUTSIDE the Shambala Gate, Rudi glanced back. The bonfires looked like tiny holes drilled into the black mass of the mountain, and one would think that it was filled with molten gold. But the lama, the main source of light, was not to be seen.

Rudi told Abby he was leaving the next day and taking Ayushi with him.

"Already?" she cried out in disappointment, but instantly changed her expression to fake friendly enthusiasm. "Well, I sure am glad for you. Good luck."

For a while, they kept bouncing on the dirt road without saying a word.

"What did you make of Margi?" Abby asked as they reached the blacktop. "Everybody's crazy about her. You, too?"

He shook his head with faked indifference. "Why?"

"She's a witch," Abby said passionately. "After she came back in the morning, I sort of kidded her: How come every time you come here the Rinpoche goes to the mountains? She just said, 'Husbands go to the mountains to escape their wives. Gurus go to the mountains to escape themselves.' The nerve of that woman!" She sniffled and dried her eyes.

You started, he was about to say, but kept it to himself.

He thought how way back in the sixties the commune residents could be dregs individually, immersed in drugs and sex and other kinds of what society called sins—yet collectively they were an ideal of spiritual communion. Now spirituality had become an individual matter, while collectively these wonderful spiritual individuals created a shit heap of a community, with alienation and tariffs for everything, including fireside group meditations. The values of today included self-improvement of the individual, not for the collective. Hence Margi's solitude. Then again, what if it was the adult way to truth and happiness? The sixties suggested radical solutions, and those who stuck to them, those who did not defect to Wall Street or became community activists, got old without growing up: Abby, for example. But what about him, Rudi-Rudra—where was he on that continuum between riot and reflection?

"DO you want to come up?" Abby asked when they stopped by the library.

Rudi shook his head. "I'm beat."

"Well . . ." Her voice was trembling with tears. "Now that you know the way, you can make it back to the retreat on your own. Good luck!" She slammed the door.

IN the morning he called Gwen again. No one picked up: neither she nor the answering machine. Had she left, unable to stand the stress? Where would she go? He called her girlfriend's number but got the machine. He did not have her mother's number in California. He thought about calling the police to look for her, but he was going back today. It could wait till New York, he decided.

"How's our librarian?" the motel keeper asked when he settled the bill. Despite the early hour, she was fully made up and ready to break hearts.

"She's not a happy woman," he said coldly. "What's with her husband getting killed?"

"Killed my ass." The woman sneered. "She drove him to it! He was a hell of a handsome guy, and she was eaten up by jealousy. She wanted to hide him in that Chinese monastery up the hill so that no woman would ever see him. He spent ten years taking this shit from her until he just could not take it. He killed himself—that's what happened!"

"You mean it was no accident?"

"No one around here believes it. She's been crazy as a loon ever since. Once she tried to poison herself with gas, almost blew up the library. . . ."

Rudi knew how nosy a small town could be, yet something about the woman's remarks rang true. He had experienced enough jealousy from his own girlfriend to take such things lightly. Anything could trigger Gwen's suspicions: a call from an attractive classmate, a smile from a waitress in a restaurant. She did not smash dishes or begin screaming matches; she withdrew, and only her silence and her bulging eyes told him something was going on. He investigated, and, once he found out the real "reason," he would talk to her quietly and calm her down. But peace never lasted.

But ever since that fateful Halloween and the intrusion of the mantra in their lives, their relationship had deteriorated dramatically. It was as if the voice in the phone receiver summoned two invisible cobras that reared their heads and hissed in Rudi's and Gwen's souls. What was this chorus of Tune Ra—or *Thunrwa*—a magical weapon that was luring evil to the surface of their minds?

He rolled down the window, exposing his face to the cold wind, hoping it would blow the tormenting thoughts out of his mind. The mountains watched his attempts with sneering sarcasm, it seemed to him. If only he were not burdened with the trial, the testimony, the witnesses . . . He could stay here, hide out like the Unabomber, go visit Ayushi on his rock. Instead, he had to return and unravel the mess his life had become.

25

BY the time Rudi reached the retreat, he was in a philosophical state of mind. Whether he was about to end up in jail or not, his life would always be a winding ascent along the edge of the cliff towards an invisible peak, with white fog all the way. Whatever you do, you cannot see beyond the next curve in the road.

There was a crowd outside the lama's hut. Between their heads, Rudi saw Margi, seated on the ground and reading from a book. Group meditation, he thought, pricking up his ears and trying to recall the Tibetan he had studied under Schechter.

"Now, Master," she read, "as you contemplate Original Clear Light—"

The Book of the Dead was an odd choice for a morning

meditation, he thought. "Studying Bardo?" he asked the manager.

"A mournful but enlightening event," Cliff said with a thin smile. "The Rinpoche has left us—"

"Left? How?"

Something in the tourists' blandly pious faces made him push to the forefront.

Next to Margi was a body covered with a bloody gray robe. He could not see the face, only the bare dirty heels, which the manager's dog was licking with delight.

"Margi went to see him in the morning," the manager murmured, "but he wasn't on his rock. We found his body below. He must have fallen off at night."

"Fallen?" Rudi cried out, causing the tourists' displeased looks. What if someone called him, he was about to say, but then stopped himself: the lama did not have a phone. "How could he fall?"

The manager was unperturbed. "It gets gusty up there. Or he may have tried to get away from the lynx."

"He was supposed to come with me." Rudi tried to keep himself in check. "Are you sure that no one came to see him?"

"You were the last one," Cliff said.

"What are you saying?" Rudi swallowed. "He was fine when I left." He kneeled in front of Margi, who had just finished reading from a tablet. "What happened?"

"I don't know." She eyed him without expression. "The lama has been preparing himself for the transition for some time. Is this your *pun'ya?*" She handed him the voice recorder. "Time for you to go now. Maybe I'll see you when you obtain freedom."

Freedom? She had to mean Nirvana—freeing himself from his ego. Unless—but how could she know he was headed for jail? Now, with his key witness dead, he was sure to lose. Instinctively, he quickened his pace and pushed his way out of the crowd.

As he wheeled out of the parking lot, he glanced in the rearview mirror. The manager was staring after him, while talking into his cell phone.

The lying sonuvabitch. Rudi slammed his fist on the dash.

Wild animals did not touch Ayushi. Gusty winds were nothing new to him. No, the lama's death could not have been a coincidence. It had to be related to his, Rudi's, arrival, and their traveling plans. He groaned. *If it had not been for me, Ayushi would still be alive.*

The moment the gate with the billowing flags disappeared from view, the lump of fear and despair shot up to his throat. What was the point of going back to New York? And how was he going there? Where was Denver? The road blurred in front of him. He had to pause in front of the sign. What were these weird arrows on it?

Upon closer examination, the arrows turned out to be bullet marks. Abby had mentioned this was the local militia's favorite training exercise. He remembered the tipsy car mechanic: *"We don't care for Nips here."*

Sonuvabitches! This was something he could take straight to the feds in New York! And what good would it do him?

The pressure was building in his chest. As he tried to take a deep breath, he felt the seat strap cutting into his stomach. He reached to unbuckle himself and felt a small object—the voice recorder. Idiot, he didn't even tape the lama chanting the *thunrwa* mantra! You messed up but good, boy.

He was about to toss the recorder on the passenger seat when he noticed that the tape had been advanced. When he had presented the gadget to Ayushi, it had been at the start point. He pulled over, and, his fingers shaking, pushed the Play button.

Ayushi's voice came out, drowned out by the howling wind. Wincing, Rudi tried to remember his scant Tibetan, snatching isolated words. *Clear Moon—clouds in the sky—fears in the young guest's mind—happiness—death comes soon—force gathers like dew—*or is it *day?—Gathers in 309 days since Great Moon of Third Month—read after second turn—*could it be *thunrwa,* the horn?—*and before last—the joy of the fall that delivers upward—*

The tape rustled quietly. The recording was over. Ayushi had done his best to help.

The engine roared as Rudi pulled out and raced back to Yampa.

*   *   *

OUTSIDE Abby's house, he passed the tow truck from the gas station. The freckled young mechanic chuckled and tipped his baseball hat in greeting.

"Abby!" Rudi cried out, alarmed.

She was where he had seen her the first time—painting at her desk. At the sight of him, her hand shifted mechanically, sending a water bottle to the floor.

Just like me with the vase, he thought.

"I knew you'd be back"—she beamed at him—"but so soon! I was so upset we didn't part well."

"The Rinpoche is dead," he said. "I'm sure he was killed. But he taped something before his death. I need your help."

THE tiny kitchenette was strewn with almanacs and old papers. Sipping coffee from a cracked mug and sniffing at the faint gas leak, Rudi was doing the calculations: the third month of the Tibetan year, full moon—last year it fell on March 15. According to *Newsweek*, Tune Ra's "I Just Wanna Uh-Oh You," featuring "the amusing chorus that has since swept the country," entered the weekly charts on March 18. It had to have been released in the preceding week . . . close enough for you, Mr. Rudi, P.I.?

So—the fifteenth. The Ides of March. Tune Ra started chanting the mantra on its Force Date.

"Read after the second horn and before the last one." Tibetan monks blow the *dun* seashell—the second horn— from the roof to greet the sunrise. According to the almanac, in March the sun rose between seven and eight, just before Tune Ra's eight A.M. morning show on MTV. The last horn was sounded at midnight, right after his late-evening show.

Rudi's head swam. Was he going insane? The schedules of MTV, the apotheosis of modernity, arranged to fit ancient Buddhist rituals?

". . . will mature two hundred sixty-six days after the Big Moon of the Third Month . . ."

March 15 plus 309 days is January 18. Today was November 30.

In forty-nine days, something was going to happen.

What was it?

*   *   *

THE phone rang.

"I'm fine, Sheriff," Abby said. "No, I don't know where he is. . . . He just stopped by to ask for directions to the retreat. . . . I sure will. Byyye. . . ."

She turned to face Rudi, her face chalk-white. "They're looking for you."

"It's the retreat manager." Rudi got to his feet. "They need a scapegoat. And I was the last one to see Ayushi."

"Then you must run!" She opened her arms for a farewell hug.

He kissed her on the cheek. Her soft skin smelled of powder and herbal creams.

"We'll meet in Shambala, Rudra!" she whispered dramatically. "Now, run!"

Twenty minutes later he slowed down on the pass to catch his breath and take a last glance at the necklace of Yampa around the blue neck of the lake.

What was this sense of kinship that sparked in his hand when he held her for, perhaps, the last time? As we run into people, they come into view the way your own body parts show up in the foam when you're lying in your bathtub—and then they disappear again, but you know you still have them. Now, too, a new part of him called "Abby" (a gland, a capillary, a wrinkle?) was about to disappear. But he knew he would always feel her.

He peered into the distance. Inexplicably, he ached to see her out on the stoop.

He turned the ignition, and the car responded explosively.

But the sound came from behind. He turned to look again.

The white bead of the library house burst into the sky in red-and-black flames.

26

NOT until Rudi heard the sirens and saw red fire trucks approaching the library could he force himself to turn the wheel towards Denver.

The rain started and, in Rudi's mind, the car turned into a large sieve: jets of fear and grief, sent by an invisible sniper, shot at him, and there was no magic shield for him to protect himself. He had never subscribed to conspiracy theories, and his mind refused to organize the events of the last month—the fall in the subway, the fatal fire in the professor's home, the fall of the lama, and now Abby—into a logical sequence. But how could he not blame himself? He was not merely afraid for his own life; he feared for whoever would come in touch with him. If he as much as slowed down, what would happen to whoever tried to pass him? He flew like a cannonball, and damn the speed limit.

At the airline terminal, his mouth went dry at the sight of uniformed policemen. Surely the sheriff had alerted the state police, and now there was an APB out for him. After a moment of hesitation, he picked the longest X-ray check line and resolutely stepped forward, his heart beating a tattoo. You don't have to believe in conspiracies to behave as if you were in one.

"PLEASE buckle your belt, sir."

"Sorry," he murmured mechanically. Lady, what's the point? If these guys could send Ayushi tumbling down the cliff, you think they'd balk at blowing up the plane? You think the belt will help?

He dialed Gwen's number on the airplane's phone in the back of the seat in front of him. Still no answer. Please answer—pack a suitcase—come to the airport—we'll get on another plane and be out of here—

Forty-nine days left—enough of this nonsense. Let's just get out of here.

ON the other hand, he thought, swaying as his Sikh cab-driver slalomed past the potholes on Grand Central, the epidemic of deaths at every turn could be the best validation of his research. His heart sank at the realization of his pettiness. He should be saving mankind—seriously, now. Go get Gwen.

AS he fumbled with the key, he heard the phone ringing inside the apartment. He entered, turned on the lights, and stopped, shocked.

Gwen was sitting on the bed, her legs crossed, looking at him—rather, through him—with her eyes wide open.

"Are you okay?"

"Om mani padme hum." Her voice was quiet, her smile Buddha-like blissful. "How was your trip?"

"Not too good." The phone kept ringing, but neither of them would pick it up.

"That's wonderful." Not a muscle in her face moved. "I'm in *samadhi,* beloved."

I must be dreaming, he thought, equally unable to move. They must have thrown me in jail in Denver, and now I'm just having a dream. "Why don't you pick up the phone?"

"Because I'm in fucking *samadhi!*" she yelled, then grabbed the phone and smashed it into the wall.

"What's wrong?" he yelled back, shielding his face from the rain of shards that flew across the room.

"Are you okay, Gwen?" a neighbor called outside.

"You have an admirer now?" Rudi opened the door a crack, yelled, "She's fine!" and slammed it shut in the face of a towheaded youth.

Gwen was weeping, covering her face with her hands.

"What's wrong, baby?" He knelt in front of her and, trembling with fear, went to kiss her wet face.

"I'll talk to you in the shower." She rose from the bed.

HAD they ever taken a shower together? Maybe during her first week in New York, if at all.

Gwen turned up the water full blast, both in the tub and in the sink, and pressed a finger to his lips. Then she embraced him and started whispering in his ear.

THE phone rang soon after he left for the airport. Five rings. Two more. Five again. Their new code. "I thought you were calling from the airport."

The familiar chanting sent her screaming on the floor. Remembering Rudi's instructions, she pressed Record on the answering machine and hung up.

The chanting stopped immediately.

"You shouldn't be using the answering machine," said a low male voice. "Taping kills communication. I'd like to speak to you live—"

"I never picked up the phone again," she whispered, pressing her wet cold body against him. "Our room is bugged, that's how they learned our code. . . ."

"Who are 'they'?" he whispered back. "Why the shower? We could've played the music loudly—"

"I wanted to feel close to you," she murmured. "We're like twins in a uterus here. I was so afraid for you. . . ."

BY the time he finished his story, the bathroom was as foggy as the mountain road in Colorado.

"We must run away," she whispered. "The hell with the bail! We'll go to Canada, we'll live in the woods, like in an ashram, didn't you want that? We'll have a baby, we'll gather herbs, pick mushrooms, you'll be writing your songs. . . . I've got it all figured out: there's a train for Toronto that leaves at a quarter to eleven."

Rudi swallowed, to kill the bitter taste of shame in his mouth. While he had been thinking about leaving her, she was forsaking her life for him. He kissed her tenderly amid the streams of water. She had not felt so desirable in a long time—

"This can wait!" She shrank away, her eyes shining feverishly. "Now we must figure out how to leave the house unnoticed. We can't afford to lead them to the station."

Seeing skepticism in his eyes, she added, "Don't question me! I know we're being watched!"

In the living room, she began throwing her things into a suitcase. "Why did you open the window?" she yelled. "Step away! Listen . . . go to the basement. There're some old blankets on top of our bikes, remember? We'll make holes in them, turn them into ponchos, pretend we're Latinos, leave through the back entrance—"

"What are you—" He almost said "babbling," but checked himself.

"The language school!"

He gasped. She was crazy as a fox! Indeed, the ground floor of the building housed a language school, and most of the students were off-the-boat South Americans. If they could merge with the crowd, they had a chance to sneak to Broadway unnoticed.

"Go, quick!"

EN route to the elevator, he tried the door to the back stairs next door to their apartment. It was essential to slipping out of the building. After a few tugs on the door handle, it gave way. He sighed with relief.

The elevator door opened on the first floor.

"Going down," Rudi snapped at a tall man in a raincoat and pushed the button to close the doors.

Within a few minutes, he retrieved the dusty blankets and, suppressing a sneeze, returned to the elevator, his heart beating violently. An enormous wave of relief kept him afloat. For the first time in months, he did not feel alone. Between the two of them, they could move the Himalayas. The forty-nine–day threat was nothing.

As the elevator doors slid open on his floor, he heard the clang of the back-stairs door. Must be the wind, he thought, to calm himself against the suspicion that was growing with every step.

He pushed the door to the apartment, only to catch the wind from the window open wide.

"Gwen!" And once again, more quietly, "Gwen. Gwen."

No answer. Somehow *knowing,* he stumbled over to the open window, his hands dropping the blankets on the way.

"Gwen!" But the red spot below, spread on the roof of a car, did not respond.

"Gwen!" The crowd that had gathered around looked up quizzically.

"Gwen!" And all Broadway—who would not pause for the presidential cortege or a thousand sirens howling at the same time—came to a standstill in response to his wail.

IT had to be a dream, and he had to wake up as soon as possible. He leapt to the door—the reality had to be on the other side—and slammed into two men: the towheaded neighbor and a black linebacker in shades.

"He killed her!" the neighbor yelled, pointing his finger. "They had a fight! He pushed her!"

Before Rudi could shove him away, the black guy barked, "NYPD," and clicked the handcuffs around his wrists.

On the way out, he writhed and tried to scream, but words would not leave his mouth. The doorman's eyes—the crowd—the red spot atop the car—all swam past him in a mesh of colors. A strong hand pressed down on his head and pushed him inside a police cruiser. He made one last lunge to freedom, and someone delivered a chop on his neck, just below his ear.

27

RUDI floated back to consciousness to see the Manhattan streetlights rushing by at a breakneck speed.

"You don't recognize an old pal?" The linebacker removed his shades.

The driver was none other than Detective Martin Rivers, Tarakis's partner. He pulled over and opened the rear door. "Come on, get in the front. You don't have much time. And stop shaking. Jesus, look at yourself. If you've pissed in my car, I'm gonna get really upset. You don't want that."

"I didn't do it," Rudi murmured.

"I know that."

"But it's all my fault!" Rudi dropped on the ground, howling and wheezing. "It's—my fault."

Rivers calmly jerked Rudi to his feet and rolled up his sleeve. "You'll feel better." A needle went into Rudi's arm, making him twitch.

SLOWLY Rudi's face regained its original color, his breath grew even, his shaking stopped. A blissful smile touched his features.

"All right," Rivers said. "Spit it out. Where have you been?"

Rudi nodded. Whatever was in the needle, it suppressed his will completely: the events of the last three days flowed out of him like a calm river through the plains. All his suffering and torment seemed childish and unimportant: interrogating Larry, hugging the rock, sitting in the shower with Gwen . . .

The detective listened closely without interrupting.

The peace Rudi had aspired to was all over him. He had been in a comedy thriller; now it was over, and a cute childish tune was playing over the closing credits. "What was this stuff in the needle?"

"Bliss-D. Fifty bucks on any street corner uptown. Run these numbers by me again three hundred–something days?"

"Three hundred nine. Forty-nine days left."

"Not much of a margin for error," remarked Rivers as he put the car in gear.

"Where are you taking me?" As if I care. I'm already feeling pretty good . . .

"To Russia." Rivers turned onto 125th Street.

Rudi broke up. Slapping the dashboard and groaning with laughter, he slid down on the floor. "You—are—killing me. You're a regular fucking comedian, you know that? This is the most politically incorrect joke I ever heard! Black Russian, like a drink, right? And then what? The Tibet of the South Bronx?"

"I could never work out the proper dosage of these

things," Rivers said gloomily as he pulled over to the curb next to a hot-dog vendor.

"Let me borrow this." Rivers indicated the ice bucket, where soda cans were floating in ice water.

Such were the detective's heft and streetwise bearing that he did not even have to flash his badge.

"Yeah, sure, brother." The diminutive Mexican sounded relieved at not being robbed.

Rivers pulled Rudi out of the car and with one brisk movement pushed his face into the bucket. While he held the younger man down with one hand, he ordered two hot dogs with everything and consumed them on the spot.

"Hm." He critically assessed Rudi's condition. "I guess maybe now we can talk. Want a hot dog?"

Rudi nodded. He remembered he had not eaten in two days.

ONLY a few years ago, Special Agent Martin Rivers was in charge of a clandestine FBI unit involved in the infamous White River standoff. Running out of options, taking the heat from Washington, the bureau dared the unthinkable: at the CIA's suggestion, they enlisted the services of an Oleg Ruslanov, the former KGB's top expert in psychological warfare. Mr. Ruslanov's task was to develop a program with a subliminal suggestion that would cause the cult to surrender. The command would be encoded into a most trivial conversation—

"Or music," Rudi said.

Rivers nodded approvingly. "You're getting there."

As in a good novel, things went well at first. There were indications that the resolve of the cult leaders was softening. A couple more days, and they would surrender.

"And then there was a leak," Rivers said. "Some reporter guy found out we had a KGB man working for us. The bosses had a shit fit. One, loss of face; two, the Red Menace; three . . . whatever. Within twenty-four hours, Oleg was on a plane. And you know what happened next."

"You guys went in," Rudi said. "And they all got torched."

"Eighty-seven, all told. Including women and children. To say nothing of six of my agents."

In a fit of rage, Rivers committed an act of high insubordination. There was talk of throwing the book at him—it is not every day that an FBI agent puts a superior in the hospital with a broken jaw—but eventually it was decided that the incident was best swept under the rug. Thus Rivers's FBI career came to an end. He was lucky to get a job with New York's Finest.

"And this is how I ended up partners with Tarakis." Rivers added. "Who is actually not a bad guy, once you get to know him. It's not his fault that Atlantic City is the farthest he has ever been outside New York."

When Rivers heard Rudi's ravings at the precinct, he immediately flashed back on White River. The special agent and the Russian scientist had become quite friendly during the siege, and Rivers had been so impressed with Ruslanov's research that he'd actually drafted a memo to his FBI boss, arguing that the Russian be hired on a long-term basis. With Russian scientists being destitute, why test the man's moral resolve and wait till he got hungry enough and sold out to the highest bidder? But that was before the famous punch that cost Rivers his job and career. As for now, any reference to anything that took place at White River would be an automatic no-go.

"But see"—Rivers's voice rose in excitement—"Oleg, he's such a smart cookie, he predicted things. We were sitting in a bar, and there was some shit video clip playing on TV, and Oleg pointed at it and said, 'If I wanted to take over the world, that's the route to take.' See what I mean?"

"Great," Rudi murmured. "It has only taken me five bodies so far to come to the same conclusion."

"But you did the most important thing." Rivers patted him on the knee. "You figured out which clip it is." Then, seeing that Rudi's eyes were swelling up, he added, "There will be always bodies. Collateral damage, you know? You should think less of the body count that's already happened—none of which you're directly responsible for, by the way—and more of how many bodies you'll be able to save."

But it was too late. "You—don't—know! Only a god-damn killer can talk like that! They're *not* collateral damage! If you only knew what a wonderful man the professor was! And the lama: he was a real-life saint! And G-g-g—" Rudi's sniffles were about to turn into full-fledged hysterics.

Rivers watched him disapprovingly. It occurred to him that, in fact, his chances for advancement with the bureau had been limited even without White River and the punch. He was just too damn intolerant of amateurs. Especially this milquetoast. He sighed and reached for the needle.

"YOU keep forcing me to do this, you're gonna end up a real-life junkie," he warned Rudi.

"I don't see a problem." Rudi stretched and yawned.

"That's what they all say. Listen to me, you dummy. Now, we don't know who's behind this. You've mentioned Colorado militias, right? Let's say your Tune Man's working for them. What do they want? They want to wipe this country clean of everybody who's not like them, right? The easiest way to do it is, start a riot. Look at these homeboys." He nodded towards a bunch of rowdy black teenagers outside a nightclub. "They're already listening to plenty of racial hatred. But let's say your Tune Man, or whoever's running him, has coded in a command: *Kill the Crackers.* Believe me, it's as easy as this!" He snapped his fingers. "One spark will do it. Then what do we have? We have L.A. riots multiplied by a hundred. And then the militias come into play. The Rescuers. You know what? Nice, liberal white people, registered Democrats all, will be begging the scumbags to come in."

"You're talking some kind of apocalypse."

"That's exactly right, my man." Rivers squinted. "Now, don't you think this is something worth hauling your sorry Buddhist ass five thousand miles for?"

Rudi was silent. An apocalypse—no, an Armageddon—was taking place in his own head. He felt sooo good, but he knew it was a temporary condition; it, too, had to pass. Suddenly a comedy thriller turned into a regular *Your Karma Forever,* and he was a suave Brit listening to an old guy with an initial for a name explain how to fart through ten-foot-thick cement walls.

"I'm not who you think I am," he forced himself to say. "I just create messes."

"Yeah, well—I don't have much of a choice. And you, you have even less. You stay here, your face will be on the wall in every post office." Rivers put the car in gear and headed east.

I'm a fugitive from justice, Rudi thought wistfully. And I don't look or act anything like Harrison Ford.

At the first light Rivers squinted, as if assessing Rudi's condition. "I think I'm getting the hang of this dosage business."

"If all else fails, you'll make a helluva drug dealer."

"Now you're talking."

As they drove across the East River, Rivers wrapped up the briefing. "Oleg is a brilliant guy, a generous guy, but things are tough over there, so . . . you have to assume the worst. Always. What if he's in some kind of money trouble, big time? Or someone has taken his wife hostage? What I'm saying is, in theory it's possible that whoever is behind the Tune Man has already availed himself of Oleg's services. So, be careful."

"I still don't understand what he's—what we're—supposed to do for you."

"Where there's a mantra, there's a countermantra. Isn't that what your lama told you?"

"But the only lama who knows it is in Chinese jail. He's as good as dead."

Rivers chuckled. "That doesn't mean you can't create a countermantra on a computer. If Oleg can code any command into gibberish, he should be able to do the reverse, too. Brother, if medical researchers, instead of synthesizing drugs, were waiting for Mother Nature to hand them medication, we would all be dead now."

"Speaking of which," Rudi murmured, watching the lights of LaGuardia float by, "how about one more shot. One for the road?"

"Now you're talking like a real junkie snitch." Rivers patted himself on the jacket. "Not until you clear Customs."

* * *

FLASHING his badge right and left, Rivers led his still-high protégé past every JFK uniform. Pretty cool, Rudi thought boyishly.

Finally, they stepped inside a small cubicle with a PERSONNEL ONLY sign, where Rivers issued Rudi a folder with a new passport in the name of Xavier Kosinski, his NYPD mugshot ("A slapdash job, but that's the best I could get in a hurry; besides, Oleg will take care of you at his end"), and a Russian entry visa.

"Why didn't you give me this before?"

"So that you could lose it? Roll up your sleeve."

Book Two

MOSCOW

28

RUSLANOV had a stubbly gray beard and eyes that were sunken gray periscopes under a high, almost concave, forehead. His face had been sculpted by the rough hands of an ancient God. They left fingerprints in the form of deep wrinkles. A da Vinci with his breath visible in the bone-piercing Russian cold.

They left the airport, and Ruslanov stepped on the gas, weaving in and out of lanes. "You do look like—like a shit, right?" he said.

"My wife got killed."

"I know. You have my sympathy. Martin called me. In America, you are Vanted Man. Martin's orders are: sit kvietly, not leave my side, give me your passport, and not call anybody in America. All your friends' and family's phones are bugged. Now we find out vot is your mantra made of."

Rudi gasped. "But you don't have its recording!"

"You can hear it on any station. Even special one opened, Tune Russia. He is good businessman, your Tune Ra."

Ruslanov turned on the radio. Tune Ra's voice screamed out like a SWAT team knocking down the doors to Rudi's head.

Rudi groaned. "You don't have any Bliss-D? Rivers shot me some."

Ruslanov shook his head, then nodded at Rudi's beads. "Are you Buddhist?"

"Used to be."

RUSLANOV'S office was in the basement of a psychiatric clinic. He tossed a threadbare lab coat, gray after many a wash, around Rudi's shoulders, and led him down the corridors stinking of carbolic acid and rotten cabbage. Patients were everywhere: mental cases in soiled pajamas and worn-out slippers, stroke victims with canes, emaciated pimpled youths. . . .

The basement was a maze of low-ceilinged dark, narrow hallways, with damp stucco, leaky pipes, and steam coming from the boiler room. Their destination was two tiny offices, with bare wires sticking out of the walls with chipped tiles.

"It was boiler room before revolution," Ruslanov explained; "then morgue, and finally it was gifted to our lab."

His office was a tiny windowless cubicle: a table with a forest of papers, a computer, dust-covered brain scanners, floor-to-ceiling rusting file cabinets.

"So where's the supersecret KGB lab?"

"Oh, one day you're supersecret lab"—Ruslanov grinned sadly—"then *pfff!* No more Soviet Union, and someone stole all money. So we had to move. That's okay. We're Russians, we're strays of humanity. We can do with pencil and pad."

He turned on the monitor. "Let me give you a run-through. Instead of a shot." He seated Rudi on a hard chair with torn upholstery and an array of wires.

"This chair has seen very much," Ruslanov orated as he covered Rudi's head and body with electrodes. "Generals, ministers, addicts, murderers. And now you. What we must do is test your reactions in normal condition. Then we apply your mantra and test you again. This is how we discover if mantra has subliminal message."

"In general tonality, nothing happens," Rudi murmured. "I mean, its effect is cumulative. Rivers must have told you."

"We discover what cumulates, okay?" Ruslanov said cheerfully. "Machine is more sensitive than man."

"I'm not a good candidate for testing," Rudi said weakly. "I'm barely here, after two days without sleep."

"This is excellent. You have less control over your consciousness. Look at screen and not become distracted."

Sequences of green figures began scrolling down the screen. Scrolling like heaven, Rudi thought. The Supreme Scientist, too, will straighten the contours of constellations into lines, roll them into a scroll—or, rather, will record them digitally and save them in a directory called Being. The directory will contain myriad folders, the Milky Way one of them; Earth, a subdirectory; People, yet another. Finally, my file . . . But what if all the files have been damaged by the virus—the mantra, that is?

Rudi's eyes swelled with tears, both from peering at the screen and from recalling Schechter, who loved this kind of philosophizing. "Do I have to do this much longer?"

Ruslanov froze the screen. "Be patient. It takes about ten minutes to get chart of your immortal soul. Then two days to analyze. Then I test about hundred patients, that's three to four months; only then we can say with degree of confidence if your mantra has subliminal message or not."

"Four months? And how long before you can figure out what the message is?"

"That could take years."

"But we only have forty-eight days!"

"To what?"

Rudi grabbed his temples, brushing the electrodes off on the way. "I wish I knew."

"All I can tell is if your mantra has subliminal message or not. What kind of message, almost impossible to say. I could do it in months maybe, instead of years, if I had supercomputer like Cray. But"—he spread his arms—"no bucks!"

Suddenly, Rudi was cold and indifferent. The latest outburst consumed what was left of his energy. What did he care? He was a dead man. If this mantra indeed threatened someone and was not a figment of his imagination—let the living save the living.

He removed the electrodes and headed for the men's room. Inside, he climbed on the john and removed his belt. Someone knocked on the door. He tied the belt into a noose. The knocking grew more insistent, accompanied by angry Russian words. The belt kept sliding off the hook. The voice started yelling. *I can't do it*, Rudi said to himself, and restored the belt to his pants.

Outside, a youngish man with a thin mustache was grimacing eloquently. He barked at Rudi in Russian and slammed the toilet door behind him.

"I'm not the only impatient client here," Rudi said to Ruslanov. "Some nutcase has just chased me out of the john."

"He's no nutcase," Ruslanov said grimly. "He's Fedot, official KGB observer. Nutcase here is you. Sit down and let us finish test."

29

RUDY was awakened by the low moaning sound of the mantra. The anonymous voice came from the next room. His heart leapt as he sat up; he was not sure where he was.

He was seated on a narrow single bed, with pictures of teenage idols on the wall above it. Tune Ra's picture was in the middle, and the mantra seemed to come out of his white-toothed grin. A gray contour of a Russian housing project loomed behind the toile window curtain. The clock showed four: he was still jet-lagged.

He tiptoed outside. A young girl was sleeping on the living-room couch. Although Rudi could not remember her, the sight of her blonde braid draped over the carpet had a strangely calming effect. He was at the Ruslanovs', he remembered, as he moved towards the quiet sound of the mantra, which was coming out of the scientist's study.

"Come in." Ruslanov spotted bewilderment in Rudi's eyes as he stared at the speaker—the source of the sound. "I synthesized it by hand after we got home. I have tape with Tuvan throat singing, so I broke down its tonality and inserted your mantra."

"But it's dangerous to be listening to it in this tonality!"

"If it contains something dangerous, it can be effective only over a long period of time, the way teenagers listen to their idols. To cause fast damage, one must feed it directly into the subconscious."

"Is it possible?"

"Why not? Here's mantra, and here's your immortal soul." Ruslanov pointed at the computer screen, where a colored picture of a maze was rotating slowly.

"I don't understand." Rudi was still in shock.

"Briefly: what your psychoanalysts do on couch I do on computer—but much, much faster, preciser, and more objectively. Of course they don't like my method because it ruins their business—millions dollars, right? Remember, you saw numbers on screen in clinic, yes? There were words between them: you did not see them, but your unconscious—I call it *uncon*—reacted to them. At speed of thirty milliseconds your mind didn't have time to censor the word, and the electrodes used your brain signals and heartbeat to measure your real attitude to these notions."

Ruslanov lit a cigarette. "After I spoke to Martin, I assembled list of components—I call them *clusters*—of your personality. I included standard ones—money, family, sex, drugs, suicide—and your specific clusters—Gwen, professor, mantra, Ayushi, Tune Ra, then—Abigail, right?—murder and so on. Then computer sorts reactions of your brain scan according to level of anxiety."

"So this maze represents my soul?"

"Built by order of King Minos—that is, ego—by his engineer Daedalus—that is, brain! Inside hides Minotaur, or conception of 'I.' "

While outlining his favorite metaphor, the scientist got excited, and was now squinting contentedly as he puffed on his cigarette.

"In order to get out of labyrinth you must understand how it is built. Minotaur looks at everything from one point of view: is it tasty food or threat? So he creates links to fear and pleasure. You can see it on your suicide cluster. See long purple disc? You both want it and afraid of it at same time."

Rudi paled: the computer knew about his suicide attempt at the men's room.

Ruslanov spotted his reaction. "Suicide does not free from labyrinth. I work much with postclinical death cases, and they tell me they went through it, too. I can confirm—I was clinical dead after stroke—that door to grave is dead end. This is my formula: 'If you don't get treatment in life, you get suffering after death.' "

"So you can use your method to find out all about any person?"

Ruslanov chuckled. "Actually, you can make just about any person do just about anything. I have come up with something I call *confids*. Like in *confidence*, yes? They are not coherent phrases, but rather combinations of important words for each individual; ones that turn off his brain and generate absolute confidence."

"But that's exactly how mantras work!" Rudy exclaimed.

"Perhaps." Ruslanov nodded. "Ancient Hindus figured their *confid* mantras by hand through thousands years, but we—we have computers. My programs find these archetypes specific for each person and code them into noises. These noises serve as distraction that allows confids to enter uncon subliminally. For example, doctor can suggest to addict that his happiness does not depend on needle, or to lame person that he can walk. They receive it as Voice of God and act on it; one throws away needle, another his crutch. So you can suggest to soul anything you want."

"You mean you can encode these subliminal messages in TV, in noises, in radio signals?"

"Exactly. That is how I met Mr. Rivers and now you."

"So you can really send a message suggesting . . . anything?"

"Subliminal message can send crowd rioting in fifteen seconds. But decoding it, that takes years."

Put the mantra out, Rudi remembered Ayushi's words. The *nagpas* knew the formulas that could stop a mantra in its tracks. "How about neutralizing it?"

Ruslanov sighed patiently. "I told you: first I must know its exact message. There are two ways to find out. One is through comparison. We must find person's reactions to words we know and compare to reaction to mantra, which we don't. We must put at least five hundred people through this procedure. But to process this much information we need Cray."

"And the second one?"

"We can take risk and introduce this mantra, taped in

correct tonality, as second background—that is, directly into patient's uncon—and concurrently follow changes in his clusters. Then control group can be narrowed down. But in view of very unpleasant things that happened to your professor and others, it involves risk. We need volunteers."

"You already have one," Rudy said.

30

WHEN Rudi woke up again, Ruslanov and the girl with the braid were already gone. He was driven to the lab by Masha—Maria, that is—the doctor's wife. On the way, she got talking about her husband.

Ruslanov became a psychologist to pursue his dream of curing people of their shortcomings. But the KGB, acting through the informers they had in every research institute, learned of Ruslanov's experiments and deemed his computer models useful for psychological warfare. Instantly, his research became classified. Ruslanov hated his new masters, but their generosity made him grin and bear it. They wanted him to create weapons to render the SDI, or Star Wars, ineffective: coded messages to incite mass panic, riots, assassinations of political leaders. Or special coded signals that could be sent from planes and subvert the consciousness of nuclear missile operators. Finally, signals could be encoded in radio and TV scripts.

"This is how Communists would counter Hollywood." She smiled. "Terrorist weapon for twenty-first century: no blood, no traces. Better than quietest nuclear sub."

"Why didn't he stop?"

"Why didn't Einstein? Why didn't Oppenheimer? For scientist, to stop working on his idea is like for mother to stop feeding her baby. Oleg says it's like to forbid Prometheus to give people fire, because it burns some people. Or it's like banning knives because some people cut throats.

But some knives cut bread, you understand? Also, he had patients—cancer, epilepsy, schizophrenia—on whom other doctors gave up. But he saved them with his confids."

Without abandoning his research, he became an internal dissident of sorts: he demanded that his work be declassified and turned over to an international committee. The KGB was considering whether they should arrest him and confine him to a prison lab, the way Stalin used to do it; but then came glasnost, perestroika, and the committee's budget was slashed. The financing of Ruslanov's research was reduced to nickels and dimes. The lab was moved to the basement; yet the KGB maintained a degree of control, applying pressure through orders, threats, and blackmail. Their greatest fear was that he would be recruited by foreign intelligence. Yet Ruslanov steadily refused offers of money and facilities from various Western universities.

"He is patriot!" His wife shrugged, as if wondering what kind of naif she had there. But her pride shone through this minor attempt at acting. "He really wants his discovery to be Russian. When he went to America—when he met Martin—KGB sent whole troop along to prevent that he defects. We never planned! But they still watch and watch." Not for the first time during the drive she glanced at the rearview mirror.

"Now that we have an ex-KGB man for president," Maria went on, "the anti-Western mood and spy mania are on the rise again. They have their own man in lab now, to keep tab, yes? Fedot is disgusting character who sticks his nose everywhere and spends nights pawing nurses and writing reports on Oleg. He saw you yesterday, so it's High Alert in KGB: foreigner in lab!"

"I'm sorry to be causing you trouble," Rudi murmured.

She waved him off. "We are used to trouble. We receive people from all over, both at home and at lab. Last year, peasant woman came to see him, her daughter has schizophrenia. She wanted to sell her cow to pay us. So we cured Varya and she stayed with us, yes—where would she go? Back to village? Besides, she still needs supervision. So she helps us at lab, takes care of patients."

Varya had to be the girl on the couch. He must have slept in her bed.

"We don't have our own children," Maria said after a pause. "For me, too late." She fell silent.

Rudi was flustered. Why was she telling this to him—a perfect stranger? Was this the courage and honesty of a scientist facing herself? He glanced at her: a fiftyish blonde with a soft Slavic profile and an imprint of chronic fatigue and patience on her face.

But she loves him so much! he thought, casting another glance. *He is both a philosopher and a passionate child. She is his student and mother at the same time; he is her guru and son. Gwen and I never had it—was it because we never had a common cause the way they do?*

"So," Rudi murmured, to change the subject. "The secrets of psychological weaponry are stored in your, er, modest basement?"

"Full know-how Oleg keeps here." She tapped on her forehead. "Computer is not enough to discover which words are key to individual's subcon. You need intuition and genius, so that all fits in just right. Oleg has gift that, fortunately, no one else has. Mafia characters come to plot against rivals and menace him. How do you say, 'Suggestion you can't turn down,' yes? Does this happen in your country, eh? Can you imagine Italian Mafia don coming up to MIT and menace scientist? Aah"—she waved a hand, exasperated—"it's hard for you to understand what kind of hell this life is.

"Listen," she went on excitedly, "KGB, government officials—they come to him in secret for treatment from alcoholism, impotence, all sorts of nerve conditions. Now we have elections coming, so politicians are going crazy. Oleg had an assistant who betrayed him. He hired himself to candidates and now settled on TV, putting propaganda messages in broadcasts. Make millions!

"And then there's business. They use subliminals in advertising. You know it has crippling effect on children's psychology? Oleg tried to expose them, he asked for parliamentary investigation. Twice already they did something to his car brakes. And threatening to sue for high treason. And here you come with your mantra-shmantra!"

HER monologue had a thoroughly humbling effect on Rudi. Until then, he had imagined that his experiments with mantras and pop music constituted a tiny unique world. Now, the Big Picture unfolded, where stupid greedy mortals were reaching for the weapon of the gods. Could it be that all of his woes came about because he had endangered some corporate campaign that used Tune Ra to pitch its product?

31

BEFORE turning on the computer, Ruslanov pulled back Rudi's headset and whispered, "If you feel sick, raise finger."

Rudi gave himself to the flow of blinking lines on the screen and the steady soporific rustling in the headphones.

So he was the first volunteer to have a mantra being fed directly into his subconscious. Camouflaged by the din in the headphones, the mantra was not being chewed carefully by the conscious; rather, it was swallowed by his soul in a lump. He was the first one to drink the poison by the glass, rather than being fed through a dropper.

As he listened, the fear sneaked up on him; cold sweat formed on his back and shoulders. Then he felt nauseous; his innards were tumbling down, and the armchair was melting and shifting away. He clenched his teeth and gripped the arm of the chair to prevent himself from raising a finger. In the corner of his eye, he spotted Maria's pale face, the syringe, the green lab coat . . . suddenly, all went dark.

Something exploded in his head, spreading a pungent odor that woke him up.

"You okay?" Ruslanov moved a smelly cotton ball under his nose. "Nothing good old ammonium chloride cannot handle," he said reassuringly to Maria, her syringes at the ready.

"Feeling better now? Look—" Ruslanov pointed at the floating color discs on the screen. "Your soul against mantra background."

"What's that?" Rudi pointed at the raspberry-colored disc in the center.

Ruslanov cracked his knuckles. "There it is, your Bon command. It generates fear. I understand that. But curious thing is that mantra serves like trigger. I mean, it provokes explosion of stress that has been building up. You know how each of us explodes at sound of certain word: for jealous man, it's his rival's name; for our Communists, it's democracy. Each cluster has its own trigger. But this mantra affected all your clusters."

He glanced at the screen and shrugged. "Very, very strange. It turned everything upside down. What used to generate fear generates pleasure. What was pleasant before is now terrifying. But it makes no sense! What kind of horsey trade-off is this?" He eyed Rudi questioningly.

It's true, Rudi thought, gazing at the image of his soul. The sensation resembled some kind of painful internal topsy-turvy motion. Was it pernicious? Desirable? Or painfully senseless?

"That's one smart invention. I think this is not main purpose of authors." Ruslanov tapped on the keyboard, and the color lines—the mantra's diagram—emerged on the screen. "But purpose of your ancient Tibetans and how they did it is still big question. Syllables of mantra carry sense, but consciousness cannot see it."

He explained, seeing incomprehension in Rudi's eyes: "One reason I agreed I help Martin was—well, I made experiment couple years ago. Objects were male volunteers— KGB cadets. I handed them various senseless combinations of letters I picked in random. I expected, reactions will be neutral. But suddenly I discovered that some combination caused anomalous reactions. I remember very well combinations: *malin, rzar, tsoshp.* Complete abracadabra! I was forced to accept as hypothesis that these combinations are equivalent of some words that have archetypal attributes;

that is, genetically meaningful. But what they mean specifically—right now we have no resources to determine."

"But we know the translation of syllables in the mantra!" Rudi countered.

"I think the problem is not translating these *ram*s and *hum*s from Sanskrit, but that they mean something in Urlanguage, once common for everybody. This meaning must be determined experimentally. What I really find troubling is that this mantra is being played on radio and TV day and night."

Rudi raised his hand, like a student. "What if you made a statement for the international media that Tune Ra's songs carry an unconscious suggestion?"

Ruslanov waved him off. "First, I would be made laughingstock like you are now. We cannot explain coherently what suggestion is and why it is bad! Second, even if we succeed to bar this song from airwaves, it would make things even worse. It would become forbidden fruit. It would be like not thinking about white elephant, you know?"

He paced the room, shaking his head and cracking his knuckles nervously. "Masha, get on phone. We need at least twenty more volunteers."

"Where will you get them?" Rudi asked.

Ruslanov grinned. "People stand in line for my spiritual makeover."

32

THE flow of patients to the lab started the next morning. Posing as an assistant, Rudi donned a white lab coat and settled in front of the computer, playing video poker and sneaking silent glances at the visitors.

Judging by Ruslanov's terse descriptions—"alcoholic crook," "sadistic general," "epileptic banker"—his clientele was diverse, but mostly high and mighty. They were neurotic film stars, depressed banker's wives, and even the DJ from Tune Russia. There was an ex-Soviet member of the cabinet, regularly wheeled in by his grandchildren, who believed that the KGB had installed some kind of an obstacle in the old man's psyche, and decoding it would lead them to the Party's secret Swiss bank accounts. There was even the Speaker of the Duma, the Russian Parliament, who plotted against the Department of Justice, which had been investigating him for corruption.

Ruslanov played the mantra for every patient, and the pattern repeated: "cretinous topsy-turvy of clusters," as he put it.

The patients arrived in Jeep Cherokees that they parked right at the entrance, pushing aside ambulances. The bosses, in long cashmere coats, disembarked and proceeded with squeamish expressions to Ruslanov's basement, closely followed by giant-jawed bodyguards in short leather jackets with fur collars.

They emerged from behind the curtain transformed. After dropping a wad of dollars on the computer, their hands could barely find their pockets. Enraged, they banged their heads on the pipes and pulled the door handle, disregarding the PUSH sign. Rudi peered in their faces, but all he saw seemed to reflect his own sensations: guilt burning through him, the feeling of doom, the earth opening underfoot—*If I'm bound to fall, let it be now.*

There were exceptions. One, a stocky, heavily cologned man with narrow slits for eyes, squeezed words in Ruslanov's face, and then slammed the door shut, setting the tiny room a-trembling.

"What did he say?"

Ruslanov chuckled. "This Cro-Magnon capitalist threatens me! He understands power of word, too! All I did was call him *kozyol*—normally, it means goat, but among criminals in camps it means, how you say—well, homosexual. Personally, I believe they get upset not so much because they are called homosexual as because they have memories of being animals in previous reincarnations."

"But what did he want from you?"

"He wanted me to code a command to his competition, so that they sign contract he wants. But you cannot work with these gentlemen—not just for ethical reasons, but safety as well. They can kill you afterwards. Why? Because you're witness! I recommended that he get treatment for himself instead—he didn't want."

But others did want the treatment and paid for it handsomely. "New Russians," the doctor explained, "do not have time to meditate or pray. If they have emotional problem, they want it solved pronto—with one audiotape, never mind the cost.

"Healthy man," Ruslanov said pensively, "must be able to untangle his clusters by himself. My method is only for sick people who can't do it: psychopaths, cancer patients. Also, special cases: cosmonauts who spent months in close quarters, or nuclear power station operators. But rich people, they want to try out latest stuff before everybody else."

He waved in despair. "The idiots don't understand: what if I make one littlest mistake? Who knows what happens? Souls are complicated business! I try to cut out his greed— what if his sex appetite shoots up? I try to cut out his lust— sadism will pop out! And if someone thinks I did that because his rivals paid me—*pfft!* Kaput Ruslanov!"

He crossed the room, stopped abruptly, and stared at Rudi. "This is what worries me about your mantra. If it changes everything, like arms instead of legs—what happens then?"

"Freaks," Rudi murmured. "Shouldn't you warn them you're feeding them the mantra? What about patients' rights?"

Ruslanov chuckled. "For better or worse, Russians do not believe that human rights are more important than those of mankind."

What kind of plastic surgery would I ask for my soul, Rudi wondered, stretching his legs outside the lab. To have my guilt lopped off? My guilt for having sacrificed, however involuntarily (did I?), my dear ones to save mankind (will I)? What if my soul gets lopped off along with guilt?

His contemplations were interrupted by yelling and the noise of tumbling furniture. He rushed back to see a group of bearded men shaking their fists at Ruslanov.

"Bros besovstvo! Bros!"

His nose bleeding, Ruslanov reached under his lab coat and pulled a hand grenade from his pocket. The yelling stopped. In the ensuing silence, the only sound was that of the tap dripping water in the bathroom.

"Von!" Ruslanov pointed at the door.

The visitors recoiled and withdrew to the hall. The door slammed. Once again, all was quiet.

"Specially for violent nutcases." Ruslanov returned the grenade to his pocket. "Excellent therapy. Don't tell Masha. She's afraid of any weapon. Though words are more dangerous, I think."

Rudi surveyed the mess: chairs on the floor, files and diskettes strewn all over. "Who were these people?"

"Ah . . ." Ruslanov waved. "My fault. So-called Orthodox militia. It's insult to their dogmas: doctor penetrates soul! Ten, maybe twenty, years from now it will be general practice. For now, it's like birth agony." He applied a wet napkin to his nosebleed. "Embryo is afraid of light of day."

The bleeding did not stop. Ruslanov sat down and tossed his head back. Rudi knelt to pick up the printouts from the floor.

"I'm worried about another thing," Ruslanov said. "They yelled, 'Stop your Satanic curses!' They claim I hypnotize believers and inject their souls with devil's curse."

Rudi gasped. "How did they find out?"

Ruslanov was still studying the ceiling. "Could they have a bug here?"

33

FORTY-SEVEN, forty-six, forty-five . . . The mantra deadline was coming closer. Although Ruslanov used to pooh-pooh the "old lama's nonsense," he was growing more anxious and irritable. He often sneaked out of the lab to have a smoke and to gaze into the calming darkness of the boiler room. Occasionally he would cup his hands for the dripping water and wash his face, muttering in Russian.

For Rudi, the only respite from the endless and useless musings about the mantra came in the person of Varya, the country girl whom the Ruslanovs had pretty much adopted. He did not run into her at the Ruslanovs'. By the time they got back, she was already in bed, and she left for the hospital early in the morning. On the second day of his basement vigil Rudi ran into her as she was escorting a diminutive old alcoholic in threadbare red pajamas with saliva-soaked lapels. Beaming blissfully, the wino was trying to lie down on the floor. Rudi caught him just as he was about to slip away from Varya's arm.

"Tank you much." She nodded, smiling.

Unexpectedly, Rudi smiled back, realizing that he had not smiled in a month. They escorted the old man together.

Soon, whenever he was not helping Ruslanov, Rudi hurried to see Varya, busy with the elderly patients. He perched on the windowsill and chatted with her, teaching her some English, picking up some Russian.

Somehow, her soft pale face with childish freckles on her nose and small brown eyes that blinked as she strained to understand him always put a smile on his face, too, as if he were one of her patients. She hears the mantra, he thought; but she's truly immune to its effects. She has no guilt, no clusters. She's like the angels; after all, they, too, are mortals who got cured and came to care for patients.

Upon closer examination, her freckles turned out to be tiny pimples. She was shy, but she had none of the teenage anxiety he remembered about himself when he was her age. Like her ash-blonde braid smelling of simple Russian soap, she exuded peace and clarity.

He caught himself wanting to touch her, to feel her hand. Could I be in love? he asked himself, horrified; what kind of monster are you, only days after Gwen's death?

No, he calmed himself; this was a new feeling for him, rare and ephemeral. He had never treated a girl like this. Her appearance alone, the very thought of her filled him with quiet joy, just like the sight of a deserted fog-bound field makes a neurotic urbanite stop and, smiling sadly, look around.

And that was exactly what happened to him: he started looking around. He saw he was amid people who were far more miserable than he had ever been. These people had gone through the deaths of their entire families (not just a girlfriend and a teacher), through torture and violence, through fatal diseases, through lives of black despair and hereditary alcoholism. With a smile, a kind word, a touch of compassion—as she straightened out their beds, damp like freshly dug graves—Varya scattered the clouds, and the true self, the clear and empty light of oblivion, shone in the faces of the wretches.

IN three days, sixteen volunteers were unwittingly subjected to the mantra. Late at night, Rudi and Varya stood on the porch, waiting for the Ruslanovs to go home. Feeling a strange bond growing between them, they silently marveled at the huge frozen moon over the roof and the dancing snowflakes, yellow in the light of the streetlamps.

"Come on, folks!" Ruslanov called out, slamming the door, and walked briskly towards the car. He stared at a piece of paper stuck behind the windshield wiper. "I'll be damned—a ticket!"

Varya ran over to take a look.

Ruslanov reached for the paper—

An explosion rocked Rudi, the snow rose underfoot, and, lying on the ground, he saw a gray cloud rising where the car was.

"Varya!" His was no human voice; rather, it was the bark of a chained dog. He struggled to his feet and stumbled towards the car. Ruslanov sat on the ground, his back against the wheel, his mouth wide open, pressing snow against his cheek. The snow was turning red.

"Oleg!" Maria yelled from the stoop.

Deafened by the explosion, her husband did not turn his head.

The girl was lying prone next to the car hood. Rudi tried to lift her. "Varya!"

Her head tilted limply. Snowflakes landed on her blonde

hair without melting. Her eyes remained shut.

Rudi pressed his hand on her throat; he had seen people doing this to check for pulse. She wheezed and, jerking her neck, opened her eyes.

"Oh . . ." Blinking, she looked around. "What—?"

For a moment Rudi held her by the shoulders; then he grabbed a handful of snow and dipped his face into it.

"Rudi," Ruslanov called out weakly. "We're okay. Crawl over here."

Brushing off his wife's hand while she was trying to wipe blood off his neck, he held up what he had mistaken for a ticket in his bloody fingers. The message consisted of three words printed on a piece of cardboard.

" 'Abandon Satanic Curse,' " he translated. "I know who this is." He indicated the torn wire over the windshield. "So this message triggered explosive—bang! Don't tell them—" He nodded at the police cars approaching, their lights flashing.

THERE were ambulances and janitors, barking dogs and KGB men in camouflage, headed by Fedot the Observer. The hospital windows were lit up, many of them blown out by the explosion, and the nurses chased away the panicky patients in pajamas. The KGB team were checking the stoop and the window niches of the basement, wary about additional charges.

Rudi registered the scene with a sense of déjà vu. The postaccident atmosphere was similar to the one at 79th and Riverside, though the cast was different. Most importantly, his life was concentrated in his right hand, which gripped Varya's thin cold fingers. He never let it go from the moment he had picked her up . . . lest she repeat Gwen's fate.

"We alive," she said suddenly, shaking his hand, as if he were a schoolmate.

He saw her childlike shiny eyes—no, there would be no replay of Gwen—and shook her hand in reponse. "We alive, yes."

Finally all grew quiet. The orderlies chased the patients back to bed, the lights went out, the KGB and the police raced off, sirens blaring.

"What cretin!" Ruslanov spat at the Volga sedan that carried off the observer. "All he can think of is finding lowly American spy. In new KGB, old habits die hard!" He winked at Rudi. "He asked me where was my *Amerikanski* friend at moment of explosion. I told him, Far from the car, and he ran off to scribe his report. You are suspect, Mister Rudi!"

"Many times over." Rudi nodded. "Who do *you* suspect?"

"What suspect? I know. Who else but patriots—*satanic curse* is their vocabulary!"

"I hope so," Maria murmured.

34

ON the way home Rudi decided that now it seemed ridiculous to heed Martin's warning and suspect Ruslanov of working together with international militias. He went into detail: his trip to Colorado, Abby and the militias, and Martin's theories of a racial explosion.

"He could be right," Maria said, and recited ironically: " 'Patriots of the world, unite against international Judeo-Masonic-nonwhite conspiracy, mass-media zombification, against pseudoscience and pseudotechnology' . . . This is from our favorite newspaper, *International Patriot.*"

"Ah!" Ruslanov waved her off, staring at the TUNE RULE graffiti in the subway car. "What's interesting is that KGB said blast was professional job. That there was minimum explosive. That it was simple scare: if they wanted to, they could blow us to pieces."

AS they left the train, they were greeted by Tune Ra again. The long underground pass that led to the exit echoed with the Tune Ra chorus, which came from a number of tape-and-CD kiosks. A few teenagers were posing as rappers, imitating Tune Ra's jerky body movements and screaming out the chorus. The passengers slowed their steps to encourage the performers and drop change into a chamber pot that served to collect tips.

Ruslanov paused, too, eyeing the dancers, and, as one of the boys approached for a contribution, grimly stared him in the eye. The kid stepped back and menacingly reached into his pocket.

The music stopped.

Maria dragged Ruslanov away to the nearest kiosk, whispering, "Don't you see it in his face: disposition to sadism, early schizophrenia, high pain threshold—"

"Of course!" He stroked her back. "Toss in inherited alcoholism and heroin addiction, right? You don't need computer, we see his kind every day. . . ."

"Can you diagnose *him?*" Rudi pointed at the smiling face of Tune Ra on the CD cover.

"Hm . . . interesting." Ruslanov gazed at the singer's face. "You know," he addressed Rudi, "you two have many things in common. Lust of flesh: you have searched and experienced various sensations—drugs, yes? And sex, too . . ."

Rudi lowered his eyes. Varya kept smiling at his side, unable to understand Ruslanov's English.

"Both of you are still searching to give yourself away—to someone's will, or idea. Something feminine—"

"What makes you say that?" Rudi murmured.

"I don't know—both of you have it in your eyes. Destructive potential of giving yourself away. People who break away from rationalism in order to live according to inspiration. Such people harm themselves and others, but if they succeed, the force to which they surrender will help them. Kind of ideal artist, spiritual seeker." Ruslanov nudged Rudi playfully. "One who submits to director's will. Somewhat like woman who took leap into pool of passion. Orgasmic surrender . . . He is not junkie, Maria?"

"I don't think so." She peered at the picture. "Sober rational side. Domination complex, but it looks as if he broke it to let someone else in."

"He must have guru or something," Ruslanov agreed. "Ninety percent probability."

"Guru . . ." Something about this hypothesis was familiar, Rudi thought.

HE was interrupted before he could remember.

"Hey, peoples!" The heavily accented voice belonged to a man who stuck his round face out of the kiosk's tiny window. "You are from America?"

"He is." Ruslanov nodded at Rudi.

"Hey, what is up, dude?" A hand with short stubby fingers and a gold signet ring came out for a handshake. "How is happening? Ooh"—the vendor spotted Rudi's beads— "cool stuff! Where did you get?"

"Tibet."

The face vanished, the side door opened, and a young Oriental-looking man with a crew cut and an earring came out. "What is your name? I'm Yendon! You been to Tibet?" Despite his accent, his speed and intonations were sheer MTV. "I have not, too! But I'm going, dude! I'm from nearby! Ever heard of Buryatia? Buddhist republic, dude! You studied Buddhism in America—wow, like—" He took a deep breath, barely able to control his emotions.

Yendon was a small-business owner who, following spiritual fashions, wanted to open a Buddhist store in Moscow. Exploiting the East's thirst for things Western, he was taking American records like Tune Ra and Lauryn Hill to Tibet to trade them for beads and incense. "You heard Tune Ra's latest? Coolest! I'll give you one—gift! I love Americans!"

"No, thanks . . ." Rudi felt Varya's fingers squeeze his elbow. He traced her look to a couple kissing passionately a few feet away. As if feeling their eyes on him, the man, an athletic type in camouflage, turned and spat out something in Russian.

Varya blushed.

"Let's go!" Maria pulled them away. "People are going berserk around here."

"Hey!" The Buryat pushed a business card in Rudi's hand. "Come back, all of you! Check it out, okay?"

35

BACK at the apartment, Ruslanov took one look at the red *16* glowing on the answering machine panel and whistled. "Hm, condolences about unsuccessful assassination!" He pressed the Play button. A weeping female voice came up.

"This is Speaker's wife," the doctor translated, getting purple in the face. "One who was looking to turn the attorney general into a zombie. This morning, he protested military invasion of Tatarstan. President ignored and sent troops. So this afternoon in middle of a Duma debate Speaker poured gasoline on himself and struck match. Died of burning. That was on all news programs just as our car blew up."

"Who could expect?" Maria shook her head. "He was always crooked."

"That's why his wife called me—to find out what I did to him."

At the sound of the next message, Ruslanov and his wife dropped on the couch, and Varya hid her face in her hands.

The next victim was the Mafia banker who had taken umbrage at being called "goat." After being exposed to the mantra, he sold his company and handed the proceeds to the investors whom he had swindled five years earlier. Later in the day, his partners blew him up in his car.

The widows' taped weeping went on. . . . After visiting Ruslanov, the retired Soviet minister wrote up a confession, listing the numbers of Swiss bank accounts that held the Party funds. The next day he left for his dacha, where he mysteriously burned up in his sauna.

The next one was the Tune Russia manager. At the concert, his DJ, Tune Ra's lookalike, suddenly lost his voice. The next day, he burned up, too. A possible explanation was that he had been gargling with something particularly inflammable and then lit a cigarette.

The list went on: bankers, gangsters, politicians . . . Out of sixteen people Ruslanov had tested, all had died, and in each case, the cause of death was related to fire and explosions. In each case, wives and partners were aware of the visit to Ruslanov and now demanded explanations or threatened him.

After the last message was played, they all stared quietly at the red *0*, when the phone rang. They shuddered, as if at an explosion. All three held their breath. Who could it be, after midnight?

Maria pressed the Speaker button, then Record. "Hello?" she said calmly.

The sounds of Tune Ra's chorus flowed into the room.

Rudi leapt to his feet. But then the roaring laughter came out.

"Oleg, you sonuvabitch—have they put out the fire yet?" Inexplicably, Martin Rivers was in a rollicking mood.

However, his information was more puzzling than amusing.

Using his former connections, Rivers had managed to get the FBI interested in Ayushi's and Abby's deaths. Moreover, he had flown to Yampa to help with the investigation. They failed to determine the cause of Ayushi's fall; but Rudi's theory—the sniper's bullet—was ruled out.

"Did you speak to Margi, the Swiss girl?" Rudi shouted.

"She was gone the next day," Martin shouted back. "So if you had any designs on her, you missed your chance."

Rudi's version of Abby's death was knocked down, too. According to the forensics experts, the cause of explosion was a gas leak and an internal source of fire, rather than a bomb. Moreover, according to Martin's friends at the bureau, the Colorado militia was a pathetic little outfit, long penetrated by the bureau's informers, and could hardly have had resources for anything as sophisticated as installing bugs or paying a DJ to put a subliminal message on the air. Nor did they have international contacts and friends among Russian militia.

"I called Martin for advice after that first pogrom," Ruslanov explained.

"The Russian KGB have an informer inside the group,"

Martin went on, "who willingly shared his information with the FBI. First, the Russian group do not have contacts in local law enforcement, so they do not dare resort to terrorism—so far. Second, like the Coloradans, they're not sophisticated enough to install bugs nor rich enough to pay informers.

"If your Russki fascists got hold of some information on the mantra, they must have received it from a third party who is using them as a cover," Martin concluded. "Hang in there, buddy! I'll keep digging for more clues! That's it— I'm calling from a pay phone—I don't think my home phone is safe!"

For a while, they sat in silence. Martin had raised more questions than he had answered. If it was not international neo-Nazis, who was it?

"What's weird is that every caller says 'perhaps burned' or 'possibly arson,' " Rudi said. "But no one knows for sure."

"What do you mean?" Ruslanov frowned. "Self-immolation caused by mantra? Nonsense."

"But nothing happened while they were listening," Maria said.

"Ayushi said," Rudi murmured slowly, trying to recall the late lama's words; "he said something like, 'drip-drop.' The suggestion penetrates the unconscious and works on it cumulatively. You introduced it directly, as second background—this should speed up its effect."

"Suggestion for what?" Ruslanov cried out.

"I don't know. . . . Forty-four days left."

Rudi felt unbearably hot. *Here it comes,* flashed through his mind. He gripped the arms of the chair. I shouldn't singe Ruslanov and Maria! He shifted back.

"What's wrong?" Both rushed to him.

"I—I thought I was catching fire—"

Maria gasped and reached for the phone. "Let me call ambulance!"

"Don't be crazy now!" Ruslanov tore away the receiver. "What good doctors can do if it's psychic? He needs to be deprogrammed. . . . We need Cray."

"We have no choice, Oleg." Maria squeezed his fingers.

"Call up KGB and agree to do job. They can have Cray tomorrow."

"You see"—Maria turned to face Rudi—"KGB offered to buy Cray for us in exchange for one job. They're looking for mole, very deeply situated. They would not even say who he is spying for: it is supersecret. Mole is so smart he can fool any lie detector. But he cannot fool Oleg's method. This mole has already caused KGB damage in millions dollars, so it's cheaper for them to buy Cray. Especially now for our new president to get rid of mole in midst of his organization is matter of honor. But Oleg has been turning them down."

"Why?" Rudi glanced at the doctor.

"They want me to test every cluster relating to treason. But every spy has subliminal thoughts of treason—so what they're talking about is purge! I can figure out mole but I cannot turn my research against him—this is immoral!"

"Being a mole is immoral," Maria said. "In general I didn't know you believed that human rights are more important than security of mankind. . . ."

Ruslanov shot her an angry look. "You didn't want it either!"

"I had different reasons. This mole is very smart. He finds out that officers are being tested for 'psychological stamina'—this is cover story—he will, how you say, smell mouse. And he'll try to kill it!" she concluded emphatically.

"Let him try!" her husband spat out and picked up the phone.

36

NEXT morning Rudi woke up with a jolt and a horrifying thought: he was doomed! He fully expected to see nurses around his burned and bandaged body.

But his arm was bare, and he felt a sheet under it. He

opened his eyes and suddenly realized that his state of well-being was nothing short of a miracle that could end any second.

He had to hold his breath. Fire is started by oxygen. First, he imagined, pleasant warmth, as if from a glass of whiskey, would spread through his body. The temperature would go up, like in a sauna. Then the warmth would change to heat and pain—excruciating pain with the smells of singed flesh and hair, with the hissing of blackening, curdling skin—no warmth, no heat, nothing but pain. Finally, dark oblivion . . .

But so far the miracle was holding. Cool, sweet air entered his nose, his throat, opened up his lungs, and left. Nothing happened. No meditation had ever brought him this wondrous feeling: breathing without fear. All things around him were breathing: the gills of the curtains were rustling, the window was gulping the frosty air through a narrow open crack, the snowflakes on the ledge were inhaling, the dust in the corner was heaving—the entire apartment was fearlessly circulating the air.

He struggled to get up and then froze. Like Ruslanov's other patients, he would catch fire from an awkward movement, which would strike a spark from an invisible flint inside him. Later the explosion would be imputed to a gas leak or an electric short or a bomb.

Yet if the roots of this mantra arson were psychic, he did not even have to move: any thought could cause self-immolation. And the longer he stayed in bed, the higher the likelihood of a careless thought.

OVERNIGHT, the hospital looked different. The gate was manned by guards with submachine guns. The courtyard was filled with military jeeps and black sedans, and there was even an imported bright-colored ambulance. There were guards at the entrance to the basement, too, and more at the lab door, where their presence was reinforced by a metal detector.

The miracle computer was a commanding presence: a tall, shiny steel box in the middle of the room was humming businesslike, as a technician was connecting the wires to the old equipment.

Ruslanov was at the monitor, his huge scooplike hand soaring and diving over the keyboard.

"Are you okay?" He rose, searching Rudi's face. "Thank God. You have to stay fireproof just little longer. This crazy machine plays out more combinations in second than person has in his life!"

The door slammed behind Rudi as Fedot marched in, his face a furious pink, his pencil-thin mustache bristling. He started whispering to Ruslanov angrily.

The scientist raised his hands—*Enough*—and took Rudi's coat off the rack. "You go home now."

As he walked Rudi to the door, he whispered, "You're making our bureaucrat nervous. KGB people among whom I shall look for mole on new computer will be here any minute; you're not supposed to see them. Who knows— what if you put them on fire?"

37

IT was already dark outside, and Ruslanov still had not called. Which meant he had no good news.

Varya was cramming for exams in her room. Rudi stayed at the telephone, melting slowly by the torment of the wait.

At first, he simply sat there, monitoring his condition, ready to grab the extinguisher at the first sign of his body warming. But the wait was wearing him out. To calm down, he poured himself a glass of ice-cold vodka. But it had the opposite effect, sending fire arrows through his gut and raising his apprehension. He lit up, but the sight of the flame from the match and the burning tip of the cigarette scared him even more.

The combined wait for the ring and the pain was unbearable. His ears were pricked at the slightest noise: the ticking of the clock, the creaking of the chair in Varya's room. But, instead of calming him, these peaceful stirrings added to the fear. He could not stand the thought of wreaking destruction on this quiet little world.

He was on a fool's errand, looking for a miracle that might not come. Even Ruslanov, despite all his bluster, never counted on the computer as a panacea. No: he had to take an honorable way out.

This time, he would make his exit open and rational. The first reason for suicide: he no longer wanted to cause harm to others around him. Second, Buddhism permitted suicide if external conditions precluded clearing your consciousness. If, as a result of self-immolation, he did not die right away, but would persist, with heavy, painful burns, then his suffering—he already knew he had a low pain threshold—would cloud his mind completely and . . . He did not need Dr. Kevorkian to know which way was up. Or, rather, out.

There was a third reason—the escape from guilt that tormented him like an internal burn—but he could not bring himself to include it. Two reasons would be enough.

He tore out a page from his diary book and wrote, his hand shaking: *Dear Oleg, Masha, and Varya—*

The letters came out in a chicken scrawl. He half-closed his eyes: his head swam with a low buzzing sound—or perhaps it was the humming of the refrigerator. He was not being honest, he thought. There was a fourth reason: the fear of what would happen forty-one days from now.

He did not fear the apocalypse, racial or otherwise; he yearned for it. More precisely, he was afraid that *nothing* would happen—and then all these lives would have been lost for nothing. It was this fear of the senselessness of sacrifice that he was fleeing.

OUTSIDE on the terrace, the cold air sobered him up. Gray high-rises stuck out of the snow like so many *Titanic*s out of the ocean. The streetlights were out, and the stars fanned across the sky like bullet holes centered around the huge shell-hole of the moon.

Please understand my decision, he wrote.

"Poetry, yes?" Varya's voice came from behind. "Oh, stars!" She stood in the doorway, a plaid blanket around her shoulders. "Read poetry! Improvisation, please!" She nudged him lightly.

Rudi reached over the railing and broke off a long clear dagger of an icicle. He stuck it in his palm—it was sharp enough to use as a weapon—and brushed it against his feverish forehead.

It seemed like once again he had failed to escape.

"Don't eat! Cold!" Varya laughed, and her laugh was as clear and ringing as the icicle itself.

"I was an icicle once: shiny and cold, set apart from my kin, but a warm wind blew, and I began to melt," Rudi intoned, daubing his closed eyelids with the icicle. "Then, to prevent other icicles from melting the way I had, I decided to split away and fall."

He let the icicle go, and after a few seconds they heard a distinct ringing sound as it hit the roof of a car below. He gripped the railing. It had been a long descent.

He glanced at Varya. She giggled and shook her head, as if trying to get rid of water in her ears; then she burst out a spate of strange sounds—

"This is not Russian?" he asked, semirhetorically.

Her eyes, dark blue in the moonlight, were wide open, as she came close, still spouting a flow of odd, meaningless sounds that seemed to devour her completely.

He held his breath as he tried to understand. Her gibberish was not unlike what Schechter had spouted in mantric trance, but it was not a product of a mental exercise; rather, it was a natural sound—this was how she was giving vent to her feelings.

With a laugh, she rushed at him and threw the blanket on top of both of them. "Marry me. Please!"

The abracadabra she was spouting was a declaration of love. A love at first sight. All this time she was falling in love. First with fright, distrust, then with increasing tenderness; something wonderful and silent was being born in her.

The earth, too, does not believe the wind initially and tries to resist the storm; but then it tosses back its waves, and in the morning, all is still, and new isles have emerged from the ocean, still wet and bare, but already bearing life.

*   *   *

HER pupils wide, her head thrown back, she pressed her warm breasts against him. He felt cold little fingers on his shoulders, and, once again, he smelled the childlike smell of soap and milk.

A warmth—not menacing, but becalming and at the same time inebriating—spread through his chest. He went to kiss her lips, her cheeks, salty with tears, icy with cold, and ultimately sweet. He remembered the taste of love; it had happened only once, when he was fourteen. Many things followed—affection, passion, lust—but he had never experienced this dizzying, overwhelming tenderness again. As his lips latched on to hers, the instinct of love and life buried the thoughts of the mantra—the virus that had infected him. Behind her, he saw the terrace railing; beyond, lay the darkness of his guilt. He drew Varya to the door, away from the abyss.

She interpreted the gesture differently. She led him to the kitchen, where she tossed the blanket on the floor, and drew him to her. His heart beating in his throat, he knelt in front of her as she pulled up her skirt.

"N-nno—" He shook his head desperately.

"Come!" She pulled the front of his pants.

And then—once again—the phone rang.

"Ru-dol-fo," the familiar basso roared. "You must see this! Come right away! This is fucking fantastic! I don't understand it! Come!"

38

HE ran out in the street without buttoning his coat.

"Rudi!" Varya shouted out of the window. "Hat!"

He waved, *Never mind*.

Half an hour later, he got out of the taxi outside the hospital. The place was asleep, the only light provided by the ambulance outside. The camouflaged guards were gone.

They must have discovered the nurses by now, Rudi thought, flying up the steps; or even female patients.

Risking his neck, he ran down the cold dark basement stairs and through the bleakly lit maze.

He flung the door of the lab open.

What he saw made him recoil.

"NO!" Like in a dream, the syllables could not leave his throat.

Ruslanov's head lay lifelessly on the keyboard, columns of numbers still scrolling down the screen. Maria was lying prone next to the couch. Their bodies were being licked by slow bluish flames.

The fire had to have started recently: it had consumed the white lab coats and was now spreading to the clothes below, emitting a horrid smell of burnt flesh and hair. The tiled floor prevented it from spreading to the furniture.

But there were no traces of violence—they could still be alive! Rudi grabbed a bedsheet; if he threw it on top of them, perhaps he could still put out the fire.

The door slammed open. "Freeze!" hollered Fedot the Observer. A guard in camouflage leveled his submachine gun at Rudi's chest.

"Fuckink spy of bitch!" the KGB man kept yelling. "Assignment Impossible, yes? Killed scientists? I warned!"

Fedot barked orders into his walkie-talkie. Then at Rudi: "You are arrested!"

He jumped away as he noticed his trousers were smoking, having caught fire from Maria's body. The place was quickly becoming hot. The guard yelled something, pointing his gun at the door. Fedot produced a small camera and pointed it at Rudi: "Evidence! Scene of crime!"

He circled the room, trying to find the right spot, so that the camera would catch both Rudi and the dead bodies.

Rudi stared at Ruslanov's trousers. A pin and a ring were sticking out of his pocket. The flames were crawling closer.

"Cheese!" shouted Fedot, and Rudi dived to the ground, behind the tall steel box of the Cray computer.

The exploding grenade drowned out the flash of Fedot's camera.

39

LATER, Rudi would have no memory at all of how he had made it outside. Deafened by the explosion, brushing blood and shreds of bone off his face, he limped clumsily through the basement and then found himself on a deserted street flanked by monotonous black boxes of buildings.

From behind came shouts and a siren. Falling and rising, he limped on through the snowdrifts of the courtyards, past playgrounds and garbage bins. He reached the safety of a glass phone booth and tore the receiver off the hook. A mad search of his pockets yielded a matchbook, a crumpled pack of cigarettes, a scrap of paper with someone's name—and two telephone tokens.

Ring—ring—ring. Then the answering machine came up.

"Varya!" he yelled. "Wake up! Pick up the phone! There's been an accident! I had nothing to do with it! Be careful! Don't leave the house! Varya—Varya—Varya!"

End of message.

It made no sense. Even if Varya had fallen asleep, the phone was at her bedside, the ringing had to wake her up. Had she left the house? Or—

RUDI walked for hours without stopping. He had no idea where he was heading as he crossed deserted avenues and got deeper into the narrow lanes of the old Moscow. A new day was dawning: the cold darkness was turning blue, and the orange beetles of snow removers crawled along the white grooves of the streets.

He did not feel the cold, either in his bare hands or on his uncovered head.

Unable to go on, he dropped onto a snow-covered bench. His frozen fingers were hurting; he rubbed snow on them, washing off the blood. It was not his, it occurred to him.

He washed his face with snow; it came out pink with blood, too. But the blood was not his. He was not wounded. Not even scratched. In the end, he had been saved by Cray the Computer, a vital component of Ruslanov's plan.

I survived, he told himself; but why—and what for?

He reviewed his options.

Before dying, Fedot had called in to inform his bosses that he had caught Rudi red-handed. Hence, turning himself in to the KGB or police was out.

As a fugitive from justice, he could not go to the American Embassy either.

Either the KGB or the doctor's killers must have already visited the Ruslanovs' apartment, so there was no point in trying to go there.

He had no money. He had no papers: the forged passport, Martin's gift, was left in the lab's safebox. He had no friends in Moscow. He could not get out of town.

Yet he had to do just that. The KGB had to assume that the four bodies in the lab were his doing. With the help of the police, they would find him within hours.

Finally, even if he evaded the famous Russian secret police, there was no getting away from those who broadcast the mantra: they had chased him to Colorado, to Moscow— they would chase him to Mars, it seemed.

No: they were just humans. He had heard at least one of them on the telephone on West 100th Street. He was afraid of them; but they were afraid of him, too. Rather, they were afraid he would decode the mantra. Had been afraid ever since he showed his hand that night at DeoMorte.

On both sides, the fear would last another forty days.

HIS thoughts were interrupted by the sounds of a slammed door and a child crying. A woman was dragging a sleepy boy, aged seven or so, towards a car—perhaps to drop him off at school.

The car refused to start. The woman stepped out and lifted the hood. The boy got out, too, wiped his tears, and went on to toss snowballs at a snowman at the edge of the playground.

Rudi watched the scene numbly. The boy kept aiming for

the snowman's nose—a frozen carrot—and missing.

"Sum of knowledge lies in center." Ruslanov pointed his red pencil in the middle of a circle. *"Access to spheres of meaning of your ancient Asians. . . ."*

The woman carefully rolled back the side of her coat and lay down in the snow to peek under the car. Some Amazon, Rudi thought.

"The first solution of your expert problem," Schechter mused, lying on the floor next to his fireplace, *"is to find a written source that says that such and such mantra means this and this. Since we're talking Shaman Bon, which precedes the written language, this option is out. The second solution is to find a man who stores such information—a* nagpa. *But all the* nagpas *were executed by the Chinese."*

The woman rose, shaking the snow off her coat.

"Message in the wind!" Laughing, Ayushi slapped his sides. *"Rinpoche is alive!"*

"Gotcha!" The snowball hit the snowman straight on the carrot.

As if on cue, Rudi rose from the bench and for the last time went through his pockets. Cigarettes—matches—a telephone token—and the scrap of paper that in fact turned out to be a business card, printed on cheap gray paper.

YENDON BABAYEV, it said. TIBETAN CRAFTS.

Book Three

LHASA

40

HE was lying in the dark, his eyes closed. The alien words he heard made no sense, but the intonation was familiar. He stirred, trying to recall what had happened.

His whole body was numb, save for his heart. Or, perhaps, it had been numb and came back, he thought, as he felt it bump into his rib cage. But now his sense of smell came back: the sweet fumes of a bonfire and incense.

He forced his eyes open a peek, only to squint at the boundless blue of the sky. Next to him, a solid stone wall. Above, dark red cloths flowing, and a man's shaven head.

"Tibet," he attempted to whisper, and moaned.

His lips were chapped, covered with a crust, and oozed blood at the slightest effort.

"Hey, Professor!" The smiling saucer-round face of Yendon the Buryat trader came into view. "Welcome to Lhasa!"

The dazzling blueness above made Rudi close his eyes again. He was coming back to life like the newborn and the dying do: immobile, mute, having lost everything and calmly waiting to receive their due.

He was curled like a pretzel inside a square plywood crate, amid cassettes, CDs, and wood chips. The crate was one of many in a spacious walled courtyard. Copper-faced, slit-eyed men in quilted jackets pried the lids open; bony, mangy dogs roamed around.

Rudi attempted to get up, and his moan made the workers look up in silence. Yendon waved and said something to them.

"Don't worry, Professor." He softly patted Rudi's bleeding lips with a paper tissue. "They're Tibetans, they don't talk to government. How are you feeling?"

Rudi opened his mouth, but only a wheezing sound came

out. He gulped air and moaned again. His throat felt as if he had swallowed a nail.

RUDI had called Yendon from a pay phone in the Moscow courtyard.

Luckily, the trader was at home and, though sleepy, welcomed him cheerfully. "Hey, Professor! How is your tricks? You want to make some Russki rubles? Come to club, read us lecture. C'mon, it's your last chance: I'm flying to Tibet tomorrow."

"I need to come along." Rudi's voice and words were as hoary as the pay phone itself.

"Why?"

"I'll explain later. Can you help me? I've got no money or passport."

After a pause, Yendon said, "Write down the address."

YENDON met him at a warehouse outside the airport. After much head-scratching, he confessed he could not help with papers. Instead, he offered to ship Rudi to Tibet along with his merchandise. "CDs, tapes—that kind of stuff."

"In this box?" Rudi pointed at the largest crate. "You wouldn't be shipping Tune Ra's CDs in it?"

"How did you know?"

Rudi eyed the crate silently. It resembled a coffin. Gwen was in a coffin, too. He did not even dare ask Martin about her funeral on the phone.

How could he be roaming the world while she was in the ground? This, then, will be his coffin. God did have a sense of humor, after all. He will be interred next to the offending tapes and CDs. He will go to sleep and wake up next to her. And beg her forgiveness.

"Thanks," he said. "But I can't pay you. You'll be losing money on me."

The Buryat grinned. "Maybe I pay you back. Maybe you were my mother in past reincarnation."

A memory of his recent woes made Rudi frown. "What if I set the cargo on fire?"

"You'll sleep, not smoke."

"You don't stop thinking in your sleep."

Yendon paused, trying to grasp the meaning of Rudi's words. Then he said seriously, "What fire? Cargo section is much cold."

HE was right. Now, still in the crate, watching the white tents hover above the low stone roofs, Rudi felt as if he had returned to his childhood. He was back in the mountains with his mother: it was late fall, he was four or five, not old enough for school yet. Everything was familiar: the early frost, the smell of smoke, the dogs. There he was: a Tibetan kid, a boy—or a girl—wrapped in something that looked like tree bark, his face smudged with soot, came up and stared at Rudi, picking his nose in silence.

He had hoped to wake up with Gwen: anywhere, be it heaven or hell. But here he was, in Lhasa, once again awake on earth, and alone. Because she could not awake. He clenched his teeth to keep himself from crying.

Scared by his grimace, the child ran away.

"Hey, they got disco here now!" Yendon scooped a few CDs from the heap. "We drop off goodies and go to hotel, right? Wash, get warm—"

Slowly, Rudi began to straighten up, holding on to the wall. "Nah," he wheezed. "I'll go."

"Hey, you got no voice yet! Look at you!" Yendon skeptically regarded his ward's bloodstained coat with wood chips stuck to it. "Where you go? You got no money, no papers."

An odd thought shot through Rudi's mind: was he indeed in Tibet? Could he still be in one of those former Soviet republics, like Yendon's native Buryatia?

Yendon sighed and stuck a few Chinese yuans in Rudi's pocket. "You can pay in Bardo. Where do I find you here?"

A scratchy rag was still smoldering in Rudi's throat, preventing him from speaking. He carefully brought his palms together, held them at his chest, and bowed to Yendon.

The trader held his hands in response. "Let me hear from you, Professor. You need anything, I'll be at Holiday Inn."

"Hey, wait!" he shouted as Rudi was about to leave. "One for the road!" He held out a flask.

Frowning, Rudi took a gulp of fiery liquid and headed out.

41

RUDI found himself on a narrow street—rather, a wide path through the frozen mud, flanked by one-floor yellow-and-gray stone shacks with flat roofs. It was quiet, save for the crackling noise made by prayer banners, pieces of colored silk flapping in the wind. Filled out like minisails, they were all over the place—on roofs' eaves, on wooden window ledges, and on the jambs of the black square niches that served as entrances.

Across the path, he saw a middle-aged woman squatting outside. Her face was copper-red, with high cheekbones. Rough blue stones were woven into her heavy black braids, carefully arranged atop her head. Her soiled brown coat was tucked in the front, with a smooth brown crescent of flesh visible. A yellow streamlet was coming from between her legs. She was urinating!

The woman met Rudi's eyes squarely and smiled, baring surprisingly strong white teeth. She was not drunk. Rudi folded his hands and bowed slightly.

Yep. He was in Tibet all right.

HE turned left without any idea where he was going. A piercing icy wind carried the odors of stove smoke and excrement—that's what the frozen mud underfoot was. He walked on, holding on to the stone walls, oblivious to where he was. But the stone was cold, the wind burned his face, and the sun was blinding. He recognized the altitude sickness symptoms: his entire body filled with heavy warm lead that made every step an ordeal.

He looked around. The sun—the flags—the dust—the Asian somnolence. And, encircling it all, the mountains. Gimavat, the Roof of the World, climbing past the clouds, with nothing but an aqua-blue sky with shades of black above it. The cosmos, outer space, was nearby. It was as windswept and deserted as any roof. Lhasa . . .

Remembering a poem of his youth, he murmured, *"Mountains, you're my father and mother / Meeting you fills my eyes with tears / Where the sky begins, the earth ends / Mountains, the frozen flame."*

Here they were, the Himalayas of his dreams. Here was Tibet, the object of his reverie. But the tears in his eyes came from the icy wind, rather than happiness. In his heart, there was nothing but guilt and pain, frozen like excrement underfoot.

Life seemed to make dreams come true only after making sure you could not enjoy them—why? But it did not respond, it merely smiled dispassionately, like this cold blind sun.

Three locals, feral-looking men in gray animal hides, walked by, spinning prayer drums: small copper cylinders on wooden sticks. As they passed, they eyed Rudi with curiosity and grinned, baring white teeth.

They are spinning their drums to atone for their sins, he thought; what did he have to do to atone for his?

Soon he came to a crowded market street, with stalls set out along the buildings' walls, and a human river of shoppers flowing past them in one direction. Despite his dark thoughts, Rudi could not help being struck by the faces around him. He seemed to have stepped into long-forgotten ancient times. Here they were, people whose culture he had been studying from afar! The locals' faces were sheer bronze, the wrinkles seemingly carved by a knife on the bone. They wore roughly sewn, untreated hides, tossed on one shoulder, belted with yarn of red wool and wide strips of skin, with silver daggers tucked in. Men wore silver and bluestone necklaces and carried prayer drums; women, fox hats, with the animals' faces and nails intact.

The merchandise was two-thirds Bronze Age, one-third modern. Locals in sheepskins sold animal hides, aquamarine gems, silver decorations, prayer bells, and other Buddhist paraphernalia; at other stands, pale-faced Chinese in triple-fat parkas sold acrylic sweaters and cheap electronics.

Nomad women, fascinated by the products of town craftsmen, crowded the stands, giggling with excitement, sweating under their fur coats made of yaks' hairy behinds. He recognized full-figured women from Amdo in the northeast, with thin braids and bright clothing and cascading silver jewelry. Tall, fierce-looking men in silver fox hats and swaths of wool braided into their hair were warriors from Kham. Smaller, shabbily dressed peasants came from central Tibet. They seem to be the most uncomfortable in the crowd.

Rudi's ears were burning with cold. Although sunny and snowless, Lhasa was colder than Moscow. Nearby, a fox-skin vendor, a strapping Tibetan with a pug nose and a huge turquoise earring, was advertising his product by tying a fox hide into a knot and mounting it on his head.

"Tashi delek." Rudi mastered the greeting in his still wheezy voice. Then he muttered, *"Gong gatsai ray?"*— How much?—hoping his college Tibetan would hold up.

"Gantsare!" The vendor roared with laughter, whether he was correcting or mimicking Rudi was unclear. He crammed the hat on Rudi's head and shoved a shard of a dirty mirror in his hand.

Rudi's sooty pale face half-disappeared under the hat. In Ruslanov's soiled worn-out sheepskin, he did not look much different from the locals. He produced Yendon's yuans; still chuckling, the vendor picked a few from his hand and shouted to other vendors.

In a moment, a crowd formed a small isle around Rudi. They pushed closer to see him; once they did, they scowled gleefully and left, letting others take a look. The vendor kept chuckling and commenting, whether at Rudy's clumsy attempts to speak Tibetan or at the sight of a towheaded Anglo who had just miraculously turned into a Tibetan.

A *dzogchen,* a spontaneous reaction, Rudi mused as he, smiling weakly, struggled outside the commotion. The locals had a childlike directness, whether urinating or demonstrating their curiosity, all without a touch of shyness. Their guileless faces were nature itself, and the sight filled him with peace.

*   *   *

THE stone wall behind the stalls came to a three-floor temple with red columns and two white mortars at the entrance. Golden deer on the yellow roof held up the Dharma Wheel with their noses, and yellow flags billowed overhead. The temple overlooked a spacious cobblestone square.

It was Johang, Rudi realized; Tibet's holiest temple, and it dated from the seventh century.

Now he remembered: the street was no mere shopping mall, but Barkhor, the famous trading street that constituted Johang's outer circle. The people, who were moving clockwise, were not mere shoppers: they were pilgrims.

Having completed the circle, the pilgrims faced the temple, attached small rectangular strips of wood to their arms, spread their rugs, and prostrated. While touching their heads, lips, and chests with their hands folded, they lowered themselves on the ground, the strips sliding on the stones, polished through the centuries of wear. Finally, they came to rest, their heads motionless between their outstretched arms. It was as if they were extracting the dirt, handful by handful, from their heads, mouths, and hearts, and burying it in the ground.

Exhausted, Rudi dropped on the ground, leaning against the mortar.

Except for two green Chinese military jeeps, the square was empty, yellow and gray with sun and dust. There were no tourists—it was the dead season. The only sound came from the rustling garments of prone pilgrims.

If mankind could be represented by one person, Rudi thought, then here, in the middle of the holy city of Lhasa, must be the top of his head; a static center of the never-ending movement of human losses and aspirations. It was as if one faced the sun with one's eyes closed and then started walking, slightly dizzy with a smile etched on one's face.

Why were Tibetans the ones living here? he wondered. By our standards, they were primitive people. Yet they sheltered the most refined philosophy lost by their more civilized neighbors. Why was it that these nomads—but not the Indians or the Chinese—supplied the West with teachers of this most complex, yet crystal-clear spiritual teaching? Was

it a case of the last becoming the first? Perhaps one had to
be a primitive, a tabula rasa, to accept the truth without
reservations. Compared to the Egyptians, Mosaic Jews were
primitives, too, and so were the fishermen of Galilee compared to the Pharisees. If he could become one of them . . .
perhaps then he would know how to atone for his guilt.

He stared at an old woman hunched next to him—brown
coat, brown skin, a long gray braid with turquoise stones,
a wrinkled face with a toothless mouth and deep-set narrow
black eyes.

A witch, he thought; if Nagpa had a wife, she would
qualify. Her face was one big ruin. The things she must
have lived through! Yet now she is eyeing Buddha with
quiet joy, she is prone in the dust as she thanks the Blessed
One. If he, Rudi, stayed here—could his grief, too, melt
with time into this silent light of love?

At the entrance, the statue of Buddha welcomed the faith-
ful. What was He saying to the woman with his Mona Lisa
smile? Rudi tried to fathom the words, but as his pen
touched the paper of his diary, a different kind of writing
came out:

*Johang and the yellow whirl, my dear Asians, I made it
here—their faces high-cheeked from the constant half-smile
of understanding—their eyes barely open, easy to close
them for the prayer. It is as if the aqua sky crumbled on
your head. Its pieces whirl in your head, like so many
thoughts; suddenly, you disappear and then reappear as
Everything. You're a giant, you're the world: in you, pilgrims wade through the dust, mountains rest, a candle is
smoking, and a dog is scratching at the door—all of them
are in you, and you're responsible for everything: for peace
and harmony in your endless domain—for the tranquility of
your mind. . . .*

RUDI closed the diary, separated himself from the wall, and
knelt. For a moment he, too, stared at the Buddha—and then
he understood what the latter was trying to tell him with
His smile. When he understood, he burst into tears. Fever,
hunger, oxygen deprivation, nervous exhaustion—all took
their toll. The tears were forming a salty film on his cheeks,

burning his chapped lips, freezing in the wind—but he had no strength to wipe them. Through the fog, he noticed the old toothless woman smile at him; he prostrated himself on the cold dusty rocks, hiding his head between his hands.

"I am freeing myself, Lord," he whispered. "You allow me to let go of my pain and guilt. You are letting me go. . . ."

Indeed, the pain flowed into the ground, as he was being absorbed in the earth's huge silent body, melting in its peace, and a white lotus flower was opening, its petals moving Rudi's lips into a smile. The bliss of becoming dust! The sweetness of remaining on the ground—even more so when you don't have any strength left! He had attained his objective; he had come to die in the city of his dreams. By becoming dust, he will become one with Gwen, and win her forgiveness.

Rudi pressed himself closer to the ground—and suddenly heard the sounds of the mantra coming out of it. The earth was throbbing with Tune Ra's voice!

He hollered, jumping to his knees. This was no hallucination: its sounds carried all over the square, and the pilgrims were turning their heads, too. The old woman, smiling, nodded at the two-floor white building at the opposite end of the square.

Of course! Unlit neon letters—BAR—were attached to the top of the building. Yendon had made his delivery.

The old woman leaned to him, muttering something. Rudi could swear that some of the words were *Nagpa* and *lu*—song.

"Nagpa?" he asked. *"Lu?"*

Nodding, the woman raised the palm of her hand up and forward, as if both inviting and showing the way, and then headed for the entrance to the temple. Rudi rushed after her, but at the door he was cut off by a group of the boy monks carrying bundled pillows. When he finally made his way through the crowd, the old woman was no longer there. She had disappeared in Johang's black mazes.

Inside the temple, one could walk only clockwise. Once again, Rudi joined the flow of the pilgrims.

42

INSIDE, the temple was a gigantic beehive. The darkness
was speckled with hundreds of tiny candles, smoldering
wicks in saucers with yak butter. Above, they illuminated
the impassionate faces of Buddhas and Boddhisattvas,
golden silk-draped queen bees. Below, they cast light on a
tightly pressed swarm of worker bees: confined by the
sooted temple walls and the seats for monks, sectioned off
by columns, the pilgrims crawled at a snail's pace from
statue to statue, carrying the pollen of good thoughts they
had gathered and muttering their mantras. The temple
seemed like a large dark flower, filled with the humming of
the swarm that was feeding off its aroma of incense, the
smell of the yak butter, and the odor of hundreds of sweating bodies.

NOW and then, Rudi, another worker bee in the swarm,
would get on his tiptoes, trying to find the old woman; but
soon, weary and drenched in sweat, he gave himself to the
dreamy viscous flow of bodies. For a moment, he thought
of Ruslanov's basement—another black labyrinth.
    Everything repeats itself, he thought; a man's thought is
capable of turning the same darkness into heaven or hell.
Here, amid the mantra-muttering Tibetan peasants, are the
thick black circles of heaven, complete with a Dante-like
LEAVE ALL HOPE. In order to enter heaven, one must leave
behind all hopes and desires, including one of entering
heaven. Just as these tribesmen did, having surrendered their
simple lots to Buddha's mercy. Holding on to hope is damn-
ing yourself to hell. And I, I hope that these tribesmen are
in heaven, though I doubt that they would have ever left
behind any of their desires. On the contrary, each of them
has come with the hope that his offerings, this stinking yak

butter they keep pouring into candle saucers, would make his desires—money, cattle, health, crops—come true. It is no different from any other place.

A few minutes or hours later, as he eyed the fierce faces of gods looming in the dark and dried the feverish sweat off his forehead with his new hat, Rudi thought that his latest wandering was merely a continuation of other similar wanderings through the incomprehensible chaos of life, with images of others' dramas flashing by: Schechter, Gwen, Abby, Ruslanov, himself. It was up to him to grasp the sense of the dark, to connect the images, to see the plan of the temple—as if it were lit up by powerful klieg lights, rather than by weak candles, with himself, Rudi, peering from above like an architect. There had to be a plan. There had to be more to it than an obsolete ritual of pointless circling and bumping in the dark.

The flow came to a stop. Rudi stepped to the side to take a look. The line was heading for a tiny cave in the temple wall. An elderly lama with a long nose admitted the pilgrims one by one, so they could touch Buddha's statue with their foreheads.

The lama caught sight of Rudi and made an inviting gesture to get ahead of the line.

Uncertainly, Rudi stepped up to the niche and, leaning over, pressed his forehead against the worn-out gold-plated surface. When he straightened up, he was amazed that his fever was gone, along with the scratching sensation in his throat. The lama, his large youthful eyes shining, placed a swath of soiled white silk around his neck. Like tagging a newborn baby, Rudi thought.

He bowed to the monk. "*Tuche-che,* thank you." As he mechanically looked up, he saw a gray braid on the upper gallery.

He pushed against the flow towards the entrance, where he had spotted the stairs to the upper tier. One flight, another—he pushed the heavy iron-plated door open. He was standing on the roof. Narrow wooden steps descended back into the shopping anthill of Barkhor. The old woman was gone.

*   *   *

THE weakness, the fever, the lump in the throat all came back. He leaned on the stone rail, waist-high, to take in the view. To the side of the belly of Johang stretched out the intestines of old Lhasa—long rows of shacks without a person in sight, a yellow-and-blue emptiness. Below was the dust, hole-ridden prayer flags on stunted trees, and puddles of frozen urine. Above was the icy aqua-blue of the sky. An alien, frozen city. Impassionate Asia was asleep. *If I used to be as "free" from other people's pain,* he thought with sudden clarity, *as Lhasa is from mine, then I really had it coming.*

He returned inside. At the end of the corridor he entered a room with stacks of wooden and paper plates—just like Schechter's—on the shelves. An elderly gaunt-faced monk with a silvery crew cut was hunched over the plates in a corner. *A library,* Rudi thought; *perhaps one of these stacks contained the mantra he was looking for. Moreover, the elderly lama could be the librarian and might know the mantra. But he, Rudi, would never know. His Tibetan was a mere "passable." With that, I was planning my trip to Tibet,* he thought; *the arrogance of the West.* Suddenly, he was seized with unbearable thirst.

As if on cue, the lama poured out of a small aluminum teapot and, noticing Rudi, gestured with a smile for him to come over.

Rudi settled on a threadbare pillow nearby. The old man's arms were bare, tanned, and specked with bluish pigment spots. He rubbed a sooted aluminum mug with the edge of his dark red robe, poured the grayish-yellow liquid, and handed the mug to Rudi, his hand slightly trembling.

"*Tuche-che.*" Rudi took a small sip and moaned with pleasure as *cha,* the heavy mix of black Chinese tea and yak butter, pushed back the scratchy lump in his throat.

"*Tuche-che.*" The lama nodded, grinning as he studied Rudi.

Now he'll ask something and realize I barely know the language. But the lama was merely smiling in silence.

Rudi finished the mug, and the old man refilled it. After the fourth mug, Rudi remembered: in order to stop the outpouring of hospitality, he had to dip his middle finger and shake off the drops. *"Mei-mei-tochei."*

Once again, the lama nodded and grinned.

Rudi racked his memory. How do you say such a simple thing as *Father, have you heard of Nagpa?*

Actually, this was the only problem he had to solve. If Schechter was right—if Nagpa had been executed, and the "message on the wind" was senile Ayushi's hallucination—then what would he do? Stay in Johang, offer to become this old man's servant, wash his feet . . .

Perhaps it was the best way out. Perhaps it had been his dream all along. He had to ask to become the old man's disciple. But how do you say it in Tibetan? His memory was failing him.

Rudi kept nodding off, waking up, drinking tea, sweating, and nodding off to the pervasive sound of the pilgrims' humming. On one awakening he discovered that the old man was gone. Instead, he was looking at a tall, heavyset monk with a sleepy sallow face. He jangled the keys and said something in Tibetan.

"Excuse me?"

The monk nodded at the door. "Please. You go now."

43

THE square was deserted. Johang had closed for the night, the pilgrims had scattered, and the wind was chasing the torn flags—someone's failed prayers—along the cobblestones. The light of the mountaintops had gone out, and, just before Lhasa plunged into darkness, it became purple—strikingly quiet and solitary. The only sound heard from time to time came from the tiny bells on Johang's roof eaves, unheard in the daytime.

What a beautiful cold light, Rudi thought. He decided not to look for shelter. He would simply lie down next to the

wall and go to sleep. Perhaps by morning he would freeze . . .
and then he would join Gwen.

He glanced around, looking for a suitable wall, but then
he saw a light. The building across the square, dark only a
second earlier, now had the letters BAR lit on its facade.

Well—if it started in a disco, it might as well end there.
Why shun symmetry?

HE passed an army jeep parked outside and climbed the
stairs. As he pulled on the tight doorspring, he felt a physical pleasure in the pain of stretching his chapped lips, the
taste of blood on his tongue, the red light in his eyes. It was
good to hear his old enemy Tune Ra's voice, good to inhale
the familiar aroma of marijuana. For a moment he wondered
whether he was in DeoMorte or in Lhasa: the sensations
had the same cold emptiness to them—they were just like
memoirs.

Inside, it was as cold as outside. Like in DeoMorte, the
darkness exploded in multicolored light beams, man-made
smoke rose from the floor, and a glass ball spinned under
the ceiling. The music roared, someone was shrieking the
mantra, and, illuminated by strobe lights, the local youths
were clumsily trying to marry local folklore dances to MTV
steps.

The men and women stood in two lines facing each other,
seemingly amazed at their own daring and trying not to
giggle, as they chopped the air in rapper imitations. Passing
the mike, the men took turns screaming out Tune Ra's mantra, their eyes closed, their expressions frozen. The girls
laughed and applauded.

A young Tibetan punk girl, with yellow hair, raspberry
highlights, and a pierced lip, was yawning behind the bar.

Rudi scooped out the rest of his yuans. "Double Scotch,
please."

"American?" She looked at him closely.

He nodded. The Scotch had a moonshine taste to it, but
the fire flowed into the tundra recesses of his body, and he
was thankful. *To you, Yendon.*

Instantly, he heard the Buryat's voice: "Professor!"

Yendon emerged from the clouds of smoke, wearing a

Barkhor-bought ethnically correct robe, embroidered with rocks and silver, and a golden-threaded Mongol hat.

I summoned him with a mantra of my toast, Rudi thought, taken aback. *Like a ghost. The closeness to death must bring out psychic gifts.*

Wobbly on his feet, the Moscow Buddhist gestured with his glass. "Come on! We celebrate good business!"

YENDON'S friends were young men in leather jackets who, sucking on their joints, roared with laughter at the trader's every word. Their arms were around their women: all short, slit-eyed, with tons of makeup, in net stockings and short fur coats. They laughed, too, baring uneven teeth between raspberry lips.

The trader was bragging about having killed two birds with one stone. He had managed to pass off Rudi as cargo to his Tibetan partners, who accepted the charges before they reached the crate in question. The second bird was, he had secured himself a good reincarnation by saving an American from the KGB's clutches. "They would have burned him alive in Moscow!"

Both the hookers and the traders giggled, oohed and aa-hed, made eyes at Rudi, clinked glasses. To him their faces were Johang's frescoes come alive. Deities, semideities, demons, hungry ghosts—all were whirling around him, the glittering ball under the ceiling was spinning, and Tune Ra was screaming. The only unrelated sound was that of a door slammed open, as the Chinese MPs came in for some warmth.

One of Yendon's friends stumbled to the floor, accepted the mike from his predecessor, and, squinting, went on to yell the mantra. Rudi gripped his temples. Was Nagpa alive? He was the only one who knew what this nonsense meant. He glanced at the Chinese soldiers at the bar—could they be the answer?

Rudi leapt to his feet and, tearing the mike out of the man's hands, declared he was going to show them how to do it right. Drenched with sweat, he cast off his coat and went into a Tune Ra–like seizure, while the rest stood around, clapping their hands. To stop the room from swimming, he closed his eyes as he orated, rap-style, "What are you applauding? What are you mimicking? You traded Nagpa for Chinese whores! Buddha is your DJ! Buddha is your rapper! *Om-mani-padme-hum!* I want fire! Huh-huh-huh!"

The hookers giggled and tried to get in sync with his contortions. Yendon collapsed on the floor, shaking like a cross between Elvis and a Cossack dancer.

"I want you to burn!" Rudi rapped on. "But without dying! I want to bring you freedom, cunts! Freedom comes from the barrel of the mantra! Bring me to Nagpa!"

Suddenly he stopped. Alone amid the giggling and dancing. "Do you know if he's alive?" he murmured. "He would teach you how to burn the Chinese with your mantras. Why am I still not arrested?"

He was choking. His heart, still unused to the altitude, stressed by the dance, leapt to his throat, trying to get out. The room turned red, the faces narrowed and broadened like in a funhouse, and he still could not inhale!

He bent to pick up his coat, but lost balance and collapsed on the floor.

Yendon shouted for help to drag him out for some air.

Someone dragged him to the door. Outside was a Lhasa night, with blistering wind and a thousand dogs barking. The army jeep was gone.

A blurry face in dark glasses was flashing in front of Rudi.

"I'm looking for Nagpa. . . ." Rudi addressed the face, which seemed to belong to Yendon's right-hand man. "I'm looking for the magician of Bon—of Bon Po."

"Go, go, Bon Po . . ." The man waved.

They dragged him down a dark narrow alley, his shoulders catching the walls. Slack on the Tibetan's shoulder, Rudi kept trying to lift his head and enjoy the view of the tungsten moon with the crystal necklace of the stars; but soon his head dropped back, forcing him to look at the frozen excrements, covered with a film of hoar and dust.

His head hit the door frame as they pulled him inside and laid him down on a low couch. He fell on the floor and was allowed to stay there. The voices around him grew animated; hands went through his pockets, pulled him by the wrists . . . and, finally, tied him up!

"Bon Po, Bon Po," the Tibetan who had dragged him in mimicked Rudi's pronunciation.

Rudi's heart beat hard, his breath quickened—he realized that someone very important, very mysterious and horrifying was about to arrive! Tying him up was a part of the plan, too! But the person he had been looking for was here, about to walk in!

He heard a rustling sound—

The door flung open, a giant shadow burst in, and a perfectly American voice yelled: "Freeze!"

Rudi paused—he knew the voice—but another shadow dashed for the door, the visitor's arm came up, and Rudi was buried under a strange body.

Then everything went dark.

44

RUDI attempted to move his head and cringed at the pain in his temple. Lying on his back, he observed his new surroundings. He was buried in a heap of soiled blankets. Across the room was another bed, also unmade, with a *tanka* on the wall—a large yellow rag with a roughly sketched black web of a mandala. Between the beds, in the middle of the tiny white room, was a table, and above the table loomed a broad coal-black back.

Once again, Rudi attempted to sit up. His left wrist felt empty: Schechter's beads were gone. Helpless, he fell back and burst into a coughing fit.

"Feeling better?" Rivers said, without turning his head.

The policeman was shaving, pouring boiled water from a huge thermos into a shaving mug. As he scrubbed his cheek, he moaned softly and immediately applied cream to the rash. His soaped cheek turned his wide black face into a yin-and-yang sign.

How did you get here? Rudi tried to ask, but only a hiss came out.

"First we take care of your voice." Martin held up the thermos. "Tibetan butter tea with Jamaican rum. The tea's free, the rum's duty-free. This, my friends"—he went on to wipe his cheek clear—"is the stinkingest hotel in the whole of Lhasa. No running water, but they're not interested in your passport, either."

Rudi held his oddly light hand to his temple. "Where's the beads?"

"You've been robbed, buddy. At least you've got your ass intact."

Rudi felt the pocket of his coat. The diary was in place. "Do you know what happened to the Ruslanovs?"

Martin nodded silently. "But I'll listen to your version, too."

Moving his mouth muscles carefully, Rudi gave his new guardian angel the account of the last week and a half. "What about you?"

AS Rudi emptied mug after mug of the vile yellow concoction, he tried to follow the detective's story, but it was not easy. He was swimming in sweat, the bed kept sinking, and Martin's head was losing focus in his eyes and coming to be replaced with tiny figures scattered along the perimeter of the mandala behind Martin's back. The mini icons of Buddha and Boddhisattva landed on Martin's shoulders and expanded to take over the detective's body.

According to Rivers, the Colorado trail led nowhere. "Nothing but boredom in your Shambala. Not even a decent woman in sight."

"The Swiss one—Margi—?"

"I told you: she disappeared the day after Ayushi's death. No one knows where she went, where she came from, or what her real name was."

"Odd."

"More than odd. So I went back to New York to take another look at the poor brother you tossed under the train.

Kidding," he added, seeing mute protest in Rudi's eyes.

The homeless man's body showed signs of frostbite, which must have been the cause of amputation of his leg.

So what, Tarakis had countered: all the homeless spent nights in the snow from time to time. It could have happened on Fifth Avenue! Yet the forensics experts uncovered something odd again: the incisions, the seams—none of the techniques had been used in the States for a long time. The amputation had to have been performed abroad.

Rudi flashed on a tan narrow hand with a pink stub for a finger; an ankle bracelet . . . But he could not hold on to the image.

"Also, he had track marks," Martin went on; "and they were not from heroin, either. No sir: our poor, underprivileged brother had been using acetazolamide! This expensive medication, a learned doc at NYU advised me, is used by mountain climbers to compensate for lack of oxygen. Now, before you jump to the conclusion that our poor brother used to be a ski bum—no, you don't need AZA to ski in the Rockies or even in the Alps! You don't need it before twenty-five thousand feet—which leaves us with the Andes or the Himalayas!"

Since there was no file on the homeless man, Martin turned his attention to Tune Ra: could there be a connection? In the absence of a legitimate police investigation, he could not get hold of an enormous database of the rock star's comings and goings. Instead, he fell back on good old legwork and located a pilot who had, until recently, flown Tune Ra's personal Lear Jet.

"Sure enough"—Martin's voice fell dramatically—"the only places our famous friend ever flies to are L.A., Beijing—and Lhasa!

"The moment I found out, I went to call Ruslanov. No response. Not at home, not at the lab. I had a bad feeling, so I called the FBI's Moscow guy—I know him from way back—who told me that everybody was dead, and the local police and the KGB were looking for an American accused of murder.

"At least you were alive, I figured. Then I thought: where would you go? All approach routes to the mantra have been blown. But I remembered you talking about some crazy lama who would decode the damn thing. Well . . . to find a good crazy lama you go either to California—and you did not have papers for that—or Tibet. Right?" He burst out in laughter at his ingenuity.

Once Martin arrived in Lhasa, it was only a matter of time: in the off-season, an American would stick out. Martin spread a little goodwill in greenbacks around the handful of hotels and the karaoke bar—the only game in town. Sure enough, soon a messenger arrived to report Rudi's arrival.

"Then I just followed when those guys dragged you outside. First, I thought maybe they were your friends—to put you up or something. But when I saw them going through your pockets . . ."

"Did you kill them?" Rudi groaned. Some Buddhist— killing over stolen beads!

"Nah. Just roughed them up. After I got you out, I called for the Chinese cops—it's their job to handle the natives. Listen, if I hadn't shown up, they'd've thrown you outside—by morning, you'd have been a corpse."

"I wanted that." Suddenly, Rudi started crying.

Martin was taken aback enough to set down his tea mug and stare. Rudi turned to the wall, unwilling to embarrass a relative stranger with his outburst; his body was trembling uncontrollably, and his face was wet with tears.

"Calm down, man," Martin said quietly. "Take it easy."

"Easy?" Rudi sat up, his face distorted with pain. "How can I take it easy if she's dead?"

"You're talking about your girlfriend? Well, she—" Martin hesitated.

"She what?" Rudi's windpipe made a supreme effort to push the words through.

"I didn't want to tell you on the phone." Martin looked away, where the windswept square was filling up with pilgrims. "She ain't dead, man. But she's as good as. She's in a coma, man; she's being kept alive by life support—"

Rudi's face was a mix of pain—for his voice was gone, once again—and triumph. He leapt up to his feet and scooped up his clothes.

"Where do you think you're going?" Martin inquired.

The sight of Rudi's bulging eyes was giving him the willies.

"I—I must be with her," Rudi whispered, trying to get his feet in his pants and tearing them in the process.

"Get a grip, man." Rivers poured himself more tea. The gesture was purely symbolic—he still hated the taste—but he had had his share of dealing with people in extreme conditions and knew that every trivial gesture would help.

"You can't even get on the plane without money or papers," he continued in the most neutral voice he could manage. "And if, by a stroke of luck, you get some sympathetic asshole in the U.S. Consulate to help you out, all you'll see in the States will be a cell in the maximum-security prison. You just don't know when—or if—your girlfriend will be well enough to tell the police that you were not the pusher. Why don't you take it easy and fix your pants first. Here."

Martin took a huge army knife out of his sack, unscrewed the handle, and handed Rudi a needle with a thread. "Don't leave home without it, heh-heh."

Rudi mutely accepted. The touch of the needle seemed to work. "How do I prove it, then?"

"Go back to plan B. Or C. I'm confused myself a bit here. First, find out if the Nagpa guy is still alive in jail."

"I knew it"—Rudi gripped the needle tightly, as if his whole life depended on it—"I knew she was alive. Last night at the bar, I was hoping to create a scene, get arrested by the Chinese. Maybe, once in jail, I would learn about Nagpa—isn't he supposed to be held there?"

"Oh yeah," Rivers drawled ironically. "Go interview the jail warden. Also, find out if Tune Ra visits Nagpa in jail—or someone else."

Rudi glanced at the detective, puzzled.

"What, you never thought about it? By the way, he adopted his stage name after he visited Tibet for the first time. *Before* his career took off. The pilot says he heard it from Tune himself. Now, what we have to do is to interview everybody around here who's connected to the jail—"

Rudi looked down, embarrassed. While he was going through hysterics, Martin was actually doing all the thinking and the legwork.

"—the guards, the cleaning men, the ex-cons. You never

know—one of them may have something. How's your Tibetan?"

"I passed the course, but—"

"I hear you. So we need an interpreter. Let's go back to the karaoke place. I've got a job candidate who's just right for us."

45

RUDI found the only john in the hotel at the end of the hall. It was freezing, with petrified feces in the hole in the floor. Outside, a bunch of stray dogs, as sleepy as the sun, stared at the bleak sign on the cloth over a porch of a cozy white ruin. AMDO HOTEL. The shadows were getting longer; it had to be close to three. On the flat roofs, the evil northern wind tormented the sails of the prayer flags, as if trying to push the ships of the shacks, wrecked on the mountain slopes, into the ocean of the sky below.

A cross-eyed old wretch murmured with his toothless mouth. . . .

"Sorry," Rudi mumbled; he had no money. "Martin, do you have change?"

His black angel merely snarled as he crammed his bags into the dirtiest jeep Rudi had ever seen.

The wretch chatted with Tsendin, their Tibetan driver, who was thirty or so and had a hole in the mouth that seemed to be cut especially for a cigarette. He smoked non-stop. Cheap tobacco was a gift from the Chinese Red Army.

The car would not start: the driver had not warmed up the engine. What's the rush, when you are on the roof of the world?

Slowly, the engine began to turn.

Lord, you have brought Gwen back to life. You have answered my prayers. Now, don't let her die.

*   *   *

ONCE outside the hotel courtyard, Tsendin promptly turned on the radio. At the sound of Tune Ra, Rudi tried to grin, but his mouth, still chapped, made him groan.

"Cut it out, fuckhead!" Martin clicked the switch and silently stared outside.

The narrow potholed street was flanked by yellow-and-gray rocky ruins, mysterious and tranquil, nameless and ageless. Perhaps they were the remnants of Atlantis, decorated with bright rags and the inhabitants' carved copper-red faces peeking out of gaping black holes of the doors; the whole thing might as well have been an exhibit at the Museum of Natural History.

At another time, this quiet ancient wilderness would have touched Rudi's heart with a feeling of kinship: a delayed rendezvous with his childhood, with the dusty world of the fairy tales his mother read to him in her quiet voice, with a smile, invisible and at the same time blinding like the Tibetan sun hiding behind the mountains. But now all he saw before him was a hospital room, an IV feeder, and Gwen's motionless body in the bed.

As they traveled west, they entered the Chinese part of town. The streets were busy with Chinese on bikes, all in identical blue jackets, their faces half-covered with gauze masks to protect their mouths from the sun and the dust. Music roared from the record stalls. A green military truck with a red flag on the hood passed, raising a dust cloud and honking at the bikers in irritation.

The trucks, the stalls, the bikes, the gaudy posters, the sounds of rap from the stalls . . . Like so many idle thoughts, the West was penetrating the pores and devouring the ruins. The road went uphill, allowing a panoramic view of Lhasa with Potala, the Dalai Lama's thousand room residence: a glittering brown-and-white colussus set under the aqua sky.

"What the hell . . . ?" Martin cursed.

A Chinese roadblock. An officer in a long coat with a Kalashnikov waved them to the curb.

"Damn. You don't have papers. Okay, pretend you're asleep."

Rudi obediently closed his eyes. The Chinese spoke close by. The driver answered. The rustling of papers . . .

What if she's not in a coma? he thought. *Her eyes may be closed because she's paralyzed, but she could hear—she might know what happened—she might know she's paralyzed!*

The terror of the thought almost made him open his eyes. Tears, warm and stinging, flowed from under his lids.

"How come there's a roadblock?" Martin asked the driver as the car took off.

Tsendin erupted in machine-gun Tibetan.

"Tibetan Tigers," Rudi translated uncertainly. "Explosion . . ."

"Guerrillas." Martin nodded. "Jesus, there's more. . . ."

Ahead they saw a commotion of military and fire trucks outside the smoking ruin of a familiar two-floor structure. The karaoke bar was no more. Tsendin slowed down.

"They sure know what they're doing," Martin commented. "Lotsa tourists, right next door to the temple—that's publicity. Hold it!" He spun the wheel, bringing the car to the curb about a hundred yards away from the scene. "We don't want another ID check."

He took out his binoculars and peered at the crowd. "There she is." He passed the binoculars to Rudi. "My snitch. In the denim jacket, on the left."

The yellow-haired girl bartender from the night before was talking to a Chinese officer, her childlike high-cheeked face distorted in pain, her hands flying in the air with emotion. Her left wrist was bandaged.

"Bring her over," Martin ordered the driver.

With a wink, Tsendin stepped out.

Martin shook his head. "One-track minds."

"Does she feel anything?" Rudi asked.

"You bet. Asian women are hot in the sack."

"I'm talking about Gwen. Does she feel anything? Is there hope? Have you talked to the doctors?"

Rivers looked down. "Uh, no. What can she feel? She's in a coma. There you are! What happened, Nyima?"

The girl warily peeked inside, then recognized Martin and, sighing relief, climbed in.

According to the girl, the bomb went off half an hour after Rudi was spirited away. Glancing at the Chinese officers in the distance, she whispered in broken English: "Tigers did that! They warned, they left flyers. They said they revenge. Many of their comrades was arrested, taken to Rating."

"You got lucky with your muggers," Martin remarked to Rudi.

"Much people dead," the girl went on. "Buddha saved me: I just reached over counter for rag to wipe—kaboom! Russian businessman died, too."

"Yendon!" Rudi exclaimed.

"Now his turn to go back in a crate," Martin said. "What are you shaking for?" He patted the girl on the neck. "Enjoy being among the living."

She bit her lilac lower lip, pierced with a tiny ring. She looked like she was about to burst into tears any minute. She was eighteen, tops, Rudi reflected; she looked older due to two steel teeth in the upper row. Rudi wondered if this was a local punk affectation.

She noticed his look and turned away, wiping her tears. "No work now," she said darkly. "Big family. No money."

Martin patted her on the knee. "What about our deal?"

She blushed. "I must to feed my family now."

"No problem." Martin placed an arm around her shoulders. "We hire you as an interpreter, for a week or two. How does a hundred bucks a day sound?"

Her expression grew wary—*a hundred dollars?*

"You'll be more than an interpreter," Martin explained. "You'll help us make contact with the Tigers."

Nyima recoiled. "I go to jail! Why you need Tigers?"

"That's none of your business. You need the money or not?"

She was silent.

Martin measured her with a cold look. "As for jail, you can find yourself there right now. What if I step out of this car and tell the Chinese that you work with the thieves who rip off foreigners? I've got a witness right here." He nodded at Rudi. "Who do you think they're gonna believe: two rich tourists or an unemployed local girl?"

She stared at him, terrified.

Rudi intervened: "He's joking. But we need your help.

You see, Nyima . . ." He swallowed. "Sorry, my throat's not too good. You see, there are bad people who use Bon mantra—you know Bon Po—to do harm. To kill people. They killed my friends, Martin's friends. They killed the Russian in the karaoke place. . . . It's all about the mantra."

The girl's frightened eyes made him think she believed his words. He went on, heatedly: "My wife is paralyzed, in a coma. She can't move. It is all because of the mantra. I can't go back to see her till I find the mantra. I need to see her while she's still alive. Please help me. . . ."

He locked his hands together in the same way she did.

"Yagpo," the girl murmured, her mouth barely moving. "Okay."

"Good girl." Martin patted her on the knee. "So can you lead us to the Tigers?"

Rudi and Martin spent God knows how many days combing through endless hole-in-the-wall dives frequented by Lhasa's underclass. As Nyima chatted up the toothless old hags who sat outside the establishments, the two men kept out of sight, staying in the jeep and gradually sliding into a state of utter listlessness. Finally, one day Nyima returned with her eyes flashing. "We go to market!" she commanded.

THE jeep turned onto the avenue, barely missing a collision with a large gray tank. A whole column were slowly progressing to the center of the town. The roar of the engines drowned out the dogs' barking, and the pedestrians had to press themselves against the trembling walls of the shacks, protecting their mouths, as if in horror, against the foul bluish exhaust that mixed with the yellow dust.

"What do they need tanks for?" Martin chuckled. "To catch guerrillas in the alleys?"

"For fear," Nyima said. "Butcher likes make people afraid."

The Butcher, she explained, was the local nickname for General Yuin, the head of the Public Security Bureau—Tibet's secret police. She nodded left at a huge green gate with a red star painted in the middle.

Martin rolled down the dirty window. A barbed wire was stretched atop a long cement wall. Behind the wire, they could see the tops of the trees and, glittering in the sun, a gold-plated roof in the style of a Chinese pagoda.

"The Reds must be feeling pretty cozy," Martin commented. "Is this their HQ?"

"This is Rating Jail," the girl said.

46

OUR mind takes us to the market of destiny, where we trade our raw flesh and tangled nerves for the gold called "spirituality"—is it a fair deal? . . .

"HEY, thinker!" Martin patted Rudi on the shoulder. "Wake up and smell the roses!"

Rudi looked up from his diary. The market was a noisy hub with the smell of blood as overpowering as in a slaughterhouse—which was the bulk of the market business. The market was in the Muslim part of town, whose inhabitants made a living rearing and slaughtering fowl and livestock. Geese, chicken, sheep, both live and freshly slaughtered, were sold on the stalls manned by the Muslim Lhasans, who were as copper-faced as Tibetans, but had thick mustaches and slightly wider eyes. The Chinese sold rice, vegetables, and even fish, which, though abundant in local rivers, was still a curiosity to Tibetans.

Among the vendors, the few Tibetan nomads, their faces a burgundy red, stood out. They wore silver necklaces and turquoise earrings, and under their threadbare yak hides one could see a dagger stuck behind the belt; to Rudi, they looked terrifying. From their alpine meadows, they brought huge yellow boulders of real yak butter, preserved in the beasts' hollowed-out stomachs, and yak meat, smoked by the sun and kept edible by the cold in the weeks it had taken them to reach the city.

Most of the customers were the Chinese military, who

had more money than the locals. In their green pajamalike uniforms, they drove their motorcycles straight to the stalls, stuffing the sidecars with chicken and geese, shoving aside the local women shopping for the smoked yak meat.

Martin advanced Nyima a hundred-dollar note and dispatched her to do reconnaissance.

"How come your Tibetans are such big meat eaters?" He sank his teeth into a kebab.

"You can't grow vegetables here." Rudi felt nauseous from the combined din of clucking and bleating, the odor of the meat, the smoke of the incense, and the persistent local aroma of dried dung burning in stoves.

"So they eat it, but they wouldn't kill it? Hypocrites, like everybody on this continent."

Rudi silently stared at the reddening sun rays forming a pattern on a soiled stall. "Are you married?" he suddenly asked Martin.

Rivers stopped chewing, took a sip of rum from his flask, and offered one to Rudi. The young man shook his head.

"Widowed," Martin said finally. "She died in an accident. There's our girl. . . ."

Nyima dragged a huge gray sheep on a leash. "Gift," she explained, then whispered, "we take it to family where Chinese arrested son. I learned address."

"A live one . . . ?" Martin nodded at the sheep.

"This is custom."

LOCKED in the back, the lamb would not stop bleating, and soon the car was filled with suffocating stink.

"Some fucking gift!" Martin cursed. "Fucking sheep shits like a horse!"

Nyima silently stared out of the window.

"She is offended by your cursing," Rudi whispered. "Buddhists consider it a case of speech pollution."

"Fuck 'em. Tell her it's my mantra. To clear my consciousness." After a moment, Martin patted the girl on the back. "C'mon, Agent Nyima! Gimme a smile! What do they say about the Tigers at the market?"

"Nothing," the girl said reluctantly. "They say at night

Chinese tow big boats to mountains. People are afraid Chinese turn around Yarlung Tsampo."

"The local river—Brahmaputra," Rudi explained.

"Crap," Martin commented with a sneer. "Although you never know. Ruslanov told me the Bolsheviks tried that with their rivers. Except for all the funds got stolen."

The sun went down, and a slice of the moon, an orange fin of a black whale, showed over the mountain ahead.

The car came to a stop on a cul-de-sac. The dogs went berserk from the headlights; when Tsendin turned them off, a silvery film of moonlight formed on the stone walls of the one-floor shacks, which showed no signs of life. If there were people inside, the solid wooden shutters kept the places impenetrably dark. Despite the barking, no one came out.

Martin told the driver to stay inside and keep the engine running. "Go first," he told the girl as he checked the action on his handgun. "Don't do anything silly, okay?"

She shrugged and dragged the sheep to the gate.

"I don't like this," Martin whispered to Rudi. "She claims she's never been here, but she found it real easy in the dark. And without any street signs, too."

"I thought so, too," Rudi whispered back, "the first time I got lost in the Bronx. This is real antiquity, Martin! Pre-Atlantis architecture!"

The three carefully made their way along a narrow alley between the shacks; rather, it was a gutter, with mini towers and stone walkways between the roofs overhead, profiled mysteriously against the moonlit silvery sky.

Martin groaned as he bumped into something. "Fucking architecture."

Nyima abruptly turned left. A door screeched.

"Here," she called.

They lowered their heads as they entered a hole in the wall. They turned towards a flickering red light and found themselves in a large dark room, with a bonfire going on in the middle. The smoke rose in a gray column, meeting moonlight in the hole in the ceiling.

The family—an old man, a woman with two babies, and a boy about eight—were seated on rugs and pillows around the fire, where a pot was boiling; an older woman—perhaps the mother of the arrested boy—was stirring the brew. Rudi recognized the smell of the black tea with yak butter and salt.

Both women wore colorful kerchiefs and sleeveless sweaters, their faces flushed by the proximity to the fire, their bracelets flickering in the light. The old man and the boy gaped at the guests, their teeth sparse. There was no table in the room; the cups and gaudily painted Chinese-made thermoses were on the floor.

Although no one rose to meet the guests, no one seemed afraid or even taken aback at the sheep. They merely viewed the strangers with gentle curiosity.

"*Tashi delek,*" Nyima greeted the hosts as she tied the sheep to a ring in the wall.

Rudi echoed the greeting in his still barely audible voice. Martin merely nodded and put away his gun, warily casing the place.

The old man chuckled and nodded to the older woman, who was pouring out the thick white concoction. The younger woman with the babies shifted from her position to make room for the guests.

"*Tuche-che,*" Nyima thanked her.

Still nodding, the old man pushed forward a large bowl with *tsampa,* baked barley, a local staple.

For a while, the two sides eyed each other in silence.

Then Nyima took a sip and spoke quickly in Tibetan, bowing lightly and nodding at the sheep. The hosts chuckled approval.

Rudi wondered if their hosts were amused, not by the presence of the sheep but, rather, by the unexpected nature of the situation. One moment they sit quietly by the fire, about to have tea with *tsampa*—suddenly strangers barge in, people of whose existence they had been unaware, and bring a gift, too. In New York, people knew exactly with whom they would be having drinks a month in advance, and the slightest deviation from these schedules, broken down to fifteen-minute segments, was fraught with stress; Tibetans seemed to be unfazed by the idea that they could not know what the next moment would bring.

Finally, the old man stopped chuckling and said something in a serious voice.

"He says he won't kill the sheep," Nyima translated; "maybe Chinese spare his son."

Martin looked at the old man closely. "Ask him to take us to his son's Tiger pals. I'll pay."

Nyima translated. The old man was silent. The dung crackled in the fire, and the dark red shadows were bouncing off the rough-hewn faces, which protruded from the darkness like the smoked stones of Johang with the mantra etched on them.

FINALLY, the old man spoke.

"He doesn't know about Tigers. His son is innocent."

Martin shifted closer to the fire, peering at the old man: tousled gray hair, a soiled dark red sweater. The man held his cup close to his face as he drank, and all one could see was his eyes: red whites and yellow dots deep in the black pupils.

"Tell him I'll give him a hundred dollars. This is the kind of money he'll probably never see in his life. Tell him, all we want to know is whatever the Tigers know about Nagpa."

The old man set his cup down. The fire lit up his thin wrinkled face, the hollow cheeks, the sparse gray hairs of his mustache—the gaunt face of a man half-dead, if it were not for a youthful glint in his eyes. These windows into the soul of a child were now turned to Rudi, and the glint began slowly reviving in Rudi a hope that Gwen had a chance, after all. . . .

Suddenly, the old man broke into a laugh.

"What's wrong with him?" Martin exclaimed.

Nyima shrugged.

"Hey!" He addressed Rudi, who was half-lying on his side, his fox hat under his head. "Are you dozing off?"

"No, I'm not." Yet he had a feeling that the conversation was flowing into vague visions in his head—like Gwen, staring at him now, with a smile, across the fire. Perhaps he was nodding off, after all.

How do I know whether I'm awake or not, he wondered,

trying to keep his eyes open. No: it's the old woman staring at me. But I must love her the way I love Gwen. One must stay awake to see the Buddha in all things and all people. One must stay awake to make an effort to love. I have to make this effort. I can't fall asleep and leave it to Martin: he's rude towards them.

The lull continued. The hosts were eating in silence. Martin was picking glumly through his *tsampa*.

The only way for me to know I'm awake is to write, Rudi thought. I never write in my dreams. He took out his diary and a pen.

What if I were the mother of this old man? Would he be the moon that shines into the cup? And I was the cup—and you were the white crumb in his mustache? Perhaps there's a reason why we're here, and eventually God will teach us to recognize each other the way dishes recognize food . . .

THE boy, instantly fascinated, sidled over to Rudi and, his mouth agape, stared at the letters appearing on the paper.

"*Kairang to mingla?*" Rudi whispered. "What's your name?"

"Dondup." The kid gazed at the Bic pen in Rudi's hand, ignoring a huge transparent drop swelling outside his nostril.

"*Len-pa.*" Rudi handed him a pen and tore out a page. "Draw."

The old man spoke, nodding at Rudi.

"He says his guest lies like a tiger in his lair. If his son is a Tiger he would act like one: he would keep hunters away from his lair."

"We're not hunters!" Martin exclaimed. "Tell him we're friends!"

"He means Chinese are hunters," Nyima explained. "He means son knew it was dangerous to bring Tigers here."

"Well, ask him some other way!" Martin demanded, irritated.

But the old man was no longer paying attention. His grandson had already brought him the new gifts and asked him to draw. His mouth open wide, the old man dragged the pen across the page.

"The fucker is senile." Martin pulled Rudi to his feet and, without bothering with good-byes, headed for the door, where he promptly bumped his head once again into the frame. "Shee-it."

The old man chuckled. Rivers glared at him and drew Rudi outside.

TSENDIN turned on the lights, and the car slowly backed downhill. Suddenly, a rock bounced off the window. Martin jumped out and pointed his gun and flashlight at the thrower.

"Don't shoot!" Rudi spotted the soot-covered face in the circle of light. "Dondup?"

The boy approached and, grinning, handed Rudi the piece of paper. Martin held up the light.

They saw an uneven circle drawn on the paper. Next to it, a tiny triangle.

"Well"—Martin sighed—"I assume it means something." He glanced at Nyima.

She spoke to the boy and then said, "The old man drew this. He said, Go to Namtso. Nam Lake. There's a small Bon Po Utse, that's like mastra—montra—"

"Monastery," Rudi prompted.

"Yes. An old Bon lama lives there. He was recently released from Rating. He was friend of Nagpa."

47

AT five in the morning, the sun was not up yet, and the moon shone bright over Potala: a round bullet hole leading into the next world. Icy puddles of urine were creaking under the wheels of the jeep as it was tumbling over the potholes en route to Nam Lake. . . .

*   *   *

EARLIER, Rudi stopped by Martin's room.

"So, what did you get for me?" The detective glanced at Rudi bemusedly.

"Huh?"

"Don't you know what day it is? December twenty-fifth. Christmas morning. Should be emptying the fucking stockings. So—what do I get? Nothing but coal?"

"I'm sorry," Rudi wheezed, his chest congested by both the cold and the shame. "I had no idea—"

"Yeah, yeah . . . All you Buddhists are the same." Martin reached in his bag and brought out a package wrapped in a Chinese newspaper. "Merry Christmas, bro'."

"Merry Christmas, Martin. I—I'm really—"

"Why don't you unwrap it first."

It was a knife, Martin's old Marine knife, with a special groove at the edge. Not entirely appropriate, Rudi thought; but it's the thought that counts.

"I was thinking of a tie," Martin went on coolly as he zipped up his parka, "but the Lhasa Barney's is closed for inventory. Anyway, considering where we are now, this sucker may come in handier."

IN the front seat, Rivers had a couple of shots of rum and snored happily. Rudi stayed in the back with Nyima, his chest racked by a dry cough, his ears blue from the cold, his hat left behind at the old man's house. As Tsendin steered the car up into the mountains, the girl nodded off, too. Rudi looked out of the window, with the stars close by: they were riding along the edge of the abyss.

LAST night he dreamed he was falling out of the window. As he flew, he saw he was about to land right on top of Gwen. Alive, she was waiting for him below, looking at him in a quiet, loving way. He screamed for her to move away, but she did not hear him. He writhed in the air, trying to change direction, but her face was coming closer—

He screamed and woke up: drenched in sweat under a pile of blankets, his head cold, his heart beating wildly.

She's in a coma, Martin had said. She is asleep.

Then she must be seeing dreams? What kind of dreams? What if she's seeing nightmares where he continues to torment her the way he had lately?

He closed his eyes. He had already tried to join her in the next world. But now—what could he do to bring her back? Keep looking for Nagpa, what else?

The mantra had another thirty-seven days till the blowup. Could this be the last Christmas?

Jesus was born in a village that was as ramshackle as any Tibetan one. Perhaps he, too, strode along mountain passes, looking for the Answer. . . .

He comes out into the cold to save people, Rudi wrote. *The cold nips at his ears—he left his hat behind—but look at the stars!*

Christ was not a god, but a yogi: he soars over Potala, clad in white, delivering his mantra of good tidings: "Every day is Christmas, every mortal a savior!"

How do I save her?

IN the first place, he had to stay awake.

He looked back and saw two lights in the distance. A car had been following them at an even distance since Lhasa. The magi or Herod's guards? How could one worry about that, with their jeep moving along the edge of the abyss?

The snow stopped. The mountains were turning a mysterious shade of lilac: the sun, still invisible, was quietly adding the tints of red to the blueness of the night. The stars were dying out, but one—the Star of Bethlehem?—shone brightly, like a striking pang of conscience.

"You like this, yes?" Nyima said suddenly. "I lived in village when little. We got up early. I like this time best, when mountains change color. I would close my eyes and try to guess what color is mountain when I open them again."

Something about the girl's dreamy, faintly sad expression reminded him of Gwen; he turned to the window.

"You are sad all the time," Nyima said. "What do you think about?"

Thank God they haven't acquired our respect for privacy yet, he thought. "About my guilt."

"I too." She sighed.

He turned to face her, the way a patient in a waiting room faces another one. "What's your guilt?"

"I have many." She grinned slyly, baring her steel teeth. "I'm liar."

The car hit another pothole, and Nyima was thrown into Rudi's lap. She gripped his hand and held on to it. He looked in the rear window. The two headlights were stubbornly trailing behind.

THE jeep climbed the plateau and came to a stop near a small rock pile. The pile was crowned with a huge yak skull with blackened antlers. The skull bone was gray, with yellow spots and the letters of a mantra etched into it.

Tsendin climbed on the pile to look around. Each antler pointed to a different dusty road. They had arrived at the fork in the road; now they had to decide whether they should circle the lake along the north or along the south. They did not know which direction was closer to the Bon lamasery, and the difference could cost them up to six hours. The driver mutely stared at the old man's drawing, then at the roads ahead. There simply was no telling which way to go.

Rudi ran his way along the letters sketched on the skull. *Om Mani Padme Hum.* Hail to the pearl in the lotus. A reminder to stay awake and observe the essence in all things. Just like these dots in the letters, etched with a mason's gentle strength. No dot knew to which letter it belonged. No letter knew which syllable it was a part of. No syllable knew what mantra it went into. Just like the mason did not know all the symbolism of the mantra, and the yak's head, of course, did not have the remotest idea what sort of a puzzle it would present to a traveler. A dot is a hint at the true volume of man's knowledge of the world, the late Schechter used to say.

His ruminations were broken by Martin, who had climbed onto the hood of the car and peered into the valley through his binoculars. "What is this crap?"

Rudi joined him. The car that had followed them was descending the last valley and would reach the plateau in another ten minutes. In the dark, it was forced to go slowly; now, it raced down a dangerous mountain road, raising clouds of dust.

"Everybody into the car," Martin commanded. "If it's the Chinese, and they ask for your papers," he addressed Rudi, "tell them you left them back at the hotel. If they tell us to go back, keep your cool. And stay out of the line of fire."

For ten minutes or so, they sat in a suspenseful silence, listening to the engine idling. Finally, a yellow jeep barreled up the plateau and, its driver seeing them, came to an abrupt stop. Then it slowly moved towards them and came to a stop about a hundred feet away.

Whoever was in it had nothing to do with the Chinese police.

A young man in a baseball hat and a safari jacket climbed out of the car and walked towards them, his hands in his pockets. Martin clicked the safety. Yet there was something familiar about the way the man walked, the way his feet carefully touched the ground. . . .

"Margi?" Rudi called.

She removed her hat and waved. Her hair was cut close to the skull.

"How did you get here?"

Ayushi's disciple did not seem to be fazed by the meeting. She appeared to be the same as in Colorado, still in a clear, mocking state of balance.

"After the Rinpoche's death, I went to Europe. A magazine assigned me to take pictures of Tibetan nomads. So I rented a jeep and have been chasing them ever since. I heard they pitched tents to the north of Namtso. What about you?"

"We"—Rudi turned to glance at Martin—"we're going to Bon Po Utse. It's on the lake, too. We're just not sure which one's a better route."

"Utse?" Margi reflected. "I don't know about it. But a house would be more likely to be built on the south side of the lake—it's warmer. I have to go north. Good seeing you. Good luck!" She gave him a hard handshake and headed for her car.

"Where can one find you?" Rudi called to her back.

"I don't know—I'm a nomad myself!" She opened the door of her jeep.

"What's your last name?"

She did not hear—or chose not to hear. The engine roared, and the yellow jeep disappeared in a cloud of yellow dust.

Rudi glanced at Martin, who was grimly copying down the jeep's license number.

"Your friend is liar." Nyima quietly came up. "This is not rented car. Rental agency has different license plates."

THE road from the plateau wound around the mountain. Directly below, a huge piece of dark blue matter filled a yellow-grayish enclosure. "Namtso," the driver said.

It was one of seven holy Tibetan lakes. The silence of its unperturbed blue surface at this altitude, among these giant rocks, was so natural and proud that one could believe that the lake was not the result of melting snows, but, rather, a leftover of the primordial ocean that used to cover these ranges. Not even a leftover, but a reminder that one day the waters would come back. A drop of blue yin in the huge yellow hemisphere of yang. A pearl in the lotus.

"I feel as if I've been here before," Rudi murmured. "I had a dream in New York, where I was atop a mountain peak with my guitar, with waters all around me."

"Whatever you were smoking, boy." After a pause, Martin added, "That's some view, yes. If it was in California, a house here would go for a few million."

RUDI remembered his fights with Gwen about their living conditions: the richer the person, the more peace and quiet he has around him. But after a while the peace and quiet reach a point where wealth is irrelevant and belong to those without property, like hermits or Tibetans. On the other hand, he who surrenders his main asset—his "I"—will always have his peace and quiet, even in the middle of the noisiest marketplace.

Had he not achieved his dream, driving through the Tibetan desert to see local anchorites? But peace and quiet were eluding him; all he had was pain and despair. The only way out was to be at her side in Manhattan, to surrender his "I" to her so that it would revive her.

FIVE hours later, they were still on the road, but the mon-astery was nowhere in sight. They were exhausted, covered with the film of gray dust that penetrated the car, tasting grit on their tongues. Either the old man was lying, Rivers cursed, or he was confused. In another three hours, they drove along the northern side, too. And just as the sun began setting on the distant ridges, they saw in their binoculars a small structure behind a stone wall. On its roof, a gold-leafed circle, flanked with two deer, glinted in the sun. A few yaks wandered outside. It had to be Namtso Utse.

Before they had a chance to rejoice, they saw a yellow jeep exiting the monastery gate and turning on the road to Lhasa. Martin cursed.

"Maybe she didn't know," Rudi said. "Maybe she ran into it by accident."

"Scavenger birds." Nyima pointed at the sky. "Bad omen."

48

LIKE many lamaseries all over Tibet, Utse was likely to have been destroyed by the Chinese. Judging by the shell holes in the outside wall, the temple had been used as an artillery target during maneuvers. Behind the wall was a half-destroyed blackened structure that served as both a temple and the living quarters for the lamas. Through the black hole of the doorway they could see flickering candles. A diminutive old man sat at the entrance, seemingly cold in his fur coat, which was impossibly old and dirty. His coat, his tousled gray hair, his gray moustache—he seemed to merge with the wall, looking like a fungus on a rock.

Trying to get warm, he held his black venous fingers to

the bonfire. The fire hissed on the pile of scrap, letting dirty smoke up into the sky.

"What is this shit they're burning?" Martin frowned.

"They fire clay for fixing things," Nyima explained.

Two boys in rags, their shaven heads smudged with soot, carried pieces of clay from the breach in the wall and dropped them in the fire. Instantly, they stopped their work and joined the guests, grinning curiously.

The old man responded to their greeting with a low sound. Nyima asked him if he had indeed been in jail. The man opened his mouth and pointed inside.

"Sonuvabitch," Martin muttered. "He's got no tongue."

The boys giggled and shouted explanations, interrupting each other.

"They say he bit off his own tongue in Rating."

Martin shook his head. "Can't do it by yourself. Had to be the Chinese. Ask him if he knows Nagpa."

The old man nodded happily.

"So Nagpa is alive?"

The hermit angrily shook his head; then he froze and, staring over the guests' heads, went to pat himself on the sides.

"Is he, like, a few dung bricks shy of a load?" Martin asked Rudi.

The boys yelled again, inviting the guests to follow them around the corner.

"They say there's another old man here. He also was in jail, but he's got a tongue."

POCKMARKED *yellow walls,* Rudi wrote, *covered with brown spots of old age. Sparse rocks/teeth in the walls/ monks' mouths. The little bell rings like a token in God's pay phone.*

Behind the house was a dusty, dirty backyard with more dogs and boulders and a row of prayer drums, broken and charred. An old man in a dark red sheepskin sleeveless sweater, somewhat younger and taller than the first one, wandered about, spinning the drums and muttering.

Followed by Rudi and Martin, Nyima tried to draw the man's attention. "What's your name?"

His round dark face spread in a smile, making his caved-in nose appear even wider. With a cough, he muttered, *"Ngey nor-tul rey . . ."* Sorry, can't remember.

Blocking his way, she asked him about Nagpa.

"Nagpa?" the man echoed the question. "Nagpa—" He spread his arms, as if tossing something to the winds, the way the pilgrims outside Johang had spread bits of incense over the candle saucers.

"Burned and tossed the ashes to the winds," Rudi made a guess.

"Can you ask him straight up if Nagpa is in Rating?" Martin said, his expression darkening. "A simple yes or no."

The old man wheezed a few words out.

"No," Nyima translated. "Nagpa flew away."

The boys broke out laughing, leaping up and waving their hands.

Martin spat. "He's jerking us around."

Indeed, for a moment Rudi felt the old man was teasing them, the dark slits of his eyes flickering through the spinning drums.

Rivers whipped out his wallet.

"Ask if your goddamn magician has disciples. Tell him we'd like to make a contribution to the foundation dedicated to his goddamn memory. But he better be straight."

At the sight of the money, the old man grew animated and extended his wrinkled dark hand through the space between the drums. Rivers put in a few notes. The man giggled, spat on his fingers to count the yuans, then placed them to his forehead, said something, and, limping, disappeared around the corner.

"He says Nagpa left something for him," Nyima said.

"Works every time, buddy," Martin said. "Brooklyn or Tib—"

An explosion shook the ground so hard that it knocked the guests and the boys off their feet, with rocks and scraps raining on their heads.

Nyima looked up and hollered in terror. All that remained of Utse was one wall. They rushed to the front yard. Amid the scattered rocks, a shell hole gaped in the ground on the spot where the old man had been warming his hands at the fire. In the rock pile, Nyima spotted pieces of bleeding flesh and the fur coat; she covered her face with her hands and dropped on her knees. In the distance, the boys were weeping, pressing close to each other.

"Could be a leftover shell," Martin mused, shaking off pieces of scrap. "You said the Chinese used this place for practice. It was here, unexploded, till the old guy placed it in the fire. Or . . . it could be your Swiss girlfriend."

"What about the second one? He might be still alive under the wreckage! We should try to get him out!"

"We should get our asses out of here pronto," Martin said. "Before the Chinese come and charge us with terrorism. C'mon, Nyima, you can bawl in the car!" He grabbed the girl and dragged her away.

"What about the kids?"

"I bet they got families in the village! C'mon!"

When the car had climbed atop the hill, Rudi tapped Tsendin on the back to stop.

"Listen," he addressed Martin. "I have a feeling we're to blame for this. If we hadn't come to see them, they'd still be alive. I'm afraid of myself."

"Welcome to the club," Martin said angrily.

49

ON the way back, it started snowing again. In the middle of the storm, two boy lamas in knitted ski hats came out of nowhere to wave at the jeep and toss a few snowballs.

The travelers were silent. Every time Rudi closed his eyes he saw the torn flesh in the scraps of gray coat. His coughing felt like hundreds of small dry explosions in his chest. Nyima buried herself in her wraps in the corner, so that only her eyes were visible.

Tsendin seemed to recover from the shock before the others and tried to sing, but Martin cut him short.

"Jesus. They're practically extinct, and what are they do-ing? Robbing tourists and singing songs, instead of joining the guerrillas."

The rest of the way everyone was silent. Just before Lhasa they were stopped by a police patrol. Following the karaoke bar explosion the night before, the authorities had declared a curfew.

"Competition." Martin chuckled. "Just like us, looking for the Tigers."

The roadblocks were a mile apart. Every time an army truck and soldiers in long overcoats with Kalashnikovs loomed ahead, Rudi spread himself along the cold floor of the jeep under Nyima's coat, and froze still. Listening to the Chinese barking orders outside, he closed his eyes and fought back a cough. He felt Nyima pressing her legs against him, as if to protect and calm him down.

They were lucky; the Chinese never looked inside the car. They checked the offered IDs and waved them on.

At the hotel, Rudi realized that the cough would keep him awake all night.

He asked Martin to drop off Nyima and stop by the phar-macy. "I saw one yesterday next door to the Holiday Inn."

"The driver can drop her off," Martin said grimly. "You take a few shots of rum, it'll go away."

Suddenly, Nyima came alive. "I have yak butter—I brought it for candles at monastery. I'll give you rubdown." She ran to the back to retrieve her bag.

Martin ordered Tsendin to stay and wait for the girl. "Watch out for her," he told Rudi.

What's that about? Rudi glanced at him, but the girl was already back. "Let's go, patient!"

RUDI lay in bed, looking on as Nyima filled a tin cup with the butter and set in on the stove to heat it up. Then she closed the window and turned on the heater. His mind went back to his life with Gwen.

He used to think that bliss was fire and passion. No, bliss was tears; it was repentance.

"C'mon, lift your sweater," Nyima ordered, grinning.

He studied the girl's face, so close to his: pockmarked

skin the color of light coffee, beads of sweat on her forehead, dirty fingernails on her hands rubbing his chest with
the stubborn diligence of a laundress getting rid of a spot.
Her bristly yellow hair showed black roots; her eyebrows
were bushy and black, too, and she seemed to have no eyelashes. Her eyes did not look narrow: just covered halfway
by her eyelids.

If I cannot serve Gwen, then I should serve the one who
is next to me; somehow, through the cosmos, it will get to
her. But how do I serve Nyima? Take her to America? From
the way she was hungrily drinking in their words, her careful use of MTV locutions, her mimicry of Western fashions,
her lack of money—he thought she would surely like that.
But he was not in a position to help her now. It was odd
how Western touches—the ring in her lip, the raspberry
streak in her hair—actually made her face more Oriental,
looking more like a predatory nomad.

Outside, the flags were snapping in the wind, reminding
him of the sound the laundry made in the ashram where he
lived with his mother. Nyima was quietly humming the song
on the radio—to Rudi, the words were nonsensical, it was
like a lullaby. . . . She had already forgotten about the explosions, about how close she had come to being killed.

She noticed his gaze. "What do you think about?"

"I wonder how I can make you happy."

She paused to stare at him. Then, realizing he was serious, she grinned widely.

"You're kind. But your friend is mean."

"I'm not kind. And he's not mean."

"No, I saw: anything not right, he fights right away. I had
boyfriend like him. We had fight, he knocked my teeth.
See?" She demonstrated her steel teeth.

"Can you teach me to dance?" she asked slyly. "Like you
did in karaoke."

"Sure," he said dejectedly, remembering the last time he
had danced before the karaoke bar: on the quad at Columbia—with Gwen.

"O-kay!" She clapped her hands, turned up the volume,
and marched to the window. The room was stifling. She
opened the window and stuck her hands out for snowflakes

that were falling quietly. She washed her face and resumed her treatment. The melted snow was streaking down her face, but she kept grinning.

Once again, this reminded him of Gwen coming in from the rain, her face wet and aglow with a young girl's bliss. Engrossed in his thoughts about lack of money and dependence on her, he'd snapped at her. She'd looked away and wept. If he could only go back—

"You have a wife?" Nyima asked, as if reading his thoughts. "In America?"

He nodded.

"That's far away."

He felt her fingers move down, below his waist.

"Don't." He stopped her.

Her hands, dark and slim, smelling of butter and smoke, slid up to his face. He had a sense of déjà vu: it had already happened, with Varya in Moscow . . .

"You don't like love?" she insisted.

"It's dangerous." The only thing he could do for her was to cause her no harm. Send her home—

"Dangerous? In America you use protection, no?"

"Go home, Nyima." He drew away and sat up. "The driver will take you home."

She slowly wiped her fingers, one by one. "You said you want to make me happy."

Although her expression was calm, even a bit flirtatious, he could tell she was upset. "Please, Nyima. It's dangerous for you to be here."

She grabbed her jacket. At the door, she snapped: "You're like all foreigners in karaoke."

Did I give her a reason? he wondered, listening to her steps dying in the hall. *Thank God she's gone, and nothing has happened. I'll have to ask Martin for an extra hundred and hire another interpreter. She's a good kid. It's too dangerous for her to be with us.*

SUDDENLY, an engine roared outside. A shriek, a blow—

Rudi tossed off his blankets and ran out to the gallery overlooking the street. Tsendin stood outside his car, rubbing his eyes sleepily. A cloud of dust was settling. A part of the gate was askew, as if hit by a car.

Martin ran out of his room. "What happened?"

"I think—" Of course! "I think Nyima got kidnapped."

A moment later, their car was leaping on the potholes, following the taillights ahead. Just as they were about to catch up with the kidnappers, the other car turned abruptly. They followed—and came to a stop. The car was in a dark cul-de-sac. The other one was nowhere to be seen.

"We'll never find them like this," Martin declared. "Let's climb one of these hills."

Indeed, traffic would be nonexistent at three A.M. in wintertime Lhasa—and with a curfew, too. The lights of the other car would be easy to see.

ATOP Chokpori Hill, the icy wind was humming persistently. A wide rocky plateau was strewn with ruins of *chortens*, low-set mortars. Once this was the site of a lama medical school, destroyed by the Chinese; now it housed the antenna for the local radio station. Martin climbed a few steps and peered downhill through his binoculars. The few lights of streetlamps and buildings were static: not one moving vehicle.

Finally, he spotted two tiny red dots approaching a well-lit rectangle in the center of the town. They entered it and disappeared.

"What's that?" Martin passed the binoculars to Tsendin.

The driver took his time learning to use the Western gadget. Finally, he announced with a bit of awe, whether at the news itself or at the power of the toy: "Rating."

"SHE got arrested because of us!" Rudi exclaimed. "I knew she would be in danger! They'll torture her, and she'll give us up!"

Martin shook his head. "Don't give me this damsel in distress shit, boy. The bitch has always worked for them, as does anybody in contact with foreigners."

"But she cursed at the Chinese!"

"A slave always curses his master, but that doesn't prevent him from serving."

"So why did you hire her?"

"I didn't *hire* her. I *re-recruited* her. The way you recruit women: get her drunk and screw the bejesus out of her."

"That makes no sense." Rudi paced the hill. "Why would they kidnap her in that case?"

"Well, I suspect . . ." Martin hesitated, as if unsure whether this was something he cared to divulge. "They may suspect she went over to our side. After all, I did promise her I would take her to America. Part of the recruiting routine, you know. That was the deal: she helps me here, I take her over there."

"She tried to seduce me, too."

"Oh well, a fallback position. I told you to watch out. I hope you at least got to give it to her."

Rudi looked away, blushing.

"Well, this whole thing sucks," Martin said, tactfully changing the subject. "If she told them we're looking for the Tigers, we can't go back to the hotel. The Chinese get hold of two Americans helping a terrorist organization—bingo! So whatever we got back at the hotel—forget it. Now we're both illegal here."

"So what do we do?"

"We take a nap. There should be enough space here. It's a good thing I didn't get one of them Corollas."

50

MARTIN and Tsendin were snoring within minutes, but Rudi could not fall asleep. He could not stretch out on the floor in the back; he kept shifting his legs, which kept going to sleep; he kept covering his ears to block out Martin's snoring. For a few seconds, he managed to fall into the darkness, but then the familiar pictures—Gwen on IV, the burning floor at the Russian lab, the ruins of Utse—started rolling, and he was ejected back to reality.

The heater kept going. A gas leak filled the car with a nauseous odor, enhanced by the stink from Tsendin's quilt jacket. Finally, Rudi had to step out for air.

At dawn, Lhasa was no longer a cup of black coffee, with streetlamps like dots of undissolved sugar, but, rather, a cup of smoky gray-and-yellow yak tea. So far, he had failed to fish out the tea leaf—Nagpa—that would take him back to Gwen.

If the girl had told the cops about their attempts to contact the Tigers, the police would be looking for them. There's no place to run—and should they run? If they get caught, at least they would be taken to Rating, where he would definitely find out if Nagpa was alive.

In the car, Rudi carefully extracted the binoculars from under Martin's elbow and pointed them at Rating.

A tall white wall bobbed into the view; then the guard towers, and a large green gate with a red star. Outside, he saw a man leaning against a long wheelbarrow.

Rudi was about to quit, when a window opened in the gate. The man outside must have heard something, for he donned his hat and limped towards the window. Weird-looking hat, white and yellow . . .

That was his—*Rudi's*—fox hat!

The man at the gate was the father of the arrested Tiger.

RUDI dashed to the car to wake up Martin. When they both had another look, the old man was still outside.

"Either he's got a visitor," Martin suggested, "or his son's being released."

Rather than letting the old man in, the guard inside opened a hole in the door, and a long, rolled green sack slid out. The old man grabbed it and dragged it to the cart.

"That's a body bag," Martin said grimly. "The sheep didn't help."

At first the old man dragged the sack in a businesslike fashion, as if it were a potato bag. But, as he was loading it on the barrow, the edge of the tarpaulin rolled up, revealing a human head.

"Let's go!" Rudi turned to the car.

"Let's not. Let's wait for the funeral. His son's pals

should show up. Let's give it a last try. Whatever they say about Nagpa . . ."

THE old man loaded the sack on the wheelbarrow and pushed it along the deserted street—to their surprise, he was not taking it home. The old man pushed the barrow with difficulty, pausing frequently and looking down in front of him.

The traffic was sparse, and they had no trouble staying on the man's tail. An hour later, they were out of the city. The road rose into the mountains. To avoid detection, Martin commanded they get out and continue on foot.

They climbed a yellow rocky hill, grabbing the sparse bushes on the way. In the middle of the next slope, a huge flat rock formed a semblance of a terrace. Under the withered bushes speckled with scraps of prayer flags, two old men and three women, seated on gray boulders—Rudi recognized the family—waved to the old man.

"I don't get it," Martin murmured. "How are they going to dig a grave? They've got no spades, no picks."

Suddenly, Rudi realized what was about to happen. "It's called 'sky burial.' "

THE vultures were motionless, only occasionally turning their beaks towards the flat rock. There were a few dozen of the huge fat birds, their color merging with gray boulders. They had no fear of people, while the latter refrained from making abrupt movements, so as not to disturb the "grave-diggers." Both parties were waiting for the old man to deliver his load.

FINALLY, he arrived, and, helped by the other two old men, dragged the sack to the center of the gray rock. The women remained seated. They must have known the terrible news. Or, perhaps, one did not show grief in this ritual.

"That's weird," Rudi whispered. "They're supposed to read Bardo first. The Tibetan Book of the Dead. For three days at least . . . Unless the body needs to be buried right away."

Martin grinned slyly. His grin was his bullet-proof vest, always in place to protect him from fear.

"I'm afraid it needs that," he said. "Look."

The old men emptied the sack. Rudi peered through his binoculars: a red spot, raw, in black rags, with a bluish human arm protruding—and looked away, unable to fight nausea.

With a shriek, one of the women dashed towards the rock and had to be restrained by the two others.

The ax caught a glint of sunshine in the air—and a blue arm flew off, to the perimeter of the rock. Cawing, the scavengers flapped their wings and sidled closer. The heavenly funeral got under way.

THE body was chopped finely, the flesh shaven off the bones. Then, using hammers, the men smashed the skull and the bones, so that the birds and the dogs could finish it all up.

"Fuckin' savages," Martin commented. He lay down and closed his eyes. "Wake me up when it's over."

Rudi watched closely, with disgust and painful curiosity. He imagined himself being buried in this manner, and, to his surprise, did not find it horrifying. Dead, he wouldn't feel the axes and the beaks. From above, he would be taking in a beautiful Himalayan day. . . . And the day was fine indeed: sunny, clear, cold, and peaceful. The cerulean sky was not disturbed by a single cloud, and somehow the funeral did not look like a horrible bloody ritual, but a quiet, legitimate natural phenomenon. Once the consciousness flowed out of the body, it turned into a piece of meat. It could and had to be used to sustain life in other living creatures; it had to go back into the circle of life. All its life it had been sustained by animals; now was the time to settle the debt.

How glorious is a bird's-eye view of the mountains, he wrote in the diary; *even if the bird is the scavenger that has devoured your body.*

Ultimately, he felt a little terrified. He tried to hold on to the thought of the impermanency of things, of compassion towards other creatures. Still, he could not help worrying:

what did the deceased have to go through before death? He, Rudi, knew he could not stand pain. . . .

The vultures were waiting for the old men to finish their work, from time to time uttering strident shrieks that sent chills down Rudi's spine. They were like muscle men for nature, he thought, telling the men to hurry and pay up.

Finally, the men were finished. They returned to join the women on the boulders. Then the entire slope bristled as dozens of wings flapped and descended to attack the red mess below. The dogs obediently waited on the sidelines, like infantry waiting for the air force to finish leveling the city.

AT last, the birds were shooed away with sticks, and the dogs were given their turn. Then the women came out to pour white powder—*tsampa*—to clean the blood and guts. It was time for the third shift to dig in. Rudi was surprised to find ordinary sparrows in Tibet. Like brown hail, they hopped all over the rock, picking at the flour mixed with blood. The vultures' gullets filled, they watched contentedly from the sidelines. One of them, a piece of ligament still hanging from its beak, glanced at Rudi, and for a moment the two gazes locked: two cold unwinking dilated pupils stared straight at the binoculars. Stared with expectation.

Rudi felt sick. To fight his fear, he set down the binoculars and wrote down:

Sky has become my grave. One must live as if one's body has been picked by angels.

When he looked up, the relatives were up and waving.

A troop of horsemen was coming from behind the hill.

51

THERE were about a dozen horsemen on small long-haired horses, wearing torn fur hats and worn-out sheepskins. They appeared to be armed solely with short daggers in faded silver scabbards, tucked in behind pieces of rope used for belts. All but the leader looked like textbook Tibetan nomads. The leader, however, wore a green Chinese military coat and a dark red ski hat. His tanned face appeared smudged.

Was this handful of ragged primitives posing as the liberators of Tibet? Rudi wondered. The fearless, impassionate warriors of Shambala? The Knights of Great Asia who emerged, ghostlike, from their mountain retreats and, aided by the spirits, fought for the New Era and its new Buddha—Maytreya?

At the ritual rock, they dismounted; two were sent out for sentry duty. They removed plastic canisters and approached the family. With a bow, the leader handed the old man a white scarf. Then they returned to the rock and tossed up pinches of *tsampa*. Finally, they took seats with the family and poured a white milky liquid out of their canisters.

"Looks like sperm," Martin cracked.

"*Chang*—milk beer," Rudi said.

As he peeked in on the wake, he felt envy: the guerrillas may have been in hiding, but they were in their own element, exuding confidence, while he was doomed to be an unsure guest, a witness, wherever he went. With all the information on the religion he digested, he used textbooks to hide from it.

"We can't go down there just like that," Martin whispered. "Either they'll run away or chop us up with their daggers. We should ambush them."

He suggested they return to the jeep and block the mountain road. When the guerrillas headed back, they'd have no choice but to talk, with him having them in the crosshairs of his sight.

Every time I tried to ambush happiness, I failed, Rudi thought; just like it was with Gwen.

"You're right," he said, and straightened up.

"Are you nuts?" Martin grabbed his leg. But it was too late. He was spotted. In an instant, the guerrillas were on their feet.

CURSING, Martin followed Rudi down the hill. The guerrillas pulled sawed-off shotguns from under their sheepskins and took position behind the rocks.

"*Tashi delek!*" Rudi shouted, and the *"ek"* skipped through the valley like a rock on the water.

The barrels of the guns were still pointed at him.

"Motherfucker thinks he's Clint Eastwood," Martin murmured.

The rocks in the distance were brown, like Gwen's eyes; the air was icy and sweet, like her lips as she walked in from the street on a winter day. A shot was bound to come any minute. But not yet.

With another fifteen feet between him and the Tibetans, it was time to shout something—and then he realized he could not remember a single phrase in Tibetan.

A dog was rolling on the rock, covered in leftover white *tsampa. Ka-bo.* The Tibetan word for "white." That's it.

Suddenly, the leader in the purple hat shouted something and, emerging from behind the rock, took aim. Martin dropped on the ground and pulled Rudi along.

A shot rang out. Martin rolled behind the rock and fired back.

"Don't shoot!" Rudi shouted, his temple pressed painfully to the cold rock. "We need help! Does anybody speak English here?"

PEER *into the strangers' faces,* he would write later. *Each is a messenger of a secret brotherhood, but has been on the road for so long, he no longer remembers his mission or who sent him, where he is coming from or where he is*

*going. Help him remember. Perhaps in this way you'll help
yourself remember, too. . . .*

"What do you want?" a voice shouted.

It had to be the leader in the purple hat. "We're your
friends. We need your help." Rudi glanced at Martin,
crouched behind the rock. "We can pay!"

After a few seconds, they were told to raise their hands
and toss their weapons aside.

AT close quarters, the leader turned out to be quite young,
with a face that reminded Rudi of a scoop of chocolate ice
cream protruding from a cone. His eyes, unusually soft and
brown for a Tibetan, were bloodshot and round with anger
as they slid back and forth between Rudi and Martin. The
smudge on his cheek was an ointment that covered a raw
pink scar stretching from the corner of his mouth. The scar
turned his expression into an ugly scowl of an angry Tibetan
deity.

"What are you doing here?" He had a strong Indian accent. "This is Tibetan ritual burial place. No foreigners allowed. How did you get here?"

Rudi joined his hands in front, as if about to bow. "We
need to know about Nagpa—the Bon Po lama? We need to
know if he's alive in Rating?"

"We don't know anything about Nagpa," the man spat
out angrily.

"We asked him." Rudi nodded at the old man. "He knows
who we are. We know that you have friends in Rating. You
have our sympathy. We are friends of Tibet."

The leader glanced at the old man questioningly. The
latter squinted, grinned at Rudi, and began talking to the
leader, gently holding the shotgun away. Then he removed
the hat, revealing sparse gray hairs, and handed Rudi the
fur hat.

"No, please." Rudi moved the man's hand away. "Gift.
Tuche-sig."

The leader chuckled and spoke to the old man. Gradually
the grin disappeared; his lower jaw trembled; he grabbed
his dagger and stepped up to Martin.

"What's wrong, old man?" Martin said calmly.

"It is because of you that his son died!" said the leader. "You knocked him out—you called Chinese police. They arrested him and found explosives. Because he fought for free Tibet. And you, 'friends of Tibet,' you handed him over."

With these words, he put the gun in the old man's hand. Unsteadily, the old man pointed the barrel at Martin's stomach.

"So you call yourself a freedom fighter," said Martin slowly, his eyes focused on the old man's hand. "I thought you were a plain mugger—didn't you try to rip off my friend?"

"I saw you in the karaoke bar!" Rudi gasped. "You were the interpreter! You wore glasses!"

"We were not trying to rob you." Noticing that the old man's grip was weakening, the leader propped the gun, still pointed at Martin. "We wanted to take you hostage, to trade for our comrades who are now in Rating. You just got lucky. We wanted to kidnap the Russian businessman, but then you showed up, and we figured we'd get more for an American. If we had taken him, you'd have been the one to die in the karaoke bar bombing—instead of him."

"There were innocent people there," Rudi murmured, blood ebbing away from his face.

"That's okay," Martin said in a conciliatory manner. "Hey, can't make an omelette without cracking the eggs, right? I'm happy you got away from the Chink cops. And you've got us now, right? So why can't we talk?"

"Okay." The guerrilla nodded after a pause. "Call me Mamatri."

"I am Martin—we sound alike, right?"

"Maybe. But first we search you."

SOME Tigers were put to work collecting dung and brushwood to build a fire on the edge of the burial rock, while others tipsily played with the jeep, sliding windows up and down and toying with the radio. Tune Ra's mantra came and went in the static.

"If there's anything worse than being a prisoner," Martin whispered out of the leader's earshot, "it's being held pris-

oner by a bunch of drunks. I bet their leader spotted a wad
of dollars when we were being searched. Or they could
poison us." He nodded at the pot brewing over the fire.

"LISTEN," Martin said to the leader, "I'm sorry about tearing up your mug. It's nothing personal, no hard feelings,
okay?"

The leader remained silent.

"I know from national-liberation struggle. My uncle was
a Black Panther in Oakland. And I could help with more
than money. I put in years with the FBI hunting down terrorists—we're not going to bog down in semantics, okay?
Now why do you think the Chinese would trade guerrillas
for a foreigner?"

Mamatri blew on the mix of hot beer and smoked meat
in his mug. "Have you heard of General Yuin?"

"The Butcher of Lhasa?"

"The Butcher of the whole Tibet. Also, a highway robber.
He's got palaces in the mountains, his own jet, foreign bank
accounts. Now, if newspapers wrote that Yuin would not
save a foreigner and had allowed these savages"—he nodded at his comrades, petrified with awe at funny sounds
coming out of their leader's mouth—"to torture to death a
tourist . . . for example, to saw him in pieces alive, like the
Chinese did Norbu . . ."

He nodded at the flat rock, where the sparrows were un-
hurriedly picking the last of the flour, revealing the fresh
bloodstains.

The old men and women heard the name of Norbu and
glanced at the leader.

"That sounds reasonable," Rivers remarked. "How do
you make contacts with the Western media?"

"I have studied in India," the young man said, somewhat
irritated. "I have my contacts."

"India, hm . . ." Martin nodded. "Right. The Chinese general would feel really bad about an article in, uh, *Tandoori
Telegraph.*"

Mamatri stared at the twig with which Rivers was stirring
his stew.

Before he could figure out whether he was being made

fun of, Rivers said, "I have a better plan. Your general might or might not care about a tourist, but every general has someone he cares about."

"Who's that?" Mamatri sat up. "Chinese General Secretary?"

Martin shook his head. "Only one person—himself. You've got to take *him* hostage."

Startled, Rudi stared at Martin.

The latter did not budge an inch, still eyeing the guerrilla with a kind of fierce bemusement. "That's right: Yuin. Now, him we can trade for both your friends and this old fart Nagpa, if he hasn't kicked the bucket yet." And, detecting a sparkle in the young man's eyes, forged on: "We find out his regular routes and cut off his security escorts. We place mines. You've got all these cute narrow alleys that are perfect. . . ."

He started drawing a map with the twig. The guerrillas crowded around, staring in amazement.

Rudi stared at his steaming mug.

Smoking ruins of Schechter's apartment—Abby's library—Ruslanov's lab—the karaoke bar . . . These Buddhist terrorists (what nonsense!) who'd turned Yendon and other bar visitors into burnt flesh. And now Martin suggests that they follow this route: more explosions, blood, horrors—for what? To liberate Nagpa, who might or might not be alive—might not exist, for that matter? To figure out the mantra? No one else is to be sacrificed but him.

Rudi moved closer to the fire. What should he offer for sacrifice?

The flames hummed and danced, like so many monks in yellow toques. Sweat formed on his brow, trickled on his eyebrows, and dripped into the *chang* cup.

The Creator did not think the whole thing through, Rudi mused, when he gave man self-consciousness. It turned into intelligence—a dangerous weapon. Then God changed his mind and asked for it back, promising to trade it for happiness. What if I lose something, thinks the man, choking with fear. Choking . . . How the throat hurts. There must be some kind of tumor. I have to get the knife—Martin's gift—and cut it out. Why are they staring at me?

"Hey!" Martin patted him on the knee. "What are you muttering there? Jeez, you're all wet."

"I'm fine." Rudi struggled to his feet. The fire moved to let him pass, and he fell, hurting his head on the mug he was holding.

Someone brought a mug to his lips. He tried to take a sip, but pain shot through his throat; his head jerked back, scattering the liquid.

"Jesus, you're on fire!" Martin slapped him on the cheek. "Hey, Mamatri, you got a hospital here?"

They walked him to the car. "Don't," he whispered, "if you lay me down, I'll go back to sleep."

Martin's powerful hand grabbed his wrist. "Buddy, don't worry. Tsendin's gonna take you to the hospital, they'll take care of you. I've got to stay here, iron out some details. You'll be all right. It's no big deal. Look, a present from Mamatri . . ." He put an object in Rudi's hand. "Compensation."

Bouncing over potholes, the car drove down the road. The object in his hand felt like a pile of ground bones. What does he need with them? Why don't the birds pick them? What are they waiting for?

With an effort, he peeled his eyes open. In his hand, he held Schechter's beads.

52

THE hospital was a two-floor cement cinderblock box. Tibetan hoi-polloi—pilgrims with canes, peasants, beggars— filled the reception room with coughing and sneezing, with blood and pus.

With Rudi in tow, Tsendin made a beeline for the doctor's office; other patients straightened up against the wall, gazing curiously at the foreigner.

"I go back help Martin," Tsendin said. "Okay?"

The sun barely penetrated the dark tiny office through the unwashed windows. The air was thick with incense and filled with particles of dust that danced to an unknown rhythm. The white walls were lined with colored rags and myriad tiny drawers.

The physician was an old man with a neat Western haircut above a native tanned face. When Rudi entered, he was using his right hand to examine a baby writhing on its mother's lap, screaming its lungs out. He kept his other hand warm in his grayish quilted robe; like any other room in Lhasa, the office was cold.

The man smiled at Rudi with his thin lilac mouth, nodded to a bench in the corner, and shuffled off to concoct a medication. He produced various colored rags out of the drawers, poured tiny balls in his hand, combined them, and quickly ground them in a small copper mortar.

A stack of medical *tanka*s was hanging off a hook over the bench. Rudi recalled Schechter's lectures: medieval Tibetan masters used these canvases, strung between rods, to copy down the Blue Beryl, a treasure of the human body's composition and its treatment, passed down from ancient Indian sages. The top *tanka* in the stack featured a skinned human, with red and blue threads of organs, veins, and ligatures. Rudi's mind slid back to the burial site; he felt nauseous again.

A medicine ball rolled under the chest of drawers, and the doctor tried to pull it back with a wooden stick. I am that ball, Rudi thought, and fate painfully hits me with a stick. Finally, the healer got the ball out, along with a huge dustball; on the way, he tapped on Rudi's bench. *"Ngalsogyab."*

Right, he needed rest. He lay down and watched the doctor dissolve powders in a cup of tea and pour the concoction into the baby's mouth. In a second, the child grew quiet.

Rudi got out his diary. *Dried intestines and animal feces. The superior creatures cure themselves with whatever they have squeezed out of the inferior ones. God, too, treats Himself with human residue—with their spirits. He slowly grinds humans in the mortar of losses, imperceptibly steams them over the fire of time, and patiently squeezes them*

*through the strainer of conscience—all of this to procure
an ounce of spirit.* . . .

"*PU!*" *Son!* Grinning, the doctor called Rudi as the baby's
mother, bowing incessantly, backed to the door.

Before Rudi could open his mouth, the healer pointed at
his own throat. "*Migpa?*"

"Yes, it's my throat, but also—"

The doctor placed a finger on his lips, caught Rudi's wrist
with his other hand, and felt the pulse with three fingers, as
if holding a violin.

Can you feel her pulse through mine? Rudi thought. Can
you roll a little magic ball to cure her? You can use me as
material—

"It's for my wife—" he started.

"*Gug-pa!*" the doctor hushed him and took the other
hand.

Of course: *wait.* God has no silver bullet to heal everybody at once. No, he wants to string people out, He wants
them to heal slowly, paying as they go. That's what sustains
Him: the crumpled notes of our prayers. He lives off our
groans, pleas, efforts to get better. . . .

Finally, after feeling the pulse for what seemed like eternity, the doctor shook his head and spoke. The only word
Rudi could distinguish was *fire.*

He shook his head. "I don't understand!"

The healer drew Rudi across the room, where he un-
hooked the stack of *tanka*s, spread them on the bench, and
went over them one by one.

"*Dey!*" Aha! The healer pointed at a miniature picture
where a doctor in a purple lama robe was bleeding a naked
patient, painted in blue. Another *tanka* showed a double
mandala, which looked like two daisies: two large circles,
each surrounded by six smaller ones.

The large circle on the left showed a vertical cross section
of a man with his internal organs: brain, heart, liver. The
one on the right showed a cross section of the earth. In the
center was a cracked lacquered circle of magma; farther out
were orange rings, brown plates, black platforms, green
covers, and blue waters—which, to Rudi, more or less

squared with high-school diagrams. The two drawings were connected with a web of tiny black arrows: one went from a man's groin to the earth's nucleus; another, from the bones to tectonic plates; yet another, from the skin to the soil.

The healer pointed at the man's groin, where a coiled red snake was sticking its head with a bared tongue into the coccyx, at the base of the man's spine. Then he drew Rudi's attention to a smaller circle to the left, where the snake's head rose to the stomach: the man was holding his stomach, his face distorted in pain.

This circle was, in turn, linked to a small circle outside the earth, where our planet was held in the claws of the fierce, scowling demon Yamantaka, decorated with human skulls. Like the snake, the magma flowed upward, its arrows rising in all directions to pierce the next ring.

To drive his point home, the healer made a mournful face and traced the upward path of the snake with his hands along his body. Like in a comic strip, the tiny circles, too, showed the advance of the magma arrows to the surface, with Yamantaka scowling worse and worse. Then he dabbed his finger on the circle with the man holding on to his throat in pain and shifted it to the original bloodletting *tanka.*

Rudi realized that he was being shown the genesis of the disease. In the Tibetan medical canon, it was most frequently traced to a lack of balance between human energies; the major one, which Indian yogis called *kundalini,* was depicted as a red snake coiled in the coccyx. If the snake went through a rude awakening and rose through the body too abruptly, it was bound to get stuck in the internal organs and cause them to be inflamed. Hence, bloodletting, one of the mainstays of Tibetan medicine.

Rudi shook his head: the scalpel he saw in the copper tub at the door looked anything but hygienic.

The healer spread his hands in despair, then dragged Rudi back to the *tanka* and again dabbed his finger on the two last small circles. In the penultimate one, the man gripped his head in terrible pain. In the last one, the snake's sting was going through his head.

Rudi peered at the picture more closely. Under closer

examination, the sting branched out in thousands of tongues and rivulets that embraced the man from head to toe—

The man was on fire!

Rudi's head swam; he had to kneel at the bench. Every tongue of a flame opened up into a larger picture: Schechter's charred body, Ayushi's body in the fire, Abby's house going up in flames, the fire in Ruslanov's lab. Schechter's words came back from a lecture: *"unsupervised tantra studies can be dangerous . . . danger may arise from an abrupt rise of the kundalini caused by incorrect exercises or a mantra."*

Watching Rudi's expression, the healer nodded happily. *"Me, me . . ."*

Fire. Then, his finger crawling up, the doctor read, one by one, the doodle-like letters at the earth's cross section.

"What did you say?" Rudi exclaimed. "Read it again! *Yang-kia!"*

But there was no need. The old man had just recited the DJ's mantra.

THE puzzle that had coated his life with an oozing film of uncertainty suddenly took shape, solidified, and was transformed into a precise four-color chart.

The *tu* syllable—the occult force—had been the stumbling stone for both Schechter and Ayushi, preventing them from grasping the meaning of the mantra. But it was not *tu*—it was *dhu!* The healer enunciated it clearly. And that's what Tune Ra had been singing all along; but the experts, naturally drawn to *tu,* took the aspiration to be just that: a singer's affectation.

Rudi remembered what the old man had muttered as he spun the drums at Utse. *"Om mati muye sale dhu."* It was the main Bon mantra, whose syllables connected the body's energy centers from top to bottom. If *om* referred to the top—the lotus—then the last syllable, *dhu,* referred to the coccyx, where the life force was concentrated, and where also the creative and destroying red snake was coiled. Human magma!

Rudi glanced at the man in flames and traced the arrow to the corresponding small circle on the right. Roaring with laughter, Yamantaka held the planet in his hands. The globe was covered with cracks.

53

AS Rudi walked out of the hospital, Schechter's words resonated in his ears: *"If words are recited frequently, the sound waves created are embedded in the subconscious of a human being or an object and develop a behavior pattern."*

Rudi almost got run over by a car, a dusty green truck with a red star on the hood. His savior, a tall young man with long hair, shouted and pushed him towards the wall. The onlookers laughed at the woolgathering foreigner.

With his entire body, he knew he had the answer. The fever was gone, and not just from the balls that the healer insisted he take; his body and his mind were filled with clarity, frozen and large-grained like the mud underfoot.

We all deem mankind to be the center of Creation, he thought; *I was no different. When I was trying to grasp the effect of the mantra on human beings, I neglected the mother of all: Mother Earth.*

WHAT did it all mean? That the earth will crack up in thirty-six days?

The earth, however, lay underfoot solid and indifferent, and the way it had lain for billions of years, and the way it would for billions of years thereafter. Trucks roared by, the crowd clamored, the sun blinded him, the dust tasted gritty in his mouth. How could all of this turn to dust and ashes—because of one word?

Just as Rudi appeared on the verge of translating this ringing clarity into a neat formula, something in the air awakened his stomach, made it growl, and the moment was gone. He sniffed and turned to see a food stall. A woman was quickly molding flour into little balls and tossing them into sizzling oil; a few moments later, she dropped them into the customers' open palms, picking up their coins with her fat oily fingers.

Rudi put a salty Tibetan doughnut in his mouth and groaned. It was unbearably hot. He remembered Larry Schechter molding Play-Doh balls and breaking them with one hand as he drove. The orange peel covered with broken pen lines in his office . . .

"It doesn't matter now." Larry put a plastic cup over the hot electric bulb; it turned black, smoking, charred. Larry kept talking about his mother, who was about to do something irreversible. But his mother had been long dead.

Was Mr. Schechter of Columbia Seismology Lab talking about *his* birth mother—or, perhaps, the birth mother of us all? Perhaps he was talking about the earth.

WASN'T it a miracle he got Larry on the phone? Then again, what is a miracle but a turning point designed by someone high above?

The sleepy, gaudily made-up girl at the Holiday Inn refused to sell Rudi an international calling card without seeing his passport.

Well, he was in a Communist country, after all. What would Ruslanov do? He laid a five-dollar note in front of her. "I really need to talk to my wife." Which was not really a lie; whomever he would be speaking to, Gwen was the real interlocutor.

The girl peered at the bill perhaps with more attention than she should have. "Passport."

Rudi laid down another note. Without batting an eye, she swept them off the desk.

FORTUNATELY, Larry's number was listed. Only as he was dialing did he realize it was four in the morning in New York. But Larry was not asleep.

"Ah, the theologian detective." His calm chuckle came

through the roaring static. "Where are you? Then again, what's the difference?"

The remark, and especially the tone of his voice, made Rudi's knees buckle.

"I'm—" He looked out of the booth, just to make sure. The girl was about to nod off. "I'm in Lhasa. In Tibet."

"That's a hell of place to go to deliver my father's diaries to Ayushi."

"Ayushi's dead. Killed, actually. Which is another story. Or, rather, the same one—look . . ." Rudi swallowed and squinted. The outward madness of what he was about to say— "Look, you kept talking about your mother. But your real mother's dead—Ayushi told me. Are you talking about . . . Mother Earth, perhaps? As a seismologist—are you talking about some kind of cataclysm, like an earthquake?"

For a moment, all he could hear was the gargling noise of the static.

"It's not a widely shared opinion," Larry said quietly.

"But what do you believe?"

"I'm one hundred percent sure. But no one, I tell you, no one believes me—and thank God for that. There's nothing anyone can do about it. And it's better to leave this life with dignity—without creating mass hysteria."

"So the earth will crack up . . . ?" Rudi grabbed the cardboard wall, covered with incomprehensible graffiti.

"I'm afraid so—but where did you get that information?"

"It started about March fifteen last year, right?"

"Yeah—" For the first time Larry seemed to lose his cool. "When Greenland shifted—"

"And it will end in thirty-six days, right?"

"App—approximately. Not *end—begin!* But how do you know? Did you steal my calculations? Did you show them to anyone?"

"I didn't take a damn thing!" Rudi was sitting on the floor, his eyes closed, fireballs shooting through the black space in his mind. "Can you just explain this thing to me? I'm on a pay phone, for Chrissake!"

LARRY compared the earth to an orange, the pulp covered with a peel—the lithosphere, or the upper crust—fifty to seventy kilometers deep. A shake-up in the pulp can cause a shift in the rotation axis: the equator and the poles will trade places. The Ice Age will come to tropics; heat, to the poles.

"This is the only theory that can explain the death of dinosaurs and the remains of the jungle found in the polar areas," Larry added. "Commonly, this is known as apocalypse."

One possible factor for unbalancing the pulp can be ice, which accumulates around the poles asymmetrically. The centrifugal momentum will be passed to the crust, which will shift in relation to the magma. The polar ice aims to become perpendicular to the rotation axis.

Currently, the cycle between the floods was almost over, give or take a few thousand years. The water level in the world ocean was rising, though due not only to the greenhouse effect, but also to the shift of Greenland ice. The first tremor took place on April 21; according to Larry's calculations, with the shift accelerating, in thirty-six days the process would become irreversible.

"Then what?" Rudi's scream broke through the double static of the line and his own congestion. Exhausted, he lay on the floor, refusing to believe what he heard.

"The earth is an ellipse; the peel will shift tens of miles a day . . . volcanic eruptions, tsunamis, tornadoes . . . famine, epidemics, chaos . . . in a year—"

"What?"

"A new earth, a new sky . . . Although we won't see them."

"But what causes the imbalance you mentioned?"

"I told you—the ice on the poles exceeds critical mass—"

"Just the ice?"

The line went dead.

"Miss!" Rudi hollered, opening the door. "I can't hear a thing!"

Larry came back on the line: "—can be a meteor or an underground bomb test—"

"What about the sound?" Rudi yelled, watching out of the corner of his eye the girl stare at him in curiosity. "Sound vibrations?"

"All cosmic vibrations affect the earth through the membrane of the atmosphere—"

"What about a sound *from* the earth? Like, a mantra?"

"You're insa—"

"Your telephone time is finished," the girl announced.

54

I'M not insane, thought Rudi as he asked for another phone card. I remember the lab. Why was this reversal of psychic poles senseless? There's the answer to your question, Dr. Ruslanov. Perhaps you had discovered it that last night when you hollered into the phone about the computer providing you with a sensational answer. The mantra penetrated the conscious all right, but it was aimed at the magma— not at the humans.

"You want for all this money?" the operator asked flirtatiously.

Rudi nodded absently.

What is she so happy about? he wondered. Her rouged cheeks, her brightly colored lips: a gold digger's childish ruses. She's no corrupt bureaucrat; she's just a kid, lost in an empty cement box in the Himalayas, dreaming of her own utopia: a well-appointed home, foreign school for the kids, a trip to Beijing. If she really plays her cards right, perhaps even the West, where they have indoor heating in the winter. Now it will remain a utopia. All that makeup for nothing. The death of her clients caused by the reversed polarity will be a mere sideshow to the Main Event.

He remembered the pictures of the dragon at the hospital. What he had taken to be cracks on the globe could well be the contours of the new continents—according to Larry, it had already happened, and more than once. Then the ancient Bon magicians had to know about it, along with the mantra that would unhinge the Ice Dumbbell. So who is this person who is using it now—who pushed Gwen—who needs a new sky with new continents—and why?

"Why?" he echoed mechanically as he collected the card. "I mean, thanks."

I should have realized it right away, he cursed himself as he dialed. Neither he nor Schechter nor Ruslanov remembered that the change starts with the smallest step—oneself.

When Larry answered, Rudi was already posing the question that he had had no time to realize: could he influence things by stopping the reversal in himself?

"Larry." He talked at a machine-gun pace, aware of seconds ticking by. "You kept working on it, you kept telling me you had no time—you tried to stop the reversal, right?"

"I built models to see if a nuclear explosion could cause the earth to quake in the counterphase and stop the ice from sliding. But it can't be calculated—"

"But the vibration method exists, Larry! It's the mantra!"

Larry's groan spanned the continents. "The same horseshit that obsessed Dad—"

"It's a mantra that would counter the first one! Ayushi told me—and Nagpa might know it. He could be right here in Lhasa!"

Larry's tone was bitter. "The same old quack who got my mother killed. Yeah, sure."

Rudi stopped short—he had forgotten all about it.

"Look," Larry said coolly, "as a scientist—if one chance in a million existed, I would have made it public. But the chance doesn't exist. I went on with the calculations merely to distract myself."

"But in theory," Rudi pleaded, "in theory, a counter-something, a counter*phase*—it could reverse the process?"

After a pause, Schechter Junior chuckled. "*In theory*. But it's more of a sci-fi proposition. Listen, Disciple Number One, why are you so concerned? It had to happen sooner or later. Every system has a built-in element of self-destruction. That's an immutable law of nature."

"Not in this case! This was done by people—who killed your father! Except for"—now he got it—"they were after you! They were afraid you would make your discovery public! Weren't you supposed to stay at your father's house that night? *You* were the real target—not your father!"

"Do you want a bit of advice, Rudolph?" said Larry dryly. "Don't waste your money on long-distance calls. Go back to your girlfriend, get into bed, and wait for the end. A few couples will surely survive for procreation. Who knows, you might get lucky."

"No!" Rudi yelled, trembling. "She's in a coma! Pushed out of the window by the same people who killed your father!"

"It doesn't matter," Larry said. "Just be patient. It will be over in another month—"

"It will not! The consciousness goes on!"

When Larry spoke again, there was quiet but distinct pain in his voice. It was as if the hissing and croaking space between them was listening in with compassion.

"You know, I hate to admit it—I never forgave my father for my mother's death. And I wanted his death, too. But then I calculated this thing with the poles—everyone will be gone. So all these notions of justice, retribution for my mother's death—they make no difference."

After a pause, he went on, "You said the consciousness does not die. That's what I'm afraid of, too, as a scientist. I drive around New York at night, I set the radio in a search mode, two seconds per station. That's what will be left of us: the music of our thoughts, the sounds we uttered, forever flying through the universe. Perhaps that's what the next world is, like a radio: whatever frequency you lived on—"

The card ran out.

THE girl giggled. "How's your wife?"

Rudi stared at her inky slits of eyes, unable to open his mouth. Subconsciously, he was a coward: spent all the money talking to Larry—more than he really had to—instead of calling Gwen's mother. Will the Great Flood wash away his chance to atone?

Outside the hotel, he sat on a cement block—and froze. At first he was afraid: his soul was leaving him. No: it was his body taking in the environment. He felt a part of the cement block; he expanded into the hotel, the sky, the galaxy . . . Then he recited the mantra. The earth shook; he fell on the ground and woke up.

How odd to be the only one to know that everybody is doomed—and to hide it. This is how a child learns about death and asks his mother: "Will I die, too?" "Of course not, you silly thing." God, too, tries to comfort us with the notion of the immortality of the soul.

Two green army jeeps barreled down the avenue straight at him. So, should he locate Martin and arrange to blow them up? Turn them into a mess of steel and burnt flesh?

The brakes screeching, the cars came to a stop at the curb. Three policemen stepped out of each one and confidently headed for the hotel. Involuntarily, Rudi turned to see the operator jump up and head for the door—but then she froze, too. He turned back; the policemen were heading straight for him.

He rose and, his heart beating hard, walked along the facade of the hotel. Someone called in Chinese from behind. He walked faster; then broke into a run. Just as he was about to turn the corner, a blow came down on his head, the asphalt flew up to meet him, and everything went dark.

55

RUDI was awakened by the pain in his wrists. He groaned and tried to twist free, but his hands were cuffed. He tried to open his eyes, but he was only halfway successful: his eyelids were glued shut with something viscous. He realized it was blood: his forehead stung, and warm liquid was dripping on his eyebrows. Through the slits of his eyes he saw black boots with brown rifle butts.

He looked up. He was in the courtyard of a seven-floor stone well; overhead, the blue sky was specked with red flags and barbed wire. The bottom seemed like a checker-board, where shaven-headed men in identical black quilt

jackets, set apart evenly, made some sort of ritual movements—not unlike old men doing tai chi in Chinatown,
Rudi thought. Except that they were moving to the music
blaring through the loudspeakers, and the music was . . .

. . . it was the mantra! It was a slower version of Tune
Ra's rap tune, arranged for Chinese string instruments. The
men had to be inmates, and every time one stared upward
and stumbled, one of the soldiers in green overcoats who
lined the perimeter would come up and strike him on the
head with a long yellow nightstick.

Rudi tried to follow their stares, but from his position he
could not see anything. He heard a command barked. An
officer in sunglasses gestured to the guards, and they
dragged Rudi inside, along a narrow hallway, past iron
doors with peepholes. The lock clanged. He was pushed
inside a cold stone-walled pen with a narrow bench.
Through the bars, he could see the lilac sky; the sun was
setting. He was in Rating.

He dropped on the bench. Before using his diary for a
pillow, he wrote: *God conducts a dance class, and we try
to follow His movements, but we are blinded by His light.
We should simply listen to the music; the tone-deaf and the
clumsy will be corrected by the stick. . . .*

He fell asleep with his pen in his hand.

When he opened his eyes, the sun was already up. Once
again, the door opened with a clang, a command was
barked, and two guards led by a colonel took him up the
steps, polished to a fault by the thousands of feet that had
preceded his. At every landing, armed guards saluted the
colonel and opened the steel bars. For many before him,
Rudi thought, it had been the last walk.

At the top floor, there were twice as many guards. As he
was searched, he glanced through the bars: down in the
yard, the tai chi went on. Spurred by the blows of the sticks,
the black checkers rose on their toes, flung their arms,
crawled into the invisible sea, crouched under the gusts of
the invisible wind.

On the roof, Rudi squinted in the bright sunshine. It was
a helicopter pad, with a large green chopper with a red star,
antennas, radars, and a red narrow carpet leading to a po-

dium where he made out a dancing figure. The inmates below must have been mimicking its movements.

The guards brought Rudi to the podium and stepped back.
The man on the podium turned to face the prisoner.

He was a tall thin man in his midforties, in a gray pajamalike jacket over the purple skirt of a monastic robe. The
narrow skull, sculpted with a strong hand, seemed familiar,
as did the high forehead, the receding black crew cut with
strands of gray, hollow cheeks, and eyes too wide for a
Chinese.

The eyes gazed at him sternly. The man came up and
placed his hands on Rudi's shoulders.

Below, the checkers placed their hands on invisible shoulders.

"What took you so long, my dear boy?" His voice was
even and rich, with a strong British accent.

"Who are you?" Rudi's voice trembled.

"I am General Yuin. Head of the Public Security Bureau
of the Tibetan Autonomous Area of the People's Republic
of China. But surely you recognize me?"

Rudi's eyes focused on the man's widening black pupils.

"Of course, our encounter was brief—a mere instant . . ."

The general grinned, baring large yellowish teeth; suddenly the words came out of his mouth—it was the anonymous voice chanting the mantra. "The elevator on the
ground floor at West One Hundredth Street—"

Rudi recoiled, then grabbed the general's jacket; another
movement, another push—and, joined together, they would
collapse to the cement ground. But, rather than resisting, the
general removed his hands from Rudi's shoulders and
stepped to the edge.

"Push," he ordered, his eyes focused on his prisoner's.

The guards were motionless, apparently following a previous order.

Below, the inmates obediently assumed the general's posture.

Rudi stood, clutching the lapels of the man's jacket,
choking on his hatred, unable to take his eyes off the man's
face—or push him into the blinding abyss.

"Push," the general repeated quietly. "But then who will set you free?"

Rudi's hands were still glued to the lapels.

"Who will liberate you from your guilt?"

Rudi's hands fell away.

The general straightened out his jacket and dispassionately gestured towards the exit. "Would you mind having a cup of tea with me?"

56

THEY descended to the basement, where they negotiated a maze of corridors. Finally, Yuin opened a steel-plated door and gestured Rudi to come in.

Rudi stopped in disbelief. The room was like outer space, with suspended transparent blue globes glowing in the dark, illuminated charts and diagrams on the walls, flickering computer screens, and TV screens tuned to CNN and BBC. The temperature was set at a perfect comfort level, a faint aroma of incense floated through the air, and a Chinese lute was playing quietly in the background. These globes reminded him of his favorite illustration from the Bhagavad Gita: Brahma resting in the field of galaxies—and only a few feet away from the dank cells where prisoners were being tortured and executed.

"Let me make tea. It's not something you leave to an orderly."

After the general disappeared behind the curtain, Rudi approached the globes and stopped dumbstruck. Each showed "alternative world maps"—just like the ones in Larry's office.

On Yuin's globes, too, the earth was missing Europe, India merged with Australia, and South America joined Africa. Another globe had disaster areas in different colors: Water Pollution, Air Pollution, Water Diversion, Ozone

Content, Toxic Water, Acid Rain, Radiation, Species Extinction, Greenhouse Effect, Fisheries Depletion, Deforestation, Population Explosion, Desertification. . . .

"FEAR and loathing?" the general said behind him.

He carried in a tray with a tea set and first-aid supplies.

"You feel you've seen yourself in the mirror, haven't you? Now, sit back and let me tend to your heroic wounds."

The general wiped Rudi's face with a damp napkin, then rubbed it with alcohol, and applied a Band-Aid on the scar. His hands were strong and warm and moved quickly and confidently, like those of a surgeon who would not flinch at causing pain.

"Sorry we had to get physical with you. But you seemed to be so taken with Larry's discovery, there was a risk of you making further calls and spreading a panic that both Larry and I are trying to prevent. If only I'd known you had no money left. . . ."

Seeing dismay in his prisoner's face, Yuin added, "Be patient. You will realize that my ignorance of your current financial status was the only thing I did not know about you. In fact, I know more about you than you do. Some of your recent life doesn't make sense to you—well, it will. But first: aren't you the slightest bit curious to know about me?"

Judging by the confidence with which Yuin picked up his cup and paced between the globes, the question was rhetorical.

"So, a little background on General Ming Yuin, popularly known as the Butcher of Tibet. Paradoxically, my father was a composer. Yes: the Shanghai Music Academy, the usual leftist-student nonsense . . . Comes the revolution—bingo! Comrade Yuin ends up as a court composer, penning music that glorified the Great Leader. With each of these sonorous cantatas and operas, he believed we were getting one step closer to the beautiful Communist future, the ultimate brotherhood of man—and so did I. But I was impatient. When I graduated, I realized that even Beethoven's sonatas couldn't bring about paradise on earth by themselves. What paradise needed was men of action; men with honor, will, and courage. Which naturally brought me to work for Chinese Intelligence."

The general seemed so enchanted with his voice, his pronunciation, his syntax, that Rudi wondered if any of his words were true. Could Yuin be a standard psychopath practicing his English in front of an educated native speaker?

"I was sent to England, where I attended Oxford, All Souls' College, which I admired very much—so much, in fact, that upon graduation I stayed to work at the embassy. Ah, to be in England . . . Unfortunately, my performance was found impressive, which meant promotion and a subsequent transfer to Beijing. And that was, my dear fellow, when the disillusionment of this young Chinese Werther set in. While our billion-strong peasants were starving for the promise of paradise, our leadership was already living in one. The Politburo country homes, the orgies in the Forbidden City . . . Believe me, no emperor had had it so good. I learned the dark side of life, too: a woman lost to my superior, backstabbing, the death of my parents . . . Sound familiar? Be patient; more parallels will emerge as we proceed. Every loss left a scar. Hence, I dreamed of mankind with no ties: not to one's body, not to ideas, not to leaders. Only then could mankind build the communism I dreamed of as a child."

I *am* dreaming, Rudi told himself, watching the silhouette wend its way among the flickering globes. I have been tortured and beaten, I'm about to pass into the next world, but to protect myself from further suffering, my mind is offering me these beautiful, absolutely ludicrous tableaux. . . .

Only the Band-Aid that puckered on his forehead was a proof of reality.

"As my star went into descent," Yuin continued in the same deep theatrical voice, "my boss, an ignorant peasant who never even learned proper Mandarin, exiled me to a place where many a functionary's career had died—Tibet. Here I learned about Buddha; here I learned about the Valley of Shambala. About the clear light of Nothingness."

Yuin paused next to the farthest globe. "I don't think Larry had time to break down the coming disaster into stages. Here's the first one . . . No, the cataclysm will not start on the day when the mantra's reading ends. On that day the ice will move. And then, approximately a week later, the water will begin arriving in New York Harbor. . . .

"Nothing is new under the sun. Twelve thousand years ago, Atlantean society pursued technological progress aimed at achieving utmost personal luxury. This created a sick society, stricken with cancer—and the high priests acted. They provoked an earthquake that turned the earth's crust the way an orange peel might turn around the pulp: Antarctica slammed into Atlantis, while Canada and northern Eurasia were freed from the polar yoke of the Arctic. New continents emerged. That was the Flood that made Noah famous.

"Some people believe that the movement of the lithosphere was caused by nuclear explosions. My money, however, is on the mantra—the great secret passed from one civilization's priests to another. You know that local Bon Po lamas go back to Atlantis priests. I heard local legends of remnants of three-eyed Boddhisattvas found in Himalayan caves—they might well be Atlantis priests. Anyway, we are witnessing a new turn of the spiral: the old continents will disappear, and our disciples will survive on the islands formed by the mountains."

"God made a covenant with Noah," Rudi murmured; "no more Floods."

"You know your Bible! But people broke the covenant first: they built their own Babylon and kept God out of it. More importantly, God could not have made such a covenant. He cannot cancel the disintegration stage, which inevitably follows creation and accomplishment. This civilization has accomplished all that is constructive, it has created all it could—and now it's time for it to sink. In fact, this is what people want: if there is no end of the world, then all the talk of its beginning and existence loses meaning.

"Why are you so afraid of dissolving? Ah, the Western— the pagan—cult of eternal youth! Disintegration is beautiful! Together, the disturbances that will come during various stages of the cataclysm will form a catharsis so global in scale that your favorite question, To Be or Not to Be, will lose its meaning, too! The cataclysm will make saints of

both the deceased and the survivors! Look at what's to
come!"

Yuin turned the globe for Rudi to see it.

"North Arctic Ocean and Greenland move south. The Atlantic will flood the Eastern Seaboard like all hurricanes put
together. The stock market collapses, both dollars and gold
lose value. The only world currency is food. Plus the right
to live on nonflooded areas."

He gave the globe a light whirl and stepped aside. "But
I'm not done with the curriculum of my vitae yet. Here in
Tibet I came to believe that Shambala was real. Our senile
politburo leaders, too, knew that somewhere in these savage
mountains grows the seedling of real communism that poses
more danger to them than all the Russian and American
rockets put together. They believed that a small group of
top Tibetan lamas were conspiring to use occult forces for
a coup d'etat; they wanted me to uncover and destroy it. I
wanted the opposite: I wanted to nurture this conspiracy. I
looked for it in all seriousness: I combed the entire area
with paratroopers, I recruited hundreds of sherpas and lamas. If only I met one of these teachers, I could convince
him to let me come aboard; together, we would turn China
upside down, and then a new civilization would be born—a
bridge between humans and angels.

"But I could not find any of these elders. Fine, I said, the
Buddhist books must be right: first, you locate Shambala in
your mind. I had to learn meditation and all this occult
hocus-pocus. I arrested lamas, delivered them here, and
forced them to teach me. I have many ways of forcing my
will, believe me. But most lamas taught me without coer-
cion: they believed that Dharma would change me. And it
did: I have learned a thousand little tricks of manipulating
one's conscious. But I also realized that the Dharma way
of creating Shambala will take thousands of years. While I
wanted to have it here and now.

"But first let me tell you about stage two." Smiling gently, Yuin passed to the next globe.

57

"NOW, a super tsunami will drive the waters of the Atlantic back north," Yuin continued, his expression so blissful it seemed he would be smacking his lips any minute.

"The tsunami enters the Arctic Ocean and floods Russian lowlands . . . Speaking of Russia: I learned of Ruslanov's research from my colleagues working in Moscow. I recognized it as a chance to accelerate the revolution in the collective conscious. The consciousness is but a microcircuit, and therefore can be speeded up by computers. I knew with Ruslanov's help, I could achieve here and now what used to take lamas lifetimes of meditation.

"Fortunately, I was not hurting for money to pay my sources. Fate was on my side: as you know, Tibet contains huge deposits of uranium ore. I took over the distribution; finding a couple of partners inside the politburo was not a problem. Alas, our Communist rulers have no idea what to do with their money! They keep buying seaside villas and penthouses in European capitals—both will be the first ones to vanish!

"By contrast, I spent every penny on my cause, and I can account for it. I paid my agents handsomely. The question was, could Ruslanov come up with a suggestion that would change the microcircuitry in human minds? The more I studied my agents' reports, the more I realized that his mind was a crawling snail of a scientist, rather than a soaring eagle of a prophet. . . . And then, a coup! Near the Bhutan border, in the heart of the mountains, where few men ever set foot, by pure accident my agents swept up the greatest living practitioner of Bon. Yes, I'm talking about Nagpa, the same one whose name has brought you here. . . .

"But let's move on to stage three." Yuin sidled over to the next globe. "Now, the lithosphere—the earth's crust—

has turned twenty degrees. The warm ocean floods cause major warming in northern and eastern Europe. The rest of the continent moves into a tropical climate, with nonstop rain and heavy mists. While the North is being flooded, the South engages in a battle with Arabs for living space.

"But I digress. Speaking of Nagpa: at first, I didn't pay much attention to him. I've seen enough top lamas, and, frankly, most of them are sheer dross. There's only a handful that are good for a scrap of wisdom: a mantra here, an incantation there. Most of which were of no use to me in the long run.

"Nagpa, however, struck me as being absolutely impervious to the best torture I had designed. He pretended he was mute—and that was the end of it. I was about to get rid of him, pardon the euphemism—when I got some interesting reports from Moscow.

"Ruslanov may have told you that his number-one disciple, Igor—did he mention him?—betrayed him for the Russian Mafia. He was wrong—I can outbid any old Russian thug. So, just for the hell of it, I decided to test some of Ruslanov's methods on the old man. I flew the Russki to Tibet, we put Nagpa in front of the terminal, clipped his eyelids up—remember *A Clockwork Orange*?—and soon enough we discovered a blocked cluster in the old man's brain. Now I got interested; we purchased a Cray computer from the Americans, and eventually we figured it out. By substituting Sanskrit and Tibetan words, Ruslanov's student discovered the sound of this mystery in his brain. And that was the mantra you already know.

"The lamas translated it for me: *The lotus and the snake change places.* Now, I had read about pole reversal before. But now, as I was poring over the Blue Beryl maps, it dawned on me: we were talking not about human chakras, or energy centers, but those of the earth! You saw those *tanka*s at the hospital. . . ." Yuin chuckled contentedly. "Do you still have doubts that Chinese intelligence is the best in the world?

"But let us not digress. The main champion of the pole-reversal theory was an obscure American geologist named Larry Schechter. After I familiarized myself with his works,

I wondered if this mantra could do the trick of affecting the ice poles. Incidentally, what was this mantra doing in Nagpa's head? Unfortunately, I never had a chance to find out. The old shaman must have realized that something important had been extracted from his brain and he hanged himself. We burned the body in the prison crematorium—

"Oh, come now." Yuin made a face at Rudi's petrified expression. "I would have set the old man free. Besides, I was beset by doubts: I wanted to create a new world—did I need to destroy the old one? But then I realized: the new mankind will start not from general changes in the collective conscious, but from a critical mass of the spirits that belong to a group of individuals—the bearers of the New Spirit!

"The acolytes must be gleaned from all over the world, and their spirits must be compressed in order to create a critical mass that would lead to an explosion—a Big Bang of sorts—that would send forth the waves of the New Conscious. It will not take much; the important point is that the explosion must take place in the right medium, open to the irradiation of the New Spirit. Now, this medium will be created by the Flood—the cataclysm of the earth's crust!

"Hence, stage four: due to the changes in the axis rotation, the world's oceans will flood the lowlands on all the continents, including eastern Siberia and the Far East. The Atlantic will pour into the Pacific through the Bering Straits. Farewell, my Heavenly Motherland!"

58

"NOW. I had to resolve the main question: will this mantra really affect the polar ice? According to the best specialist in esoteric history, the answer was right here, in Tibet! The books, or rather, tablets of Padmasambhava, written by ancient Indian *rishi,* the successors of Atlantean priests, and hidden during the persecution of Buddhism, were found in

Himalayan caves next to the remnants of fishes and marine animals. One of these books belonged to a certain professor of Buddhism named . . . can you guess? Michael Schechter. Alas, he did not communicate with his son, and they never had a chance to compare their information. A coincidence? Hardly. The Hand of God, as you're so fond of saying in the West.

"The book says that the priests of Atlantis destroyed their continent through magic—and what is a mantra?—when their civilization became fascinated with technology at the expense of mankind's final objective. They used the magic to accelerate the Flood, and then escaped; like Noahs, they sailed their arks in different directions, in order to re-create mankind on their Ararats.

"I realized that this describes our world as well. Look at the metastases of our civilization: genetic engineering, cloning, space travel, and the general collapse of morals. In my hand, I'm holding the scalpel to remove the tumor and lead mankind to a new race of angels . . . Please pay attention: stage five!"

As he proceeded to the next globe, he licked his lips nervously and even patted his brow with a handkerchief.

"Where were we? Ah yes: American Eastern Seaboard gone, Midwest—ditto. The Rockies still standing. Fleeing the Arctic cold, my countrymen head for India, where—surprise! It rains nonstop, no roads, no communications, no food, no medicine. By the way, I'm glad this will happen *after* the year 2000. People were getting ready for the Millennium—but now even the fiercest fanatics have relaxed. What an ambush! 'Beware, for ye shall not know when I return!' Ha! While they still try to figure it out by reading the stars! No"—Yuin chuckled at Rudi's expression—"I'm not Christ! Rather, I am the King of the Mongols that Nostradamus wrote about.

"In the coming apocalypse, the sources of energy—coal mines and oil fields—will be paralyzed. This should have happened long ago. Production of coal, gas, and oil is equivalent to vandalizing a cemetery. For millions of years, corpses of plants, animals, and humans have been turning into fuel, taking their karma deeper into the earth. But modern man dug it up and thus opened the Pandora's box."

Yuin passed to the next globe.

"And what about the pollution of world airwaves? You consider dumping physical garbage harmful yet you ignore the dumping of verbal garbage. I did not start the mantra; modern people—and I don't mean just the media and Internet—launch millions of destructive mantras a second. Ah, the words. Whatever created the problem must resolve it. If in the beginning was the Word—"

For the first time Rudi opened his mouth. "Perhaps the mantra affected the earth only because the people themselves were affected. The earth reacts to mass feelings. When paradise reigned in people's consciousness, the earth was a paradise, too. But it becomes hell as hell triumphs in people's minds."

"Bravo!" Yuin snapped his fingers. "I can indeed have a conversation with you. I agree: the New Consciousness always arrives via the Word. Before it came through Logos, or Christ. Now, through the Mantra."

59

"IN stage six, the South American pampas are flooded, and the south of the continent is made extinct by super-low temperatures. But"—Yuin shrugged—"who will miss the Hispanics? Although I did make good use of them at an early stage; they filled up the discos where Tune Ra was playing. . . .

"I had to resolve two problems. First, I had to spread the mantra and test it. Fate sent me Tune Ra, who at the time was called Frankie Mastromauro, a sometime DJ at a club in Jersey. He was visiting Nepal and decided to take a side trip to Tibet. Sure enough, our brave Customs agents busted him for possession of a couple of joints. When I was looking through the lists of the arrested—I do not shirk from my official duties, you know—I saw that he had stated *disk jockey* as his occupation. Something clicked."

As if to illustrate, Yuin cracked his fingers.

"I put him through Ruslanov's machine. I learned of his poverty, his overpowering thirst for fame, his talents, his fears . . ." Yuin chuckled, recalling the poor Frankie with electrodes on his head. "And then I realized: the mantra should be inserted into a tune. Let the people die through their own weakness.

"He was my first acolyte. It was here, at Rating, that the mantra debuted on the air: we used the antenna on Chokpori Hill. I made up a name for him, Tune Ra—sounded like *thun wra,* the old magic horn for mantra-throwing. I financed his career; I bought radio stations, recording studios, DJs from coast to coast. What is the media but today's pulpit? But the only priests who make it to the pulpit are the toughest scoundrels around, and I shall smite them with their own weapon.

"The mantra went on to conquer the world. I hired the best geophysicists and paid top dollar for their silence. They confirmed: the ice of Greenland was shifting! The shift was barely detectable by common sensors, and other scientists would consider it normal. But I already knew that Nagpa had good reasons to maintain silence! The mantra was working!"

Animated, Yuin paced faster.

"My second task was assembling a new group of priests, a Shambala ashram, who would declare themselves to the world after the catastrophe, who would lead the survivors to our objective. I had to gather those who would bring the people together into one spiritual essence.

"But how would I select them from among the sleeping terrestrials? What would lead them to battle? What would be the criterion for selection?

"And I realized: the answer was still the mantra.

"My acolytes should be the ones who would feel the mantra as more than a simple tune. For them, it would be the call of Shambala!

"I waited . . . soon, they came.

"They came here in a variety of ways. Most of them

could not even explain what drew them in the first place. They were of different ages, and came from different countries.

"My imprisoned lamas selected a place, a holy valley in the mountains, where I built my Shambala. Yes, there are rumors in the bazaar that I have a palace. The lamas also calculated that critical mass can be achieved with one hundred and eight followers. But first, let us hear about stage seven!"

60

"SO stage seven. The Sahara is at the bottom of the ocean, with the Atlas Mountains forming small islets, just like other mountains in the Middle East. Southern Siberia is all that's left of Russia, but it's warm, and the new Russians will live under the palm trees on the shores of the tropical Russian Sea. While the Japanese will end up on the North Pole. The new Santa will have narrow eyes!

"By the way: have you ever wondered why the main stations airing the mantra are in New York and other major cities? That's right: because these places have the highest concentration of antennas. These air hogs—not Greenland—have become the lever that cracked up the crust. These cities, the crowning achievements of your civilizations, will be the first ones to collapse, for they stand right on the fault line.

"The main problem mankind faces does not lie in interethnic conflicts or ecology or even genetic engineering. The main problem is that people do not have a clear understanding of the sense of their lives, of the raison d'etre for the earth itself. As the military and the spies are fond of saying, one must have a clear sense of the mission. By that I mean a coherent system of views that will replace the chaos in the minds of earthlings: genetics, Buddhism, capitalism, theosophy, UFOlogy, and so on. The madness caused by this chaos will soon destroy the earth without any mantra.

"In China, we have a saying, You cannot make a horse out of a hundred rabbits. The multiplying facts and ideas need to be melded into a new consciousness. We need the fire of the spirit, the effort of the will provided by the great prophets like Rama, Krishna, Moses, or Jesus. Now such fire can be introduced by us: the New Shambala."

"You're not the only one concerned about the sores of the modern world," Rudi said wearily. "But you propose to kill the patient instead of cutting them out."

"If the sores take up nine-tenths of the patient's body . . ." Yuin shrugged. "Have you ever been to Mexico, next door to your California? The slums of Rio? Africa? Calcutta? Inland China or Russia? Let me tell you, my friend: with the exception of a handful of white people, this world is rotting physically. While the white people are rotting in their souls. . . .

"But let us return to you. You, too, heard the call. You dreamed of it, of coming to Tibet, of finding a holy community and becoming a part of it, a cell in the throbbing heart of the new world. You dreamed of breaking free of New York and Gwen. This is why you showed up at DeoMorte. But when you arrived, you were already Number 109. You were the fifth wheel, an extra rock in the pyramid that can sometimes bring down the whole structure. Tune Ra followed instructions—a new arrival is too late—and ordered your removal.

"However, you killed Demis. That's right, you don't even know the name of the poor black man, my first and most devoted disciple. He was the first one I brought to my ashram, where he froze off his foot. He was a devotee, yet you managed to kill him. To me, this was a sign; I considered having you replace him. I flew to New York to investigate. I vetted each of one hundred and eight candidates personally. I bought your police file, I ordered a background investigation, and then I realized that you are not merely the last disciple. You're my double!"

61

"BUT first, for the grand finale. As the water level in the Mediterranean grows, the tsunami destroys every seaport. Storms and floods finish off the infrastructure. Farewell, arrogant Europe!

"That's what the Last Judgment is: a lithospheric catastrophe. The ground will stand on its rear legs, and its roar will be powerful enough to kill anyone who hears it. At the same time, the earth layers struggling upward will generate tremendous electric charges. The radon, imprisoned in rock, will break free, causing the radiation level to skyrocket.

"You will not recognize the map of the new world. Scandinavia, Spain, and Italy will be islands in the ocean. The equator will be somewhere in the Urals. Yet so many lands will enjoy warm climes! The polar radius will increase, along with the earth's rotation speed, while the days will grow shorter. The survivors will see a new land and a new sky: because the northerners will be living in the Southern Hemisphere, and vice versa.

"The prophecy will come true: the Iron Age and the Era of Nations will be gone completely. The survivors will be living in the true Kingdom of Heaven."

"And you'll be the one to decide who survives?"

Yuin shook his head. "You must understand: our race has accomplished its historical mission, and now must leave, in the same fashion as the ones that preceded it: by being cleansed with the Flood. Only the virtuous men who trust their instinct—like Noah—will be saved. We are the new Noahs. My ashram is the new Noah's Ark. And you can be my first mate!"

Rudi was not stirring. He caught himself; he was no longer able to distinguish his captor's maniacal fantasies from reality; he was no longer able to grasp his role in the general's plans. Perhaps he, Rudi, had been covered in blood all along. He had been the first mate, however unwittingly.

Yuin lowered himself in front of Rudi and took the young man's hand.

"You are more than my first mate: you're my doppelgänger. On the one hand, you're like the other Chosen. A typical specimen of your hemisphere, a former rocker and junkie, currently a politically correct Ivy Leaguer, a rational American.

"On the other hand, you're the only person in the world besides me who arrived at the mantra through your intelligence rather than through your spirit. You're my antipode double. I'm the typical specimen of the Orient. (That's right; contrary to what you think, I'm not trying to pass for a Brit.) I am a muckety-muck of a totalitarian system, a slit-eyed despot who denies all your 'moral values.' So perhaps fate has sent you to destroy my plan. Perhaps your mind would make a different use of my discovery.

"This is why I brought you here—do you understand? If I am wrong, you will find the Original Argument. Then I will stop airing the mantra, I'll launch the countermantra, which will put out the vibrations, and the ice will stop shifting—for now. Because one day it will shift by itself. I unearthed this brake in Nagpa's head, too; perhaps it is stored as a miracle, heh-heh, for the rather improbable eventuality of mankind atoning as one person. You know about it, which is why you came here. Unfortunately, by now *I* am the only one who knows it. If I am right and you fail to find the Original Argument, my doubts will be gone, and the new era will dawn here and now."

Yuin squatted in front of Rudi, looking at him expectantly.

Rudi's head was still spinning, refusing to accept what he had just heard. On the other hand, the nine globes fluorescing in the dark were analogous to the maps in Larry's lab.

"What is this Original Argument you are looking for?" he asked finally.

"In the beginning, there was the Word. I want to under-

stand why the Creator did what He did; I want to understand
His motivation. Then I will refrain from destroying the Creation by the same means with which it was created."

Overcome by a sense of unreality, Rudi peered into the
general's eyes, and his look ran into an opposing identical
look that was every bit as intent.

"Remember the fairy tales?" Yuin whispered. "All you
need is the magic word. Just whisper it; and I will crumble
down like Golem."

Yet, despite his mocking tone, Yuin was not joking. Nor
was he a maniac. But he was asking the kind of question
that not even a Brahmin could answer. And who, besides
Yuin himself, could say whether the explanation would be
convincing? Could he pass off his own doubts as God's?
But Rudi's life and millions of others were in the general's
hands. . . .

"If I win, then you—"

Yuin grinned. "Even if I cheat you, what do you stand
to lose? In a few weeks—if you don't find the argument,
that is—you will be gone anyway, along with your world.
You still disbelieve me? As I said, you have nothing to lose.
Consider: currently you are under arrest for illegally entering the People's Republic of China. You have no passport.
You are involved in the bombing of the karaoke bar outside
Johang, the explosion at Namtso Utse, and conspiring to
kidnap General Yuin. So, even if you don't believe in the
Flood, I can still sentence you to fifty years in prison. Or I
could deport you. Take your pick: Russia? You're the main
suspect in the bombing of Ruslanov's lab and a series of
suspicious arson accidents. The U.S.? The list goes on and
on. See, you stand to lose nothing by venturing an argument. But if you lose, our minds will merge—and you will
join our ashram."

"What if I don't want to join?"

"You'll still gain. Weren't you looking for an acquittal,
but not by a jury—by your own conscience—for all the
deaths you had caused? I'll provide you with arguments for
your defense . . . Or prosecution."

62

YUIN sent Rudi back to the cell to bone up for the "debate." Rudi was so shocked by what he had heard that he could barely walk. All he wanted to do was to drop on the bunk and sleep; perhaps sleep would bring a plan of action, he thought.

The cell was a cement pen, cold, dark, and narrow. When Rudi was shoved in, a familiar voice came from one of the three benches: "I need a doctor, motherfucker!"

The moment the door clanged shut, Rudi leapt to the bench to hug the speaker's black shaven head.

With a groan, Rivers pushed him away. His head—his entire body—was covered with bruises.

Barely had Rudi left Martin and the Tigers near the burial rock when they were surrounded by the Chinese. Martin was sure they had been watched all along.

Some of the Tigers were shot on the spot, while others, including the family of the deceased and Mamatri, who was wounded while trying to escape, were beaten and brought to Rating.

"But what about your diplomatic passport?"

Martin glanced into the corner. There was another prisoner, whom Rudi had not noticed at first. His eyes were closed, and he was perfectly immobile, so that, his black jacket merging into the wall, his corner seemed empty. In the dim light, his young face was bedraggled but tranquil.

"He must be a lama," Martin whisperred in response to Rudi's mute question. "On the other hand, everybody gets their heads shaven here. You'll get yours, too. I tried to talk to him, but he doesn't move. Must be meditating."

"Could be. But what about your passport?"

"Oh, they spotted a forgery right away. The colonel with the glasses? The guard commander? He showed me a fax from the embassy: no diplomat named Martin Rivers listed. Nyima sold us out. They must have tailed us since the karaoke bar."

"Much earlier," Rudi said. "Try DeoMorte."

RUDI sat next to Martin, their bodies pressed to each other, side by side, to keep warm, as he filled his friend in on the story: the healer, the call to Larry, the imminent cataclysm, and its architect—the anonymous voice on the phone.

"Do you remember when you were taking me to the airport and we were crossing Harlem? You were talking about the explosion at the bottom of society? Well, it's the bottom all right—but miles deeper."

"Then it's like Chinese water torture," Martin concluded gloomily. "Dripping on a person's mind until he blows up."

"Right. Just imagine the earth has the same composition as a human being: body, skin, hair, internal organs—the magma—and the invisible ones, like the soul. And then there are glands—the energy centers. Two of them are poles. Like, the North Pole is the top of your head, the lotus, the intelligence center. The South Pole is your coccyx, the knot of the life force. From time to time, they shift to the equator. Your reason descends into your heart, making it wise, while your instinct rises, and the man—that is, the earth—begins to love rather than desire. There comes the harmony—the New Mankind."

"You sound like you're approving of this nutcake."

"No! These things must come in their own good time. But Yuin is jumping the gun. And the trigger is the mantra."

Martin nodded. "I've seen it happen: a word can drive you berserk."

"But it takes a word to calm you down, too. If Nagpa was alive, we could learn the countermantra. But now, Yuin is the only one who knows it."

RUDI told his friend of Yuin's proposal of debate, leaving out the offer to join the ashram. He did not want Martin even to suspect that he was on the side of "the nutcake."

"Keep debating him," Martin advised. "Stalling is a prisoner's only tactic."

They heard the guards shouting and pots clanging outside: it was dinnertime. Their cellmate came out of his trance and introduced himself, smiling, "Dorje." Otherwise, he remained incommunicado. He did not appear to understand English or Rudi's pigeon Tibetan.

The dinner arrived: bowls of malodorous hot barley gruel. The colonel with the glasses stopped by, too. At his arrival, Dorje shot up to attention. Rudi struggled up, too, but Martin stayed prone. Grinning maliciously, the colonel splashed gruel in Martin's face. With a holler, he leapt up; the colonel grabbed him by the throat and forced his arm behind his back.

"Did you burn yourself? We put on cold, yes?"

He dragged Martin into the corner and dipped his face into the bucket that served as a toilet. "Maybe in America when boss comes in, you don't get up. In Rating you get up!"

Before he left, he said to Rudi, "Get ready for a wash. They take you to general now."

Martin lay on the floor, holding on to his scalded face and moaning. Suddenly, they heard chanting. Dorje had climbed on his bench and, rocking imperceptibly, was reciting mantras. A moment later, Martin stopped moaning and took his hands off his face.

"Feeling better?" Rudi asked, his mouth agape.

"It's gone."

They stared at the monk. Dorje opened his eyes and smiled.

"Mantra natsha chaya-kiy men?" Rudi asked. *Mantra, she kill pain?*

Dorje nodded happily.

"Kairang lungba kaney yin?" Rudi insisted, trying to find out what sect Dorje belonged to. *"Geluk? Kagyu?"*

"Bon Po." Dorje bowed, lay down, and turned to the wall.

"DO you understand?" Rudi turned to Martin, his eyes flashing. "We've got us a real Bon lama!"

"I'll take a cake of soap instead," Martin grumbled, wiping the gruel. "Try to steal one when they take you to the wash."

"What do they do at the wash?"

"Shave your head, take your personal effects, down to your underwear, give you these rags instead."

"They take everything?" Rudi mechanically reached to his pocket. "Diary, too?"

"You bet. Might as well eat it up. Or tear it up and dunk it in the bucket."

Rudi took out his notebook and paused over the smelly bucket. Then he went back to the bench and started writing feverishly. "I'll just make the last entry, and after that they can have it. Maybe some deep-sea diver will find it after the Flood."

63

HE was eventually taken to the shower room, which looked like a combination of an underground garage and a circle of hell, with disinfectant smells, clouds of steam, bedraggled shadows, and guards shouting. Even the soap came in a smelly brown lump, too large to be smuggled back to the cell.

Then he was shoved in a barber chair, and watched his blond locks join the dark cuttings of his predecessors on the dirty cement floor. They kept his personal belongings—the only thing he was allowed were Schechter's beads—and issued him a black robe. Then, through a maze of flights of stairs he was led to his first interrogation—what Yuin called a "debate." Martin called it a warm-up act. To Rudi, it was torture, plain and simple.

The "debates" went on for two weeks, or perhaps longer. . . .

NOW. as his cellmates went to sleep, Rudi stayed up, waiting for the guard commander to take him to the general. But this time Yuin came in person.

He sat down on the bench next to Rudi. For a while they eyed each other in silence.

"You haven't found the Original Argument," Yuin said finally. "The mantra has another twenty days to go. To-morrow, I'm leaving for my ashram for the last prepara-tions. I'm not coming back. I'll have to become Number 108 myself. You'll drown here, like a rat. It's a pity. I've grown quite fond of you. But you failed to find the argu-ment against my plan, and you still refuse to accept it—or, perhaps, you've changed your mind?"

Rudi stared back silently. In the weeks of torture, his hatred of Yuin had solidified to the extent where it ceased to be a mere emotion; instead, it had turned into a block of cement, solid like the blocks that made up the floor.

"You haven't recovered from our last debate yet?" Yuin chuckled. "Or you just don't want to talk to me—you've crossed me off the roster of humans? Too bad. I do want you to save both them and yourself. Here's your last chance. The argument is right here." He held up a small orange-covered book.

Rudi recognized his diary.

"I read it," Yuin said. "To my great astonishment, the argument is right here. Aha! Finally, a spark of disbelief in your face—a step up from the dull hatred you've been dis-playing recently. I'm telling you the truth: the argument is right here. But you must find it yourself. Here's your last chance. You've got till morning."

Rudi glanced at the diary extended to him; then, without accepting it, at Yuin.

"You don't want to take it?" The latter grinned. "You prefer to drown along with the rest of humanity? I under-stand. But I'm disappointed, too, in your Western analytical mind. Are you really giving up on finding an answer, even with a little prompt from me? No *Eureka*, no leaping up with joy? Will you indeed peer blindly into your own diary with-out seeing it? In that case, you and your world are indeed hopeless, and no one will miss them."

Yuin peered in Rudi's face, trying to find a foothold, a break in the cement. Then he frowned. "All right. Let us raise the ante. You will not have to wait for the Flood.

Unless you find the argument or agree to follow me in the morning, you and your Negro pal—are you lovers, by any chance?—will die in the morning. I'll make sure that your death will be much harsher than the Flood and totally devoid of any spiritual content."

Yuin tossed the diary on the bench and headed for the exit. In the doorway, he paused. "How odd. The argument came up in our debates. You just never noticed it."

RUDI shifted closer to the dim light of the lamp. At first, he read slowly, pausing and staring at the darkness outside for long periods of time. As the moon shifted, too, spraying its metallic sheen across the slopes of the mountain, he leafed faster. By the time they changed the guards in the hall, he finished his last entry, made on his first day at Rating.

The diary did not contain a single thought that he had not voiced during his "debates." The general was lying. The thought of dying brought about nausea and cold sweat. He closed his eyes, but this heightened the feeling of horror. He had to wake up his friends.

Motionless, Dorje was in the corner. Rivers was snoring rhythmically. They had agreed they would try to end their lives on their own terms before the execution. Martin promised he would break Rudi's neck—the way he had been taught at the FBI academy—and then his own.

Now it seemed like the moment for Martin to recall his skills. Yet Rudi hesitated. The soiled floor shimmered in the moonlight, and the shadows of the bars across it seemed like a Chinese hieroglyph. Neither the stars nor the moon knew they were shining into a jail cell; they were calm, peaceful, dispassionate.

That's just life itself treating our suffering: calmly and dispassionately, Rudi thought. His eyes became teary from staring at the lamp. The world blurred, filling with rainbow-like circles. That's the real thing, Rudi thought, open only to those who view the world through a lens of compassion.

Drawing on what was left of his determination, he woke up Martin to tell him of the morning execution. "I had a chance to save us . . . but I couldn't."

"Come on, kid." Martin patted Rudi's arm. His hand was large and warm. "Don't torment yourself. The guy's a psycho."

"Let's do it." Rudi turned his back on Martin and got on his knees.

Martin sighed and wiped his hands on his pants. Rudi's stomach was getting weak; he fought to keep himself from dashing to the toilet bucket. Finally, he felt Martin's hand on his ear, and the other one under his chin.

"Don't be afraid, baby." Martin patted Rudi's cheek, wet with tears. But his hands, too, grew moist and trembling. He tried to take them away, but Rudi grabbed them and would not let go.

"I'm not afraid, Marty. I just wish . . . I have never been either hot or cold; I just lingered on the doorstep. I have never really pushed the envelope. And now the door has been slammed shut on me."

"At least you've been halfway there," Martin responded. "I'm just sitting here in my own shit."

They chuckled about this last-minute confession. Rudi stopped trembling. "Come on, buddy." He kissed Martin's hand and let it go. "Just do it, right?" He felt the pressure from Martin's hands and closed his eyes.

"Guro-nang!" Dorje cried out. "Wait!"

Rudi opened his eyes.

"Sonuvabitch always pretends he's asleep." Martin glared at the monk.

"Nagpa's alive," Dorje whispered. "I wanted to kill myself, too, so Yuin not torment anymore, but Rinpoche would not let me. Just now he sent me message on the wind. He helps us escape."

Book Four

TIBET

RUDRA'S DIARY

64

I was writing these lines at dawn two days later, in a stone shed in a nameless valley. None of what had happened to me in Rating, none of what I was entering in the diary, could be true, I thought; they were episodes in a nightmare that I needed to awaken from. And the only way to do it was to recall as much detail as I could.

ACCORDING to Dorje, his teacher, while meditating in the cell, had turned into a *jalus,* a rainbow body, and disappeared from Rating. He materialized in a faraway cave monastery on the Indian border. Yuin spread the rumor that Nagpa had killed himself and his body was burned in the prison crematorium. He even burned the body of another prisoner. But none of this could fool Dorje.

"If Nagpa wants to die, he doesn't need a noose. He just sits down and dies."

Also, Dorje claimed, he was in touch with Nagpa through "messages in the wind," or telepathically.

Martin was skeptical, as befits an NYPD cop, regardless of location. But I had doubts, too. True, ancient Tibetan magi were said to have teleported themselves; but in this case it could well have been self-suggestion on Dorje's part. Or was he communicating with the spirit of the dead?

"Why didn't you tell us before?" Martin was still holding my head.

"The teacher was studying you."

His intonation was so convincingly sincere that for a split second Martin's fingers loosened their grip.

"So how will he help us escape?"

"I will have to begin reciting a mantra."

Dorje asked me for my beads—his own had been confiscated—and began to finger them while chanting quietly.

Martin shrugged and let my head go.

Bereft of all hope, we waited in the dark, our ears pricked up for the guard's steps outside. What if Yuin decided to take us out for execution before the regular wake-up?

Yet our vigilance was short-lived. It was past four in the morning, the light gone, the moon all but disappeared behind the watchtowers. The cell was pitch-dark, the lama's incantation was soporific, and we dozed off, leaning against each other.

I was dreaming that I was leafing through my diary once again, but all the pages were black. In vain I looked for at least one spot of white—

"Hey!"

Nothing but blackness—

"Look!" Martin nudged me hard.

I opened my eyes and grew numb.

A garland was shimmering in the moonlight in Dorje's corner. We came closer. Dorje kept chanting, going through the beads carefully . . . but they were no longer beads—they were a shiny necklace! The only reminder of our humble past was an orange thread that connected the beads.

"*Diy su rei?*" I whispered, touching Dorje's knee. *Who is it?*

The monk opened his eyes. "Dorje."

"No: who is it?" Realizing I could not remember the Tibetan for *what,* I touched the large transparent beads.

"Dorje," the lama repeated, still smiling.

Now it dawned on me: *dor ge*—a diamond. He had turned the bone beads into a diamond necklace. "How did you do it?"

"Nagpa." The monk bowed into the darkness. *"Tu."*

Yes, this time it was *tu*—the occult force.

I kept fingering the cold sparkling pieces, still unable to believe in their reality. Even Martin was convinced, after he tried biting on one. "Shit. That's real rocks, man. What now?"

Dorje pointed at the door. *"Mig-shey."*

The glasses. He meant the commanding guard.

Martin pulled Dorje by the ears and bussed his shaven head.

*   *   *

THE colonel's greed lived up to our expectations. He even took off his black-framed glasses, revealing narrow slits of eyes without eyelashes, in order to take a good look at the gems.

"I knew you'd be hiding beads! What kind of a monk without beads!"

Martin tried to take the diamonds back, but the colonel's fist was clenched tightly. Martin grinned. "General Yuin will be up in a few hours. He'll be happy to learn of your acquisition. But you can keep them if you take us outside."

The officer did not hesitate long. He would not arouse suspicion: he often took prisoners out on work detail.

HALF an hour later, to the guards' delighted laughter, the colonel shoved the three prisoners into his jeep outside the prison gate.

"I told them I'm going to shoot you," the colonel said, chuckling. "Maybe I will, heh?"

The driver turned on the siren and raced across nighttime Lhasa. Still incredulous about the release, I devoured the rare streetlights with my eyes. The colonel roared in delight, peeking into his coat sleeve every few minutes, just as incredulous of his fortune. Dorje was silent, his eyes half-shut, seemingly oblivious to his surroundings.

Soon we were speeding on a deserted highway.

"Are we going to the airport—Gonggar?" Martin asked.

"I am!" The colonel slapped his knee. "In one hour, flight to Katmandu!"

"So take us with you!"

"You're dreaming!"

"But you won't get through the passport check. We'll take you to the American consul—he'll give you asylum—a ticket to the U.S.—"

"I can buy my own fucking asylum! Wherever I want!"

The highway began climbing into the mountains, not a person or a vehicle in sight. The colonel told the driver to stop. "It's a thousand miles to Nepal! You can make it! Black people can run fast—I watched the Olympics!"

"You fuckhead—" Martin cursed.

The colonel drew his gun. "Say thank you, nigger."

Martin swallowed. "Thank you."

But the colonel had already waved to the driver. When you're on the cusp of the life of a Hong Kong millionaire, why care about the ingratitude of a stupid American.

"Here!" He tossed Martin's knife—his gift to Rudi—out of the window. "I can't take it on the plane anyway! You can fight among you who dies first!"

"What do we do now?" I asked.

"Catch a ride." Martin was still seething. "We've got a couple of hours."

Dorje shook his head. "We run to mountains now." He waved into the darkness. *"Mik-shei gyok-po tshu-logpa."*

"Why is the Glasses coming back soon?"

"Mala yidam," the monk said.

"Mala yidam," I echoed. What?

Yidam was a suggested object! The diamondness of the beads was a suggestion—hypnosis! The beads remained made of bone, but people saw them as diamonds as long as the person who generated the image kept maintaining the illusion. Dorje must have sensed that he—or Nagpa—could not or would not continue focusing.

"Run!" I pushed Martin along. "Our friend's holding nothing but pieces of bone in his hands!"

We started climbing, cutting our hands. We crawled behind the crag that hid us from the highway and dropped, exhausted, on the hoary rocks. Immediately, the red-and-yellow reflections of the revolving lights on the colonel's car came into view, and in a second the car itself roared by—back to Lhasa.

"Running off to confess . . . In another half hour they're gonna block all the roads," Martin gasped. He glanced at Dorje, and his expression grew into a smile filled with awe. "You son of a bitch. I always said: can't trust an Asian."

65

WE halted the climb to catch our breath and took a farewell glance at the sparse lights of Lhasa and the huge Potala, a moonlit white boat in the black waves of the mountains.

Tibetans believe, I recalled, that the round towers along its perimeter are the wings that will fly Potala away from the Flood. A catastrophe of one era becomes a fairy tale for the next.

"Enough slacking!" Martin commanded. "What are you grinning about?"

"It's ironic that I'm fleeing Yuin, rather than the Flood." I wheezed, keeping up the pace. "The end of reason is more terrible than the end of the world. Because the end of the world is actually a beginning of a different reason that is being shed on everything, even if it's done with the Flood. Can you imagine how in the next world we will see the usefulness of what happened to us at Rating?"

Martin shrugged. "Sounds to me like your reason is already gone. Come on, step lively."

BEFORE dawn, we had to get as far away from the highway as possible. We climbed down one mountain and then had to start up the next one immediately. Overcome with altitude sickness, I was running out of breath; my head ached, as if filled with lead; I kept stumbling and pausing to rest. Each time was harder than the previous one, and I wondered whether I would be able to keep going.

"White boy!" Martin hissed at me, though himself barely breathing. "You're gonna get to the breakdown point—then what? Sambo will carry you?"

"Not yet," I gasped. "I know where my breakdown point is."

"And?"

"When we see Nagpa." I nodded at Dorje, whose brisk walk suggested a promenade at sea level.

Three hours later, I collapsed. Martin lowered himself to the ground next to me. Dorje paused, too, and sat down quietly. There was nothing around us but silence and darkness.

Still, better to die here of altitude sickness, I thought, listening to the heartbeat shattering my rib cage, than from torture at Rating. I found solace in knowing that it was earth under my body—cold and rock-hard, but still better than the stinking cement of that cell. I had an absurd feeling that somehow the earth would save me: it would open up and hide me from the Chinese.

"Which way?" I asked Dorje, rising to resume the journey.

"Tell him we have to make sure we're not going in circles," Martin muttered.

After a pause, Dorje declared: "*Shar-gya.* Straight."

AT forks in the road, I thought, you must be like Dorje, who relied on his instinct. Calm down, refill yourself with beauty—and the choice will be made for you. Instinctively, I looked up at the stars—something I had been denied in Rating. Oddly, the view reminded me of an old screen saver, a black background with flickering white points, on my computer back in New York. Once, as I stared at the screen after hours of burning the midnight oil, I thought that the starry sky was a symbol of life: one light is born while another goes out. If you go back to the light, you will find darkness. And where there was darkness, there is suddenly a light. We chase freedom the way we chase this light, and this is wrong. Perhaps this was what I was really afraid of: failing to find freedom where I thought I would find it. Freedom should be obtained by contemplation in place; yet we keep running. . . .

THE second wind died fast. At the next slope, I realized we had traded an instant death in Rating for a slow one in the mountains. A mere four hours out of Lhasa, the landscape became positively lunar, without a hint of man's existence.

Around us were wide-ranging rock floes and refrigerator-like cold; the air was like steaming dry ice removed from the freezer. In anticipation of dawn, the sky turned a tender green, with milky pale stars across. The sun was bound to show up any minute. To us, it meant both warmth and death.

Once it became light, Yuin would send out the helicopters and cut off all the roads and the passes. The only way to escape detection was to find a cave and hide out till dark.

I could not go on. Under the gusts of wind, tears flowed out of my eyes and froze on my cheeks; stuck in my pockets, my hands were numb, along with my nose—my ears—my cheeks . . . I felt no pain as I kicked the rock with my rough prisoner boot. The cold penetrated the marrow of my bone; my insides were lined with an icy stucco, and it seemed to me that with every step, my frozen parts would start falling off.

Once again, I fell and could not get up.

"Get up." Martin crouched next to me, breathing heavily.

"I can't. You've got to break my neck now."

"I can't. My hands are frozen. You remember what Yuin does to the escapees he catches?"

A cheerful smile played on the general's face when I was brought in for his first interrogation.

"Look—a shaven head and a black robe really become you! You're a monk in a real Tibetan monastery, Rating-gompa! Your dream has come true, Rudi. . . . Don't be surprised: I know a lot about you. But be patient. Let me show you something first."

The inmates were lined up in the courtyard. A man lay in the middle, his limbs tied to four jeeps pointed outwards. He was a guerrilla from Mamatri's unit: the one who'd poured out the food at the burial site.

"This is what we do to those who try to escape," Yuin said without expression.

The drivers started their engines, and the prisoner screamed. Even before the cars had moved an inch, his soul was already on its way out, scratching his insides and uttering the unbearable inhuman howl.

The drivers were experienced, and the jeeps moved imperceptibly, an inch a minute. While the guerrilla kept screaming, Yuin whispered in my ear:

"It is yourself you see stretched out on the ground. . . . You're the one suspended between passion, compassion, money, wisdom—there is an infinite number of cars, and, as long as you breathe, your every brain cell screams out in torment. The history of the world is the history of torment handed out by God in the name of ecstasy of pain and enlightenment. When you know it's the end, your scream of despair changes into one of ecstasy. . . ."

Finally, Yuin waved, the cars roared forward, and the inmates along the perimeter trembled and then froze from the final scream.

"But mostly, it's this silence . . ." Yuin whispered again.

The engines died, and the cars stopped, bloody mess hanging from their ropes. The resulting silence was something from outer space—

"I can't cut the ropes for everybody," Yuin went on, his voice empty of sentiment. "I can be generous enough to turn on the gas and liberate humanity with fanfare, volcanoes spouting the lava of blood. But you—I can help cut off your ropes from this world. At first you'll feel like a stump. Then you'll feel like a vacuum. Which means, you'll be whole."

DORJE squatted next to me. "Afraid your feet-hands?"

I nodded.

"Is your name foot-hand?"

"*Mindu.* No."

"Is your name head?"

"No."

"Stomach?"

"No."

With a patiently serious expression, Dorje patted me down. "What's your name? Where are you?" And I giggled. Behind him was the sky, icy and empty.

Somehow I rose and, holding on to Dorje, stumbled on. Just as we climbed another hill, the monk pushed us down.

A dirt road wove its way below. At the turn was a small white house with a stone fence and barbed wire. A red star was visible on the green gate. Gray smoke billowed from the chimney.

It was a Chinese guard house. There were people, and they had to be warm.

"Gyabla," Dorje whispered. "Back." He tugged Martin by the sleeve, indicating they had to crawl back and pick a different route.

"No way, Jose. I can't stand cold too good, man." Martin's cracked lips moved slowly. "I am from Africa. You've got to respect your roots, man. *Shar-gya.* Full speed. Wait here."

WE did not have time to stop him. He walked up to the house without crouching or trying to hide, and Dorje murmured the mantra, trying to keep pace with Martin. Behind the gate, a dog barked, first warily, then wilder, scratching its claws on the metal of the gate. Martin lay down and covered his head. Dorje chanted faster.

The gate opened, and a German shepherd leapt forward, its jaws clenching the sleeve of Martin's jacket. Dorje chanted as fast and loud as he could.

A soldier in a green overcoat came out, yawning and scratching; he had clearly spent the night in his coat and was not yet quite awake. He barked an order to the dog and tapped it with the bayonet of his automatic rifle. Growling, the dog stepped back.

The soldier addressed Martin, but the American did not move. The Chinese stuck the barrel at his head and yelled. Still, no movement. The soldier slung the weapon over his shoulder and leaned forward.

Martin was so fast that even the dog did not move. He swung the guard around and gripped his head from the back. The crack of the neck made a crisp sound in the morning silence. Dorje trembled and fell silent.

The dog leapt at Martin. He hid behind the dead man's body and tore off the automatic. At the next leap, the dog was met with the bayonet.

Rivers waved to us and disappeared behind the gate.

*   *   *

INSIDE, the tiny room was dark save for the kerosene lamp. The stove cast a reddish glow in the corner. Before I could melt from the heavenly warmth, Martin yelled, "Tie them up!" He pointed his automatic at the three Chinese soldiers crouching in the corner.

"What shall I tie them with?" I murmured, fighting the impulse to drop on the floor and embrace the stove. The Chinese already seemed to be paralyzed with fear.

"Take their belts off!"

My hands still numb with cold, I fumbled with the pants of a pimply Chinese teenager in uniform. The soldier's pants fell down, and he screamed in fear.

"Shut the fuck up!" I yelled, but the kid bawled even louder.

Martin smashed the stock of the gun in his face. The blood shot up in a geyser. The two other soldiers stared in numb fear as I tied them up, trying to remember the knots I had not used in years. The older one exuded a sharp odor of urine.

Finally, the prisoners were stacked against the wall, and we collapsed at the stove. Cursing and crying, Martin held his hands to the scalding surface. I clenched my teeth as I felt the pain of life returning to my limbs. Only after our toes thawed off a little, we realized that Dorje was not in the room.

WE found him outside, whispering into the dead guard's ear.

"He's dead!" Martin shouted. "You dumb fuck."

"He's reading Bardo," I ventured a guess. "Leading the deceased towards a better reincarnation."

"What does he need with that?"

"Maybe we need it more than he does. He needs to be helped either not to be reborn, or to find a good reincarnation. So that in the next life he doesn't break your neck. Or that he isn't reborn a dog who would tear you into pieces."

66

HOWEVER tempting, the guardhouse was not a safe place. After a day's rest, we equipped ourselves with food, clothes, and weapons, and left for the mountains.

As we were leaving the guardhouse, Martin and Dorje got into a fight. The monk tried to loosen the prisoners' ropes. "If it's too tight, they might lose their hands," he explained. "What you do will come back to you."

"Are you crazy?" Martin pushed him away. "Did they take care of me?"

"Maybe you hurt innocent in your previous life. Or in this one."

"Shut your mouth!"

I caught Martin's hand before he struck the lama. "Dorje saved you."

Martin stormed out in a huff.

Things work in chains, I later wrote in my diary. First, I was tied; then, I had to do the tying. The colonel hit Martin in the face; now Martin would have hit the monk. I squatted near one of the Chinese soldiers to loosen his ropes, and when he realized I was not going to kill him, he began to cry.

AFTER an all-night march, by dawn Dorje spotted a cave cut into the slope. We barely had a chance to explore our new shelter when the roar of the helicopters came from behind the mountain.

The cave was as cold as the outside, but at least there was no wind. We bundled ourselves into the long army overcoats and settled for a night's sleep.

AFTER the four-jeep execution, I could not move. A guard had to drag me to Yuin's office.

The general followed with a dispassionate expression. In the office, he indicated that I should sit down. The iron stool must have been designed with jail in mind, for its rough edges cut into my flesh. But I was too exhausted to pay attention. The guard drew my arms behind my back and locked the handcuffs to the stool.

The general took his favorite seat, next to the water globe. He gave it a light spin, and the water came into motion, flooding the familiar contours of continents. In the light of the lamp that represented the sun, the shadow of the general's head was like Atlantis emerging from the ocean.

"The turn in the earth's crust is a turn in your brain," Yuin said. "Do not be afraid to turn your conscious. Let your peaks, your ideals, become flooded; let the mysterious continents of your subconscious come to light. God wants the man's different sides to trade places, until they all become equal. Why did you kill the black man?" He turned abruptly.

"I didn't kill him. It was an accident. I wanted to trade places with him."

Yuin frowned. "You know there's no such thing as an accident. Why did you want to trade places with him?"

"He was chanting a mantra that would have made me fall under the train."

"That's just the outside. A man is a libertine who hires thoughts like whores to massage his ego—his soul. The difference between noble and lowly thoughts is one between a pricey call girl and a drug-ravaged street hooker. But a pure soul needs no whores; it chooses the emptiness of no-mind. . . . Remember what you thought about in New York? Let me remind you."

He rose to face me, his arms crossed on his chest.

"Perhaps you could no longer stand the mantra of the metropolis—the vibes of a culture grounded in competition. Perhaps you wanted to trade places with an outsider. Hence your dreams of an ashram, Tibet, monastery." He caught my look of surprise. "I read a few pages from your diary. But, perhaps, this desire to trade coexisted with the subconscious fear of becoming a bum that is common to all law-abiding citizens.

"Or were you trying to escape your racial karma? If so,

you failed: once again, the white man killed the black one. The karma includes repetition. The victim avenges himself by re-becoming the victim, again and again, condemning the guilty party to a circle of guilt.

"The neo-Nazis are off the mark when they talk of the impending black revolt. When the Flood comes, Africa will be a logical place for the whites to escape to and form the United States of Africa. Your much-vaunted civilization will collapse when your cultured countrymen start bidding for seats on every ship and boat across the ocean. And then they'll fight one another tooth and claw for the remainder. . . ."

MY writing was interrupted by Martin, who went for a leak outside and now could not go back to sleep. He was still bitter about being unable to account for the miracle with the beads.

"These lamas are well-trained bastards," he mused. "Has to be the climate; good for this telepathy business. You think a thousand times: should I climb this glacier to send a message or should I just think hard about it? One thing I don't get: if they're such tough psychics, how come they can't get rid of the Chinese?"

I reflected on this paradox, but by the time I felt I had an answer, Martin was snoring away.

Perhaps they have been granted these powers for divine purposes, I wrote. *And then they are sparing with these powers for their own personal purposes. God has no divine interest; there's only common good. In the same way, lamas pray to end suffering for every living creature, instead of for a victory of Buddhism over Communism and recovery of Buddhist statehood. If the need arises, the victory will come back by itself. . . .*

"SO what kind of conclusion should be drawn?" Yuin asked, to wrap up his trading-places theory.

"It seems that an attempt to force trading places leads to the death of one party and eternal guilt for the other. So why do you insist on forcing a new Flood? It will happen of its own accord. Perhaps the new civilization should be born of those who survived by accident. How do you know the proper balance between applying one's will and letting go?"

The general smiled thinly. He unlocked my cuffs and motioned me to take a look at the globe.

I attempted to get up—and instantly collapsed on the floor.

I did not feel my legs.

I felt as if, instead of legs, I had two scraps of paper below my waist. It seemed that the jail stool was designed to apply pressure to certain points in one's body, which would result in paralysis.

Yuin sat down next to me. "The earth and the spirit of mankind have gone dead from staying in the same position; we should stretch them a bit. As for 'letting go' . . . Moses could wait for the natural end of slavery, too. Yet he heeded God's will and, using violence, he took the Chosen to freedom. Why not do the same? Like Moses, I forge noble spirits. I lead them to the desert: hunger, poverty, the physical pain of the Himalayan ashram—they are all gates to freedom.

"In the subway, you were afraid to enter. It was not a gimpy black man you pushed away: you pushed away spiritual freedom. The first thing this freedom brings is not a rose of bliss, but misery; this freedom is ragged and stinking, like that homeless man, and places your body in peril. You, too, were afraid for your body. Even now, as I tell you to walk—with your spirit, not your body—you can't. Your spirit is numb, it has gone to sleep, and, despite your efforts, you cannot stand on your legs of spirit. Your spirit has been choked by the straps of your ego. I'll help you get up and follow me and enter the gate right here."

He called for the guards to take his prisoner back to the cell.

THE cell was empty: Martin and Dorje had been taken to work duty. For a long time, I lay on the floor, waiting for the painful sensation to come back to my legs. In my eyes, the cell was upside down.

As a baby comes out of the womb, it sees the world in a vertical reverse, and so does a dying man in his last moments. The circle closes. Perhaps their view is the true one, and it is we the living who see the world upside down.

67

FROM the cave, we can see helicopters over the mountains and army trucks in the valley. They are hunting us like animals, to be shot on the spot or tossed back into the cage. We are afraid to start a fire lest they spot the smoke. Brimming with fury, Martin threatens to tear apart every Chinese in sight. By contrast, Dorje does not seem to hate them. In my previous lives, he says, I preyed on someone, too.

Weren't you always a lama?

Not always . . . I might have chased someone in my mind.

I suspect that Dorje sees the Chinese as his own mirror image: a pursuing army of thoughts, each capable of throwing you in jail, of torturing and killing you.

It is better to perish in the cave, with a wide view of the mountains. The chances of reaching our destination are slim. Dorje does not seem to know the way too well; Nagpa will get us there, he says. Nagpa lives in a cave monastery somewhere close to the Indian border. The nearest border with India is almost a thousand miles away. The mantra has less than two weeks to go; there's not enough time.

The cold does not let us sleep. We rub one another's hands. Just to think that I used to dream of fleeing the Upper West Side and settling in a cave in Tibet, where I would be singing songs à la Milarepa! I would gladly trade his whole repertory for a hot shower and the safety of my tiny studio on 100th Street.

IT takes the moon only a few minutes to soar over the mountains. First, its pink rim shows up—it is as if the dark slope got singed. Then you see a section of a saffron tangerine, which turns into a half of an ocher Vidalia onion. The moonball rose, wobbling, on the slope, and then broke away from it. The blue strip between the ball and the mountain widened, and soon the moon shone in the crystal-clear black sky, like a diamond on the black velvet in a jewelry box.

Dispassionately, the moon has witnessed eruptions, floods, collapsing civilizations—not one of them has altered her shining state.

Time to go, Dorje says. Until we put enough distance between Lhasa and us, we can move only by night.

MARTIN was the first to leave the cave. He tripped and tumbled down the slope. Luckily, his fall was stopped by a rock. He cursed out loud as he got up. Dorje hushed him: any loud sound would be reported to the Chinese for a bribe by shepherds or nomads in the area . . . Man is more dangerous than nature.

The backpacks are heavy, forcing us to stop often. We can't start a fire, either. At stops, Martin stretches on the rocks and nods towards the sitting Dorje: "If they can reach heaven by sheer willpower, why do they put up with all this torment here?"

I give him the textbook version: "Like your Marines, they have a clear understanding of their mission: people are sent into the darkness of the world to bring enlightenment."

"Lights make good targets," Martin said.

He has a point.

THE moonlit plateau is dusty, cold, and covered with sheets of granite. A mix of the Sahara and the Arctic; or, perhaps, the bottom of a mountainous Atlantis—a silent silvery ocean, petrified long ago. Now I understand why the concept of Emptiness is specific to Tibet: a territory larger than Europe populated by a mere four million people. It takes days of travel to go from village to village. You feel like a wood chip in an ocean, except that instead of seasickness you suffer from altitude: dizziness, slowness of movement, and shortage of air. And yet it's so much better here than in the stifling Chinese jail. Still, I have to remember all that was said there. Yuin said that we had used the argument in the course of the debate. Could I have missed my chance?

THE second interrogation took place at night. When I arrived, Yuin stood at the window, eyeing the moon, as bright as on the night of our escape.

"Do you remember the vow of Boddhisattva?" he asked without turning. "All will turn to nothing: me, the moon . . . I am the doctor and the nanny to the world. I am the boat that will carry everybody to the shore of freedom. I will keep being reborn until I have saved each and every one.

"Imagine a plot." He turned to face me. "This saint comes back for the last soul, and this last soul does not want to be saved. The saint drags him, fights him, is tempted to leave— and then he suddenly realizes that he has spent his entire life in violence. He was saving those who did not wish to be saved; he was tearing off the chains that the prisoners loved. Now, facing his last prisoner, the saint turns around: I'm tired of being the nanny, he says; I want to be a sick child myself. Healing is a sweet dream. Health is boredom. Perhaps our whole life is someone's dream of being cured. Perhaps we all are God's enjoyment of his sickness."

JUST after we left yet another cave at dusk, we ran into a storm. The wind was slashing our faces with icy, dusty razors. We could barely breathe. We had to get behind the rocks, Martin yelled, and wait it out. We would have died of exposure, had Dorje not spotted the ruins of a monastery up the mountain.

I always dreamed of the ruins as a kid. Darkness, silence—a regular mother's womb. A storm rages outside, while here you can roll into a ball and go to sleep. But maybe it's too cold for a mother's womb. Martin ordered us to get torchlights and scout the monastery for wood and branches to build a fire.

We came up empty. Had to settle for some dubious canned beans. Martin and I shared some vile-tasting Chinese vodka. I had a sip, while he gulped down a jarful and went straight to sleep. Dorje, as always, quietly turned immobile near the wall.

The cold would not let me sleep. Through a hole in the roof, moonlight showed a cracked fresco of Yab-Yum, Buddha's archetypes in the union of mother and father.

"—WHAT if I want to be sick, too, and skip school?" Yuin grinned at me. "Are you ready with your argument?"

"You were talking about the gate of deprivation," I wheezed. "In our cell, we're so cold, we have to hug one another to fall asleep. If you have similar conditions in your ashram, how are you planning to bring up your generations of children? They'll freeze to death. The Flood will wash out all fuel sources, right? Unless you've stashed some away, in which case you're no different from the end-of-the-world American nuts in Montana."

"But we're different." Yuin grinned again. "We shall preserve the integrity of the experiment. No stashing. The earth's final tremor will help the capable ones—the ones I picked—reveal a multitude of gifts. Including the one using the 'winged dragon,' or internal heat. My ashram is already prepared to be sustained by this kind of fuel. But we cannot wait for too long for the transfer. Once you gather the spiritual energy in a mass, it must be used; or else it will evaporate, and man will lose his spiritual potential. Look at the Jews: they've been waiting for their Messiah for so long that their spiritual muscle has wizened. You, too, can learn how to live off your internal heat. I'll teach you."

He signaled to the guards.

"Why?" I shouted when I was stripped and tied up.

"You have overcome your first tie, one to your body." Yuin pulled on a rubber glove. "Now it's time to give up on the second one. . . . Do you feel the Finger of God?"

He picked up my genitals and toyed with them.

"God toys with galaxies and planets and our destinies as He chants His mantra and shines with bliss. Do you feel His joy? Do you hear His song? Do you?"

He clenched his fist, forcing a moan out of me.

"All right, enough pain for now. Now, a little fun."

*   *   *

THE guards pushed in the next prisoner—shaven head, standard black uniform, caked blood from beatings. He had to be utterly exhausted: when the guard let him go, he fell on his knees and froze, his head on his chest. I glanced at Yuin quizzically.

"Not familiar?" The general lifted the prisoner's chin. "This is how people refuse to recognize the consequences of their deeds. Take a good look."

I cried out in surprise.

The ring had been torn out from the lip, and raw blood still smudged the chin; the yellow hair with a raspberry streak was gone—but I recognized Nyima's jaws, her freckled skin, her eyes, barely covered with narrow eyelids.

"Say hi to your former guide," Yuin said.

I closed my eyes.

Yuin interpreted it his own way. "You think she betrayed you? Not at all; she wouldn't talk about her ties to the Americans. The silly girl did not know I already knew everything. She fell for you—and now you're being so ungrateful. But I'll give you another chance."

He gestured the guards to pull her closer to me.

"What's the matter? Are you ashamed of your nudity? Ah, you're a man, she's a woman . . . But that's an illusion. Now she will give you, uh, a fellatio. While you'll be holding back for, shall we say, ten minutes—fair enough? If you don't . . ."

I heard a click and opened my eyes. Yuin held a gun in one hand; a stopwatch in the other.

"In order to enter the ashram, you must master the tantra. If you blow your stack too fast, I'll shoot her." He pressed the barrel against Nyima's temple. "And you, little Tibetan whore, if you don't make him come in ten, I'm going to cut off his balls. Understood? Let me put on some cream. It's completely wilted with fear. . . . Let's go."

Nyima obediently reached forward.

I pulled away. "Why do you need this?"

"We are moving on to your second charge," Yuin explained. "You ran off to Tibet to prove your innocence, right? Let me show you the proof of your guilt. And give you a chance to atone. After the black bum, your next vic-

tim was Professor Schechter. What we're witnessing here is
no different from what you were doing to the professor. You
kept exciting him without letting him come. You tormented
him. But one is seen as a sex object only if he sees somebody else that way. After your body, your sex is the greatest
obstacle to being empty. I'll teach you how to get rid of it.
Come on, Nyima!"

Straining every rope, I screamed my lungs out. I
screamed I would tear Yuin's throat and stir-fry his slanted
eyes. I called him a bastard, a nothing, a monkey, a worm,
a stinking Chink, a worthless imitator, a provincial slit-eyed
satrap. I screamed in the hope that Yuin would lose his cool
and shoot me.

Not a muscle moved in the general's face.

"See how this is a metaphor for what's to come?" Yuin
said when I collapsed on the ropes in exhaustion. "Tectonic
plates have shifted, and the magma of fury flowed up! How
beautiful will be this fury of truth on the global scale! Humanity will scream insults in the face of its reason—this
dirty, snotty nothing, this stinking monkey—and break free
of its chains. Naked and bleeding, it will crawl to us and
beg us to lead it to the light. But, before you can lead, my
friend, you have to learn a thing or two. Let's go!"

I jerked again, but my flesh was already in Nyima's
mouth, her tongue whirling around it. Covered with sweat,
I clenched my teeth and fists. I had to hold back; I could
not cause yet another death.

The grin of pleasure did not leave Yuin's face. "Seven
more minutes. A sweet pain, isn't it? Torment and anticipation; the foretaste of apocalypse. Another minute, and
your being will be splintered in a million particles, and
then—silence. Which pretty much sums up my plans for
mankind: I want to relieve the sweet torment of life and
bring it to peace. Hard to hold back, isn't it?"

It was. Nyima knew what she was doing, making me
tremble with strain.

"Three more minutes," Yuin announced. "The marriage
of Shiva and Shakhti is about to be consummated—but
Shiva is still holding back! Aha, so you know that you must
parlay the sexual orgasm into a spiritual one in order to

ascend to angels. If this is just spilling seed, it amounts to a throwback to animals. So the torment is in your own head, after all! You embody modernity's most significant conflict: the constant itching of instinct and the mind's constant attempts to rein it in. Mankind keeps exciting itself with more and more pleasures, yet it knows how dangerous it can be and so it keeps passing laws against it. If it gives free rein to instinct, this will be the end of civilization, here represented by Nyima. While getting rid of instinct means losing your procreation mechanism—and, eventually, life. Did not your God order you to "fruit and multiply"? And now"— he glanced at the watch—"she failed!"

He fired at my crotch.

I screamed.

Nyima froze, deafened by the explosion, her face covered with soot.

THE bullet was a blank.

"You've done well," Yuin complimented me, while I was still trembling. "But did you feel the flight? Did you understand that when the seed goes upward, you cease to be a man and a woman? The sex is gone, the shame is gone— you're an angel. My ashram lives in this constant state of flight."

Nyima was led away. I was untied and seated in a regular chair.

"Still trembling?" The general waved the gun at me the way a cornerman fans a fighter with a towel between rounds. "I'll teach you how to curb the winged dragon with an easy smile. A man and his thought must restrain themselves from procreation, from replicating the Creator's disastrous primal error. We never learned the internal act that does not involve the spilling of the seed, and therefore we end up spilling the seed on the outside—another man's blood. The same way as you spilled the professor's blood."

"But I didn't kill him," I murmured, trying to suppress the trembling.

"But you did." Yuin walked over to the bar in the corner. "I've read some more of your diary. Remember, you wrote, *The day was windy, and the ground was covered with leaves*?" He poured a glass of cognac and handed it to me.

"You were walking in the park and becoming irritated at the professor's orating. You sensed he was trying to seduce you. He was tempting you to sacrifice your gender, to make one more step towards becoming an angel. But you dared not cross the line; you turned down his invitation to stay over. You were not fleeing the professor; you were afraid to be suspended in the air, to lose your gender, to stay alone—but not as Milarepa the hermit poet of your desires, but a self-hating homo. You were scared and you brushed off the temptation. In your mind, you deleted the professor—and the professor was no more. You were the real cause of the murder. My agent was a mere instrument of your will."

"So you did have an agent."

"We have a large staff in New York. You were right to suspect the car parked across the street from Schechter's place. My agent transcribed your conversation from the vibrations of windows at the apartment. When I realized you were not staying, that you wanted to get rid of Schechter, I merely brought your desires to a practical conclusion. Yes, my agent killed Schechter and burned the apartment."

"Not true! You were trying to kill Larry! You killed the professor by mistake!"

"We don't make mistakes. In a sense, your guess is right: I did want to get rid of Larry. He calculated the coming lithospheric shift, and I was afraid he would leak the news and cause a panic. But then I realized that he, too, was waiting for the catastrophe, wishing death upon both himself and his father. On the other hand, Schechter burned by himself—literally, of shame! The mantra awakens the stress that accumulates inside both the body and the psyche. Schechter was ashamed of AIDS, though the real AIDS is the virus of human intellect, the mutation of divine wisdom. My ashram is a kind of serum against it."

Outside, the mountains were becoming gray. Yuin stood by the window.

"Clouds gray and full, float above, without spilling their seed," he recited. "What sort of motive could the Supreme

Being have for creating us, with our shameful thoughts and their shameless implementations?"

I was silent. My mind was on Riverside Drive. Yuin was not joking: had I not feared the professor would make a pass at me, I would have stayed, and Schechter could still be alive.

YUIN is a New Age Frankenstein, I wrote. *A horrifying combination of Chinese esoterica and a Communist's obsessiveness. Tao meets Mao . . . But how am I different?*

OUTSIDE the ruins, the storm had ended. It was getting light. Pistachio-colored clouds with tungsten edges floated in the sky: it was as if the mountains had broken away from their moorings.

What a lighthearted feeling, I thought; it is as if I were to die now. Clouds are like human thoughts, varying in speed, structure, color, shape. The clouds over the Midwest are as solid and unhurried as the thoughts of local farmers. The clouds over New York are fast, chased by Atlantic winds, torn by high-rise buildings and darkened, like the thoughts of its denizens, by local smog. Over Russia, the skies lie low and gray, with blue streaks—just like Russia itself, the land of heavy drinking and dour fears, interlaced with moments of sublime tenderness. But all of them disperse; what stays, like the sky over Tibet, is the blue void— the doorway to heaven.

The mountains are the greenery and the snow, the ice and the sun, all rolled in one. This is why they fascinate us so: this marriage of the opposites is not unlike our own essence—old age and youth, love and hate, passion and indifference. All of them coexist at the same time, visible through each other, like the green through the falling snow, and reflecting each other like the sun in the ice of the peaks. And the beauty! Perhaps this is why there is no local literature here: the view alone makes the heart stop in your chest.

That's what I should have told Yuin. I should have told him to take a closer look at the tender, passionate way God loves the Earth. He cannot get enough of the warmth of Her body, soft in the water and hard on the land. Nor of the sweet aromas of Her plants. Nor of the cool, gentle fingers of Her rivers. Of the shining eyes of Her glaciers . . .

Why, then, does He unleash the disasters of floods, eruptions, and meteorites? Perhaps this is a particularly violent kind of coitus, where He slaps and bites Her before the orgasm—look at the furious male deity on the frescoes. She hurts and screams, but when it's all over, She kisses him gently. An abusive relationship, some would say, but one that harkens way back, and needs no recourse.

He treats Her children, humanity, as—well, as the children that they are. If they misuse their favorite toy—life— He takes it back and sends them into the dark corner of death, so that they can discover the light of knowledge and return, wiser, to a new lesson.

68

WE decided to risk moving in the daytime; otherwise we did not have even a theoretical chance of getting to the border in time. The choppers are gone; Yuin must be thinking we're going to Nepal and so is looking for us in the west—but we are moving southeast, towards India.

Dorje makes out the Chinese characters on the field map we found at the guardhouse. We're about seventy miles away from Lhasa, near Gokhar-la Pass. It is sure to be guarded, so we'll have to detour and climb to sixteen thousand feet.

Before, we used to see scraps of prayer flags—signs of local peasants passing through—but now there's nothing but rocks and stones. It is cold. And there is never enough air.

God's thought is somewhere deep inside, in the marrow of the Absolute; sometimes it awakens and flows all over, destroying the old and generating the new. Could it be that

God would have second thoughts, as we do: what hath I wrought? That's what the Himalayas are: grandiose dreams of heroic deeds that turned into a lifeless, airless, frozen desert. The wretched death of a philosopher among the frozen boulders of his own constructs.

MY backpack weighs a ton: cans of food, a rolled-up blanket, the submachine gun with ammo. Yet Martin will not let me ditch any of it. He is barely holding up, too, with an even heavier one. Dorje is the one who maintains a steady swagger, though he is carrying the same things we are, plus a few grenades.

At a rest stop, I glance through the binoculars at the dry riverbed in the valley below and spot a cart, moving in the same direction as we are. Dorje is against making contact, but Martin issues the order to go down and catch a ride.

Yeah! We're riding! My backpack is next to me on the cart. Dorje negotiated a fare with a handful of yuans from the guardhouse. Now he is walking next to the cart, without even removing his backpack: "I and things are one." He must have felt sorry for the tiny horse, sad-looking despite the bells on the harness painted in once gay but now faded colors. The two drivers, Tujin and Norbu, walk, too. Martin and I don't have a chance of keeping up with them, so we stay on the cart.

Tujin is young, with white teeth and a red visored hat with a scarf tied over it. Norbu is older, with a small sharp face, short bowed legs, and a dagger under his belt, all of which make him look a bit like a highway robber.

Tujin sings, the wheels creak, and the dust feels gritty in our mouths. The plateau is like the bottom of the primordial ocean, and we are oceanologists in our deep-sea chamber. The rivers that run through the valleys are narrow, roaring like freight trains, and white, almost milklike, with foam. Here, every valley can be a Shambala. Which means that one of them could be hiding Yuin's ashram.

THE third interrogation took place in Rating's garage. As Yuin and the colonel watched, the guards stripped me and suspended me on a belt about twelve feet over the grease pit.

Then they brought in Nyima. She, too, had been stripped, and then oiled with axle grease from head to toe. As at our previous meeting, she was silent. When I tried to shout, Yuin nodded to the colonel, who leaned over the railing and smashed his nightstick on my kidneys. For a moment, the blinding headlights of the trucks died in my eyes.

After I regained my senses, Yuin explained his new game. Now I had to hold Nyima, slippery with oil, over the pit. "Hold tight. If she falls, she will hurt herself badly."

The guards dragged Nyima onto the platform. Then, holding her arms and legs, they swung her, and giggling, tossed her towards me.

I did catch her! She shrieked and instantly began sliding down. I yelled, too, and gripped her the only way I could: one arm under her armpit, the other one between her legs. Instinctively, she gripped me with her legs, her arms around my neck.

"Good job!" Yuin clapped his hands. "Now, you need a third point of support. Go ahead, put it in."

"I can't!" I yelled, my arms trembling with strain. "I'll drop her! Why are you doing this?"

"Try." The general smiled. "If you don't, you'll get another reminder with a stick—then you'll certainly drop your, eh, beautiful savage."

As if to illustrate his point, the colonel tapped the stick on his hip.

I closed my eyes. Even if I wanted to . . . I could not. The trembling of my hands took up all of my energy.

"Tough, huh?" Yuin inquired with fake sympathy. "There's a metaphor for you: a man tries to hold on to the object of his desires, but, just as he is about to enjoy himself, he drops it. Well?" He glanced at the colonel. "Shall we introduce a little correction here?"

Even before the place went dark in my eyes, I groaned and loosened my grip. A thud came from below.

I could not bear to look down at Nyima's body.

Yuin shrugged. "Once again, I am not doing anything to you that you did not wish upon others. Remember Gwen:

how she trembled with strain when you kept sliding out of
her arms. When you, slippery with doubts, extended her
torment with your half-absence in her arms."

"But she's the one who fell—not me!"

"You wished her to."

"I told you my wife was dead," Martin said suddenly. He
was sitting with his back to me, staring at the horse's gray
tail with red ribbons woven into it. "That's not the whole
story. I killed her."

Sharon, he told me, was painfully jealous of him. He did
not give her cause for it, he claimed; he reminded her what
their reverend had said: jealousy is the Devil's temptation.
But she was not to be reasoned with.

"If I worked in a bank . . . ," Martin said. "But in my line
of work, she could never know where I was or who I saw."

Late one night the phone rang: a snitch needed an emergency meeting. As he was getting dressed, he realized he
could not find his gun. Sharon stood at the bedroom door.
You don't need a gun, she said, wielding his Colt; unless
you need to prove yourself to your girlfriend.

I did not not have time for this nonsense, Martin said. As
if I was happy to be leaving a nice, warm house on a cold
night to see some asshole who needed fifty bucks to buy
smack.

He tried to wrest the gun from her; she resisted. He
pushed her hard. . . .

That's when she really took off, he said. She yelled and
screamed and told him he was not going to find her or their
six-year-old son when he came back from his whore.

"I have a problem controlling anger," Martin said
hoarsely, watching horse chestnuts dropping on the road. "I
turn into an animal. I feel as if I were growing a hide, claws,
fangs, whatever. I just want to sink my claws into flesh and
tear it up, blood and guts and all. All this calm is a mask.
I'm just trying to keep the beast asleep."

Finally, she blocked his way. This is an ultimatum, she
said; me or her. Your call.

They were standing at the top of the stairs. He pushed
her away. "Maybe a little too hard."

She tripped and rolled down the steps. When Martin ran down, she was not moving.

Their son, Kirk, awakened by the noise, had been watching the whole scene through a crack in the door.

"The fifteen minutes before the ambulance came," Martin said, "that was real hell. Worse than death. She could not move her lips; she was just staring at me with tears in her eyes. And Kirk—he would not let me touch him."

He jumped off the cart and walked along.

"CREATION is a spontaneous act." Yuin sipped his tea. "It's like a family scene. The father explodes, and his children—the particles—flee him in terror. . . ."

While he orated, the guards lifted the unconscious girl from the pit. Her face and shoulders were covered with blood. An army medic in a white coat knelt next to her and took a syringe from his bag.

"Let me get this straight." Yuin strolled along the edge of the pit, past me, still suspended from the hook. "You were not married to Gwen officially, so you were constantly wondering whether you should take a powder. But this is exactly where humanity stands vis-à-vis life. Humanity had never walked life down the aisle. Adam did not ask to be created. If this union was not entered into in full consciousness, then it must be sinful and perhaps should be dissolved. The temptation is always there. You wanted to buy your way out with the grant, while others pay with their lives to get out of the torment of everyday existence." He glanced at the girl. "Looks like your girlfriend has recovered enough for an encore."

SOMETIMES the cart stopped, and the drivers treated us to *chang*. They stored the gray sour-milk beer in dirty plastic canisters, perhaps used by the Chinese for gasoline.

Norbu poured himself a cup, dipped a dark calloused finger, shook it three times—offerings to Buddha, his teaching, and his community—and gulped it down. Once upon a time the cup had been a tender white-and-blue; now, it was practically black. Norbu wiped it with his soiled coat, filled it with *chang,* and handed it to me. I could not possibly turn it down. For the Tibetans, the issue of clean versus unclean was resolved the Buddhist way: all differences were relative and existed only in the eye of the beholder.

The sour brew almost made me choke. Tujin saw my expression, chuckled, patted me on the knee, and turned away to take a leak. For a child of nature, conventions do not apply.

Martin shook his head to the offer of *chang*. He went on with his story; clearly, he *had* to finish it.

Sharon saved him from going to jail. She was paralyzed. The DA wrote on a piece of paper to show her, *Did he push you?* And, *Was it an accident?* She closed her eyes to the latter. Martin spent every waking moment with her at the hospital. For a while, she seemed to be getting better.

But then he had to go to Vegas to deliver an embezzler wanted in three states. He ran into some ex-colleagues who had retired to the local PD. They would not let him leave without showing him "a good time."

After three days, he did get back to D.C., but somehow she knew that a link that had begun healing was broken. The light in her eyes was gone. A month later she was gone, too. Her mother got custody of Kirk.

ONCE again, I caught the girl. No longer could she hold on to me with her legs; her body instantly wilted in my arms, and her head fell lifelessly on my chest, smearing it with blood.

"You're wheezing as if you were having an orgasm." Yuin commented on my convulsions as I tried to hold on to the girl.

"Isn't orgasm like birth? You emerge from the trance straight into a woman's arms, just as a newborn does? You will say, A man is being born of his own free will, the same way he reaches an orgasm. In Bardo he can choose not to be born, but goes into the womb out of habitual desire to acquire a shape. But no one asked the first man if he wanted to be born! Adam's birth was not a conscious act of marrying life! Thus if we close down, or at least narrow, the gates of birth, we will spare people the sin of adultery with life.

"You will say, I deliver people from their sins by sacrificing their lives. But that's common in nature. The sun burns out to provide warmth; the cloud runs dry to give water to earth. But what can a man sacrifice but his life?"

"His own life"—I gasped—"not someone else's!"

"But that's what you did: you sacrificed someone else's life. When we met in the elevator on West One Hundredth Street, I was on my way to executing your will. You wanted to be rid of your wife. You wanted freedom from her, not from yourself."

"Noooo!" There was no struggle left in my body as my fingers were losing their grip.

WE got back on the cart. Norbu and Dorje chatted about horses. Tujin tried to talk to me, but I lacked an everyday vocabulary; all I understood was that the driver wanted to discuss the relative values of American versus Tibetan women. Tujin chortled at my strained answers and went back to singing.

Martin waited with a gloomy expression for Tujin to leave me alone. "After you talked our ears off at the precinct about the mantra, I looked up your file. I read about your father shooting your mother and getting off on temporary insanity. I read you hadn't seen him since—right?"

I nodded, eyeing dispassionately the brown fins of the mountains on the horizon. It used to be that the slightest reference to the man who called himself my father would make me seethe with hatred. Oddly, that was no longer the case. On the other hand, at that moment I did not feel sympathy even for my mother. Any thoughts of her were as remote as the dot I saw bobbing up and down across the valley—a cart, or a solitary yak.

"So I wasn't just trying to revenge myself on the boss when I got myself into your case," Martin said. "I just sort of felt the same way your father must have done. Since I can't do anything to help my own son. And then, when I found out your girlfriend fell from the window and was paralyzed—so, karma or not, we're like twins or something."

Once again, he jumped off and strode along, holding on

to the edge of the cart. "There's more. After this whole thing happened, I got into smack in a heavy way. If it wasn't for Ruslanov—"

AFTER the Russian expert was brought in to consult the FBI on the siege in Texas, he demonstrated his method. He cured one agent of alcoholism; another, of smoking. In Martin's case, it was his suicidal tendencies.

I remembered that Ruslanov had refused to discuss Martin's problems.

"I kept wondering what I should have done when she was tormenting me." Martin would not quit. "Is this your slant-eyed karma—to decide that I may have been unfaithful to her in my previous life? I could have kneeled in front of her, could have told her it was my fault, I'm the one who led you into the sin of jealousy. Maybe we would have cried a little and then hugged and made up—for good. Other times, I remember her wild eyes when she was talking shit at me—I start shaking and wishing I could do this all over again. What do you say, Mr. Theologian? Should I have kneeled or just divorced her?"

I thought: *The teacher says, Do the third choice: contemplate the Void.* But I remained silent. How much contemplation had I actually done? I remembered one of our "relationship talks"—typically, I could not remember the immediate cause—in the dusk at our studio. Finally, I had gotten over my irritation and began kissing her hands, begging her forgiveness—then, suddenly the suppressed anger broke through, I bit her knee and screamed. She cried, and her tears brought an end to it. We made up, and later went back to the never-ending routine.

"In the West, we're given to extremes," I answered. "Either we break necks or get down on our knees. In the East, they stick to the Golden Mean."

"What would that be?"

"I don't know, Martin. Maybe it's in his head." I nodded at Dorje, who strode effortlessly alongside the cart, looking forward with a smile on his face.

*   *   *

NYIMA screamed wildly as the guards pulled her out of the pit; a piece of a bone was sticking out of her knee—an open fracture. My eyes closed, I bit into my fist helplessly.

"Come on, take a look," Yuin said, strolling along the pit. "Don't you have a sense of déjà vu? This is how you let go of Gwen. I would even say, pushed her."

"You're the one who pushed her, you bastard!" I screamed so hard I thought my head would explode with hatred.

"Me?" Yuin faked curiosity. "You're forgetting that I'm merely a tool of your thoughts. As the last member of my ashram, you must see for yourself how karma and thought work together. You wanted to be rid of Gwen: and you were!"

"Not true! I wanted to get away from her!"

"That's not what your diary says. Karmic forces are like children, or madmen, or the subconscious: they respond to the words' direct sense. To be rid of someone means exactly that. I merely made your wish come true."

"But I didn't anymore!" I cried out, but my fury was no longer aimed at Yuin; rather, at a sort of turncoat inside myself. "We were going to run off to Canada!"

"Karma is like math. The sum of your old thoughts was greater than the sum of the new ones. As they say, the bill has been paid for. The fruit of your desire had ripened, and I merely shook the branch for it to fall. I mean, her to fall."

Yuin came close, calculating that I needed at least four inches to go for his throat, and said calmly, "Admit it: the thought crossed your mind during your fights. I read your diary. It did occur to you: what if I no longer hold back— break her neck—pop out these dilated eyes of hers—toss her out of the window? Don't tell me you never wanted it? You shrank away from these thoughts, for they made you no better than an animal—but you fantasized, didn't you?"

"I loved her!" I screamed. "I did!"

"Don't lie to me!" Yuin suddenly screamed back, banging his fist on the railing. "What do you know about love? You were rotting away with her; you wanted to get away, but to do it with kindness; you wanted to slip out unnoticed, as if you were greased with oil. Me—I loved so hard that

I had spasms in my fingers—to hold her! Unlike you, I did!
I held on to my loyalty!"

Veins stood out on his temples. Just as suddenly, he loosened his fist. "What nonsense. All the personal sacrifices,
all the world dramas, are boring variations on the aspirations
of one's instinct and mistakes of judgment. I was still a
Young Communist, I had a girlfriend, my boss took her
away from me, and I didn't do a thing, because Party discipline was above petty personal things. Then he returned
her to me, with a child, and suffering from syphilis. Boring,
boring . . . I took pity on her; I took her in, I had her cured,
I helped rear another man's child, and then she was jailed
for ties to dissidents. I waited for her to get out, I ignored
offers from younger women, but when she got out, she went
to live with someone else. Do you think I got mad? No: I
looked up in the sky and realized that, if I were happy, it
would be just as silent. I looked at the earth: it would be
silent, too. This silence is the only truth there is. But to
reach it, one must cease being a man; one must be like an
angel, suspended between the earth and the sky. If you drain
yourself of emotion, you can handle anything fate throws
at you."

WE'RE falling into a trance. We're forgetting that we are
escapees. The idea of the coming cataclysm no longer horrifies: this rocky brown ocean around us will merge with
the infinite blue one above, that's all. We will continue our
progress along a different valley. Everybody will continue
doing whatever they were doing, but in different worlds.
Actually, that's the only thing that's horrible. Or, rather,
sad, because neither I nor anyone else realizes that *there*
will be no different from *here*. You will be in the same state
as you continue on your way and perform the simple rituals
aimed at a slight improvement in your next life: sharing,
giving gifts, and showing deference. The ritual with *chorten*s, for example—the tiny pyramids at the side of the road;
every time we pass one, our drivers mechanically drop
pebbles and circle them three times. Those are the rules they
live by. :

Dorje is still cheerful, though. He marches tirelessly with

his heavy backpack, smiling at Martin, me, the sun. He pets the horse, trades jokes with the drivers. Can it be that he indeed sees everything and everybody as representations of Buddha?

I laughed out loud and said, in response to Martin's quizzical look, "We're playing a game. Butch Cassidy and the Sundance Kid Go to Tibet."

"I see you forgot the touch of your Chinese metal stool." Martin peered through his binoculars at the horse cart approaching in the opposite direction. "I don't like this one. One driver, but the horse barely moves its feet. Must be some cargo."

I took the binoculars. We were about three hundred feet apart. A regular Tibetan cart. A regular horse. A regular old Tibetan in a coat over one shoulder and a worn-out winter hat.

"He seems to be going to the same village where our guys came from," Martin said coldly. "But we have already crossed two rivers. Every time we had to get off and hold on to the load, so that the cart wouldn't tip over on the rocks. How does this old fart expect to get across with this kind of load and all by himself?"

They were about a hundred feet away. Once again, I peered in the binoculars. The edge of the sackcloth cover rose, and a man's face flashed underneath.

"Martin!"

The detective saw it, too. He grabbed his automatic and, with one quick movement, swung himself and me off the cart.

ON landing I hurt my ear on a rock, which, hit by a bullet, instantly rang and let out a cloud of dust. I crawled to take shelter in a ditch that ran along the road.

Everything happened at once. The oncoming cart turned to block the road, its driver holding to the reins tightly. Three Chinese soldiers tossed off the sackcloth and opened fire. A fourth one, an officer, got on the walkie-talkie.

Dorje dropped on the road and lay prone, covering his head. Tujin jerked, raised his hands to his face—and collapsed, his head in the ditch a few feet away from me. His red scarf was turning dark from the spouting blood.

Our horse, frightened by the gunfire, rose on its rear legs, neighed, and galloped off. Screaming, Norbu ran after it—his only property. A few feet later, his body was tossed forward; his hands flailed in the air, and he dropped to the ground.

Martin crawled over to Dorje and reached into the pack on the lama's back. For a moment, there came a lull as the officer barked orders to the soldiers. We crawled away from the cart to get a better aim at the enemy behind the rocks. Martin rose on his knee and tossed a grenade, but not before one of the soldiers squeezed the trigger. Martin cried out, and instantly, a fountain of fire and rocks burst out under the soldiers' feet.

When the dust settled, I saw the other horse limp and trot down the road, dragging behind the driver's dead body. A leg in an officer's soft boot extended from under the remains of the cart. The three bodies in green uniforms with red insignia were scattered across the road.

"Sonuvabitch!" Martin screamed, lying on his side. "You okay? Get me the knife! Fast! Aw shit!"

He held his hands to his hip, his fingers turning red.

"Come on, stop staring—cut my pants! The sonuvabitch is in the bone! Where's our goddamn first aid?"

"It was on the cart," I said. "But the horse took off—"

"Just my fucking luck! Come on, make a tampon—stick it in the wound—Dorje? Is the motherfucker alive? He's got my vodka!"

"It's over!" I called out to the monk. *"Sar song!"*

Only then did the monk unclench his hands over his head and rise.

We washed the wound with vodka. Then we dipped the impromptu tampon in the same murky liquid, and Dorje, muttering, abruptly shoved the tampon inside the wound.

In the anticipation of pain, Rivers stuck the knife handle in his mouth for biting.

"What do we do now, Martin?" I cried out, after he had his wound bandaged. "How could they know—?"

"They sent out recon carts. Come on, lift me up! Back to the mountains—the choppers will be here any minute!"

"Wait!" I exclaimed. "Norbu!"

In the distance, the older driver tried to crawl up, pushing with one good hand.

Dorje and I went to look. The man was dying. His clothes were soaked with blood. Pink bubbles formed in the corners of his mouth.

Dorje wiped his face. I took out my knife and began cutting strips of cloth from his overcoat.

"Leave the poor fucker alone." Martin tugged me by the shoulder. "He's got a few seconds left. Let's go, damn it! They had a radio—choppers will be here any minute!"

"And leave him like this?"

Martin glanced at Norbu's dimming eyes and raised his gun.

"YOU wanted to be rid of Gwen, yet the two of you became quite alike," Yuin said. "You might as well flee a mirror."

He pressed me with one hand against the railing, while holding smelling salts to my nose with the other. "In your moments of fury and fear your facial expression is exactly the one she had when I entered the apartment."

"But how did you learn our telephone code?"

"I told you: we have a lot of agents in New York. We rented an apartment across the street from yours—you know, a brownstone with a green tower? Modern technology is quite magnificent: it picks up the windows' vibrations and translates them into words.

"I sensed that after Colorado you would be trying to get away, and in the midst of your transition to a new life, I would be able to make a small correction and steer you the right way. Then, in a coincidence, I walked into our safe house just as you were packing. Actually, I didn't have a plan then: I was just going to pass you along to my Canadian agents.

"I went over to your building to take a look at a potential disciple. Just as I get into the lobby, I get the call on my phone: you're on your way to the basement. And this is how, on pure inspiration, I decided to pay a visit to your old lady. Especially since she was so impressionable, so scared of my phone calls.

"I got a glimpse of you in the elevator, got off on your floor. It's unlocked, she called; come in. An omen, isn't it? No difference between the master and the disciple.

"When I came in, she was airing a sweater in the window. She turned to look only when I was standing next to her."

Yuin glanced at Nyima, still unconscious as the guards pulled her out of the pit. "She's fine," he reported. "She doesn't feel anything. Neither does your Gwen. She's in bliss. You might say I lanced a boil on her mind. So much pain had accumulated there, so much stress from the uncertainty in your future; then your sudden decision to go to Canada cut the rope, and she went dizzy.

"Similarly, the earth is uncertain about man's intentions. Will you stay? Do you love her or just use her? Are you planning to take off and stop tormenting her? And you—a so-called civilization—you cannot make up your mind. I, the only gentleman, have to deliver the coup de grace and cut the rope."

He waved to the guards to pull me up. As they loosened the ropes, I moaned, but more from the memories than from the physical pain.

I knew Yuin was right. I had spent so many hours staring at the computer screen and playing out our farewell scenario—what should I say? What would she answer? What could I do to ease her suffering?

Yuin looked on as the medic put salve on my wounds. "Mankind torments itself by staying with an unloved wife. Now is the time to toss your civilization out of the window. Of course it will be painful—but you should have thought about it beforehand! I hope you understand you had no business being with with Gwen. He who has not abandoned his reason has no business picking up anyone—for surely he'll drop her!"

OUR cave is dark and narrow, like a coffin. The choppers are hovering above; we had barely time to drag Martin to the nearest rock pile and stick ourselves into this hole as they arrived. Now we are waiting for the night to fall. Dorje is meditating; Martin, groaning and cursing. I close my eyes and try to recall everything that happened before the ambush.

Dorje would not take off his backpack, saying, *I'm one with my burden.*

WHAT burdens us is the sexual instinct. Yuin suggests that it should be dealt with in a Tantric way; but you can't erase it completely. It will always linger in some remote corner of your mind, and then one day it will pop out and hurt someone else. In order to negotiate the road, one should assume the burden, one should marry, but the purpose must be to help each other become empty, rather than in making demands and fuming at the reflection of your helplessness— the way it was with me and Gwen.

69

WE keep climbing. We can't drag Martin anymore; after ten minutes, I'm ready to pass out. He tries to hobble, but keeps falling down. In order to suppress the pain, he carries the knife in his mouth, like a pirate about to board a merchant ship. The sight would be comical if it weren't tragic.

The air is all around us, yet we keep suffocating. The clouds are suspended so close I could reach up and touch them. I try to inhale them, but they will not budge. They give me visions: they are like tulle curtains in my father's house. Which means we must be close to our destination.

Oxygen deprivation is a drug, erasing every thought, every problem. The lower the oxygen level of desires, the lower the barometric pressure of one's problems, the easier, the more blissful it is to give up your worries—that is, if you've already had altitude sickness. But I'm not over it yet.

Neither Martin nor I can go on. One more pass to go,

Dorje says; there's a place to stay. A Bon Po *gompa*, a lamasery.

WHEN we saw the lamasery—a tiny pyramid of ochre-tinted cubes glued to the slope—Martin decided to pause and reconnoiter through our binoculars.

He was right: a green jeep with a driver was parked outside at a distance from the wall, with a number of black dots—pilgrims—along it. From time to time, the Chinese soldiers showed up at the gate, laden with bags that they deposited in the trunk of the car.

"Are they ransacking the place?" I asked.

The lama nodded.

"I sure wish I had a grenade launcher," Martin murmured. "These mountains are custom-made for guerrilla warfare: you find the right point, and you control the pass. When the hell are they gonna leave?"

"Can stay night," Dorje said calmly. He sat down, closed his eyes, and began chanting: *"Om-ma-ti-mu-ye-sa-le-du . . ."*

"Oh-ma-va-fa-ka-do . . . ," Martin groaned. "To die of gangrene in this shithole. You won't even give me a decent burial. Leave my body to those damn birds. I wish I had broken my neck back in Rating. Oh, fucking hell . . ."

As he kept cursing, Dorje paused in his chanting. His eyes slightly open, he watched the wounded man with a tiny smile. Either he was patiently waiting for Martin to fall silent, or he was beaming his Bon Po anesthesia at him.

"What were you praying about?" I asked.

"Gompa. Lamas. To spend night, we bring gifts."

OF course! I forgot the Tibetan custom: you can't show up at someone's home without a gift. You can't ask for things without giving first. We have no material goods to give, so Dorje is sending them a spiritual gift of prayer.

In the same way, a man is also a visitor at the abode of the Creator. He is allowing us to stay rent-free in his house, where everything is made by His hand: the floor of the soil, the walls of the mountains, the prayer space of the valleys, the baths of the oceans and rivers, and the ceiling of the sky. The only way to pay Him back is to work off the rent by improving the palace, something we hardly ever do.

All day long, I watched through binoculars the crowds of peasants arriving. They were mostly old men, leading horse carts with women and babies in rags. Today, Dorje explained, was the day for receiving the sick; the *gompa* was the only health-care place in the area. The Chinese search forced these wretches to wait outside, where the temperature was dropping precipitously as the sun went down.

I went through the stages of yearning, senselessness, freezing . . . finally, my toes were completely numb, and the sucking feeling left my stomach cold and empty. At one point, I became dizzy. I was flying in a circle, along with the rocks and the trees around me; the circle was expanding, and I began spotting familiar faces: Gwen, Schechter, Ruslanov. They all circled next to me, and I loved them all, but I could not do anything for them, because I was just like them, another patient waiting for his turn, waiting to be cured of his fever and hallucinations. The fever was melting down the borders between me and the rest of them, and I felt a closeness to people that emerges in one's last living moments, or when the body is too weak to hold on to one's thoughts.

"*Lang!*" Dorje tapped me lightly on the shoulder. "Get up!"

The jeep was gone. The purple gate of the lamasery was slowly sucking in the long flow of pilgrims.

COVERED with dust and dirt, laden with their bags, the peasants stared at us with silent curiosity. As I dragged Martin inside, my eyes met those of the old men, and their wrinkled faces smiled at me, while the women quickly looked away, hiding their swathed babies from the foreigner's evil eye.

Bon lamas looked similar to Tibetan Buddhist ones, but for the blue rather than yellow sleeves of their garments under the same purple robes. After a brief exchange with Dorje, they brought us a teapot with hot milk with a bowl of *tsampa* and left to talk to their head priest.

As we devoured our food, we looked like speleologists

who had come down into a deep cave, lit up by the flickering droplets of magma. The darkness of the temple was spotted with hundreds of candles; their crude wicks provided little light, yet filled the cave with a sweet stinking smell and the soot that through the years had blackened the temple, making it look like a coal mine.

The flow of pilgrims moved counterclockwise slowly from statue to statue, adding to each candle a few drops of liquified yak butter from each canister. The floor was in turns slippery and sticky. The pilgrims filed behind an embroidered curtain, where they would be seen by the lama doctors.

Cripples, old men, mothers with children tied to their backs—their faces were lit with childlike awe. This tiny dark temple is the center of their universe, I thought, as I tried to mix the milk with the flour into barley balls, local style. This is the real pearl in the lotus: faith, naive and tender like baby skin, hidden inside the rough nomads scattered through the world's least habitable land.

Martin moaned, pushing away his empty cup. "Where's this goddamn guy?"

"*Gom*," Dorje said. "Think."

The head lama had plenty to think about. Sheltering runaways was risky: the Chinese could arrest all the lamas and thus deprive hundreds of locals of spiritual and medical care.

Pilgrims crawled across the hall to the shiny golden statue of Tonpo Shenrab, the Bon Buddha; they kissed small silk scarves they were holding, and placed them at Buddha's feet. Crying, the women showered kisses on the divine toenails, polished by thousands of lips. Then they crawled on to greasy-looking colored rags, hanging from other statues, and pressed them to their foreheads.

Once again, I was relaxed by the darkness, the flickering lights, the golden faces of deities kind and furious, the pilgrims' exotic faces, the smell, the soot, the humming of the mantras—the quiet bubbling of the primeval mire. Life flowed slowly, in a circle, in close quarters, groping in the dark from one light to another, offering pitiful earthly gifts, and asking heavenly ones in exchange, touching the soiled sacredness and experiencing the greater spirituality they could not touch.

FINALLY, two young lamas came back and led Dorje and Martin away.

The good shepherd risked his flock to save one lost sheep, I thought. One could do a thesis how Jesus may have put in time in Tibet.

The thought made me chuckle. I had warmed up a little, put some food in my stomach, was relatively safe—and once again (perhaps for the first time since that night at DeoMorte) dreaming about my impossibly remote academic life at Columbia. . . .

MY musings were interrupted by the loud sound of two monks striking two cymbals and large yellow-and-green drums, installed in the middle of the hall on long bamboo sticks. They were calling fellow monks for the evening *pujah* or service.

The lamas seated themselves on pillows, forming two rows that faced each other. From small yellow sacks, they produced stacks of long strips of paper and, following the cymbals, began chanting, varying their pitch and rocking in a counterclockwise direction.

As I watched them from the side gallery, I involuntarily followed their motions. Then I closed my eyes. . . . The sounds flowed up and down my blood, rocking and tickling me; I felt the little hairy feet of herds of syllables crawling along my nerve endings and the curves of my brain, bubbling and swelling in my throat, gargling and spilling inside my body in a hot foamy stream.

The monks were chanting, and I felt as though each cell of my brain had acquired a voice and now spoke individually; each of the millions of my former lives chanted its own history, the dance of its ascent. I was the choir of all the lives of the universe and at the same time I was the audience, too—a clear void in whose calm the choir sounded.

*   *   *

FINALLY, the chanting was over. I opened my eyes. My jaws ached: I had been so caught up in the chant that I could not wipe the smile of bliss off my face. Little lama boys giggled at me.

Two boys walked along the rows, pouring tea—they got me a mug, too. Soon, the lamas were gone. I leaned against the wall, rearranged Dorje's backpack by moving the dissembled submachine gun and the grenades to the sides, propped my head on it—and fell asleep to the even humming of the pilgrims who were still roaming around the temple.

WHEN I woke up, it was already light. The empty hall was filled with sunlight and incense.

"How do you like my getup?" Martin asked.

"Fucking Buddha of Harlem," I murmured.

Wearing a purple lama robe, Rivers was reclining on the same pillows where the monks had held their service the night before. Dorje, who had also changed into a new robe, and another monk were tying a red piece of cloth around the patient's huge hairy leg.

"I just woke up myself," Martin said, grinning. "They fed me some kind of dried shit—had to be a painkiller. Dorje says they took the bullet out. I don't know if it's true, but the pain is gone, man! C'mon, soldier, get yourself a new uniform!" He pointed at the heap of purple rags. "You're really in Tibet now! The Chinks are looking for three guys in army coats—and we'll be wearing robes! C'mon, time to go. Dorje says the pilgrims might have already dropped the dime on us."

"Really?" I frowned, recalling my awe of the pilgrims' faces the night before.

Dorje chortled. "In Tibet people say, You don't kill, you don't steal—you don't survive. You must kill, steal, go to *gompa,* make offering—then you a man. If not, you hungry spirit in hell."

THE monks supplied us with tea and flour and walked us to the gate, giggling over our appearances: Martin was still limping and tripping over his long robe, while I kept tossing the edges of the robe over my shoulders, revealing the Chinese uniform underneath.

The monks advised us to stick to the road: Martin's leg was not strong enough for climbing. We had to follow the road uphill to a pass and, after a few more valleys, come to a village, where we could hire guides with horses to take us to the border.

"What if we run into the Chinese on the way?"

The monks burst out laughing.

"They say, Dorje will teach us how to be invisible," I translated.

Martin shot a glance at Dorje, who was laughing along with the monks, and patted the backpack with the weapons. "That's all right, I can make them invisible, too."

AT the jail hospital, Yuin announced that I was well enough for the next debate.

I grew cold inside. "If you're bent on doing good, why are you doing this through a conspiracy? Have you seen one Hollywood thriller too many?"

I did my best to sound condescending. I would do anything to anger Yuin, to make him lose his temper—and kill his prisoner. I could not take more torture.

My intention had to be written on my face. The general merely chuckled: "Creation itself is a thriller of sorts. Everything is connected to everything else, but the reader is kept in the dark."

"You're thinking like a Maoist of the most primitive kind. A hero changes the world through the power of his ideas. I find it amusing. I don't know whether you're a joke or a parody."

"The Creator is exactly that kind of a hero, creating the world by the power of his idea. You're obsessed with an idea, too. The world continues to be created by the thoughts of its inhabitants. In order to bring it to a state of harmony, the conscience of the masses needs to be put in order first.

"Intellect will be the undoing of our civilization. In the next civilization, man will conquer his mind. He will develop psychic powers to the point where he will be able to read another's thoughts, thus making sin impossible."

"Tibetan lamas read thoughts. Yet you persecute them."

"Who is 'we' here? Chinese Red Guard morons? They're aping the West—the only difference is, they chase material goods together in a crowd, not individually. They see their Communist paradise in purely material terms: a kingdom of technology. Instead of storming the spiritual peak up front, the way the lamas do it, they climb along the winding path. At the top, they'll see something that the 'savages' achieved long ago: the void of consciousness!"

"So why do you persecute these 'savages'?"

"You don't understand. . . . The idea is that everyone become like a lama. But they preach the doctrine very slowly, while man is about to clone himself and thus throw a monkey wrench into the spiritual works of the universe. We must prevent this from happening. Since I occupy a certain position, I must play my part well."

"By torturing the monks?"

"No one will ever suspect General Yuin the Butcher of Tibet of promoting the Buddhist world evolution."

AFTER the pass, the road curved into a narrow hollow. The village was supposed to be just down the road, which was good news for Martin, whose leg was acting up again. We turned around the rock—

"*Dik-song!*" Dorje exclaimed.

We froze. The road to the hollow was blocked by an armored vehicle, a Chinese soldier standing on top. The vehicle was surrounded by jeeps. The soldiers were all over the place: a roadblock. A recent one, too, since the monks at the *gompa* had not told us about it.

The guard waved. Dorje raised his arm in response.

Once we were spotted, going back would look suspicious. Within minutes, we would be picked up by a jeep.

"You were right," I said quietly to Martin. "About how easy it is to fight in the mountains. Just one roadblock . . . They must have gotten the idea from you."

"That Yuin really did a number on your brain."

"That's how karma works." I licked a sudden drop of sweat off my upper lip. "What do we do, Dorje?"

"*Dro.*" The monk took Martin's arm and led him forward. "Go."

"What are you doing?" Martin resisted. "Go how?"

"Through them."

"Cut out this shit!" Martin tore his arm away. "You mean like the number with the beads? That won't pan out, pal. They've already seen us, and diamonds we ain't!"

"We see they empty!" Dorje caught Martin's arm again, beaming a smile.

I've never seen him beam like this before, I thought— and then I stopped abruptly, as if smashing into an invisible wall.

I had not *recognized* the lama! All I saw was the smile; all I sensed was the love radiated by this face—but I could not actually see the features!

"Martin, he means—you have to feel love for them!"

"Love . . . What are you grinning about?" Martin exclaimed.

It was another two hundred feet to the checkpoint.

"I got it, Martin!" It was like at the last night's *pujah* service: once again, my face froze in a golden mask of the Blessed Buddha. My mouth stretched in a winning smile, and my eyes narrowed into barely visible slits. "I know why they're beaming! Take a look: don't I look like a monk?"

"You look like a slant-eye, but I'm black! Give me a grenade!" He reached for the backpack. "Time to rock and roll!"

"No!" I grabbed his other arm.

Now Martin was caught in the middle. Another hundred fifty feet. We could clearly see the soldiers' submachine guns.

"Make an effort!" I whispered through the spasmlike smile. "You must identify with the object! You must become one!"

"You're crazy!" Martin hissed, his dilated bloodshot eyes drilling holes in the approaching Chinese.

"If you see Buddha in them, then Buddha in them will wake up!" I slowly set one foot after another, choking from the joy of total despair. "Come on, start smiling! They can see our faces! Come on, Martin! A big smile! Say a super-cheese!"

Gritting his teeth, Martin scowled and stretched his mouth.

"No!" I gripped his elbow. "Look at the shining under their uniforms: this is our common essence—but it's very small, it's like a twig—it needs your love to grow! It needs your light!"

I whispered feverishly into Martin's ear, while my inner voice murmured, *Lord, I want to believe in this common light! I see it inside them! I believe I can see it!*

"Am I going to turn into one transparent nigger?" Martin hissed through his scowl.

Dorje said something in Tibetan. I recognized Professor Schechter's favorite phrase.

They are empty, but my karma makes me see them this way.

"Look," I whispered hotly, "our past prevents us from seeing them the way they are seen by angels: glowing with heavenly light—"

A young soldier with a bandage around his neck hopped off the truck and shifted his submachine gun to his chest.

"You have to see him as your son!" I whispered finally and fell silent.

At twenty feet away, the soldier could hear us.

The soldier took off his hat, wiped his crew cut, and stepped forward.

My heart missed a beat.

Suddenly, a light! As if my heart collapsed into the receptacle of fear: and melted gold flowed into my head and my eyes.

The soldier's face dissolved in a dazzling sunlit circle.

God—joy—ecstasy—they were all around, taking new, dazzling shapes: green coats, the armored vehicle's grilled headlights. Martin's arm shot forward to pat the soldier on the head.

The second jeep—sunbeams playing on the windshield—a hand waving us through . . .

*   *   *

WE regained our senses long after we had left the hollow.

"How do you feel?" Beaming, I asked Martin, who was still smiling, too.

With an effort, Martin replaced his smile with a derisive grimace. "Shit happens. Dorje could make a shitload in the States just from hypnosis. Actually, some Navy Seals are taught to turn into invisible ninjas. . . ."

Yet the experience had been enough of a shake-up. Unable to hold back, Martin chuckled: "But when we were passing through—phew! This was like a ten-mile high! But the Chinks—some roadblock! Didn't even check our backpacks! If that young kid went through Dorje's pack—what a schmuck!"

"He's your son," I said quietly.

"Cut the crap!" Martin spat out. "Thank God it's over. Give me your shoulder. Forward march!"

For a while, we walked in silence. Then we paused to listen—we looked at each other—and we froze.

Raising dust, the jeep was about to catch up with us.

"See?" I breathed out. "See how karma works? Who's the schmuck now?"

Before Martin had a chance to rebut, the jeep stopped, and two soldiers walked towards us. The young one with the bandaged neck shouted, pointing at Dorje's backpack.

Smiling, the lama began bowing.

"Smile!" I hissed to Martin, feeling my own will would not obey me. "They have light in them—smile, for Chrissake!"

Ripples ran through Martin's face: a smile—a scowl—a smile . . .

The second soldier changed his direction and headed for Martin, eyeing him angrily.

He was only a few feet away, when Martin's face trembled in a spasm.

With a small cry, the soldier swung his gun forward. Growling, Martin pushed the barrel aside with his left hand and swung his right.

The blade of the knife flashed in the sun.

For a moment, the soldier cleaved to Martin's arm. Then the American jerked his hand, and the Chinese fell on his back, catching the red-and-white mess spouting from his stomach.

The second soldier shrieked, dropped his gun, and ran for the car. Limping, Martin leapt forward and threw his knife.

The Chinese screamed, took a few steps, and collapsed, grabbing the bumper of the jeep.

When we came up, he was on his back, still alive, the bloody tip of the blade sticking out of his chest.

Hatless, his childlike face was not unlike that of the boys who had poured the tea at the lamasery. He attempted to push away from Martin, but he could not; he merely stared with his eyes wide with fear.

Suddenly, his eyes swelled with tears.

Martin recoiled. The Chinese gasped, reached for his bandaged throat, dropped his hands, and grew quiet.

70

AT dusk, we settled for the night on the bank of the Brahmaputra. The great Asian river, a wide brown stream that Tibetans called Yarlung Tsampo, placidly flowed below.

"Morning boat go across," Dorje said. "Now we look for cave."

We found one easily, next to a mini waterfall, a stream that descended to the river down the terraced slope. We pushed the jeep off the cliff; we had just finished toting our belongings to the cave when we heard the buzzing of the choppers. But it was too dark for the Chinese to notice the hood of the car sticking out of the water; even up close, it looked like a boulder.

We decided to stay put until complete darkness. Dorje put fresh salve, a gift from the lamasery, on Martin's wound and changed the bandage. I opened my diary.

* * *

*ONCE again, we're in a cave. It's warm, dark, and soiled
with some animal shit scattered on the floor. Things begin
in black holes, and end there as well: a grave, an explosion,
a turned-off computer screen. It is possible that a few
programmers will survive the cataclysm in caves. Deprived
of their Macs and PCs, they will carve the code on the
walls, and future archeologists will go crazy trying to read
it.*

AT darkness, the humming of the helicopters was gone,
replaced by the quick patter of the stream. We went outside
to gather wood for a fire.

The rocky slope was covered with wizened, stunted
growth. I bent aside the prickly dry branches, while Martin
cut them off. We worked in silence. At some point—inevitably—our eyes met, as Martin was wiping his knife.

"So that was his karma?" Martin asked.

For a second, I was taken aback as I realized that Martin
was sure both of us were thinking about the Chinese soldier.

"It's his karma, it's your karma . . . mine, too. I stood by,
and you did it in part for me."

"So what do we do now?"

"We investigate. Our conscious is like an investigator. It
is working on a case it has inherited from colleagues who
could not crack it: from our previous incarnations. The investigator must not be involved personally. He calls it 'my
case,' but in reality it isn't; he is merely assigned to it. If
you unravel it, you get promoted. If you fail, you'll be sent
on a similar case once again. That's what happened to you.

"Our cases are alike, which is why we share the same
cell. Our path is strewn with victims—not through our fault,
we believe. But the crimes follow a pattern, and that's the
karma. It means there's no accident, and it will go on.
That's the way karma is.

"First scenario: the killer and the victim trade places. Second: the killer is reborn as a killer again and again. The
victim, ditto. They keep each other locked within a circle.
Why? Because the motives are criminal."

Martin, up to now listening with utmost attention, recoiled. "How are they criminal if our cause is just?"

"Exactly because it is *our* cause, while it should be a neutral one." I gathered the branches and carried them to the cave. On the way I was trying to remember Schechter's explanation of karma, back at the fireside. . . .

What is life, the professor said, but a huge scale, where life situations are myriad tiny weights, with no one to balance them properly. The weights bob and spin in the most inconceivable combinations, always reaching an ideal balance. You lose money, you acquire love. You lose love, you get health. Every plus is matched with a minus, the result coming to zero. The Being does not like you to veer from this zero course and so it always adjusts this balance, cutting both your gains and your losses. The karma rule seems so obvious, yet the only way to grasp it with your guts is to get a taste of this math firsthand. You pay for everything, my boy. For every step you make for yourself, you'll have to walk a mile for someone else. . . ."

I heard Dorje call out my name. Stepping cautiously on the slippery rocks, I climbed up the stream. Soon I saw the lama, who was doing a kind of a balancing act on the bank of the stream, gesticulating oddly.

Watching him, I lost my footing and tripped.

"Ka li?" Dorje called.

"I'm fine," I called back, washing my hands.

The rocks create danger for man but they cheer up the stream. The stream needs the rocks to bubble, and man needs suffering to give voice to his soul. But the voice had to be joyful, and that part was missing in Schechter's explanations. He squinted, he smiled, but out of fear, rather than joy. Yet where there is no joy, there is no truth either.

DORJE'S dancing was in effect fishing. He built a fishing rod out of a rope, thorns, and threads from his robe. When I came close, Dorje triumphantly raised a writhing silvery fish.

Martin took upon himself the kitchen duty. His shadow, a knife in his hand, was dancing on the wall of the cave, making me feel that we had gone back thousands of years.

*   *   *

I don't know about this fish, man." Martin turned the spit over the fire and sniffed the sweetly rotting aroma of the fish with a skeptical expression.

"If the mountain can digest us," I said, "and we are straight in its belly—then we can digest the fish, too."

Finally, the fish was deemed ready. With utmost disregard of the heat, Dorje grabbed the fish, pared the purplish black skin and the bones, and placed the flesh on the freshly splashed rocks that served as plates.

We are like early Christians, I thought. *The catacombs, the fish . . .*

"Why don't you say grace or something," Martin said. "At least Dorje sprinkles water for his gods; we're like pagans or something."

I was taken aback. Despite Martin's stubborn distrust of local mysticism, some of it must have rubbed off. In the thin air of Tibet, purified from the buzzing of other people's thoughts, the receiver of your conscious picked up all signals. Unbeknownst to himself, Martin tuned in to my frequency. Perhaps because it was the only one around: Dorje was completely engrossed in the process of eating, examining every bone carefully and licking his fingers. He didn't muse; he just was.

We finished the fish, and Dorje began mixing *tsampa* in a bowl. Suddenly, as if continuing the thought, Martin said, "If everybody contains a relative of yours, then everybody partially contains you, too?"

"If we look at the big picture," I said, no longer surprised, "then not even partially—completely."

"Then the world is a hall of mirrors. You keep bumping into your reflections and breaking your nose. That's not real humanistic. Whose idea is it I'm not allowed to realize it's me in the mirror?"

"That's your karma."

After a pause, Martin said, "On the other hand, even if I knew the one in the mirror is me, I wouldn't hug him. Maybe I like myself even less than others."

"The mirrors are not for hugging or avoiding. They're for showing you your guilt."

"Aw shit!" Martin turned clumsily and overturned his tea

mug, spilling hot water on his wound. "Give me that rag!"

"Again your fuckin' guilt!" He grabbed a piece of cloth and spoke quickly as he tamped the wound to keep the bandage dry. "This is all Yuin's brainwashing! How can you believe this guy? This is some way to treat your pet follower—by torturing him! Why does he need you to talk him out of his operation? He's just a two-bit Asian dictator! Probably shoots up, too! He must have gone crazy from all this power and money."

When Martin fell silent, Dorje shook his head, grinning, and took the mugs out to wash in the stream.

"What?" Martin asked angrily. "He doesn't agree with me?"

"I don't, either. Yuin is no crazier than you or I. Don't we torment those we love—and kill them, too?"

WHEN the guards delivered me, Yuin was staring at Dore's *The Flood,* projected on the screen.

"I am fascinated by Noah," he said; "though he is not shown here. God chose him because he followed his inner voice. He believed without doubt. But I am doomed, as a modern-day Noah, to contain a grain of doubt, like a black yin in a white yang. Like any human, I am a mechanism, complete with a hidden black button. If you press this button, the program will crash.

"So did Buddha, afraid of bringing his truth to people. So did Moses with his stuttering! So did Jesus when he prayed about the Cup! Lord: stop me—give me a sign! I can stop myself anytime, but I wanted God to tell me to. But He would not. He kept sending me signs to the contrary: my job, the uranium mines, Tune Ra, Ruslanov, and, finally, you.

"When you showed up, I decided: if my conscience—for this is what God is for you in the West—if it doesn't want to give me a tangible sign and smash my doubts, then I'll make it tangible. I appointed you to be my conscience. I love you and I torment you the way my mind and my conscience love and torment each other. I want you to press the button in my mind—and I don't."

He paused to study my expression. "I know I sound

schizophrenic. But this is a psychosis shared by our entire civilization."

Yuin opened the window in his office and inhaled the frosty air. His arms were outstretched, forming a cross against the starry sky.

I wondered why a Chinese should be so enamored of the Hollywood gothic tradition.

"It is hard to be a guard in the breach," Yuin said. "Closing out one civilization and welcoming the next one. All the greats had lieutenants: Moses and Aaron, Buddha and Ananda, Jesus and Judas. I need a friend. Or an enemy—which is the same thing."

"I fit the part."

"Yes. You are my, as you say in the West, alter ego. Didn't you dream of creating a new conscience through words? For better or worse—generally worse—I'm here to make your dreams come true. Contrary to what you think, I don't deem myself a messiah who leads the people through the breach. I'm just a Chinese guide, by law assigned to a foreigner in Tibet. It's a job, do you understand?"

71

"EARTHLINGS wait for the aliens to land," Yuin said. "But we will come by water. We have speakers of all languages among us, who will travel all over the world to bring the new gospel to the survivors. Later, they will be revered as apostles."

"What will you use for ships? The speedboats you transport to the mountains?"

Yuin chuckled. "Marketplace rumors. We have other means. You will learn when you come to the ashram."

DORJE was the first to spot a black dot below. We quickly rolled down the bank. He shouted to the captain, and soon a structure made of yak skins stretched over bone supports came close.

The Yarlung ferry had no benches and was propelled with poles by two locals with faces so rough they seemed to have been torn off the ship's stern. After brief negotiations, we came aboard.

Tending to his leg, Martin made a clumsy movement, and we nearly tipped over. Even being a passenger here requires skill. You have to stick close to the side; the skin-made bottom is fragile, and you will be in the ice-cold, fast-flowing water before you know it.

The main criterion for ashram entry is intuition, Yuin says. Hence we cannot warn people and provide them with foolproof evidence of the coming Flood: only the ones whose intuition fits the standards of the new era will survive.

What about me—do I meet the criterion? And what is the difference between intuition and faith?

WE have been on the water for half a day now. Good: the Chinese expect us to go upriver to Nepal, a shorter route. While we are traveling downstream to India. You cannot see the banks anymore: just the blue-and-purple peaks of the mountains, like a giant cardiogram, on the horizon. The tide is up, the ferrymen explain. The sky is so huge as to match the tide below—is this what's coming?

IN the evening, we reached the other bank. While Dorje talks to the boatmen, Martin glances at them askew—would they sell us out to the Chinese?—as he strokes the stock of his submachine gun. I sit down next to him, try to distract him with talk. I have no illusions about them: people are people everywhere.

Dorje rejoins us and calms Martin down; he has chanted the boatmen into silence, he says. The locals respect and fear the Bon lamas. Still, we must cover our tracks: let the boatmen think we went east. In reality, we are heading west.

THERE are no Chinese patrols, but we must stay invisible. Like wild animals, we avoid all forms of human habitation: roads, villages, roadhouses.

The Himalayas are made of magma: nature's red primeval plasma, whose pulse has frozen into mountain ridges.
The blood in my ears pulsates, too, as we climb up and
down.

Or, perhaps, the Himalayas form a planet of their own.
We are three tiny alien ants crawling across the rocky Atlantis. Up and down, again and again: it feels like there's
nothing else but these solid brown waves that keep rolling
till they pass into the sky.

IN the evening, a few mountain goats crossed our path,
calmly and majestically, right under our noses. Martin
reached for the backpack, but it was too late. I took out my
diary. This was the first time I realized that the world does
not belong to man alone.

IT happened over a week after my arrival in Rating. The
guards led me to the prison garden—the treetops that we
had seen when Martin and I drove by the gate for the first
time. Sure enough, the garden houses Yuin's personal zoo.
He actually collects an Ark, couple by couple—not all the
animals, but many.

I found him teasing a cobra with a mouse on a stick.

"The snake of wisdom climbed into Eve's ear and coiled
through her brain. People heeded it, hoping to acquire *arum,*
wisdom; instead, they got *erum,* nakedness. Is my Hebrew
up to snuff, Mr. Divinity? And they got shame. To free
yourself is to kill the snake of reason."

The cobra dashed for the mouse and missed, hitting its
head against the bars of the cage.

"It's restless"—Yuin chuckled—"it feels the tremors.
People don't. The earth will move just before dawn. Fires
will start, as gas and electricity that men have stolen from
nature will take revenge on the thieves. The artificial shel-
ters, all these bunkers, will turn into tombs, burying the
arrogant human moles. The bridges will collapse. Everything man-made will vanish—can you feel Noah's ecstasy?"

His eyes were shiny, filled with—hashish?—bliss.

Martin is right, I thought. The fucker's crazy. But what's
more horrifying is that I know the ecstasy he is talking about.

* * *

WE are out of *tsampa.* Our bellies are singing a mournful song. We cannot climb any more and drag Martin, who is still limping. We're somewhere to the east of Trigu Tso Lake. To stay on course, we must go over a nameless pass marked on the map with a simple dot and a number, 6,594—the elevation in meters. It is not easy to get here even with food and oxygen.

Like a zombie, I set one foot after the other. Hunger fills my head with visions: brown mountaintops are chocolate cakes with icing, no pun intended, on top. My only recourse is filling in the diary. For Dorje, it is chanting the mantras; Martin, writhing in pain, can only bite into the leather strap of his submachine gun.

ONE of the "reeducation" sessions took place at the prison's "art gallery." Yuin, decked out in a silk robe with golden embroidery, strolled along the walls of masterworks. I am no expert, but they might well have been originals.

"At first I wanted to create a warehouse for my ashram," Yuin said; "a quintessence of world arts and sciences. I had experts compile a library on education, economics, politics, sciences . . . but then I realized that man should enter the new era naked, bringing along nothing but his consciousness.

"It is especially apt since we will not be using traditional energy systems. Instead of heating, we have *tumo,* a yoga technique to raise your body temperature. Telepathy, which my adepts have already mastered, will replace radio and telephone. Meditation will replace TV and other entertainment. And a truly open mind can compute better than a mainframe. We don't need lasers and CAT scans for medicine. Oil for transportation? Again, my followers have already mastered teleportation and telekinesis. You can, too."

"What about food?"

"Food is poison. The cataclysm will change human biology. They won't need material food."

OF course it's nonsense. Of course he's a maniac. But Dorje has been walking for three days without a bite of food—

and not slowing down, either. I eat air, he told me. True, it takes a long time to learn Pranic breathing. But perhaps the cataclysm will shock people into learning it overnight.

Martin has been obsessed with meat ever since he saw the goats. Now he has decided to stay put till he ambushes one.

Perhaps starvation has reawakened his ancestors' hunting spirits. Or perhaps he has mastered the Tibetan gift of visualization. Or, perhaps, Dorje felt sorry for him and decided to help. Or we just got lucky. But the goat appeared in a mere two hours.

It walked out on the slope to the left of us. Martin fired a salvo. The goat vanished. We ran up to look over the cliff. It was trying to crawl away, its legs riddled with bullets.

"Go get it!" Martin roared.

My hunting instinct awakened, too. I dashed down and grabbed the poor animal in flight, like a receiver in the end zone.

The goat bleated and kicked its legs, smearing me with blood. Martin hobbled over and got out the knife.

The fear in the poor animal's eyes was completely human.

"Bad," Dorje said. "You must calm him down before death. Now meat is bitter."

I suppose this was a simplified explanation of the kosher principle: ridding the blood of fear-induced adrenaline. If only I could go back to school and write a paper on similarities between Tibetan Buddhism and Judaism.

Both Yuin and Larry were wrong. People need to be warned so they have time to overcome their fears. This is why an animal offered to God is calmed and stroked before its throat is cut. We must do at least that, even if we fail with the countermantra, so that the flesh of the victims—that is, human souls—do not poison the angels. So that our today does not poison our tomorrow.

MARTIN ordered that Dorje and I help him skin the goat. I dutifully held the goat, but looked away.

"C'mon!" Martin chuckled. "We're gonna have us some nice Tibetan spare ribs!"

"That's what your back looked like in jail," I said.

With a curse, he let the goat's innards out. I had to climb off the rock to fight nausea.

ONCE again, Martin snapped at the colonel, and Yuin ordered a caning.

I joined other inmates at the courtyard. The guards made Martin kneel in front of a wooden bench.

Martin broke down after twenty blows or so. Red flesh sputtered every which way, his white bones came into view, and he wailed.

"See how black turns into red and then into white," Yuin whispered in my ear as he circled me from the other side. "That is the fate of all of us: under the blows of fate, we shed our skin, only to find ourselves in somebody else's, again and again, till we find out what it's like for everybody. A wise man will volunteer for a beating, in order to go through all the colors and turn colorless."

DERIVING pleasure from pain must be the only way of surviving the beatings. I forced myself not to squint, but then I felt I would fall any minute.

"I should actually be caning you"—Yuin propped me up—"but you're too weak. So I have to use your friend as a scapegoat. But it's all your fault.

"Remember Ayushi: the thorns on his robe, the wrinkly skin on his hands, his beatific smile? His body was smashed, too, when he fell off the rock. And you're the one who did it."

"I wasn't even there," I stammered, wincing with every blow that fell on Martin.

"Harder!" Yuin commanded. "Once again, you're thinking about the outward things," he whispered to me. "Of course, technically he was killed by my agent. He might have remembered the meaning of the mantra. But you were the one who actually did it. You were envious of his spiritual assets: his ability to go on without sleep, food, or warm clothing."

He peered at my face and winked.

"You were envious of how high he had managed to soar! You wanted to be like him: alone on the mountaintop, without family or guilt, wrapped in contemplation and delights. But deep inside, you knew that you were denied this triumph. The realization filled you with bitterness. And it was the force of this bitterness that pushed the old man down."

Once again, the cane cut into the bloody mess of Martin's back. He screamed so hard as to make me recoil.

"You're vain, which is one quality banned from my ashram," Yuin went on. "We have saints, not vain ones. This is why I have to beat your vanities, including spiritual ones, out of you. I'll start with your aspiration to achievement. The Flood will take care of the rest. The new people will have already achieved it."

"Your agent in Colorado—"

"—the one who treads without noise."

"But she's the disciple of Ayushi!"

"She's my disciple. Ayushi was her assignment."

72

WE scrambled up to another Bon lamasery after dark. An Arctic cold had set in. We groped our way across the frozen stream that surrounded the place like a natural moat. Outside, unapproachable mountains; inside, a hilly village with crooked stone streets. With the wizardly reputation of Bon monks added in, the place looked positively ominous.

Inside, we were met by a few dogs, crazed with barking, and a few elderly lamas. Apart from their robes, they looked no different from the villagers.

We were led up creaking vertical stairs, with steps missing, and no railings. One needed to be in a trance to negotiate this passage safely, or to have a guide. An outsider could break his bones—if he hasn't broken them before in the mountains.

Finally, we found ourselves in a large room upstairs, sparsely lit by candles. Martin and I collapsed on the floor.

Contrary to the custom, the lamas did not offer us tea or even start the cast-iron stove in the middle of the room.

"They go get head lama," Dorje said. Beneath his calm voice I caught a note of anxiety. Something was not right.

FINALLY, the prelate showed up: an old man in a purple ski hat with a violet birthmark on his arm. He spoke to Dorje angrily. Our lama kept folding his hands, bowing, and nodding at us. I made out "sick" and "die." But the old man was not to be cajoled. He kept interrupting Dorje and pointing at the door.

"He says we go," Dorje said finally. "Chinese came before, said if foreigners come in without papers, he must call them. Or they shut down the lamasery."

"I'm gonna shut him down." Martin pulled out his submachine gun and shoved it in the old man's stomach. "Doctor—and—food—you—understand?"

Taken aback, Dorje flailed his arms.

"Or—I—make—hole—here?" Martin continued without batting an eye.

The old man recoiled and issued orders to his underlings.

"See, everybody understands English." Martin drew the gun away.

In a few minutes, the boy lamas were already stoking the dung in the stove, the teapot was boiling, and a sleepy, fat lama was changing Martin's bandages. Martin groaned, biting into his gun handle and glancing at the prelate, who was sitting quietly in the corner.

After he was done with Martin, the healer took my pulse, nodded, and left. Soon he returned with a cup of black concoction that smelled like glue. I glanced at Dorje suspiciously: Bon lamas were famous for their poisons.

Dorje grinned encouragingly: "Tonight, you sweat. Morning, you well. No more cough."

WARM under the blanket, I studied our new quarters. The low ceiling was propped up by dark red columns in the middle; cots along the walls; narrow mica windows. No decorations: not a Buddha statue, no *tanka*, no mandalas. Just some dried gnarly branches on sooty walls. I thought

they were bundles of dried grass that the healer had used in
his medicinal concoction; or, perhaps, yak wool. But Dorje
said something to the boy monk; he removed one of these
things off the wall, pared it with his knife, and placed some
shavings into a plate.

"Yak meat," Dorje explained, handing me the plate.
"Smoked."

The smell made me nauseous. The other lamas—there
were already half a dozen in the room—devoured the meat
avidly.

First, they chanted a mantra for a while; then they ate,
slowly, silently, their eyes steadily focused on their food.

I had heard that a perfect yogi, by meditative focusing,
should be able to transform the meat of five successive degrees of rottenness and five types of vile-smelling liquids
into pure edible and potable substances. Considerations like
tasty/tasteless, pure/impure, liked/disliked do not enter the
picture.

Or it could just be a lack of refrigeration.

AS usual, we went to sleep without undressing. Dorje promised we would leave at dawn in order not to put the lamas
at peril. Three of them stayed with us in the room. Like us,
they slept on broad wooden cots with thin worn-out rugs.
While we settled down, coughing, sneezing, and groaning,
the candles died, as did the stove, and finally the room was
lit only by the Himalayan stars, the largest in the world,
hanging dangerously low, like lights in an operation room.

In their silver shining, one could distinctly see six white
streams formed by our breath: it was as cold inside as out.

IN the middle of the night, I woke up, swimming in sweat;
the medicine must have been working. I could not sleep. As
quietly as I could, I made my way out of the room. Despite
the hostile reception, I felt safe: the dark catacombs, the
ancient wildness—a childhood dream, no less. There was
also a barely perceptible smell of dung: there had to be goats
kept nearby. A typical *gompa,* I recalled, has everything
under one roof: a stable, bedrooms, a kitchen, a prayer
room. A Buddhist monastery is not a cathedral, where earth

is a foundation and God is a spire. Like their worldview, a monastery is a layered cake, where every layer contains both heaven and hell and every piece contains God's brain and his callouses, too.

At the end of a pitch-dark hallway, I heard faint sounds of chanting. Someone was holding a predawn *pujah*. I walked towards the flickering light. Through a crack in the door, I saw a yellow swastika embroidered on a black silk cloth. I peeked in.

In the dark, the monks' shaven skulls turned slowly, like planets rotating under the weight of their poles. I pricked up my ears. The mantra was familiar, "Additapariya Sutra": *All things burn due to their inconsistence. . . .*

"YOU agree," I told Yuin, "that Creation is a permanent process, and up to now the lower societies have been becoming higher ones? If our civilization frees up its evolutionary level, another one will come to occupy it. Then what are you changing but the natural course of history, and He may not like it. Regardless of Satan, the apple would have fallen anyway—due to gravity.

Yuin shrugged. "I am not convinced." He pointed his telescope at the square outside Johang, where a flickering wreath, made of the pilgrims with their candles, was slowly rotating around the temple.

"They are driven by their libidos, their desire to be one with Buddha." He pointed the telescope upward. "The stars are driven by gravitation: the libido of the universe. Think about it: unlike the stars, the earth does not even have a light of its own. It's a dark clump of matter that rotates around a sun and sends to the universe nothing but its bitter thoughts and nuclear waste. Soon, it will be over. . . . Have some coffee."

The orderly placed a silver coffee service on the table. I took a sip . . . déjà vu—

"Just like Riverside Drive with the late professor?" Yuin asked immediately. "All things repeat themselves . . . even different points of view." He dropped a lump of sugar into his cup. "Why a long face? The poor earth will dissolve like this sugar and make the galactic coffee yet sweeter."

"I don't think so. Touched by a murderer's hand, the sugar will carry the stink and despoil the taste. Aah!"

Scalding liquid splashed in my face.

"Swine! Take him to the garage!"

ONE had to love the pain of the electrical shock. There was simply no other way to survive but to become your own executioner—to torment your former "I."

"Don't make faces," Yuin said. "Everything around us smells burnt. All things burn due to their inconsistence. Let me teach you Additapariya Sutra. Repeat after me: *All burns, o bkhikhu . . .*"

THE monks finished the chanting. I climbed the stairs to the roof. The dawn had barely started, and the courtyard was still empty. The *pujah* attendees went back to catch a nap. I needed to go to the toilet; here, like in the previous lamasery, it was at the very end of the structure, straight over the cliff.

A Tibetan toilet has to be performed in a trance, since the entire amenity consists of two boards protruding three feet over the abyss. You squat with your back to the deep and concentrate on the third eye, on the tips of your shoes, on anything—as long as you don't look between your feet. If you fidget or get dizzy, your body will roll down the soiled slope.

If you turn to face the courtyard, you will see the lamasery dogs: calm as if after meditation, with a permanently hungry look, focused upon your defecations. Tactfully, they wait for you to leave before they dig in. A perfect meditation on different species feeding each other.

I lost concentration and lowered my eyes. A young lama was walking down the slope, glancing back now and then. He had chosen the back road, rather than the main one, visible through the windows in the dining room where we stayed. He must have hoped he would not be seen. . . .

73

I dashed back to the sleeping quarters to wake up Martin.

"The old fart sent him to inform the Chinese!" Martin sprang to his feet as if he had had a full night's sleep. "I'm gonna kill this sonuvabitch!"

Dorje cautioned: *Wait.* "First, we catch messenger."

After a pause, Martin agreed. "You're right. No time to lose."

OUTSIDE. Martin's expression grew bitter as he peered into his binoculars. "Too far. Can't get him."

Dorje waved. "We go forward."

The messenger was circling the mountain. In order to climb it, we had to descend into the hollow where the mountain started.

BUDDHIST monks turning into informers! Perhaps Yuin had a point, I thought, about erasing the world's hard drive. Clearly, the global computer was out of whack. But Yuin did not believe in the backup. . . .

PANTING, we scrambled up the mountain. The dot below was moving up the winding path at a clip.

The monk was not looking underfoot. He looked right ahead, or, rather, slightly upward, as if he were keeping his eye on a star on the horizon; yet he did not stumble once, maintaining the same pace as he bypassed the rocks, staying a mere few feet away from the abyss. He was clearly a *lungom-pa,* or a trance-walker. At this rate he would be passing below us in about ten minutes—long before we could cross his path.

Martin drew his submachine gun.

"No." Dorje held him back. "He stops himself."

"How's that?"

Instead of answering, Dorje sat down on a boulder and closed his eyes.

"Is he gonna pray?"

"I don't know," I said. "Maybe he'll break his concentration."

Martin sounded desperate. Clearly, he was getting fed up with Tibetan ways.

The messenger kept walking as we kept passing each other the binoculars with bated breath. Suddenly, he stumbled. His head dropped as he looked underfoot. He made a few more brisk steps—and stumbled again. He looked back with a startled expression and started running. Now he was immediately below us; another twenty feet, and he would be out of our view.

Now, something strange happened: the messenger turned abruptly, as if someone had tapped him on the shoulder, and, catching the bottom hem of his robe, he sprinted forth on the edge of the cliff. But he only made a few steps; he screamed, spread his arms, and tumbled down into the gorge.

Martin and I exchanged looks: are we dreaming? I glanced at Dorje and recoiled: I distinctly saw a scowling skull coming through his light smile. But in the next instant, he leapt up, glanced at the now empty path, and ran down.

IT took us another hour to reach the body.

"He's got his brains outside," Martin informed us, stopping a few feet away from the body. "Let's go back."

Ignoring him, Dorje came up, turned the body over, and, kneeling, leaned over the dead man's ear.

"We got no time for those wakes!" Martin exclaimed.

"He must read Bardo," I said, dropping onto the rock. "The dead man can still see and hear. Dorje must convince him he is dead. Or else the dead man keeps going, thinking nothing has changed."

"Same as with live people," Martin remarked, closing his eyes.

I opened my diary, partly to cover embarrassment. Once again, I was wrong about Martin's outward appearance.

* * *

DORJE had been reading for over an hour. I went to the stream to get a drink. The flow was carrying frozen pieces of jetsam and flotsam. Some of them stuck at the edge and instantly melted. The waste freed itself of the ice and flowed on. Just like with people, I thought: the waste that is our thoughts and feelings is held together by the ice of our bodies. When we die, the ice melts, and the flotsam races in the Bardo flow, till it freezes again, in a new combination.

"WHAT will happen in the next world to the billions of people you will dispatch there?" I asked Yuin.

"Same as here," he said with a sneer. "Each of them will just keep chewing the cud of his thoughts."

"So what will you change? A mind does not dissolve by itself; it can void itself only when it is in a shape. After your ashram mankind has fruited and multiplied, then this whole ton of crap, canned in ether, will flow down and pollute your pure babies. Wasn't Cain a reincarnation of someone before him?"

MARTIN hobbled up to the stream. "What if Nagpa doesn't exist? Maybe he"—he nodded at Dorje—"wants to bring us as an offering to his warlocks. They put us on a spit and roast—"

I waved him off.

Nonetheless, I kept my eye on Dorje. I realized I didn't know anything about him. He claimed he had been arrested together with Nagpa, whom he had not seen since. He never talked about himself. "I grew up in monastery," he said. "I was lazy. Teacher always beat me because I cannot focus." He sounded a little like Ayushi.

Although Dorje was past thirty, at times he appeared to be my junior. He was shy and curious in a childish way: for example, gazing at the submachine gun when Martin oiled it. We never discussed with him the details of what had happened to us before Tibet. When he first heard the abridged version of our story, he said, "All mantras were invented by founder of Bon, our Lord Tumposhero, twelve thousand years ago."

I was struck by a coincidence—according to Yuin, this was the last time when the crust cracked up—and peppered him with questions. He fell silent. Only just before our escape he said, *No layman can read a Bon mantra and know its meaning.*

As a career policeman, Martin had to find Dorje's silence suspicious. But the silence of the lamas has nothing to do with keeping a secret, with distrust of strangers, or even with concentration. Theirs is the silence of the mountains: they exist, rather than talk.

I was startled by a gunshot nearby. Dorje leapt up to his feet, too. Martin peered into the distance, the barrel of his gun smoking. The echo rolled away, along with the birds' sounds. A flock of vultures—I did not even see them gather around—rose in the air, flapping their wings and cackling unhappily.

"We'll eat it on the way." Martin picked up a dead bird cheerfully.

"Not good for you," Dorje spat out. "You scare dead. You shoot when his mind goes off." He returned to his kneeling position and added: "Later, he scare you, too."

"Where's that?" Martin grinned. "In the next world?"

"This or next, same difference." Dorje went back to whispering into the corpse's ear.

PERHAPS all of us are already in Bardo, roaming while our consciousness goes through a transitory stage, getting spooked by the echo of our own deeds?

74

WHILE Dorje continues to read Bardo to the corpse, I go over my first morning in Rating. The guards were handing out food, banging on the doors. Dorje was already awake, seated on his cot and staring at me. He was sitting in a conventional fashion, with his two feet on the floor: the prison authorities did not allow the monks to assume meditation positions. His face was like china; I don't know any other way to describe this glowing solidity. It was as if a ray of sunshine had fallen on his brick-red slit-eyed face and froze on its surface. It was as if his face were wearing a cast: a mask of the sun that no amount of beatings, of food and sleep deprivation, could dissolve.

He always slept with a light smile playing on his lips. He must do "night work," or lucid sleep. I heard that lamas plan their nights ahead: flying in their sleep, writing poetry, and even meditating. Just what the children claim: you want to see something in your dream—and you do.

On another morning in Rating, Martin and I woke up gloomy as usual. Dorje, just as usual, was smiling. I asked him what he had seen in his dream. Without a hint of squeamishness, he used his fingernail to draw a mandala—the circle of life—on the dirty floor.

"But then you woke up and saw this." I spread my arms to indicate the cell.

He nodded and spread his arms, too, as if gathering the cell into a giant sack; then he placed the sack in a tiny dot in the corner of the mandala.

I understood. Everything was a part of the giant mandala.

Then the lama picked up a grain of sand and pretended to blow it up like a balloon, flailing his arms to indicate first the cell, then the prison, and, finally, infinity.

It was the first time that I did not think of the cell as hell. Any part of the universe contained the entire universe. There was no difference between a grain of sand and the entire desert. And any speck of cement could tell you everything about life.

DORJE saves me and supports me in the most critical moments. Like God, he does it almost imperceptibly.

I wake up every night in nightmares: the black man in the subway, Gwen on top of the car, Ayushi on the rock. And always Yuin in the Rating garage.

Every time, I find Dorje looking at me, as if he had woken up a moment before in the knowledge that I was about to open my eyes. He smiles or lightly touches my hand. I calm down and go back to sleep.

GOING back to our first night in the mountains: at dusk, everything grew ominously quiet and became covered with a silent dark web. As if the dawn may or may not come. I thought: this is what the first morning after the cataclysm would be like.

As if reading my thoughts, Martin said, "Our unit was protecting the medical staff on an island in the Caribbean right after the earthquake. Brrr: people covered with ashes walking through a great storm. Almost as if a crematorium got blown up and the ashes poured out on the living."

We are always covered with the ashes of our past experience, I thought; neither dead nor alive, we are walking wrapped in the burial sheets of our memory.

Two days earlier, in the cave, I had a dream about these sheets. I woke up and crawled out of the cave. It was early morning, with hoary reddish grass and ice sparkling in the cracks of the rocks. The moon was like a pale window in a giant blue tent. Silence, and tears in my eyes from the cold wind and memories.

I remembered the cold dawns of my childhood. I used to wake up before the others in my mother's ashram. I sat outside, looking down on the valley, and dreaming of love and adventures. Just the way I am sitting now. No adventures, no ashram; instead of adventures, fear and the flight of an animal; instead of love, the guilt and the diary.

What had happened between these two dawns? A lot; but the most important thing—love—had not. *My angels,* I addressed them, *I am crying because I have not loved enough. It's not too late, is it?* But the sky was silent.

Suddenly, a rustling sound came from behind.

"Not late," said Dorje's silhouette.

I shivered. "What?"

"Early." He pointed at the cave. "Go sleep."

A gust of the wind blew off my tears. And I could see Dorje smile.

No, it was not a mistake in his English. He said exactly what he meant.

Go and love. It's never too late.

75

THE plateau is coated in blinding hard-packed snow. With every step, you break the crust and sink down to your knees, scraping your shins. If we are spotted, we will not make it in time to the mountains, the blue iceberg at the end of the plateau. But they seem to be thinking we went in the opposite direction. I am starving. The dazzling snow looks like a raisin cake, with the boulders scattered across the slope like raisins.

The sun and the wind have covered my face with bleeding cracks; my lips are swollen and bleeding, and every attempt to open my mouth causes pain. The fierce wind has forced us to make masks out of the rags that our robes have become. Yet the sun and the wind penetrate the holes for the eyes and the nose. Looking is painful, and breathing is hard.

This will go on and on: the plateau is followed by a pass, which is followed by another plateau. I am trying to trick myself and pretend a gorgeous valley lies beyond the horizon. In its soft, balmy air, we will peel off the stinking rags and skinny-dip in a stream. Its water will be warm and sweet as honey, and we'll drink it without having to break off the ice and gnash our teeth. We will stroll on the green grass, and the birds will sing, rather than wait for the pensive Bardo-chanting killers to leave.

I picked you, Yuin said, because you were in the doorway. With one foot, you were already in the ashram with my angels, who are relaxed, soaring, giving and taking with ease, going beyond nation, race, age, gender, immune to guilt and consequences of their actions—for they do not want anything and they love anyone without expecting love in return. This is the kind of love that children, madmen, and whores have: light and cool, like a summer breeze. Perhaps this is why they made up Jesus' followers: they cannot give themselves to a single person, because they have no selves.

THE plateau is empty, the sun is blazing, but I see the white light, and . . . a yurt! A nomad tent! Tea—warmth— *tsampa!*

"Look, Martin!" I point ahead and then see that it's just a *chorten,* a stone mortar left by whoever was here before us.

SNOW blinds, too, and turns in rainbow ovals. Like Yuin's eyes.

"In Tibetan terms," Yuin said, "we are half-gods."

"Sounds like Nazis to me. Perhaps it was no accident that Hitler consulted Bon Po lamas."

"Consciousness knows no race. We have Jews, Gypsies, blacks. We are the Reich of the spirit."

"You are advancing a new cultural revolution, where ideas replace the means of production, and psychic forces replace guns. But all revolutions are doomed, bearing the sin of impatience and violence."

Yuin sounded as if he knew the answer long ago. "Cloning and genetic engineering disasters are a much worse form of violence against nature and a worse form of impatience in mastering God's forces."

A ringing in my ears; a distinct aroma of roses. Here, in the snow? No: the ringing must come from the altitude. The smell, from the frozen blood in my nose; my thirsty exhaling injects this blood straight in the brain. Or we could be approaching Shambala.

A ripple spreads across the snow. The surface begins trembling, and then melting. I walk on the water—white milky water. I must be hallucinating. Yuin's voice in my ears: ". . . *but your other foot is with the old mankind, where love is heavy like magma, where people struggle in the course of its flow, where they smash themselves on the rap-*

ids and pull one another down to the bottom. I picked you for your typically Western dichotomy. . . ."

THE ringing of the wind in my ears grows heavier, almost like a bell. It *is* a gong, whose sound floats over a clearing with white grass. People in white sit in a circle; I can't see their faces, but I recognize their backs. Gwen, Schechter, Abby, the Ruslanovs, my mother.

Suddenly, a little boy standing among them turns around, and I recognize myself at four or five. He smiles: everything is fine, everybody's alive, everybody has forgiven one another, everybody loves one another.

And then they are gone, and there is nothing but snow.

FINALLY, the mountains on the horizon are growing. Now they look like a crown made of coral peaks. Now . . . we are entering the valley.

This is just how I pictured it: peaceful and quiet, and air is sweet, the aroma of roses in the air, and an imperceptible ringing.

But where are the ashram dwellers? I feel as if someone is watching me. I hear the steps—no, it's a stone rustling by.

Is it that no one is supposed to be here?

"THE ability to join is a sign of backwardness," I told Yuin. "If your people's will is truly advanced, they do not need to be together."

"They have come here because—like you—they heard the mantra."

"Indeed, I used to dream of the commune of the enlightened. But the urge to unite is all too human. Angels are solitary; teachers are scattered all over the world. Shambala in one place is sheer nonsense."

"In order to pour like rain and start a new race, we must gather into a cloud first."

STROLLING through the valley, I did not notice stumbling into a cave. A huge bowl is flickering in the dark, with people in glittering white around it, chanting or singing. So that's why the valley was abandoned—they're all here!

As I approach the bowl, its white emanations dazzle more and more. Squinting but curious, I come closer, I get on my tiptoes, I lose balance—and I fall.

"GET up," Dorje says. "You have *kang*—"
   "I can't see you! Where are you? It's all white—"
   "Don't afraid," he says. "Is *kang na.*"
   Kang . . . ? "Snow disease," or snow blindness.
   The valley was a mirage.

76

DORJE was leading me by the arm. I tried to shake off his hand, but I could not feel my fingers. My toes were frost-bitten, too. I saw nothing but white. The freezing punishment cell, a lamp in my eyes, and Yuin's voice:

"You must go through the extreme physical pressure in order to realize that it is the inside world that matters. If you're not a slave inside, if you're free of desires, if you're not a body—you're free. All my followers have gone through that. Mankind, too, goes through a Rating of its own, with cataclysms and epidemics. The polar switch will be an ultimate experience of prison and release. Physical strength and stashed groceries will not help you survive the Flood; only faith will."

DORJE tried to cheer me up, humming some Tibetan ditties. I could barely move my feet. I wanted only to lie down, get warm, and have someone turn off the light.
   "A tent!" Martin shouts. "I see a tent!"
   Must be another *chorten,* I thought—a mirage . . .

. . . BUT then I hear the dogs bark, a yak moo, and, finally, human voices in Tibetan. It does not smell like roses or

Shambala, but for now the warm smell of a human abode is so much sweeter.

As they lead me inside, I feel a gust of warm sour air. What a miracle! No wind! They seat me on a stack of skins. I tilt to the side, and my head touches the wall. I lean against the yak fur and listen to the wind roar outside: how thin the line between life and death is.

Dorje applies something fat and edible to my eyes. He puts on a bandage, spreads more salve over my face and cracked lips, and feeds me tea, all the while chanting his healing mantras into my ear.

Gwen is lying just like this, a horrible thought flashes through my mind. Someone else dabs at her eyes that see nothing but pain.

"Hurt?" Dorje asks. "Burn?"

I shake my head.

"Gwen?"

I nod.

I think about her all the time. If I had been recording my thoughts in the diary, I would be walking around in a circle.

I must keep going; I must overcome everything, including new guilt and new losses: any pain, any humiliation; I must chafe my soul till it bleeds like my feet in these beaten-down boots—but I must get to see her. I am not doing this in order to save mankind or stop Yuin or be exculpated by the court or avenge my friends. I am doing this in order to see her, if only for a second. To see her eyes—and if she can't see me, it will be enough to hold her hand, stand at the head of her bed. I must be there, no matter what. She will feel my presence, and understand. She will know the punishment I inflicted upon myself—every second I spent in Rating, every second since her fall. She will know how much I love her. She will know I have relived every instant I loved her a thousand times, and executed myself for each instant I did not a thousand times, too. She will know that she was the reason I survived Rating. That my soul is covered with a bloody crust, just like my face; that my heart is frozen insensitive, just like the callouses on my feet; that I no longer know what pain is, either mine or someone else's. But I still keep going, because deep below, beneath this crust, there is a burning much worse than Yuin's electric shock—caused by my guilt of and my love for her. I keep going because she is going with me. She will understand that her healing is the meaning of my life and my atonement. I'll give her my hands, my feet, my eyes—I'll give her my life to replace the one I—

"YOU okay?" Dorje touches my hand.

My eyes itch again, and salt is eating at the cracks in my cheeks. "Okay." To change the subject, I ask, "What did you show that monk? The one who fell?"

"Ha! I show monster in his mind! But in empty mind—no monster!"

But how do I remove this monstrous guilt? I must find Nagpa, then come back, see her—and then . . . Once again, I am walking in a circle.

I smell yak manure, smoked meat, cured skins, smoke. The stove crackles; its soft warmth envelopes my face and caresses my naked toes, stretched out. The cup warms my hands; the *cha* revives my innards, and I can speak again.

Why can't we stay here, a cowardly thought flashes. Why do we always need to keep striving? First, I worked hard to bring Gwen over; then I dreamed of getting rid of her. Now I am busting my ass to get her back. That's what Dorje was whispering to the dead body: do not try to come back! You are being lured back by your habit to wish things, the habit of thinking that there's something else outside you that can make you happy. But you already have it all inside yourself.

And yet the guilt hovers in the shadows, sneaks into your dreams, ambushes you when you're at peace. To atone for guilt, you must leave the tent.

77

WE spent the night in the yurt. In the morning, Dorje removed my bandages. Halleluja—I can see again.

Now I can see I was a little romantic about the yurt; but that is an inevitable part of any dream.

Our saviors are a herder family: a husband, an old man, three women—perhaps his mother and two wives—and half a dozen kids. All of them sleep in a tiny, dark, smelly space. All household items—walls, dishes, clothes, butter in the candle saucer, and the salve that saved my eyes—come from yaks, those black hillocks sleeping in the snow outside.

The kids are the ones most cheered by our arrival. As I commit to paper the memories of our white trek, they giggle fearfully at the ornament that comes out of a tiny black stick.

The adults grin, too. They look like a mix of yaks and *chorten*s come alive—smoked by the sun, swathed in their skins, unhurried like statues, guileless like their animals.

DORJE turned the occasion into a house call. He has lanced the old man's boil, chanted mantras for the kids' rashes, and burned Bon offerings: some crumbs and rolled balls crackle in the stove.

Our hosts are filled with awe and delight. A lama in their abode is like having the Pope in an Irish family's living room in Queens. They are so grateful to provide us with food and yak skins for the road, and even tiny nets made of yak wool that you tie around your head in order to shield your eyes. Now, swathed from head to toe, we look like real natives.

Back on the path, we soon catch up with a group of pilgrims prostrating in the dust. While two perform the ritual, the third one pushes the cart with their belongings. They are wearing leather aprons and yak mittens with wooden laths strapped to their arms. They bring their folded hands to the tops of their heads, then to their necks and hearts; finally, they drop on the ground and freeze for a moment. And then all over again: get up, fold your hands, and stretch—a body's length. It takes a year to get from their homes to the holy mountain in this fashion, Dorje told us. They atone for sins and get themselves a favorable next reincarnation.

Martin grinned after we passed them. "They must've sinned a shitload."

"If we had to prostrate ourselves for our sins," I countered, "we would have to circle the equator."

After a pause, Martin added, "Or more."

NOW we are being cautious and check the passes in advance. The next one, at 20,100 feet, has a Chinese roadblock. We take cover behind a rock about half a mile away and study the new obstacle through the binoculars. Unfortunately, there is no way around it: a gorge to the left, a straight drop to the right.

Martin winces and expressively pats the stock of his gun. "No more lovey-dovey stuff."

Dorje has another idea. We will wait for the prostrating pilgrims and crawl through with them.

Martin grits his teeth, but has to agree. "I've crawled in the jungle, I've crawled in the desert . . . Damn! All right: put on your face paint!"

We cover our yak skins, mittens, and faces with the whitish dust. Now we all look alike: tanned and smoked, like roadside boulders.

Finally, the pilgrims arrive. Dorje trades some choice Bon blessings for a rental of aprons and wooden laths.

"We don't have to crawl yet," Martin suggests.

Dorje says we start now—to get into the part.

MY first time prostrated. I cling to the ground—oddly, it feels like sex—and instantly grow calm. They can take me now. I have known peace.

A Chinese truck rumbles by. I remain prone, my face

submerged in the cloud of the raised dust. There is something to this self-abnegation: my pride, my self-assertion, my fear of rejection—all are in the dust now.

Martin curses nonstop, clenching his teeth and spitting out the dust. Dorje stretches like a true pro. The roadblock is coming closer: I can hear the Chinese speech. Scared, I seek cover in the ground. But with every step, my strength wanes. I can see the boom. I crawl like a recruit in a Marine boot camp. I am a tongue licking the earth. Perhaps in the hundred feet left I will please her enough that she will hide me.

Every time I get up, I see the soldiers' faces grow larger, with their contemptuous grimaces of Romans observing pagan rites. I see their boots, the paws of the German shepherds. The dogs might smell something. A body search will reveal Martin's gun—back to Rating we go. The courtyard with four jeeps and the ropes.

The officer's boots, the green pants with red piping. Coming right at me.

"WHEN the earth erupts," Yuin was fond of saying, "the resulting electromagnetic storm will release so much energy that everybody will have a vision of angels and the Second Coming—at least for a moment."

"What if you and your ashram are blown up, too?"

"So much the better!" he exclaimed. "Then it's not just civilization that is folding—but the whole universe! Game over! Then you will see the heavens folding like a scroll, and everything returning to a single point in the middle of the mandala!"

He drew his gun and shot at the *tanka* on the wall. He hit the Buddha in the middle—bull's-eye—and the echo from his shot resounded through the prison.

I thought I was petrified with fear, but here I am, getting up at a mere three feet away from the officer. Suddenly I know what I should have told Yuin: "This game is like a yo-yo. It can't fold."

I smile, and Dorje's smile of enlightenment has nothing on me. I drop into the dust at the man's feet, like a drunk—a dog—an ant. I am the denizen of these ashes; I rise from them and I return to them. Again and again, from life to life—this is my Tao. I equal dust, I am nothing—therefore, I cannot be exposed.

Ecstatic, I get up again, I fold my hands over my head, and I extend the officer an ear-to-ear smile.

For a second, his slitlike eyes study my blackened mug and become even narrower—he is smiling back.

78

FOR a day, we walked without adventures. I am not sure that pilgrims earn themselves a good karma by stretching prone; perhaps they erase the leftovers of their minds with their wooden laths, and the monotony of brown cliffs puts your mind in an enlightened but dull state. . . .

No sooner did I write this than we spotted a dozen people in black prison uniforms below the pass. They were doing roadwork, shovels in their hands, with a handful of Chinese soldiers flanking them. Through the binoculars we recognized faces of our ex–fellow inmates from Rating.

The chief guard was a dour-faced sergeant. Had it not been for his sunglasses, we might not have recognized the colonel, the former lucky owner of the diamond necklace. How the mighty had fallen! No longer was he strolling up and down the courtyard in an impeccably pressed tunic and polished shoes; now he was wearing a quilted jacket, and his boots were splattered with mud.

"Too bad Yuin has spared him," Martin said, peering at his nemesis through the binoculars.

"The general believes in purification through suffering," I said.

The sergeant yelled at a scrawny prisoner and raised his nightstick, as if to hit him. The poor man recoiled, making the sergeant stumble and fall on the rocks. He immediately got back on his feet and started striking the prisoner methodically with his stick. The echo carried the curses and the groans through the gorge.

Martin shook his head. "If the end is soon, why did Yuin send them to repave the road?"

"Labor is salvation," I quoted Yuin. *"It saves people of the stomach from beastly idleness, and people of the mind from existential horror.* He also keeps up the pretense of normal activity. I'm sure Beijing has informers here to report on him."

"Maybe that's who the colonel was," Martin mused. "Yuin never mentioned cataclysm in front of him, right? Maybe that's how the bastard survived—because Yuin did not want to alert Beijing. Sonuvabitch sure knows what he's doing.

"Anyway . . ." Martin drawled. "If we hit the targets right, the falling rocks will bury them."

Indeed, we were out of options. The road below was the only path forward. With glaciers above us, we could not take a high road.

Martin nodded at the sack on which Dorji was seated. "Give me the grenades."

Dorje did not budge, calmly watching the ex-colonel raging below.

"He make rock fall," the monk said finally, as he assumed a pose for meditation.

Martin glared at him, but, after the episode with the monk going over the cliff, he did not dare press his case.

"What about them?" I nodded at the tiny black-clad figures below.

"They anyway die." Dorje closed his eyes. His lips moved quickly and silently.

This was the first time Dorje had acknowledged that the cataclysm was inevitable. He believed in it as much as Yuin did.

"LET Nyima go," I told Yuin. "Or else no more debates."

Yuin shrugged. "Then I'll just kill her. What's the point in letting her go? When the earth crust shifts, so will the magnetic poles. Those not buried under the water or the lava will simply lose their minds or vanish in the black hole of time, the way things vanish in the Bermuda Triangle. Only the initiated will avoid this fate."

"Let her go," I repeated. "Let her die at home."

"She will be distracted there. Let the prison be her lamasery."

I forced myself to focus. "According to Bardo, your last thought before death defines the quality of your conscious in your next reincarnation. She shouldn't be in prison."

"Prison is the best place for fantasies. Come, let me show you something. . . ."

I was distracted from reminiscing by the sounds below. The colonel was still raging as he repeatedly kicked the prisoner in the groin. Finally, the man swore and flung a rock at the torturer. The colonel dodged, then pulled his gun and fired. The prisoner writhed, holding his stomach. The colonel stood over him, riddling his limbs with bullets.

I looked away, at a boulder farther up the slope. As I shuddered at a gunshot, the boulder seemed to shudder as well. Another shot—another boulder. Dorje was chanting out loud now, in a voice that seemed to grow more ominous with every note.

Another shot brought me to my feet. The mountain was stirring! Brown boulders were sliding down the slope— right at us!

"Watch out!" Martin grabbed Dorje and pushed him inside a small niche in the bushes.

The last thing I saw before joining them inside was the colonel with his arm up. It looked as though he was firing at the mountain.

I felt as if I were lying between the rails, with the freight train roaring above. The din and the crashing sound grew by the minute. Sand streamed past the entrance to our niche; then came small pebbles, and finally, boulders, one by one. And then all became dark.

"I didn't get it"—Martin shouted over the din—"was it our guy who caused it by chanting or that asshole by firing his gun?"

"It could be that he was induced by the mantra to start shooting!" I yelled.

"If the mountain collapses, we're fucked!"

"Start praying!" I rolled myself into a ball and hid my head between my hands.

AFRAID to move, we stayed in our positions for a long time after it became quiet. Gradually, the wall of dust outside dispersed, and we saw a small gray cloud. Only then did we warily crawl out of our shelter.

The road below was gone. There was a pile of brown rocks, with spots of color, where the inmates had been working.

From above, the scene reminded me of the ruins of the Colorado library in the picture.

YUIN showed me the picture. "That's all that's left of Abby's library."

I peered into it, as if hoping to find the remains of the poor poetess among the ruins. "Why did you do this?"

"You did this. You wanted to get rid of her motherly jealousy. She wanted you, you were ashamed of wanting her—you wanted to be rid of her. To dig deeper, you wanted to flee the pattern of being reborn."

"Nonsense. I—"

"Let's go back." He took a folder out of his desk. "These court-appointed doctors don't care much for patients' rights, do they?"

He leafed through pages. "You produced some choice confessions in the course of your therapy. Here's your mother: young, cheerful, devil-may-care. How could you not be totally besotted with her? In turn, she made you fall in love with music and poetry. She was unhappy with your father. Whom you hated: he was 'rude, arrogant, called her'—your mother—'lowbrow and primitive, resented her joy of life, music, flowers—' Whew."

Yuin winced. "Textbook Oedipus. Yet it was for your sake that your mother would not leave him. She was afraid you'd become a junkie, especially since you already showed some inclination in that direction. Your girlfriend was a junkie, a poet, much older, almost your mother's age—in short, a future Abby. Your mother had a jealous fit. Hm, that's quite graphic: 'she was screaming that I would never call her Mother if I didn't ditch Charlotte. . . . You're killing me, she yelled.' Sounds like she was projecting, don't you think? To her, it was incest of sorts. . . .

"You were shocked—you were unaware that so much stress had been building up. But you didn't care, did you? You went off to spend a weekend with your Charlotte. Your mother was left alone—your father was away on business—so she went to her favorite bar, where she allowed a colleague of your father's buy her a few margaritas. One thing led to another. . . .

"Unfortunately, the ending is pure farce: your father comes back earlier than planned, the colleague jumps out of the window and breaks his leg. Your mother follows him and breaks her neck. Or did your father push her? The police chose not to look too closely. God bless American family values.

"Let's see . . . the patient—Rudolph, that is—torments himself with guilt as an indirect cause of his mother's death. Never saw his father again. Heroin dependency—accident—court-ordered treatment . . ."

He noisily slapped the folder shut.

"So poor Abby had no idea of the enormity of complexes that she ran into—"

"—and I killed her." I did not have to read Yuin's mind. With time, his conclusions had become predictable. "Metaphysically speaking. And if we skip meta—?"

"She got killed by methane concentration."

"Who was it—the redneck from the gas station or the sheriff?"

"Nobody. She lit a cigarette in the kitchen, which was already filled with gas."

"She told me she never smoked there."

"She was upset. Right after you left, she got a phone call from Margi. Just to say good-bye—to tell Abby she was leaving with you to keep looking for the mantra. Margi also added that you hadn't told Abby the two of you were leaving together because you suspected Abby might be jealous."

Yuin chuckled. "If words were dynamite, women would make the best terrorists. You might entertain some notions about my omniscience now, but, honestly, I don't know what happened next. Maybe she saw the situation as a replay of the one with her husband and decided to bail out, or maybe she got nervous and needed a cigarette right away."

Or maybe Margi chanted something into the phone, I thought.

WHEN we got down the slope and approached the wreckage, I noticed scraped bloody limbs stirring among the brownish rocks. It was as if the earth were giving birth to monster plants—to these bodies, maimed, but still clinging to life.

I dropped on my knees and pushed a rock away.The young inmate was still alive: his hand was trembling, and he tried to turn his head, which lay on its side motionlessly. Dorje took the man's wrist and shook his head.

"Agony," he explained. "For Bardo no time."

"There's another one." Martin nodded at a hand reaching towards us. The fingers were grabbing the dusty side of the rock and kept slipping off.

We came close—and froze. The wrist of the hand had the professor's beads around it.

Martin lifted the rock, and for the first time we saw the colonel's eyes—the sunglasses must have fallen off. His eyes were narrow and, oddly enough, blue.

"Devil," Dorje whispered. "China devil."

The colonel moved his head slightly and squinted. He must have had a concussion.

"Forgot an old friend?" Martin sneered.

The man's blue eyes grew white with terror. "No diamonds . . ."

"They would have been diamonds—in another man's hands." Martin tore the beads off the colonel's wrist and tossed them to me. Then, as if washing his hands of the whole thing, he let the rock drop straight down.

*   *   *

AS we proceeded down the road, Martin kept wondering
about the beads. Surely the colonel would have kept them,
in the greedy hope that they might turn back into diamonds.
Yuin had not confiscated the beads; perhaps he believed in
objects that served as magic. Or, perhaps, he intuited the
beads were dangerous and let the informer have them—
sooner or later, they would become his undoing.

79

THE roads with Chinese checkpoints were too dangerous
and took too long to cover. If we were to take shortcuts, we
would be facing impossibly high passes and glaciers, and
to negotiate that terrain we needed tents and food, which
was running out. In short, we needed to hire sherpa guides
with mules. We had no choice but to approach the village
ahead.

From up the mountain, the village was a pile of shacks
that looked like a swallow's nest. For a couple of hours, we
studied it through the binoculars: a few locals passed by;
gray threads of smoke from stoves rose into the sky—the
place showed no signs of Chinese troops. Still, we were
wary as we entered the village.

THE dusty alleys, weaving in a maze between the shacks,
were just wide enough to let through a loaded yak. Now
they were abandoned, save for packs of shaggy dogs. The
villagers must have spotted us from afar and now seemed
to be hiding in their windowless fortresslike shacks of gray
stone. If they were afraid, was it of us—or of whomever
would follow us?

"You stay here, I look." Dorje disappeared in a side
street.

We rested with our backs to the wall. Martin turned to
take a look and nudged me. "I don't know about Chinks,

but they sure have some kind of Aryan Brotherhood here."

The swastika was painted Bon-style, counterclockwise. Next to it were the moon and the sun: the unity of the opposites.

"This goes back to before to the Nazis," I whispered. "Means eternity and luck. Protects the house against evil spirits."

Martin chortled. "Then how come both lamas and skinheads shave their heads?"

I shrugged. Then I looked up—and was startled.

WE were facing a small crowd. Toothless old men in fur hats, women in kerchiefs, soot-faced children in rags belted with pieces of rope—they noiselessly emerged from every crack, joining the onlookers.

Martin cleared his throat. "Well, folks—any English speakers here?"

There was a pause. And then the crowd erupted in laughter.

"What the f—" Martin's hand mechanically reached for his gun.

Yet the laughter did not seem to be aimed at us. Rather, they were having fun the way a child has fun with a new toy.

"I bet," I started uncertainly, "I bet they never heard foreign speech before."

BY the time Dorje came back with the village elder, the communication was in full swing. The kids were alternately overjoyed and frightened when Martin allowed them to trace the serrated blade of his Marine knife with their fingers.

We were invited to spend the night at the elder's house—the largest one in the village, set aside from the rest. The sherpas would come back the next day, we were told. Hospitality is a law of survival and secures a good reincarnation.

ALTHOUGH the room was dark and smoke-filled, one could tell it was spacious. In the reddish glow cast by the flames in the large stove, I gradually made out shiny eyes,

shaven heads, and red ribbons with turquoise woven into
the black braids.

Everybody bowed, and we bowed back, putting our
palms together. Even Martin got into doing it mechanically.
The gesture is a reminder to oneself: do not be a man or a
woman, but—a whole.

*I'll bring the two hemispheres together: no longer will
the world be divided into east and west, north and south. . . .*

These people *are* whole: they have no need of Yuin's
plan.

WE settled on the rug-covered benches in the corner. On
the wall above were a painting of Tara the Goddess of
Plenty and a yellowed poster of *The Terminator*. In the
kitchen across the room, the preparations for the welcoming
feast were under way. Several youths were chopping the
meat on the stone floor. Red flesh, black cleavers, white-
toothed smiles as they glanced at us. If they were chopping
our bodies for the buzzards, they would be proceeding with
equal ease and good cheer.

BLACK dishes, black hands. By now, I was so used to eating with my hands unwashed, I no longer remembered why
one did it. By contrast, dipping your finger in the water and
flicking it three times—for Buddha, for his teachings, and
for the community—seemed like the most natural thing.
Here, with the cruelest climate and lack of basic hygiene,
faith was your daily bread, your fuel, your penicillin. You
had to resort to mantras and prayers as protection against
freezing, getting poisoned, or losing your way.

I couldn't follow Dorje's machine-gun-fast Tibetan. He had
to be narrating our odyssey to the hosts. They laughed and
stared at us as they grabbed pieces of meat with their hands.

"They may be Buddhists," Martin remarked, "but they're
still primitives."

And what was civilized? Perhaps it was an ability to live
in peace with yourself without harming others?

*   *   *

MY eyes were simultaneously getting used to darkness and blurring with *chang*. There was a constant flow of people in and out—the entire village had to take a look at us. Our hosts were getting drunker and louder. Actually, I couldn't tell the hosts from the guests. Perhaps everybody was related and consciously indistinct from one another; perhaps Western individualism was in their past, rather than in their future; perhaps they had already been through it and come full circle.

The pack of Chinese cigarettes that Martin had offered our host was almost empty, and smoke seemed to have replaced oxygen. Martin's blackness fascinated them endlessly. Someone asked Dorje what kind of ointment Martin was using and where they could get some.

"They say you handsome." Dorje giggled.

Martin allowed one of the kids to rub his finger on his black skin for test purposes.

"They sure are poor, but they ain't vicious," he remarked, flattered by the attention.

I concurred. Perhaps the absence of viciousness comes from both lack of attachment to your own possessions and envy of those of others. Whoever gives, does not lose; whoever takes does not get; the keeper, the object, the receiver are all one. If all God's things belong to me, then all my things belong to God, too.

Agitated both by the compliments and the *chang,* Martin flirted with our hostess, a jolly Tibetan Brunhild, who chortled as he tried to grab her abundant waist and pushed him away. She had her duties, with guests arriving nonstop.

Nonplussed, Martin turned his attention to Dolma, the elder's daughter, a tall, strong girl who stared at us with unconcealed curiosity. With Dorje's help, he began explaining that the girl was born for the runway and magazine covers.

"Look at her cheekbones, man! All those agencies will die to have her! Ask her—she wants to come to America with me? I'll manage her personally!"

As Dorje translated, the onlookers burst into laughter.

"What do you say, girl?" Martin grabbed her hand and eyeballed her as he went on with the patter. "Want to be rich? Want to ride around in a white limo, drink champagne, stay up all night?"

Looking down, she shook her head silently and pulled away.

"What's the matter? You got a boyfriend, huh?"

He tried to get her hand back, but she recoiled and ran out of the room, to yet another outburst of laughter.

SO does the earth take fright at the attacks of the sky. It learns its lessons, and sheds leaves before the abuses of winter, so that the snow does not break the branches with its weight. After punishing droughts, it learns to hide water in underground springs. So did Gwen: the slightest whiff of a hurt drove her inside her armor.

She, too, wanted a large family, like this one in Tibet: a house upstate, where she could bring her mother and have plenty of children. I did not; she perceived it as a lack of love, and the torment drove her inside herself. I did not want my freedom to be constrained, but she wanted freedom to bloom in constraint, the way a grain can yield fruit only when it's held tightly by the soil. I was a late bloomer; a man is always slow in joining a woman's quiet dream, just like a mind is slow to understand the meaning of life.

I have been dreaming of this throughout our trek: a large family living together. The continuity of life, all its forms and stages taking place together and at the same time: animals, nature, childhood, maturity, old age. In the West, life has been carefully partitioned: nature in the park, animals in the zoo, children in the kindergarten, old folks in their "managed-living" facilities.

Yet both this village and Gwen's dreams are about the blood kinship of a clan. Me, I used to want a different kind of unity. Not unlike the one that would come in the Flood as families intermingle and survivors are brought together by fate and their spirit, rather than blood.

Hence, a man's secret yearning for the Flood: not for everything to be washed away, but for everything to merge.

I was yanked out of my contemplations by a true blast from the past. Suddenly, the humming of the human hive was shattered by the hysterical voice of Tune Ra hollering the mantra!

I leapt to my feet mechanically, but Martin calmed me down. No one paid attention: they crowded around the elder who was toying with a tuner on the cheap transistor radio. The voice of Yuin's favorite faded and came back again through the static.

"Don't they have another station here?" I gasped.

Of course they did not. The only signal that reached the village came from a Chinese station. Asking the host to turn the music off was out of the question: the radio was the high point of a feast.

The hollering brought more people inside, including Dolma and her girlfriends, decked out in brightly colored kerchiefs and turquoise necklaces. After much whispering among them, Dolma finally approached her mother, who shrieked with surprise but parlayed the request to Dorje.

"Girls say you teach them dance like in America," Dorje said, beaming.

I shook my head, but Martin drunkenly shoved me forward. "I know you ain't supposed to have rhythm, but my leg's still hurting. Besides, they've never seen *Showtime at the Apollo*—they won't know the difference."

THEY didn't, but they reacted no less ardently than an uptown crowd. "*Ray! Ray!* Go!" Tune Ra was screaming through the static—it was as if the entire planet was cracking up. Our hosts had no idea that these screams would bring on death and destruction.

Was it a shack in the Himalayas or DeoMorte in Manhattan? The same darkness, the same reddish glow, the same Bosch-like faces . . .

After a few seconds of dancing, I was soaked: sweat poured out of my body and irritated the still unhealed cracks on my lips. My heart leapt out of my chest, and I could not catch my breath, short of air, sparse at this altitude. I did some kind of clumsy curtsy, barely keeping my butt above the floor, and stumbled to the exit.

*   *   *

THE Himalayas in moonlight: majestic icebergs, frozen at the instant of collision with the boat of the village. Falling stars, dogs' barking, and the sweetish smoke of dry manure. If only Gwen could see it—she would have understood my longing for Tibet, and we would not have fought, I would not have dreamed of escaping her.

When all is said and done, the cause of our falling out— and her fall—was my dream, and nothing else.

If I could only start over! I would not need her understanding. In her, I would see my Himalayas, my heart, my song. We would be flying together because we would know that each and every one of us contains the same heavenly magnificence and awe. All you need is to see it.

80

WHEN I woke up, the sun was high over the mountains, and fresh snow sparkled with blue-and-pink light. Once again, I felt like a child, getting up before everyone else. The air at this hour was just as cold and sweet, and filled with aromas of the bonfire and burnt clay and dry leaves, not unlike that of the dried manure in the village.

The elder's wife offered to wash our clothes. I surrendered them gratefully and walked outside. In the backyard, the children were slapping together a snowman.

"Aha!" Martin patted me on the back. "You feel like you should be a daddy yet? High time, buddy. I had my first when I was twenty-one. He's just made sergeant. Yeah, kids are fun!"

He grabbed his walking stick and, holding it athwart like a lance, rushed at the kids. Within minutes, they were competing at lance-throwing, with the snowman the target.

I climbed the eroded stone steps to the top of the shack and watched Dolma carry the sack with our laundry to the creek. She walked with innate grace, balancing the sack on her head, and the sight of her tugged at my heart: I felt like Adam watching Eve, just as lonely and graceful, on the plateau of Eden. Why go that far? Not so long ago I used to watch Gwen walking with an air of solitude through the crowds of Broadway, and my heart missed a beat, full of tenderness, because I knew she was walking to see me.

Children, animals, nature, tilling the soil . . . happiness. We could have been happy, too, had I not gone to the basement.

But I was not truthful; I had turned it down of my own accord. She wanted a child. I retorted by saying, You must imagine a world where everyone's a child.

What an idiot. If everybody's a child, there's no room for the tenderness and care that only parents can provide.

I knew how to talk about the ideal world, but I never learned the art of ideal love, which consists in loving everybody as if he or she were your own child. Gwen knew that. She wanted to help me learn to love one of my own, so that I could use this art on everyone else.

DOLMA came up to the roof to hang the laundry. The kids came running, too, drawn by the bright red plastic bag with the Marlboro cowboy, in which she carried the laundry. We had confiscated it from the Chinese at the guardhouse.

I don't know what gave me the idea: perhaps the praying flags that flapped on the rope above us. I picked a clothesline, fastened two sticks to the bag, and, holding the end of the rope, tossed it in the air: a kite! A flying cowboy!

Giggling, the kids followed me as I ran down the steps, outside the gate, and down the slope to the creek. I ran, sinking in the snow, exposing my face to the sun, my ears filled with the kids' cries of excitement—and I felt the walls of Rating's cell, Yuin's arguments, and my guilt caving in. I stumbled and fell, but one of the kids caught the rope and ran off, hollering triumphantly.

I lay in the snow, gasping the frosty air, and for a moment nothing else existed: no guilt, no Yuin, no endless torture. For a moment, I felt I could live again.

"Hey, poet!" Martin called. "The sherpas are back!"

*   *   *

THE money we had taken from the Chinese was running out, and we had to bargain hard for the sherpas' services. Yet even after we paid, departure was nowhere in sight: the sherpas settled down for *cha*-and-chat with our hosts, then left to replace their gear and seemed to vanish.

The delays drove Martin berserk. Yet it is elementary physics: mass goes up, speed goes down, time goes up. The Himalayas put a brake on everything: the inhabitants' movements, the metabolism, and, finally, the thinking process. If your mind is as immobile as the mountains, you must have arrived. Time to step down and take off your shoes . . .

THE whole village came out to see us off. I am tearful: I feel as if I were leaving my own family, with the hostess representing a mother, and Dolma a sister. Perhaps the village is enchanted—a place where you forget everything and remember everything? Once, everyone was a kinsman of yours: a mother, a daughter, a friend. You loved them in equal measure; love is indivisible. That is why they're so cheerful and simple, like rocks in the sun. I wonder if I'll ever see them again—see anyone who's dear to me—see Gwen?

But the Tibetans do not seem to share the concept of sadness. They laugh. . . . Innate knowledge of the illusory nature of attachment.

81

ACCORDING to the symptoms, we had never been at this altitude before. At above twenty thousand feet, your nose bleeds, your ears are blocked, you are fighting nausea and headache. You no longer move—you crawl, gasping for air.

The two sherpas chuckled as they waited for us straggling behind. The older one, with a face like a baked potato and a bad case of farsightedness, was quieter, as befit his age;

the younger one constantly revealed his dazzling white teeth on an equally brown, though less wrinkled face. He watched Martin with an awe reserved for an ET—which Martin is, of course.

If I stay alive, I should write *Climbing for Dummies*. One should move up the mountain the way one moves through life: a) slowly; b) with a prayer, or a mantra, or at least concentrating on a single object, like this tail of a horse in front of me, with horse apples dropping underfoot; c) avoid abrupt movements and remain silent, to save energy and breath; d) stop often to admire the beauty and suppress the wheezing in your chest; e) return to pick up the stragglers, but not the things you have dropped; f) do not take offense at the mocking sherpas, who, like angels, are always above you. Finally, never take your eyes off the peak you want to conquer. And finally—finally, remember that behind it will be other peaks, even higher, and the climb is endless.

THE sherpas performed their bodily functions openly. Martin shook his head: *Primitives*. Ha! What's the sight of a bare ass compared to the murder and mayhem that fill our airwaves day and night! We are not ashamed of violence and hate, yet we blink at the beautiful human body and its natural functions. Tibetan kids who only know how to throw snowballs will stay in their mountains, but our kids who sit at their PlayStations zapping other kids will become world leaders. Is Yuin's solution the only way out?

SOMETIMES the path became so narrow as to let only one human body between the rock face and the abyss. Martin and I crawled, our eyes half-shut, pressing ourselves into the wall. Dorje used short, careful steps. The sherpas did not slow down one bit—and led the fully laden horses, too!

Skill? Yes. Habit? Yes. But also indifference to death. That is, innate understanding that death is not the worst thing that can happen to a person. Death is a transition into a new form. It is much worse to kill—to steal—to do any similar damage to your own soul, for this will lead to a bad reincarnation and resulting suffering. A complete reversal from our culture, where death is the supreme punishment.

The coldness of Tibet is not an absence of warmth, but, rather, the presence of ultimate clarity. Deserted spaces are not barren; they provide space for the most important work—all you can do here is glorify the Unity and, like the lamas, pray for the salvation of all living creatures.

Once you get used to the altitude, you slide into a condition akin to a light hangover: not a single thought, slow movement, and a humble calm in your soul. I could not tell my foot from the rock I lowered it upon. There was nothing for the mind to concentrate on, and my body seemed to be moving to the next rock of its own accord.

SUDDENLY, the sherpas came to a halt, and lay prone for the prayer.

"What's with them?" Martin asked.

Dorje nodded upward. A *menghir*—an image of a horseman engraved in the rock—protruded over the path.

"I was child, I waited for him to show up," Dorje said with his customary smile. "From blue mountains on a red horse."

"Who?"

"Rigden Japo, future Buddha. Master of Shambala."

His Sanskrit name was Rudra. I scrambled up to get a closer look. The wind had eroded most of the facial features, but the horseman's eyes were strikingly wide, and his hairline was intact, an M on a high forehead. According to Schechter, *menghir*s like this were left behind by ancient Aryans. The professor had seen one only once, not far from the lamasery, where he stayed with Nagpa.

"What does it say?" Martin nodded at the more distinct inscription—perhaps a more recent one—under the figure.

"Hail the pearl in the lotus."

"Aha, one of them mottoes." He nodded. "We used to write mottoes on our helmets in the army," he added a hundred feet later. "If you wrote one, what would that be?"

I paused. "Maybe, *I'm in Heaven.* Meaning, I don't have to achieve nothing or become no one."

"You really think that, huh?" He eyed me inquisitively.

"That's from the Vedas. What about you? What did you have?"

"Evil Is My Mirror."
"Where does that come from?"
"From experience."

I could not get enough of Himalayan sunsets. The clouds were stacked in the sky in a super-rainbow array of colors: black—red—blue—yellow—purple—pistachio—orange—red again.... This looked like a color-coded message, a spirit descending into matter. But it was only our eyes and the horizon that limited this array: the colors changed interminably.

"Wow." Even Martin was impressed. "With a view like this, I sure could use a barbecue."

As if on cue, the sherpas called a halt and began collecting twigs for the fire.

Martin ordered me to help him chop the meat we had brought from the village. Once again, I could not help feeling irritated. To him, beauty was a mere complement to stuffing his face. With his thick neck and sausagelike fingers, he looked a little like a yak himself.

Right now, he is going on about respecting the Chinese for having built an empire without bothering for all those human concerns Americans are famous for. When he talks like this, he seems to be siding with our pursuers: men whose actions are dictated by their stomachs. I'd like to think I'm on the side of men of thought. Yet look who's on my side: Yuin and other brainy chimeras, whom I have to flee. Where am I?

82

"WHY are you holding me in the cell?" I asked Yuin when I was brought in for yet another investigation, dizzy after a sleepless night in the cold cell. "You might as well put me up in a hotel. In humane conditions, I would be better suited to provide you with your arguments—if you really need them."

This suggestion was Martin's idea. With crazy Yuin, who knew what would work? At least one had a chance of escaping from the hotel.

Yuin merely grinned. "All the candidates for my ashram have gone through Rating. "Here, they have been weaned from logic, human rights, human dignity, and the satisfaction of human needs. Rating is the gate to Shambala: complete absurdity, utter hopelessness. At any time, anyone can be tortured, killed, forced to have sex with his mother or daughter, turned into a snitch or a homosexual. I am the embodiment of their karma, acting without visible reasons; in order not to go crazy from this absolute power of fate, they are forced to become Buddhas and never invest their actions with personal motives. To become the Void."

"How does that make you different from great tyrants like Mao or Stalin?"

"They made mistakes, but both of them knew that their primitive subjects would not reach enlightenment through reading books and meditating; only the master's cane can do the job. They wanted to free man from the fear of loss. Loss of friends, family, freedom, money, health, honor, conscience . . . They wanted the masses to master the Void. Unfortunately, the masses are not capable of it. Therefore, they must be removed, and I must use a handful of capable ones to grow a mankind of the Void."

"Margi passed through Rating, too?"

"With flying colors. She'll tell you all about it."

Night in the Himalayas comes abruptly: as if someone has turned off the light in a giant planetarium. All that's left is you, unknown constellations above, and the humming of the cosmos. Our bonfire is the flaming center of this universe, its heart that will go out last, the way a flicker of life dies last in the heart of a dying person.

"The black smile of the corpse is always in my eyes, Rudi; it's so beautiful. . . ."

Schechter said that as he meditated in front of the fireplace, which later was the source of his own death. Yet in New York, a fireplace is a mere decoration, while here in

Tibet, fire is life: it warms you, cooks your food, and frightens off the animals.

The sherpas were involved in a heated argument, appealing to Dorje, who listened with his customary smile.

The younger one was talking about the local rumors: people went on from here and vanished in the mountains! There had always been plenty of natural causes, of course: avalanches, falling rocks, wildcats, and even bandits. But now, the young man claimed, there was some kind of weird place, with weird people—and sherpas, whether running into these people or stumbling upon that place, were never heard from again!

"But how do you know," Dorje asked, "if they were never heard from again?"

"Not all of them were lost! I wasn't! And I saw *pi ling!*"

The elder one waved. "You're still going on about that woman."

Irritated by his partner's condescending expression and Dorje's smile, the younger one was getting excited, slurring words and spitting.

"Pi ling?" I asked. "Foreigners? Mountain climbers?"

"No—but they're like white Buddhas."

"All lies," his partner commented. "And what do they look like?"

"I saw a *kie men.* Beautiful. Woman."

"You should get married!" The elder man burst out in laughter. "All you can think about is pussy!"

"I saw her!" the youth exclaimed. "In a white sheet! Right here! A little farther, after the pass!"

"Why didn't you say so! After the pass! That's where old Nagpa used to live—when the Chinese caught him and wrecked his lamasery, he left guardian *yidam*s—spirits—here."

I glanced at Dorje, surprised. He nodded lightly.

Why hadn't he told me he grew up here with the teacher? That means the horseman statue we had run into was the same one Schechter had seen!

Before I had a chance to fully digest this new information, the sherpa youth was yelling: "This was no *yidam!* This was real! I lagged behind the caravan and stopped for a cup of *chang*. Suddenly, there was whistling behind me. There she was, standing on the rock, all in white—and her dog, too. I wanted to run after her, but I was too scared."

"Ha! That was the white woman's ghost! About the time you were born, a white woman used to come to the village—her husband studied with Nagpa, while she treated the kids. Then she got sick from the plague, and her body was burned! But her ghost hangs out here all the time!"

I almost jumped up. He was talking about Larry Schechter's mother!

"Nah"—the youth waved—"you can't really see the white woman's ghost. You just catch sight of her, she disappears right away. She has black hair, and she cries. This one was different. This one was real! Had a dog, too! You ever heard of a ghost with a dog?"

The old man laughed again. "Your eyes went crazy with fear, you took a pile of shit for a dog!"

"You're the blind one! I heard how you took a bear for Yeti the Snowman: you left your yak and ran off to the village, scared shitless!"

Enraged, the old man grabbed a burning twig and tossed it at the youth.

"Stop!" It was time for me to interfere. "*I* believe you. But what did she look like?"

"She was tall." The youth said eagerly, gratified. "Gold hair. Barefoot. And a bracelet on her ankle goes *zing-zing.*"

YUIN was in his winter garden, reading a book under a blossoming cherry tree. When the guards brought me in, he set the book aside.

"Ming Huy, one of our best romantic poets," he said indicating the book. "According to him, all the best things—inspiration, wisdom, love—can be found only in your ideal opposite. By me, that's irrational nonsense, songs of the penis. But you, too, seemed to be moving on the route from joy to discontent to escape, all among the varieties of the Ideal Woman: Gwen as a wife, Abby as a mother, Varya as a daughter, Nyima as a sister. You hoped to find them all merged into one, didn't you?"

"Impossible," I said, frowning. "An ideal opposite can be found only in your own self."

"You've learned my lessons well. But I'll let you in on a secret: if you have found your partner in yourself, you win a prize in my ashram—an ideal half."

"That doesn't exist."

"It certainly does. Moreover, you have already met yours. Look—"

At the end of the path I saw a woman in white.

THE old man was not giving in lightly. "That was just *chang* ringing in your ears!"

"And what about the children from Lukla—they were drunk, too? They got lost at night and saw *pi ling*s. And when *pi ling*s went over the pass, there was a light above it. And the sounds: toot, toot!"

"You mean, like a horn?" I asked.

"I don't know! But there was a light . . . at night in the mountains! Pink light! There!" The young sherpa leapt to his feet.

A barely distinct ringing came from the dark.

We froze. But the sound did not come back. The old sherpa picked up a burning twig and stepped into the dark. Martin followed, gripping his automatic.

MARGI had let her hair grow and dyed it a golden hue. She was wearing a white dress that came down to her knees, with a golden-colored belt. The bracelet tinkled lightly, giving away her presence. A white chow followed her.

I was petrified. Her arm came down lightly on my shoulder, and her lips brushed my cheek.

"You're back," she murmured; "and you're liberated."

I recoiled. But her aroma! She smelled of my first love, of my mother's perfume and lipstick on a cold frosty day, when she leaned to kiss me at the skating rink. A lily, sweet and cold . . .

Margi knew of the secret, shameful, forbidden room in my heart that dreamed of seeing her again—of "returning and liberating."

"Your duty and conscience push you to Gwen, but you're

drawn to me by love. Isn't love superior to everything else?"

I was silent.

"Let's go for a walk." She took me by the arm. "You can talk to me, right? That doesn't count as betrayal."

I took my arm away.

"How could you kill Ayushi?"

Her smile was light and clear. "There's no death. And the old man could get in the way."

"You really believe you're the Chosen?"

"I do. And so do you. Yuin has appointed me as your wife. In the ashram, we'll have children, and they'll create a new civilization."

As I looked at this utterly, breathtakingly beautiful face, I found it hard to believe that this angel was evil. She, and the ones like her—if Yuin is right and they exist—they may represent a truly amoral species. Genuinely beyond good and evil. They neither rise nor fall: like angels, they simply float in the cold clarity and solitude of Himalayan air.

"It is man, not angels," Schechter said, *"who is made in God's image. An angel is merely God's instrument. But man is God, and he orders the angels. He gives birth to them in his soul, and he kills them there, too."*

"THERE'S nothing there," Martin informed me as he returned to the fire.

"It was them," the youth muttered, his eyes wide and sparkling. "We must be too close to their valley. They guard the entrance. You get too close, they kill you—or, if they like your karma, they take you with them."

"And who decides that?" Dorje asked.

"Their king." The sherpa swallowed fearfully. "Rigden Japo."

"Would you like to live in that valley, too?" I asked the younger sherpa.

He laughed. "Sure I would! You don't work there!"

"That's all you want." The older man gave him a light kick in the shin. "Roll out the blankets, we go to sleep now."

"We take turns." Martin peered into the dark. "I'll take the first watch."

* * *

I couldn't sleep. "Would you like to be in that valley, too?"
I asked Martin.

"I would." His expression was grave, his body enveloped
around the submachine gun.

"In order not to work?"

"In order to live without guilt."

"You're talking about your wife?"

"I'm talking about my kids."

He got up, indicating his unwillingness to go on with the
conversation, and paced around the fire. Then he settled
back in.

"I told you I was eighteen when I got married the first
time. She was a few years older, with a boy, seven years
old. I loved her like I'll never love anyone again. But her
son—I didn't like him much. I mean, I just put up with
him. He felt it, you know? So he got closer to his mom,
and she spoiled him, which got me rankled, too. When I
joined up, I would discipline him every time I got home.
Chin-ups, push-ups . . . I thought every kid would go for it.
Tried to make a man out of him, you know?

"Didn't work out. I slapped him around a few times. He
tried to fight back. I just tried to hold him, like in self-
defense, you know? He grabs a knife—well, I'm trained for
this kind of situation, you know? He kept getting hysterical,
and I was getting more pissed off in return. So I took off
my belt, you know. . . . He keeps screaming, *I'll kill you
when I grow up. You're a mama's boy,* I told him; *you
won't kill anyone.* I let him have it good. She walks in, la-la,
Don't you dare lay a hand, all that crap. Didn't even notice
I was bleeding. So I packed up and was gone."

He fell silent, tossing twigs in the fire.

"You never heard what became of him?"

"Oh yes, I did. Once I was gone, it was all over for him.
The usual road down for a ghetto kid. Joined a gang, got
busted for possession. First night out of juvie, goes out with
homies: bang-bang. Murder Two, thirty years." He raised
his bloodshot eyes. "I feel more guilty about him than about
my two kids from the other marriages. More than about my

second wife. I broke her body, yes, but with him—like I
broke his soul, you know?"

We were silent for a while.

"I always wanted things to be right," Martin said. "I
wanted order, I wanted justice. But somehow everyone
around me got into trouble. What I want now is . . . not to
want anything. I want to stop making trouble. Live without
wanting."

"That's Buddhism," I said quietly.

"That's bull—" He cut himself short. "Whatever. Get
some shut-eye now."

ONLY an hour ago, I resented him, I thought. What a road
I have to travel to learn how to be nonjudgmental and com-
passionate. And I don't want Yuin to get in the way. That's
my motivation for getting to see Nagpa. That's my "clear
sense of the mission." Not for others—for myself. Save
yourself, and thousands around you will be saved. . . .

"What if—what if Yuin's project falls through," I said
quietly. "If we get saved. You'd want to start all over again:
a perfect wife and kids?"

"Kids," he chuckled. "Nope. There ain't nothing unique
about me to carry over into the next generation. No heritage,
no estate either. You want kids? There's plenty of fatherless
kids around—get yourself one."

"What about a wife?"

"You said an ideal one, right?" He shook his head.
"That's a laugh. Maybe you're young enough to hustle and
pick and choose. I'm tired of this shit. If we get out of this
mess, I'll take the first one who says yes. If you get rid of
your own shit, you can be happy with anyone."

"What kind of shit're you talking about?"

"I'm talking about your ideas of what a big shit you are.
So, what kind of things do you like?" he said in a whiny
imitation of a woman. Then, reverting to his former self, he
made an important face and started counting on his fingers:
"Woman, ah wan' lobster an' ah wan' mah steak well done.
An' den I wan' some Chivas an' ah wan' some good hot
lovin' to Teddy Pendergrass on all speakers. An' I wan'
some ordah in de house. An' I wan' no sass from you when

my buddies come to watch de Supah Bowl. An' I don' want yo' mama evah to show her face in mah house." He turned to me, his face a blank. "Do you hear this? *Ah wan', ah wan'* . . . Well, *ah* don't want nothin'. Whatever she sets out in front of me, I'll take it."

"You are a Buddhist, Marty, whether you like it or not."

"Whatever. You gon' sleep or what?"

AS we walked down the garden path, the trees acquired a bluish radiance, and the peaks changed their colors. The day was drawing to a close.

"A blue valley with purple mountains," Margi said; "the sky above is pistachio, with mother-of-pearl clouds; the air is sweet and cold, and you feel like taxiing off and flying . . . wouldn't you want to live there?"

She seemed to have read all of my dreams of Tibet.

"You would be sitting with me on the sun-heated slope, roaming all over the mountain, entering a cave, walking through a maze, exiting through another cave in a different embodiment—and then meeting me again, changed but still recognizable: isn't that something you would like?"

How beautiful she was in her white chiton, with her hair forming a golden aura with the cherries in the background— an Eve in the Garden of Eden. You will leave your father, your mother, and cleave to your wife. You will leave the spirit and the matter and cleave to life—to Eve. No, it's the other way around: duty and guilt are life. Life is love. And that's what drew me to Gwen. Margi was a dream, a fantasy, an illusion, a fleeting image against the backdrop of falling petals.

"No," I said.

"Coward." And she walked off, whistling as she called her dog over.

I dreamed of men hidden in steel safe boxes. Walking jail cells. They paced the Rating courtyard, trying to embrace, to see, to hear one another—but all they heard was the clanging of the metal. I could see their eyes and hear their moans through the bars in front of them: they begged that someone open the doors and let them out. Each had a large rusty key sticking out of his chest; but no one had hands, and therefore could not help another. They cried inside their boxes, but more often, enraged, they slammed into one another, trying to hurt each other.

I was one of them, and I saw the way to open the box. All it required was a bit of cooperation: two people would hold the key with their sides and turn it with slow, studied movements. And then the doors would open, and light would fill them and show the gate to the fairy-tale valley with blossoming cherries and our never-dying dear ones strolling through the gardens.

I yelled, but no one heard me. I tried to turn one man's key on my own, but I merely slammed into his steel-plated side and hurt myself.

"WAKE up!" Martin shoved his gun in my side. "Your turn."

I huddled with the gun and sat by the fire, watching its tongues flickering like the lamas' yellow hats. All we see are these flames, the searing consequences, without paying attention to the cause—the smoldering coals, the manure patties. There lies the source of dissatisfaction.

I had not fled my personal ties for freedom, but for some kind of ideal tie—a chimera created by my imagination. Martin was right: you have to take the woman sent you by fate, tied to you by your guilt. What is love but overcoming your ego, shedding blood and tears as you file away all the flaws that prevent you from joining in an ideal union. It takes years—or one brief revelation that will make you understand that the flaws are an illusion. Or bullshit, as Martin would put it.

83

IT started at dawn. Whether it was the Devil's work or God's work, I couldn't tell.

The wind blew like a hurricane; as if angels were racing one another in the sky, puffing icy gusts. And yet the sky remained impossibly clear, with not a hint of a cloud. The sun rose, but the moon was not going away; it lay in the sky like a white feather on a light-blue rug.

When we settled around for morning *cha*, we smelled an aroma—of lilies! Lilies in the mountains?

The younger sherpa smiled. "That's her—the smell of a white woman." His hand trembled, spilling the drink.

"Hallucinations," Martin muttered, frowning.

Dorje was as imperturbable as ever. But the elder sherpa moaned and rubbed his skull. When he went to saddle the horses, he picked up a bag and, confused, went in the wrong direction. He stumbled and fell down. When we ran over to pick him up, he was rocking and moaning in pain.

After an hour, the path disappeared. The old man did not know the direction! He dragged the nag one way; then he would mutter, shake his head, and reverse his steps.

"Something in my eye . . . ," he murmured. Then, once again, he stumbled and fell down.

Dorje turned him over and drew his eyelids open.

"It's all because he was making fun of Tara," the younger one whispered. "The white woman, she overheard us last night."

According to Dorje, the nerves in the old man's neck were inflamed. They were connected to the optical nerves, which caused problems with his eyesight. The only cure was ablutions made with grass, to be found in the lamasery. But how were we to get there?

FROM one glance at the general's eyes, Dorje had diagnosed Yuin with liver cancer.

"You're just a dying egoist who wants to take the world
with him to the grave," I announced at the interrogation.
"Torturing others distracts you from your own pain."

It did not take Yuin long to establish the source of my
information. "Your monk is good. Yes, like Moses or Rama,
I'm destined to die at the border of the Promised Land.

"It is hard for an ordinary person to realize that our universe is a mere cell in God's body," Yuin went on. His own
imminent end seemed just another subject for his sermons.
"It is born, develops, mutates, torments the entire body with
pain—and it needs to be cut off. Instead of a scalpel, God
uses his tender pain-soothing hand, like Filipino healers . . ."

". . . who were exposed as frauds. The same may apply
to your theory."

THE younger sherpa is leading us uncertainly: he has only
a general idea of the direction. The icy wind changes to a
warm, humid breeze. My face feels wet, but when I touch
it, it's dry. The sky turns a dark blue, an aqua, like an ocean.
Finally, we smell sea salt. An ocean in the Himalayas?

Martin gives me an intense look: he must have the same
sensations. Dorje is still unflappable. The sherpas and their
horses recoil to the rocky wall in confusion. They must be
sensing something strange; they don't know what the sea
smells like.

My heart is soaring in mute delight.

THE sky turned green. Colored flashes on the horizon. And
the ringing, quiet and clear, in the air.

"Shambala is near," the younger sherpa whispered.

But the ringing grew in intensity till it turned into the
sound of horns. The golden horns of Shambala!

"Airplanes!" Martin dived, closing his ears.

But the roar grew, and the sky was empty.

"Maybe an elephant?" Martin whispered. "Did Yuin say
he's got a private zoo here?"

The air vibrated. Neighing, the horses buckled and tore
at the bits.

Suddenly, unable to take it, the elder sherpa dropped on his knees and closed his ears. The horse soared on its hind legs.

"Ka li!" the younger sherpa yelled. "Careful!"

The old man did not react. The horse jerked aside, forcing the youth to grab the rein.

"It's Rigden Japo! That's his horse!" He struggled with the horse, trying to turn it back. "We got to go back! Rigden guards his palace well!"

"Wait," I whispered to him. "Didn't you say you want to go there? That's why Goddess Tara appeared to you—she's waiting there for you. I'll come with you. Don't be afraid."

After a moment's hesitation, he clenched my hand, barked at the horse, and turned it back forward.

The sound disappeared instantly. All was calm—deadly, auspiciously so.

"What was that, Dorje?"

"Wind," the lama said. "Go!" he shouted at the older sherpa.

The old man did not move. He was deaf.

We barely walked a hundred yards when the range ahead suddenly dropped its brown camouflage and became covered with soft purple velvet. The air was warm and filled with incense, as if we were in the dark belly of a Buddhist temple.

"What's that, Dorje?"

"Nothing. Air moves."

Martin sniffed. "Smells like gunpowder. Or gasoline."

"No, it's women. . . ." The sherpa youth grabbed my arm. "Smells milk. She's here!"

Once again, the older sherpa collapsed to his knees—and vomited violently. The younger one dashed after the horse, but it was too late: it stood on its hind legs and jumped off the cliff.

Dorje went to examine the old man, who was writhing in his vomit, muttering and shaking his head.

"He says, Smells blood," Dorje translated. "And rotten corpse."

*   *   *

HALF our supplies were gone with the horse: ammunition, grenades, food. At least we still had the second horse with the gun and the warm coats we used for sleeping bags, attached to the saddle. But the old man couldn't walk any more. We had to set him on the remaining horse and put on the coats, instantly soaking in sweat.

Even Martin stopped cursing; he merely looked back every few steps. I had never seen him scared.

Another turn in the path—and, a few feet away from us, we saw seagulls noiselessly soaring in the air. White seagulls in the Himalayas!

I froze. One of the birds—I just knew it with all my soul—was my mother. She made a circle and sat down on a rock at the edge of the cliff. She could not see me. I had to call her! But I was paralyzed with fear—what if I scare her off—she falls—

"It's them," Martin's voice was trembling. "They never burned. The guys from the cult . . . the siege in Texas . . ."

Now the entire slope was covered with white birds—except they were people whom I knew so well and who now stared at me sadly. Schechter, Abby, Ayushi, Ruslanov, Varya—they were all alive, all were forgiven, and they forgave me, too.

THE burst from the submachine gun was so sudden that we paused for a moment and only then hit the ground. The old sherpa on the horse had grabbed Martin's gun from the saddle and was firing at the rock, burst after burst, shrieking madly and ignoring the horse's neighing and twitching.

"Hold it!" Martin yelled.

For the last time, the horse stood up—and dashed towards the abyss. In another moment, still firing and shrieking, both the sherpa and the horse disappeared from view.

The sounds of shrieking, neighing, and gunshots were still echoing through the mountains, but their source—the horse and the man, a black mote on the yellow rock—was lying a few miles below.

"He was bandit when young," the other sherpa said. "Robbed caravans, killed people. I think maybe he saw his victims now. Maybe they got him."

"But it was not them on the mountain," the youth whispered to me conspiratorially. "Those were Yetis, messengers of Dharmapala. We must be real close." His eyes were completely mad. "We must look real hard for the entrance now."

84

"I was hoping you would leave the Hall of Knowledge for the Hall of Wisdom." Yuin dropped Ruslanov's picture on the table.

There was a smile in the Russian's bushy mustache, and a da Vincian spark in his eyes, the eyes of a discoverer.

"Ruslanov could have intuited the mantra if he had not been so obsessed with the American computer. When the voltmeter measures the voltage, it brings in its own index error. In order to 'measure the mantra,' he needed to empty his conscience. Yet he was too lazy to do so. It is a common human problem: they keep thinking, and they are too lazy to stop doing so and see the answer."

"Yet he did get to the answer and you got him killed."

"It was Fedot, his KGB monitor. I recruited him ages ago, when I was working out of Beijing. He was the major foreign mole in the KGB. The American computer could have exposed him."

"You killed a genius to save the mole? But you didn't save him anyway!"

The general chuckled. "I didn't care about Fedot; I paid him so much it was inevitable that he would flaunt his wealth and end up dead like any other Russian nouveau riche. In the first place, Ruslanov decoded the mantra and could have become an obstacle. Second, he wanted to create explicable happiness—a semantic resonator for everybody. But God doesn't want everybody to listen to a tape and get His conscience. He wants people to prostrate in blood and gore in front of the Godhead. Third—as usual—you're the one who killed him."

WE are lost. One gorge follows another; we climb ridges, then descend, only to discover we have made a circle.

"You know what you're doing or you just jerking us off?" Martin yells at the young sherpa.

"I listen," he says. Indeed, once in a while, he pauses and stands still.

Dorje remains silent. The map is gone with the rest of the bags. I suspect it would not have helped. All we have is the sherpa's instinct.

THIS terrain is truly strange; or else we are the strange ones. Yet its landscape mirrors the traveler's emotional condition to a T. Once we become alive with hope that we are on the right track, nature opens up vistas that are too beautiful even for Tibet: a blue ocean of mountains and white crests of glaciers like the tips of frozen waves. The moment we realize we have been going in circles, we find ourselves in a gloomy ravine or on the edge of an insurmountable glacier.

WE are descending another gorge, and it's stiflingly hot. I hear the chirping of birds—for the first time since I got here. The birds are invisible, but I am tired of being surprised. The day draws to a close, with the sun still shining brightly on the other side.

"It's purple!" I exclaim, pointing at the sun.

No one answers. The lama walks like a zombie, muttering the mantras. Martin is too tired, and so is the sherpa, scowling like a hound.

"We're close!" he winks.

I can sense it—I can hear it in the birds' chirping. But close to what?

An intense purple glow arose in front of us. As if someone had switched on a powerful light generator over the black teeth of the ridge.

"It's a sunset." Martin's voice was anything but confident.

"The sunset is behind us—look!"

The sun was on the opposite side of the ravine, and its vanishing disk was also projecting a purple-red semicircle. Yet this light was fading, while the ridge ahead was growing brighter.

Suddenly, the entire ridge burst into purple flames, as if someone had turned on a gas range inside the mountain.

"Tara!" the young sherpa exclaimed. He shed his coat and went to climb the ridge.

I saw her. . . .

A woman stood atop the ridge, in a light-purple glow.

"Gwen," I whispered.

She heard, she glanced at me—and stepped over the ridge.

I dashed after the sherpa.

"HOLD him!"

Martin, though gasping, played perfect defense by bringing me to the ground.

The young sherpa was almost there. Gwen dissolved in the glow—but I knew she was there!

Martin forced my arm back. I groaned in pain, but my eyes remained fixed on the sherpa as he stood up, full height, against the glow.

A short yell—

He waved his arms and vanished.

"YOU did want to get rid of Ruslanov," Yuin declared. "He took apart your entire psyche: shame, guilt, regret, envy, uncertainty, and conflict with everybody and everything—Gwen, your parents, your friends, your past, your future, and the teachings of the Blessed One. And you came to hate the bad-news messenger. You don't like me, either, though I'm helping you get rid of your vices better than any gizmo of Ruslanov's ever would."

"Why did Ruslanov's patients catch fire?"

"That was the doing of Fedot and his crew. They were laying the groundwork for justifying the death of Ruslanov and your disappearance. He was supposed to pack you off to Rating. But you got here yourself."

* * *

THE glow over the ridge was still visible, but the sherpa was gone.

"They've accepted him. Please let me go," I begged.

Martin held his lock firm. "You came to his Shamb—camp—without Yuin. They'll break your ass into little pieces!"

I stared at him. "So we both believe in his ashram?"

For a few moments he stared at me, too, as if trying to figure out who I was; then he shook his head, as if chasing away sleep, and pulled me to my feet.

"Let's get out of here. It's all hallucinations from oxygen deprivation. All this shit happens in the mountains. It's nothing but a cliff—and the fucking sherpa went down. There's no ashram! Yuin was bluffing! Whom of its members did you see? Your Margi is just his girlfriend. The gimpy black dude and Tune, they're on his payroll, that's all! C'mon, let's get out of here!"

"Wait, please!" I pleaded. "It's not an ashram. . . . It's something else. Something I have been looking for."

"I thought you were looking for Nagpa."

"I saw Gwen there. Means she's dead. And I don't have to go back."

Looking me straight in the eye, Martin applied more pressure to my arm. I almost fainted with pain. When I opened my eyes, he was leading me out of the ravine, gripping my elbow, as if I were just another perp busted for possession.

After a couple of hundred feet, I looked back. The glow was gone, and the landscape reverted to the familiar one: brown rocks, cold air, dour evening light.

"Was it Shambala?" I quietly asked Dorje, rubbing my arm, released by Martin.

He shrugged.

"But you saw what happened to the mountain—the rocks?"

"Mountain is mountain. Rocks are rocks."

"What about the purple sun? You saw that sun?"

"Sun is round."

"And the light over the ridge? Where did it come from?"

He glanced at me and smiled. "From the Great Mirror. We don't see what is; we only see our minds."

I kept mulling over his words till dark. Finally, the stars came out; we started settling down for the night, and I realized what was missing in Dorje's answer. "But why was the Great Mirror presented so close to us in that place, and not elsewhere?"

After a pause, he shook his head. "I don't know."

85

ONCE again, we were straggling across a plateau, without a guide or a map. The desert was an icy shade of brown, the sky was a monotonous off-white, and the wind grew colder and fiercer till it finally turned into a snowstorm.

Our knees buckled as we fought our way through the hordes of white flurries. If we broke for a stop, we'd be buried. The only question was whether we'd die of exposure or starvation first.

Dorje kept muttering his mantras.

"Do you know where you're going?" Rivers shouted. "Didn't you say you never been to Nagpa's new monastery?"

"I can see *gompa*." Dorje paused. "It's at Indian border. I don't know its name, but I can see it: two mountains, like a saddle."

"There's thousands of mountains like that!"

"Rinpoche will lead us."

"We don't need spirits—we need guides!"

"He'll send us guides—there!"

I gasped. Two horse silhouettes came into view through the curtain of snow.

Was it another mantra-induced mirage?

Were they peaceful nomads or mountain bandits?

We no longer had our gun with us. All we could do was wait and pray.

THE horsemen in worn-out coats had ancient carbines strapped to their backs. Their shaggy dogs barked like some primeval snowstorm spirits. Martin offered the horsemen his knife in exchange for their horses and sherpa services.

They laughed. "You don't have anything we need."

Yet when they learned that a Bon lama was with us, they told us to follow them. We struggled on through the storm, holding on to the horses' reins. Had we been saved or taken prisoner? The horsemen were silent.

Finally, the black triangles of a camp loomed ahead in the whiteness.

THE tribesmen wearing yak hides and turquoise necklaces lined up against the walls of the tent. Outside, the storm roared; inside, a meaty-faced youth was groaning—the reason for Dorje's presence.

The threads of red wool in the patient's hair and a cataract on his eye made him look like a fierce deity. From the way he was pressing his hands to his stomach, he may have been suffering from a poisoning. But after a few mantras, he grew quiet.

We ate meat with our hands. An old man with a goatee and only two teeth in his mouth used a nail: his finger was swollen. Again, Dorje was summoned. The lama inspected the old-timer's finger and discovered a splinter, which he easily removed with Martin's knife, with me holding the old man's hand.

Amid the numerous bows and the newfound respect of me as a healer, we learned that the tribesmen were *drokpa*s, or "salt people." They were heading for Dzong-pa Yumko salt lake, where they would load up on salt and sell it later. According to Dorje, we were traveling in the same direction.

ONCE again, I am walking, as if in a dream, across the plateau, holding on to the edge of a horse cart led by the old man with a goatee. Dorje's patient is groaning in the cart. The driver winks at me and breaks into a song. I cannot help smiling.

Even rendering minimal assistance at the splinter extraction gave me more satisfaction than my poetry ever did. Feeling compassion is more blissful than accomplishing something. Perhaps this is the true Shambala: compassion compressed to the point of explosion. Then my Shambala must be in the hospital in New York.

As I walk, I compose letters to my Shambala. Now I know she is alive. If she were dead, I would have climbed that ridge and gone over.

THE view in the distance is as transparent and multicolored as a child's dream. The mountains seem impossibly far; but the thought of you waiting for me at the horizon gives me strength. I don't have to walk anymore: I just set one foot after another, and the earth rolls up to meet me.

On our last night before I went to Denver you said you wanted to remember me exactly the way I was. Did you have a premonition you would be lying immobile, with only your memories? This thought is a torture far worse than anything in Rating.

As I look at the mountains, I remember your body, too: the valley of your stomach, the distant peaks of your breasts. The night sky makes me think of your eyes; the quietude of the mountains, of your silence; the touch of wind on my face, your lips. You kissed me the way a wave kisses the shore: rolling up quietly out of the dark and picking at my face blindly, trustfully, with all your being. Now, I kiss you back; can you sense it?

THE stone pyramids of *chortens* are scattered across the plateau. The *drokpas* pass them in a circle and toss pebbles for good luck. I feel both light and empty. As if I had imagined a chimera that had now crashed.

Happiness does not lie in scaling the ridge with euphoria awaiting you on the other side. You should just keep walking, monotonously, with a sack of salt as your objective. You don't have to achieve anything outstanding. Just get your salt, and then you'll be of some use. Some use is better than none.

What if you can't even do that?—Then just walk without doing harm.

What if you already have done harm and barely drag your feet, laden with guilt?

Keep walking, no matter what. And, step by step, keep peeling the crust off your heart. Then you'll have a hard time harming others, because your heart, newly bared, will be hurt first.

MY guilt du jour is about the young sherpa. Can it be that I seduced him with all the Shambala talk? If he had simply left, he would still be alive. But we couldn't let him leave— we needed him to show us the way. Same thing happened with Nyima: we half-tricked her into working for us—and look at all the grief we brought her in the name of our mission!

This is karma: your every thought and deed lead to consequences; and not always beneficial ones, regardless of your intentions. Buddhism teaches: Immerse your mind in Buddha and then do what you want. But in reality, who can live like that but the lamas? Who qualifies for sainthood outside a monastery? These *drokpas*?

As we in the West have concerns—careers, sex, health— so do the *drokpa*s: yaks, weather, salt. . . . But they do not seem to have anxieties: if they need to do something, they just do it. If they spot a menace in the future, they pray; but at all times, their mind is at rest.

One should not hurry up the evolution. It should advance slowly, like a *drokpa* caravan, with a song and a prayer, stopping to enjoy the rest and the food.

86

WITHOUT saying a word, the guards dressed me in a thick padded coat and a helmet with a wire mask. Then they led me to the far end of the garden, with the sounds of humming bees and something else I could not put my finger on. Yuin stood under a tree, wearing a coat and a mask, similar to mine, and fanning the trunk with a twig. The trunk was stirring . . . there was a person tied to it, whose naked body was covered with bees.

The person was Nyima.

"This is an approximation of Tibetan hell," Yuin said. "But in Bardo, a sinner is stung by his own desires while he is tied to his own ego. What is your greatest desire?"

I was paralyzed by the view. The sound I had been unable to identify was the person's groaning. "Let her go!" I yelled.

"Hah! This is what you wrote: *Honey is the effort of the bee to understand that it and the beehive are one.* This is the biggest fallacy of your culture: art that overcomes pain. Go ahead—write me a *tanka,* and I'll untie her!"

I could not take my eyes off Nyima's face; befogged with pain, her eyes remained alive. Groans kept coming out of her half-open mouth. Her head kept dropping, but Yuin kept bringing smelling salts to her nose—and the whole thing started again.

She had to be dying, and so I prayed for her soul. For his, too: I was convinced he would be reborn into suffering as many times as she was stung by the bees.

"Come on, where's your poetry? You've done this before: people close to you were suffering, while you kept writing your poetry. Are you trying to distance yourself? There's no me, no beehive. . . . Or have you decided to go mute—does it help?"

"No."

"Because you're not an Oriental freak, like your Zen idols! So give it up and think about the argument—you have two days left!"

He barked the orders to untie the girl and, smashing the twig, briskly headed for the main building.

NYIMA was unconscious. I tossed off my helmet to give her mouth-to-mouth. She opened her eyes and recognized me. Her words were barely discernible amid her groans.

"Punishment for karaoke—Tigers left bag under table—I thought, with money in it—I did not stop them—the Russian trader burned to death—he was in much pain—like me now—help me die—"

THE *drokpa*—the cart driver—sings while his friend groans with stomach pain. No one looks at him; no one gives him water.

Yuin has a point. I can't walk dispassionately the way they do. The profoundly Oriental indifference to suffering is alien to me. Perhaps I admire Tibet so much in order to suppress my fear of it. If I fell sick among them, they would not lift a finger. Their souls must be like so many tears dried by their wisdom into a salt lake, where nothing lives and nothing spoils either. The West may not know meditation and the bliss of being at rest. But the Orient does not know love and active compassion.

FINALLY, a glittering, blinding strip appeared on the horizon: the salt lake. The *drokpa*s holler in joy and toss their hats in the air.

"We split at hill over there," the old *drokpa* says. "You go straight, there's roadblock. But you bear right, towards farther hills, Kangto Tso. Then, India."

"Is there a Bon Po *gompa* on the Indian side?"

The old man nodded, surprised. "Between mountains that curve like saddle."

Dorje smiled.

Suddenly, a younger *drokpa* broke into an angry tirade at the old man. I could not understand a single word; it almost sounded like Schechter ranting in a trance on his last night.

Dorje looked puzzled, too. Other *drokpa*s joined the conversation in the same incomprehensible language.

I asked the old man about it.

He seemed to bark at his companions to shut up and then explained: it was a *drokpa* secret language. When you approach the salt lake, you must stop thinking bad thoughts, stop cursing, and switch to the secret tongue. This is a ritual, to make sure that the salt lake gods would not take offense and give up the salt.

IN a way, I'm a *drokpa*, too. I'm going after my salt. My salt consists in cleansing myself of desires, the Oriental way, but retaining love and passion, the Western way.

I don't know what lake I can find this salt in, but I keep looking.

87

WE heard the roar a few hours later, when we parted from the *drokpa*s and were halfway to the pass. We had not heard it for a week, and at first I mistook it for distant thunder. But the three dots in the sky moving at us fast left no room for doubt.

"Choppers!" Martin yelled. "Sonuvabitches sold us for a sack of salt at the roadblock! That's what they were yakking about! Some fucking ritual! We should have cut them up when they switched to their mumbo-jumbo!"

"Perhaps we should find a cave," I said uncertainly. "Hide out till dark . . ."

"They'll have a whole army here! It's a border area!"

Dorje was silent. While we were panicking, he quietly sat down on the ground, his legs crossed.

"What are you doing?" I whispered.

"Fog." He held up his hand: *Don't bother me.*

"What the fuck—" Martin started.

But there was no place to run. I lowered myself on the ground next to the monk. Gnashing his teeth, Martin joined us. I closed my eyes.

The roar grew, like a distant avalanche.

"Motherfucker," Martin whispered next to me.

I opened my eyes.

At first, I thought that someone had stoked up a fire. Wafts of gray smoke were crawling down the slope, thickening and branching out by the minute. We could barely see the helicopters.

"How did you—?"

Dorje opened his eyes and smiled. "Rinpoche helps. Come!"

THE saving fog turned mountains into hills: now the wooded foothills passed directly into the milky grayish sky. The only sounds were the rustling of a distant stream and, rarely, the chirp of a bird. How odd, I thought; all we see is a few feet of the rock road ahead, but we know that in fact we are surrounded by towering peaks. Isn't it the same with God: we see a drop, but we feel the presence of an ocean?

YUIN and I watched the fog from the roof of Rating. The roofs of Lhasa and the golden cupola of Potala dissolved in a giant cup of gray-and-white *cha:* as if the Flood had come, and the palace of a thousand rooms had flown away on the fairy-tale wings of its towers.

"The argument you are demanding," I said, "is hidden in the fog. It is like Potala: if you don't know it's there, you might think there's an emptiness. But Potala will not disappear just because we can't see it. Same with your argument: just because we don't see the cause doesn't mean it doesn't exist."

"You remember Potala being there," Yuin countered. "I want you to remember the reason."

                    *   *   *

WHETHER aided by the Rinpoche or not, Dorje may have tried too hard: not only had the fog hidden the mountains from the helicopters, but from us as well. The higher we got, the less clear was the view: soon, we were practically crawling, sensing rather than seeing the abyss on the side.

Finally, we reached the peak, and, through a hole in the fog, I saw another majestic vista: black ridges towering over the spaces white with fog, like the fins of primeval monsters who surfaced in the earth's waters. And we were separated from these black peaks by—was it an ocean or an abyss?

"RINPOCHE helped," Martin whispers. "I still can't buy it. How did his lama disappear from jail?"

"The teacher can become invisible, because his mind is liberated. If it is empty, then that's what you see: emptiness."

"I can see rocks, too. They ain't got no minds either."

"They think. They worry about erosion. But the teacher doesn't worry about a single thing."

AS we started on our descent, we plunged into the fog once again. And—once again, just like at the pseudo-Shambala earlier—I sniffed a familiar briny smell of the sea. The sensation was so strong that I closed my eyes and opened them again, fully expecting to see the ocean stretching to the horizon.

Dorje stepped off the path and climbed on a rock. "Kangto Tso!" he said, pointing downward.

Through the fog, we saw a valley filled to the rim with rippled gray mass. It was Lake Bon, the Lake of Prophets, and the opposite shore belonged to India.

In the fog, the shoreline was invisible; motionless, the water looked like *tsampa* in a stone bowl. But the smell of fish and algae was for real, oddly discordant with the snow-capped peaks and the altitude sickness.

"We have to go down and around the lake," Dorje said.

"Can't we circle it through the mountains?" Martin's face was covered with purple splotches as he was struggling to regain his breath.

"We won't find the way without sherpas."

"Once the fog is gone, the choppers are coming back," Martin said, wincing with pain as he held to his side. "If we don't make it around by then, they'll pick us off like rabbits. No place to hide at the shore."

We're rushing into the saving unknown, I thought, quickening my pace down the slope. In everyday life, we fear the fog of the unknown, but in an extreme situation, whether eluding someone or tormented by your own soul, the fog becomes your salvation; just leap into it headlong! One must simply believe that the path leads to your destination. One must simply keep moving, one foot after another. And the unknown will recede at exactly the same rate.

WE had barely walked a few hundred feet before the fog indeed began to disperse. And, just as Martin had predicted, that brought about the chirping of the helicopters. We walked faster, but there was no place to hide on an open slope.

"Come on, baldie, ask your witch doctor to bring back the fog!" Martin called.

But the fog was not coming back. The wind blew harder, pushing the black clouds to the lake.

It was as if someone had sounded an alarm in the sky. Darkness was falling fast. In the distance, we saw a flash of lightning, as if someone had been struck with a brilliant idea.

Dorje sat down, crossed his legs, and shut his eyes.

The choppers were already halfway across the lake, whose surface had turned black. Clouds of dust rose between the sky and the rippled water surface; it was as if someone were tugging hard at the curtain between the sky and the earth, and the air was filling up with the wet dust of the cloth.

AS the choppers approached, the wind blew harder, raising white crests on the lake. I could see rockets attached to their sides, but they were not firing: did they want to take us alive?

Suddenly, I saw a water drop on Dorje's shaven pate.

And then came an eruption! As if someone at the heav-

enly disco had turned on the amplifiers! Instantly, an armada
of droplets plopped on our bodies and the rocks. Then, the
armada's pace accelerated: they were racing downward,
turning into an avalanche. A bolt of thunder slashed the
mountains; a flash of lightning, and then everything—
the choppers, the lake, the mountain across—vanished in
the roaring gray storm.

"Right on, bro'!" Martin pulled up Dorje and kissed him
on the pate. "Good job, shaman!"

But it was more than a storm—it was a real flood. The
point where we stood did not feel like a mountain—rather,
we were in the middle of the ocean, surrounded by nothing
but the white mist and the roaring wind.

Yuin miscalculated, flashed through my mind; the Flood
has started.

A landing force of waves was storming a beachhead. One
after another, they crashed against the shore, but the next
row climbed higher and higher. Indeed, they were storming
the Roof of the World.

"Down!" Dorje exclaimed, but the rest of his words
drowned in yet another thunderbolt. And another bolt of
lightning.

"It's like Mount Sinai or something," Martin muttered.

The effect did seem biblical: a superior force cut a hole
through our modest, threadbare sky allowing us a peek into
the real firmament—a dazzling vision of heavenly glory that
left us standing with our mouths agape, unable to speak or
move.

Another bolt of lightning: it was as if the Creator Himself
was using a flash to take pictures of us—or, rather, our
souls: our bodies would not show when the film developed.

The lightning now was coming steadily, one bolt after
another, lighting up the sky, and the mountain peaks were
white, as if on a film negative. We ran downward, tumbling
and sliding through the mud with the rocks and the
bushes—and I was laughing like a maniac! I was seized by
an intoxicating ecstasy. Along with Mother Nature, I was
returning to childhood.

I got caught on a rock with the edge of my coat, and,
freeing myself, looked up.

The Himalayas were alive. They had turned liquid and roared downward in tsunamilike waves, crested with snow-caps—

"Mudflow!" Martin hollered. "Run!"

We had another couple of hundred feet until the lake—but it was too late. Hot and damp, the earth shuddered; the landslide spun me, closed my eyes with mud, struck me on the head, dragged me over rocks—and tossed me into the freezing water.

My head still spinning, my arms and legs seized with ice-cold water, my sodden yak coat weighing a ton—I swallowed water and began sinking.

Dorje grabbed me by the collar and pulled me towards a floating log. Martin's face flashed by. Spitting out the water, I looked up and saw a brown wall of water covering us.

The last thing I knew was Martin's arm holding me in a choke as it pressed me against the log.

88

ENTOMBED in ice, moaning and groaning, I struck myself repeatedly with a climbing stick. One after another, pieces of ice fell off, smashing against the ground like thousands of liquid nitrogen smithereens, Terminator-like. . . .

I opened my eyes. My wet clothes clung to my battered body and turned to ice. Nearby, Martin was desperately rubbing two roots against each other, trying to start a fire. We seemed to be in a cave, or, rather, hole; out of the corner of my eye I could see a grayish spot of the lake.

Looks like we're in a coffin, I thought. Didn't the Bible have something like this: Graves will open and the dead will come up?

But that's what Yuin said: The earth will open! The closing of the season will be the Greatest Show ever: today's

continents will vanish among explosions and eclipses. And
new ones, with never-seen mountains, lakes, and plains, will
emerge through the smoke and the hissing of the volcanoes.
A grand dance—a celestial ménage à trois among water,
earth, and fire! You will see the promised new world yet!

Literally—

Denying a literal sense is the refuge of a doubter.

WHILE the mudflow was carrying me down the slope, I
experienced my most frightening but most ecstatic moments. No acid had ever inspired such a mix of delight and
horror; of my complete disappearance into something vast.
What, then, will the Flood be like?

The Great Snake of Chaos will stop for an instant the
consciousness of both the victims and the survivors. So
grand would the catastrophe be that it would be a long time
before the human mind could return to its ego. By the time
it did, the Serpent of Eden would be substantially weakened.

Could all this be brought about by one person? Actually,
it had already happened. The thought made me sit up. The
whole thing was indeed created by this—by this short monk
who was now drying his robe in the corner.

"DORJE," I called. "How did you do it? The landslide?"

"I said, Rinpoche helps."

"No, seriously. Did you use Bon mantras to summon the
spirit of the mountain? Or one of the fog?"

After a pause, he chuckled. "I see truth very unclear, like
fog. I just imagine this fog of my mind and take it outside."

I sat up. "What if you were a saint? If you did not have
fog in your consciousness, you could not bring it up—and
we would have been killed."

Dorje pensively straightened his robe on the rock. "Mind
of saint is like water in mountain lake. The fog of pursuers'
conscience reflects in his water, so they see fog."

"How did you summon the rain?"

"Thought! Ka-boom!" He traced a bolt of lightning with
his hand. "I saw fog empty!"

Seemingly unwilling to go on, he sidled over to help Mar-

tin start a fire. He picked up the roots and started rubbing
them, muttering a mantra all along.

A thought—lightning—makes sense, I thought. If the
genesis of man started when a thought flashed through
God's mind . . .

Soon, the first spark flashed.

"Yak-po!" Dorje exclaimed. "Good!"

Martin just stared at the tiny tongue of a flame running
up the roots.

Now he has used a mantra to start a fire, I thought. What
if there were a lot of people with this power, and they joined
hands? Their psychic energy would present a problem as
large as nuclear energy, with as much possibility for abuse.
If Yuin could discover the secrets of mantras, so could any
other villain.

DORJE peeked outside and announced the rain was over.
"Now we go around lake."

Martin shivered and sneezed. "First we get warm."

"Sun came out. Sun warms us." The lama took another
peek. "Sky opened Maitreya Gate!"

With a groan, I turned on my stomach and crawled to the
exit. "Look!" I screamed. "You've never seen anything like
it!"

I was telling Martin the truth: no one has seen it outside
the Himalayas. The rainbow took up precisely half the sky.
It was a giant arch, the Arch of all the Triumphal Arches,
that spanned the mountain peaks from the east to the west.
The huge seven-colored semicircle divided the sky in two
parts: inside the rainbow, it was red and gold; outside, black
and blue.

So splendid was the view as to make me forget all about
cold and pain. Once again, I was a little kid believing in
fairy tales. What else but happiness could lie over this thing
of beauty?

"Holy shit." Next to me, Martin gasped.

I glanced at him, and he, too, seemed to have lowered
the mask of the cynical cop/FBI agent. Once again, he was
a kid in the Bronx, splashing about in the jets of water
coming from a hydrant.

*   *   *

WE returned to the fire, but in another ten minutes, dizzy with smoke, I had to crawl outside. The wind was blowing harder, and the rainbow was evaporating. It was dissolving from the top, but the supports rising from the east and the west held on to their colors for a long time. They were like two giant horns of a ram, whose symbol can be seen often in the Himalayas. Finally, they were two raspberry-colored columns, thinning and vanishing into the thin air.

I was brought back to earth by Dorje, who noticed that my shirt collar was covered with blood. I must have hit my head against a rock or two during the ride down the slope. The wound was sizable, and needed to be disinfected.

Dorje told me to lower my head to the ground. A moment later, I felt a warm and stinky trickle down my neck.

Martin roared with laughter at my startled expression. Yet after the initial shock I had to admit it made sense. Considering the conditions, why can't we use urine for disinfectant? Buddhists were right: there are no clean or unclean substances. It's the way one uses a substance that renders it clean or unclean.

89

CHINESE soldiers had encircled the lake along the shoreline. We had a better chance of escape if we climbed back to the glacier. From there, it was just a quick hop over to India.

WE started at nightfall in order to reach the top by dawn. The glacier was steeper and more treacherous than it had seemed from below. The faint moonlight was of little help as we groped our way up. Martin was in the lead, using his knife to break into the ice. The wind was tearing the skin off our faces; the only sound was that of our own breath—it was like digging into a deep tunnel of white noise.

Early on, after our escape from jail, it would have taken us a day and a night to make the climb. Now, spurred on by the proximity of our objective, we were moving at double pace.

As we reached the top, the sky turned a predawn pale blue. Our last Tibetan mountain! We made it!

I am you, Yuin used to say; you can't escape yourself.

But I did!

The sun peeked in from around the mountain, and the glacier sparkled, like the throne of the King of Tibet. The throne had been usurped, but we had overthrown the impostor! We had achieved the impossible!

I turned to cast my last look of triumph on Tibet—

A chopper!

It was coming in slowly, against the wind, and we had not heard its rotary blades.

Before we could move, something flickered and thundered under the stomach of the iron grasshopper; a red line shot through the air, and a cloud of explosion burst below us.

"Chinks!" Martin hollered. "Run!"

Another flicker—another cloud of snow, much closer above us. We barely had time to dive into a tiny hole in the ice.

The third cloud rose within feet of the hole. For a moment, we were blinded—

"He's got another one!" Martin shouted.

We hugged closer, our eyes closed in terror.

But the shot did not come. The chopper rose slightly and hovered overhead.

A second chopper approached slowly, too. An ugly black splash of steel—a black hieroglyph on the blue page—one man's insanity embodied against God's peaceful conscious. It lowered itself so close that the wind from its propellers pushed us into the ice.

"I am you!" the voice echoed through the mountains. "You can't escape yourself—"

The wind carried the words, and the mountain echo amplified them, creating a horrifying effect of a voice from nowhere.

"You have not found the argument." Yuin spoke through the speaker aboard the chopper, his voice tired; "but I told you: I need a full set in my ashram. You studied your cabala: without one letter, the text is incomplete. Come on up!"

A ladder started to unfold from the first chopper.

I glanced at Martin, who was looking downward, at the precipice with sharp icy spikes at the bottom. Unsurpassable ice cliffs loomed above. Without hooks and ropes we could not get out of here on our own. Within twenty-four hours, we would be dead of exposure.

"Go ahead," Martin said. "We're done for here anyway. Maybe you can push him overboard. Or give birth to a new mankind. Come on."

"What about my friends?" I shouted back.

A chuckle came through the speaker. "Nothing! They're free to freeze here! Maybe they'll even make it to the Flood—not long to wait! Jump! It's your stairway to heaven!"

The rope ladder dangled within reach.

Martin caught it and put it in my hand. "Go on—"

"My friends go first!" I shouted. "You guarantee them life; then I'll go, too!"

"I give my word!" The words tumbled through the air, followed by Yuin's laughter.

"I'd rather die of cold than get whipped to death in his jail." Once again, Martin forced the rope into my hand. "Come on—"

"If you can't leave your friends to a slow death," Yuin said, "I'll provide them with a fast one!"

A soldier with a submachine gun around his neck started descending the rope.

I stepped up on the edge of the hole. "If he moves another foot, I'll jump down!"

"But then you would reject your own argument! You said that death is not a solution. If you jump, then I am right: a quick death saves you from a long suffering, and is therefore a right choice—and that's what the Flood will do!"

The soldier nimbly inserted his feet between the rungs

and swooped down, dropping the gun into his hand and taking aim. Then I heard a whistling sound; the soldier grabbed his chest; the gun fell to the ground. The handle of Martin's knife was sticking out of the man's chest.

A burst of gunfire came from the chopper; instantly, Yuin shouted, and the firing stopped. The rope slid upward, carrying the body with it.

"Try it again, and I'll jump!" I shouted.

"No problem." Yuin chuckled. "Have it your way—a slow death. We've still got time. I'll come back to check on you at sundown. I hope you'll still have strength left to hold on to the rope."

His chopper turned around and headed back. The first one stayed on, hovering above menacingly, circling the mountain.

SUDDENLY Martin broke off a piece of ice and flung it at the chopper.

"Chink bastards!" he hollered. "We almost made it! What's the deal with this gook Buddha of his?" He nodded at Dorje, who huddled in the corner, his eyes closed, his arms crossed. "Why wouldn't He give us another half hour to cross the glacier? If your God wants the Flood, why are we messing with His will?"

"There's no God," I said quietly.

"Oh yeah?" Martin exhaled. "What is, then?"

"Just your mind. And mine. Your mind wants us to freeze to death. So that we would understand."

"Understand what?"

"That mind is everything—"

"Bull—shit!" Martin stamped his foot and groaned with pain, reminded of his wound, still unhealed. "Okay, okay." He dropped on the ice in front of the lama and folded his hands, Buddhist style. "Dorje—do something! It makes no sense, to have gone through all this shit and turn into icicles half an hour away from the end! You can do it: I believe— Holy Father, Dio, Holy Spirit—I believe in your fucking Emptiness! Just do it! You did the fog, didn't you!"

Dorje was silent.

"What do you want him to do?" I groaned. "This is a crack in our minds, and in his, too."

"But he's a fucking saint!"

"A saint could also be chased by desires. He could be chased by a desire to stop his mind from chasing and become a real saint."

"What? Okay: then I want you to blow up your mind," Martin whispered as he gently placed his hands on Dorje's knees. "Imagine your mind is Yuin's chopper! You can do it! You can jam together all your hate and then aim it at their choppers—blow them out of the air!"

"Then what?" I said. "The choppers will leave, but then we'll freeze to death anyway."

"Then—then—" Martin kept whispering as he peered into Dorje's dispassionate, seemingly sleepy face. "Then, find in your mind a rope with a hook of hope. Our preacher used to say that God lowers it for those who drown in their sins. If Baptists have hopes, you must, too. Maybe your Emptiness is not that empty. Let this rope drop from that cliff over there. If we didn't have choppers in the way—if we only had a rope with a hook—we could give it a shot! All we need is to climb that cliff! Then—India's border guards must have AA-guns or something, the gooks won't dare. . . . Just an itsy-bitsy fifty-foot climb! Come on, bro'! You can do it! I believe in you!"

Not a muscle moved in Dorje's face. With a groan, Martin dropped on his side.

90

GWEN, my love, I'm writing you from a glacier whose name I do not know. A free cryogenic burial to make the future mountaineers—or deep-water divers?—rack their brains: who were these three, and what were they after to end up in this hole in the ice?

The sun has vanished behind a cloud, and everything has turned gray: the sky, the chopper, the vultures. My body will be burned and picked to bits; my ashes will mix with the rocks, the ice, the birds' stomachs, and the ground on which they will defecate. You won't see this body again. But that's just the body—that's not me. My conscious will keep on running, delighting in its movement, fearing the traps, and—yearning for you.

Nothing will change for my "I." The vultures are waiting for my body; Yuin, for my conscious. He wants to chew his prey with verbal torment and swallow it into the stomach of his mad idea. But I don't want it; I don't want my soul to freeze up like my toes, which I no longer feel; I don't want it to stop yearning for you.

THERE'S nothing I can do but wait for death and stare at the sky. The sky in general, and the Tibetan one even more so, is endowed with a scientist's sterile lack of passion. It is God's main trait. A scientist peers into his microscope at the samples of his own blood, the struggle between natural antibiotics and human bacteria; God watches as dispassionately through the aqua lens of the firmament, at the struggle between the good and the evil. His neutrality drives the stupid man to rage, the intelligent man to insanity, and the wise man to perfect clarity and more wisdom.

DO you remember our New York days—how we used to pick a restaurant not for its cuisine or prices, but for the view from its windows? Same here, on this glacier. It doesn't matter that we are the menu. The view is sublime, as the blue mountains turn to red, gold, and finally to gray. Just like life itself: it is colorless. What changes is the lighting, as the clouds of our thoughts turn to the sun of the conscious.

AT sundown, I can barely move my fingers. Cursing, Martin keeps pricking his fingers and cheeks with a sharpened piece of ice. Dorje is meditating. . . .

We have a day left—at most—before we freeze to death. A whole day! That should be enough to understand life. I have had so many of them—but I never took the chances I had. You awaken and see the sky; you wash yourself, start a fire, cook the food, eat and drink, walk, run, see another person and greet him, do something useful, help another person or a beast—and keep on loving every being, human or not. Then you pray, you watch the sun go down, you go to sleep. After a day like this, you can't fear death. You can say: I have known life, in this body, on this earth, and now I am ready to learn it in another body, in another place.

I haven't lived a single day like this. I am afraid that this discontent will keep eating at me until I regain a body. But the conscious that has never learned to live and to love fully will be unhappy in a new wrapper, too.

THE sun hid behind the mountain. Darkness fell; the cold struck mercilessly. I may have been optimistic; we would not survive the night.

"Good-bye, Martin."

My friend could no longer even move his lips; all I got was a slight nod. We pressed closer to each other, I closed my eyes—and screamed from a blinding flash.

At first I thought that I had popped a vessel in my head. But it was a searchlight, striking us in the eye as the chopper hovered over the entrance into our cave.

"ISN'T that what you wanted?" Yuin was all but purring in the speakers. "To sit in a cave like Milarepa the poet and compose hymns? Didn't you write in your diary that it was better to be impotent than deaf: then you could be a great mystic and hear the music of the mountains? Ha! Right now, you'd settle for being an impotent deaf-mute for a chance to get out of here. I warned you to beware fantasies: even the noblest ones are dangerous! The bliss you were pursuing is only bliss as a flight from something else—the more you get of it, the more suffering it will cause you. But you don't look happy. Isn't that the hermitage you wanted: the Himalayas, a cave, and no one to get in the way of contemplation. No competition or publishers or grants or academic degrees—go on, create!

"In the civilization you have been trying to save, these

conditions can mean one thing only: the hermit will die!
Remember Namtso Utse, the lamasery with two hermits?"

Martin and I exchanged looks.

"You blew them up." Yuin's voice was clear despite the
roar of the propellers. "When you were there, you thought
that the insanity of their bliss was superior to intellect and
poetry. You thought that their insanity helped them stand
the torture. You wanted to climb to their level, but then you
saw it was nothing but greed! For a pittance, the lama was
prepared to sell you a relic; shall we say . . . an interesting
part of his teacher Nagpa's body! Ha! Naturally, you recoiled. What you took for holy madness was simple fool-
ishness and banal stupidity. You thought: What if all of my
idols, those great hermits, are nothing but a bunch of asinine
savages?

"I knew this all along. That's why I sent Margi in advance to plant a radio-controlled bomb. She camped on the
hill overlooking Utse, her camera pointed at the lamasery
below. So that I could see it in Rating, too. And the moment
I saw disgust in your face, I ordered that she push the button."

I glanced at Martin.

"It's not that complicated," he murmured.

"Do not despair!" Yuin chuckled. "The idiocy of saints
and hermits is no more of a salvation than anything else in
this society. Whatever man has, from sex to ecstatic prayer,
it leads him to suffering. My father used to say to me: When
you grow up, you'll see I was right. So does God say to
man: When you die, you'll see I was right. But I want you
to acknowledge it now—not posthumously! Stop being ridiculous and climb up!"

I had to squint as I looked into the bright light and shook
my head.

"You have till morning."

His voice had lost its joy. The savior of mankind was not
used to being defied.

The lights went out, and the chopper headed back, followed by the first one. Now we were in perfect silence and
darkness.

I pressed my palms to my face. Why? True, sometimes

a thinker gets stuck and dies in solitude on the peaks he has conjured. But there had to be something to liberate us from the prison of ice. What was it?

My hands were too shaky to block my sight completely; but when a flickering light showed between my fingers . . .

. . . Dorje's contour was emitting a faint, but distinct glow.

Semiparalyzed, I reached for the glow and recoiled as my fingers caught a pocket of warmth. The monk was radiating heat! A small puddle had formed in the ice next to him.

"Press together," he murmured, his eyes still shut. "Warm."

I had heard about *tumo,* the Tibetan art of generating heat through concentration. Now I saw it for myself. *A Warming Thought!* Truly: denying literal meaning was a doubter's refuge!

DORJE remained seated, while Martin and I coiled ourselves around him, trying to get closer to the human stove. This was not the first time I was sleeping like this with Martin, and I was no longer repelled by the odor of the mouth that had long been without a toothbrush, the smell of the unwashed body, the other person's arms on one's face. Here, the embrace was the only salvation. Not just from the cold; but in the Christian sense as well.

People should be hugging one another all the time, I thought, falling asleep; they should be like trees and soil, like sand and rocks, like meadow grass and horses. We seek the embraces of our beloved in order to feel complete. But seeking for your "unique" other half is a mistake, for our lost half can be anywhere, for the completeness of God is everywhere, too.

91

WE unclenched our arms from around Dorje, who remained motionless, at the roar of the helicopters.

"Is God's spark still warm in you, boy?"

There were four helicopters now, but I could not tell
which one Yuin's voice was coming from.

"Another night, and it will go out. Are you ready now?"

With an effort, I straightened my arm and flipped him
the finger.

Yuin chuckled. "Social morality teaches one not to leave
friends in trouble. Did no one tell you there's an abyss between a good person and a religious one? The abyss between aesthetics and mysticism—if you want to be a saint,
you jump!"

"I don't want to."

He must have lip-read my answer. "Doesn't matter. Let
me make you an offer you can't refuse, as they say." He
turned back to bark an order.

A chopper turned its side towards the cave. Two soldiers
shoved Nyima forward for me to see. Before I could react,
they pushed her out.

I did not have time to scream. Yet she did not fall; they
were holding her aloft over the abyss. The wind blew the
edge of her convict jacket over the face of one of the soldiers, and for a second he let go of her arm. But the other
one held her tightly.

"If you want her to be pulled back," Yuin said, "you'll
do as you are told."

Another helicopter came down and dropped a rope with
a wide tool belt dangling from it.

"At the count of three"—Yuin's voice suggested that the
jokes were over—"the belt goes back up—and this time you
won't catch her. One!"

I glanced at Martin. He shook his head and shouted over the noise of the propellers, "You better do it!"

"Two!"

I grabbed the belt and for the last time cast a glance of despair at Dorje.

As if on cue, the monk's eyes opened. Yet they were looking past me—at the chopper—and widening with every second.

"Three!"

The belt jerked out of my hand, and a powerful blast threw us down on the ice. A giant fireball flew past us, singeing our faces—it was the helicopter with the rope!

"You did it!" Martin hollered, kissing Dorje on the top of his head. "And there's the rope!"

A steel grapple fork on the rope struck against the edge of our cave. Somewhere above a machine gun went *rat-a-tat,* and a rocket shot through the air, barely missing the choppers. That's how the first chopper had been shot down!

"Grab it!" A familiar voice came over the noise of the gunfire, and the equally familiar face of Tsendin, our Lhasa driver, showed over the edge of the cave.

"You grab!" he shouted. "All three! We pull!"

Another explosion turned the second helicopter into a fireball. But now the remaining ones had redeployed and were returning fire.

Screaming with fear, we grabbed the fork; for a moment, we were airborne over the cliff. In another second, a missile shot from the helicopter made a direct hit on the cave where we had been hiding. By then we were safely atop the glacier.

A dozen brick-faced Tibetans in white robes were firing haphazardly at the choppers. One of them had a Stinger over his shoulder. The concentration on his face far exceeded that from any meditation.

"When you arrested, Chinese look for me, too!" Tsendin shouted happily. "I found Tigers! They hunt Yuin now! We intercepted radio: Yuin was looking for you here! You run now to India!" He waved to the end of the glacier.

"Don't shoot!" I yelled at the Stinger man, his finger dancing on the button. "Nyima's aboard!"

"Yuin's aboard!" Tsendin scowled. "Butcher of Lhasa! Run!"

Another helicopter went down. We rushed to the edge of the glacier and instantly were thrown forward by the blast wave—the Chinese hit the Tigers.

WHEN we recovered from the tumble, we were standing on the edge of a cliff. About seven feet divided the glacier from a rocky slope on the Indian side. The border police were nowhere in sight.

"Gotta jump," Martin gasped. "They got one chopper left!"

Dorje jumped first, without stepping back. Flew over like a bird.

"Go!" Rivers pushed me.

"What about your leg? You won't be able to push off!"

"You'll just have to catch me! Jump!"

I made a few steps back and jumped. I barely made it.

Martin peeled off his clothes, leaving his pants and boots on. Limping, he stepped back farther, clenched his fists, and hurtled forward with a yell.

He hit the edge and would have dropped down; but Dorje and I caught his hand and pulled him up.

"We're in India, Martin!" I cried out, kissing the top of his head.

Martin picked up a rock and bit into it to suppress the pain. He had struck his leg against the cliff, and his wound had opened up again.

"Help." Dorje nodded downward, where a green bug, an Indian border guard jeep, was climbing uphill.

Supporting Martin, we limped down the slope, when a roar came up from behind. It was the fourth helicopter. The one the Tigers did not get.

We tried to run, but the jump had taken up the last of Martin's energy. He stumbled and fell down. "Run," he wheezed, holding on to his pants, which were quickly swelling with blood.

The chopper was so close we could no longer hear one another.

"No, no," I muttered, trying to get him up, but I was spent, too.

Over the noise of the propellers, Yuin spoke from above: "I told you: you can't escape yourself."

Dorje dropped Martin's arm and ran downhill.

"Good thinking." Martin nodded. "At least he'll save his ass."

The chopper was coming down, with no shots fired. Apparently, Yuin was planning to capture us alive.

After fifty feet or so, Dorje reached a small clearing with puddles of snow: the nearest flat spot where the chopper could land. He sat down and crossed his legs.

"What is he doing?" Martin cried out.

"I don't know!" I shouted.

The helicopter hovered over the spot where Dorje was seated and slowly began coming down with tremendous noise.

"Run, Dorje!" I yelled. "He'll squash you!"

Yuin appeared in the door, a scowl on his face. We were roaches, caught on a glue pad; and he was about to wipe us out.

At a mere couple of hundred feet from the ground, the propeller started to slow down. Yuin yelled to the pilot. A frightened face under a helmet showed in the window. And then the blades were still.

For a moment, the huge green monster with a red star painted on its side hung in the air; and then it collapsed downward—right on top of Dorje.

THE helicopter did not explode when it hit the ground; it merely fell apart. We sorted through the wreckage, shoving aside the bodies of the soldiers in camouflage till we came across the bloody mess of flesh and bone in the purple robe. Dorje's dead face bore the same smile of absolute bliss that I had seen on Schechter's blackened face.

Something white showed through a crack in the lama's skull: perhaps it was his brain, or a bone, or snow. But now I could not help thinking that it was Emptiness itself that had always shone through him and that now bestowed on him the last grateful kiss of bliss.

"How did he do that?" Martin whispered.

"He identified his mind with the engine—the mind of the chopper." Tears rose to my throat, but, before they could reach my eyes, they flowed down, washing over my chest in warm, salty bliss. "The two merged completely. So, when he stopped his own mind, the engine stopped, too."

Something stirred behind us.

"Yuin!"

We turned him over onto his back.

The general was still alive. Every breath he made released a stream of bubbling blood out of his mouth; it was as if the lava from the eruption he had invoked was devouring its first victim. He opened his eyes; his lips trembled into a semblance of a smile.

"You killed me," he wheezed. "Means you loved me. You killed everyone you loved."

"So did you."

"We are two poles. Movement is everything; the objective is nothing. Or, Emptiness. God doesn't know what He wants. But *I* do."

He tried to smile once again. "I know what He wants. I'll tell you the argument."

He motioned me to lower my head. I did, my ear almost touching his bloody mouth. He took in the air; a wave of blood rose to his lips, and, without spilling out, stopped.

His yellow eyes, unusually wide for a Chinese, stared glassily at the top of the glacier.

"HE told you?" Martin asked.

I shook my head.

"Fuck him anyway." Wincing, Martin removed Yuin's blood-drenched military tunic and put it on. "Might come in handy in the course of the investigation." He went through the pockets and found an army card.

"He looks pretty damn gloomy here." Martin flicked at the photo on the card. "Now he's smiling. Death becomes him. Or maybe Dorje stopped his mind, too."

Like Schechter and Dorje, Yuin had died with a smile. But his was more like a grin of Lenin or Mao. Despite his avowed Buddhism, Yuin remained a Communist. He was tormented by the necessity to choose, the blessing and the curse of our civilization; he tried to rip off his chains and achieve Emptiness. But he was as crude and cruel as only a materialist can be, and, like his Communist predecessors, he tortured everyone he wanted to liberate. Dorje's smile was of enlightenment; Yuin's, a feral scowl.

"And yet God could extend a rope even to him," I said.

"You said there was no God."

"His Fullness is Emptiness. . . . Can you hear Him?"

In the silence, we could hear only gusts of wind, and the quiet crackling of wrecked steel. And that was God.

Suddenly, a moan came from under the wreckage. It was Nyima—covered with blood, still handcuffed, unconscious—but alive! By the time we carried her, along with Dorje's remains, away from the wreckage, which had begun smoking menacingly, the Indian border police had finally arrived. A mustachioed lieutenant in a turban demanded to see our papers.

"F—B—I!" Martin declared with unconcealed aplomb. "We need your assistance on a matter of international security. If you cooperate—and fast—you can count on a promotion and a medal . . . or a green card and a hack medallion. I have full authority as a representative of the American government. Deliver the girl to the hospital immediately. And we need to go to the Bon lamasery. A *gompa*. There's one nearby, am I right?"

"About an hour," the lieutenant uttered, completely bewildered.

"Excellent!" Martin nodded. "Contact the U.S. Embassy in New Delhi. They'll send a helicopter to pick us up. By the way, what day is it today?"

The lieutenant murmured the date.

"We have eight days left," I said quietly.

"Step on it, Lieutenant!" Martin went on. "A green card for you and your clan."

"Where's the nearest hospital?" I remembered to ask.

"About a day's travel," the Indian said.

"Then she'll have to come with us to the *gompa*. Him, too." I pointed at Dorje's body.

"We'll come back for him," the officer suggested. "His body can wait."

"The body can," I countered, "but his conscious won't. Right now it's abroad, just like we are. It needs a jeep and an escort, too. It is being awaited at the *gompa.*"

92

IN the dusty window of the jeep, the peaks merged into a yellow saddle with green reins.

"Where's the *gompa?*"

"Right there, sir." The officer pointed at a chain of caves. From the distance, they looked like tiny black nostrils, through which the mountain was inhaling the sky.

When we pulled up, Martin jotted down a message to the embassy. The officer saluted and was gone, to the barking of the dogs, who ran out to meet us.

WOODEN steps led up to the main cave, surrounded by a colorful group of barefoot Indian women and children. Like their Tibetan counterparts, they had come to be healed and blessed. At the sight of the blood-splattered tarp with the bodies, the women grabbed their children and scattered.

"Where's the damn lamas?" Martin waved to the monks watching from the cave.

With a moan, Nyima opened her eyes and recognized me. "Where are we?"

I heard the steps creaking behind me.

"In Shambala," I said.

She opened her eyes wide and saw shaven heads and purple robes.

"I knew." She smiled and closed her eyes.

"SHE needs doctor." A tall young monk tapped me on the shoulder. He had a sleepy expression on a heavy, rounded face that somehow suggested a melon. "You want us to take her up?"

He spoke confidently, with authority. His English was accented but fluent. He could well be the elder, or whatever they called the head of the *gompa*.

I nodded, and he commanded other monks to pick up Nyima and carry her up the ladder. "Would you like to bury your friend?" The young elder pointed at the blood-drenched rag with Dorje's feet sticking out.

I lifted the rag. "He's a disciple of Nagpa's. Did you know him?"

He shook his head.

"We must inform Nagpa. We must see him on a very important matter."

He remained silent.

"Nagpa is here, isn't he? He's alive, right?"

"No," the lama said.

"What do you mean, no?" I felt queasy in my stomach.

"I don't know no Nagpa."

"Dorje—our friend here—told us he was here!"

The elder glanced at the body again, and his expression grew even more somnolent. "This monk is not from our *gompa.*"

"True, but he saw Nagpa seeking shelter here. He told him on the wind. Nagpa was his teacher!"

"I don't know no Nagpa."

"Every lama knows Nagpa!" I cried out in despair. "Here—I have his beads!"

The lama glanced at my wrist, and his face became impenetrable once again.

Martin was seated on the ground, staring numbly at the monk's huge white sneakers. I knew the look: all his energy had been exhausted in the last effort. He was burned out.

Me, too: I was ready to lie down next to Dorje and become a corpse.

"He led us to Nagpa," I murmured, my eyes fixed on our friend's singed, scowling skull. "We were cell mates in Rating. Dorje helped us escape—with Nagpa's help. Then he took us through hell—again, with Nagpa's help. At the very least I would like to tell Nagpa how his disciple died."

"He knows." The elder headed back up to the cave.

WE exchanged bewildered glances. Were we supposed to follow him? Before we knew it, the white sneakers vanished from sight, and silent monks materialized from nowhere to cover up Dorje's body and carry it upstairs.

What else could we do? We climbed up and warily stepped into the darkness.

THE narrow passage was barely lit by candles on the walls. The mixed odor of incense, yak fat, and manure was overpowering. What did they do here—keep goats? Moaning sounds came from the dark, making my skin crawl as I recalled the stories of Bon poisoners. The elder was not aware we had sent the police for help. Perhaps we should wait for them . . . ?

But Martin plodded on, and the sound of his steps comforted me.

FINALLY, we entered a long narrow cave, lit with two rows of candles, like a taxiing strip at night. Along the walls, the monks rocked steadily, muttering mantras and moaning in eerie voices.

The elder, seated in the middle, caught our glances and nodded at the pillows at his side.

A group of monks with horns, drums, and kettledrums emerged from the opposite end of the cave. At the elder's order, the chanting stopped. And the band started playing.

At first, I thought that someone had grabbed the hemispheres of my brain and started banging them against each other like kettledrums, filling my entire body with a horrible growing din.

The cave had unusual acoustics: the sound came at you from six sides, rather than four. The stones under my feet hummed, and the stone ceiling was coming down on my head with a roar.

They have to be crazy to be playing here, I thought. *You can go deaf here, in this Bon disco—this is worse than DeoMorte!*

"This is torture by music!" Martin yelled in my ear. "We used it on terrorists! Let's get out of here!"

The elder's eyes fixed on me, I shook my head. The cacophony had to be aimed at us: it could be a ritual—or a test.

The sounds grew by the second. It was as if God Himself was treading on the firmament to see if it was sturdy enough; the heavenly army's war elephants were about to trample the earthlings; and the entire mountain above was collapsing on us.

The sight of Martin made me flinch. His face was distorted, his hands gripped his knees, his teeth clenched, his eyes goggled. I was reminded of Dr. Ruslanov's patients as they were listening to the mantra with their headsets on.

The horns! I was about to shut my ears, but the elder's stern look stopped me in my tracks. Apparently I was expected to withstand this audio assault.

I had this feeling once before, perhaps ten or so years ago, in Santa Clara County Municipal Auditorium. Once again, my mind was an ocean; the sound was creating tiny ripples that kept swelling till they burst in a sky-high wave that rose between me and the world. I tried to hide from it, I tried to think of myself as a dot—but there was no getting away as it crashed on top of me.

Death. Light. But I am alive! The elder's eyes seem to be directly attached to mine, millimeters between us. Now my mind turns into the earth, and the sound comes up from its belly. They swell as they rise—another minute, and the erupting lava will bury me under.

Once again, I am alive, staring into the black maws of the horns. Or are they the elder's eyes? They are humming—no, the humming is inside my head. It is a huge bonfire, my brains are crackling, my gray matter is bursting out in bubbles. It turns into a whirlwind that keeps sucking me into air funnels—

Do not fall! Stay awake! The elder's eyes are still fixed on me. And in the next instant the wind dies, the fire returns to the soil, and the water is the calm surface of a pond.

When I opened my eyes, my cheeks were wet with tears.

My eyes fixed on the elder. The music was gone, along with
the monks and their instruments.

Martin lay against the wall, his head on his chest, his
eyes closed, his breathing labored. He was unconscious.

"COME," the elder said. "You've passed the *chod.*"

"What?" I was so deafened I could hardly hear my own
voice.

"You can call it mental detector," the elder said with utter
seriousness, seemingly unaware of the pun.

As we plunged deeper into the innards of the mountain,
it occurred to me that it was no pun. The purpose of the
ritual was to identify the aggressive aspects of the testee's
conscious and bounce their energy back at him. The monks
did not react to the torment because to their clear conscious
that cacophony was the natural sound of reality, the biblical
"noise of many waters." It was a layer where all things
happen at once, creating this horrible and at the same time
wonderful polyphony. Indeed, it was a "mental detector."
That's what Ruslanov would have called it. Perhaps the elder in sneakers had been reading the Russian's thoughts. Or
perhaps the man whom I was about to see had been "getting
them on the wind."

BY the time we arrived at a small cave, we had made so
many turns that I had lost all sense of direction. The small
cave was empty save for the three big oil lamps illuminating
the *tanka* on the wall. Their faint flames trembled, as if
recoiling from the images of angry dieties, spitting fire and
drinking blood from human skulls, on the *tanka*. In the center was a ray of gray light, coming from somewhere above.
It reminded me of the holes made through pyramids in order
to let a certain star shine exactly on the tomb.

Perhaps this particular hole was an animal's hideout: a
clump of feathers or wool gently floated amid the particles
of dust. I traced its path as it slowly dropped on the floor—
right at the feet of an old man.

I shivered. How come I had not seen him right away? He
was seated only a few feet away. . . . I caught my breath and
shifted slightly to get a better look.

*   *   *

PHYSICALLY, Nagpa was a plain old peasant, the kind familiar to me by now around the Tibetan countryside: a long wind-beaten face with hollow cheeks and a few gray hairs on the chin. The trick about his face was its perfect motionlessness. He was like an African mask or an Easter Island idol.

Like the elder, Nagpa was wearing white sneakers, blue track pants, and a pink T-shirt. His wardrobe must have come from an international aid package. With his finger, he was polishing off some green goop from an aluminum plate.

I turned around, but the elder was gone, having vanished without a sound.

"*Tashi delek,*" I said timidly.

Nagpa looked up. His teary eyes slid across my face, and then he went back to his meal.

"Rinpoche . . . I am a student of Michael Schechter's. Here—" I held up the beads. "You gave them to Schechter. He gave them to me."

Nagpa glanced at the beads and, once again, went back to eating.

"I knew Lama Ayushi!"

Slurping noisily, Nagpa licked the goop off his finger.

"Dorje led us here. He's dead now—but I brought his body."

The old-timer wiped the green goop off his chin and then licked his palm.

So this was the savior of the world? The enlightened master?

But my teachers worshipped him. Could he be, well, pissed off or something?

That's right—I'd forgotten to prostrate myself.

I took a few steps back, folded my hands, touched the top of my head, my lips, my heart, and then prostrated myself, outstretching my arms and hiding my head between them. And then I heard an odd creaky sound.

I looked up to see if perhaps Nagpa was having a choking fit. But the old man was laughing, his head shaking slightly.

Embarrassed, I knelt and folded my hands again. "Rinpoche, I have very important business. I beg you to hear me out."

Then, without rising, I told him everything that had happened, beginning with the night at DeoMorte.

"Now it's up to you," I concluded. "You're the only hope. If you chant the countermantra, we can still put it on the air and prevent the catastrophe." I waited.

Without raising his eyes, the old man kept mopping clean the bowl.

"Can you hear me?"

I felt a sudden urge to turn.

THE elder, the *gompa*'s abbot, again stood behind me, his eyes fixed on me. "He can hear you," he spoke softly. "But Rinpoche's tongue is not with him. It is in Namtso Utse, preserved by the lama who was his cell mate. Nagpa bit off his own tongue in order to prevent himself from revealing the secret mantras under torture."

"Dorje never told me."

"Dorje did not know."

I sat on the floor, getting dizzy.

"How do you communicate?" I asked the elder. "Does he write?"

"Rinpoche does not know how to write. We understand what he is trying to say."

I jumped up. "So tell me his answer!"

"The answer can be understood only by him in whose mind the question has ripened." He turned around and vanished in the darkness of the maze.

I dropped back on the floor. My strength was leaving me. . . .

COULDN'T he see the torment his guest had gone through while searching for the clue to this puzzle? I eyed Nagpa's motionless face with hate. He could hear me! Couldn't he give a sign?

Didn't he feel anything at all about mankind? Perhaps he was really no sage, but a mere warlock, adept in black magic.

*   *   *

TIME went by. I kept staring at the old man, who seemed to be immersed in sleep, or else meditating. When the ray of sunshine turned to dark gray, a thought flashed through my mind.

Who the hell was I, to take upon myself the mission to save the world? This is sheer megalomania! And the old man is merely senile! It's not too late to get to the village and call the embassy. I can't save anyone; all I can do is warn. Let the government handle this, evacuate people or something.

That was nonsense: how could they evacuate everybody and where to? But the thoughts kept running around my head:

Perhaps I should kidnap Nagpa to the U.S. Perhaps—

Oh yeah. Add kidnapping on top of murder charges. If the FBI was afraid to hire Ruslanov, they'll scream with joy at the chance to explore the subconscious of this Tibetan old-timer.

What if I blackmailed him? Call Martin and communicate that he will break my neck if the old man does not crack up?

Yep. Nagpa won't lift a finger. Won't even read Bardo.

BY the time the light column turned dark red, I had a new idea: the hell with it. I'll stay here!

The cave felt like a mother's belly: warm, dark, quiet. One could spend an eternity here. Bird's down floating in the air. Odor of incense. Dusty pillar of light. Here, it did not even matter whether the cave would be flooded or not.

Oddly, the old man was not sending me away. Was he waiting for something?

FINALLY, the light was almost gone, and only then it dawned on me: I had not brought a *kato*—an offering! I was about to dash for the exit, but then I paused.

If this was indeed the crux of the problem, a banal silk scarf would not do. I had nothing of value—but my mind. It kept bombarding me with action plans that were getting in the way of listening to Nagpa. It needed to be cleared

and offered to Rinpoche. But monks in the *gompa* spent
years learning how to do that, so how was I—?

ABRUPTLY, Nagpa emerged from his immersion. He
placed his hands on his ears, the way a DJ presses an earset,
and, his eyes still shut, slowly swayed in a circle, quietly
moaning a mantra. Gradually, his swaying got wider; his
moaning, louder.

There was an unmistakable déjà vu about the scene. Ah!
I remembered.

*"AYUSHI was bad student, lazy. Ayushi ask all the time:
explain this, explain that. Rinpoche wait that Ayushi hear
without words. Then, Rinpoche send Ayushi to mountain.
He say, Go to highest mountain and sit on dangerousest
rock seven day. . . ."*

93

I asked the abbot for a thermos of *cha*. He handed it to me
silently, without bothering me with questions. Martin demanded an explanation, but I shut him up, leaving him alone
in the dark *gompa* until further instructions.

As I left the lamasery, Indian mothers with their children
were still waiting for their turn to see the healer. The women
laughed softly as I walked by.

Their laughter, their clinking bracelets, the clamor of their
children, the barking of their dogs—all the sounds of life,
simple and warm, where you hear only what is said—stayed
with me for a long time as I was climbing back into the
cold silence of the mountains. The Himalayas could get me
killed; but first I had to learn how to listen to them.

AFTER an hour, I was in a completely isolated place, where
no one could bother me. I looked around—and saw it right

away. The huge boulder hanging over the abyss was waiting for me in silence, as if lying in ambush. I cautiously patted its cold eroded surface.

"I don't know your name," I whispered as I peered into its gloomy granite brow. "Me, I'm—I'm Abraham and Isaac rolled into one."

It was on this rock that Nagpa wanted me to sacrifice my mind, which would not leave me alone with its escape schemes. What if I died, along with my mind? What if the angel did not stay my hand at the last moment?

But this "if" was exactly what I had to kill here.

I needed to move closer to the abyss, the way Ayushi had done. The drop was easily two miles long. Meditation my ass. Overcoming my fear would be a feat unto itself.

I crossed my legs and clenched my hands together, to prevent them from acting on the impulse to push away from the edge. I forced myself to be still and keep my eyes open. I had to look in front of me: directly into the yawning pale purple emptiness. And go through the worst in my mind. The slightest gust of wind could send me into a panic and over the edge.

The palms of my hands grew cold. My head was spinning. Fighting your fear . . . One hundred sixty pounds of flesh, bone, and blood that supported my conscious had no desire to fall.

I wanted to become part of the boulder. Nothing else was closer to me than this porous gray mass with pale green spots of moss, with reddish specks of iron, with white sprays of quartz. Air was death; boulder was life.

I wished someone would show up; then I would have an excuse—to crawl back from the edge, to talk, to leave. Soon, it would get dark; the chasm would become invisible. I'd fall asleep, stir, and—

There was God, and in the mountains your prayers got answered faster than in the plains. I could not tell the face of the man who was slowly climbing up the path. But he had a limp. Martin! I almost cried out—and then I recognized him.

It was the black man from the subway.

*   *   *

INSTANTLY, he was seated facing me. Rather, he was aloft in the air, his artificial leg outstretched towards the boulder. Just as I had wished a moment ago, I found myself grown into the rock. The fear made the hair on my arms stir.

"Now you know what it's like, being cold and lonely like a homeless man on a street corner?"

"Yeah," I whispered.

Not even whispered—*thought.*

He nodded understanding. "All right . . . Do you know now why you killed me?"

"Yuin said you'd been killed by my fear of trading places with you—of becoming a homeless black man. That, too— the race guilt—"

"Yeah." He nodded. "But that's not the whole story. In another life I killed you when you tried to kill me. In this one, you took revenge. We keep trading places, infinitely. You shouldn't have taken revenge; you should've let yourself get killed. But it's not too late. Come here—"

He held out his hand. So intimate, so inviting was the gesture that I extended my hand, too—and, touching the emptiness, instantly recoiled.

"You're lying!" I cried out. "You are my fear for my body. That's what killed you! My self-preservation instinct was my master! And I am here to put it in its place!"

"Hey, brother"—his tone became friendly—"you'll be a goner without it. It's too dangerous sitting here. You can fall, or get eaten by an animal, or starve to death—"

"Shut up! You are my primeval fear. But I'm stronger—"

"You'll freeze off your legs, bro'." He rolled back his pant leg. "Yuin sent me to the mountains, too, to practice *tumo*—the yoga internal heat thing, remember?"

I nodded, afraid to utter a word.

"I froze off my leg, and it got chopped off. You know how local surgeons are? Brrr . . . Listen, the Flood is a fairy tale—meantime, you'll be a cripple for the rest of your life. Get off this thing!"

"No way." I flipped him the bird. "I know where you're coming from. Thanks to you—to self-preservation instinct— we have come to live a long life. But you keep me imprisoned. I know that my spirit is immortal. It can fly; it fears nothing. 'I'm nothing but my body' is an illusion, and I'm free of it now. Understand?"

No one answered. The black man was gone. In his place was a dark blue emptiness. The night had fallen.

AS always in Tibet, the air instantly grew cold. All I could hear was an occasional gust of the wind and the murmur of a distant brook. Soon, I heard the animals, too. The sound of falling pebbles that sent my heart to my throat: a mountain goat came up and sniffed me from the distance. What if a lynx came? I began trembling.

I had to overcome the cold—the fear. I was writing my notes by touch. The abyss and the mountain merged into one dark entity, yet I still saw them, along with the images of all my thoughts. Whatever you see in life you will see in death, too. You will carry these thousands of things, tantalizing in their variety, from one dream to another, until you give up on their shapes and learn to see their essence instead. Then existence will no longer be divided into life and death.

The wind was howling, and the mountain stream bubbled nonstop, too, forming together an endless monologue that those who survived deliver to those who are gone. I could not fall asleep; then I would lose consciousness and fall. I had to look into the darkness. I had to love the darkness.

I used to love it, as a child. I used to sneak into the woods after dark and sit in the clearing, listening to the rustling sounds. It was eerie, but I felt safe. I felt the forest was on my side. Now, in the Himalayas, I felt I had sneaked out to the roof to admire the silvery stars in the velvety darkness specked with moondust. With every whisper of the wind, the nighttime darkness changed its hues; it was fleeting and dizzying, like a wave.

As night passed, I went over everything I had ever seen; all people, things, and places, now invisible in the dark.

One after another, I caressed every bead of my reminiscences with gentle fingers of memory, and gazed at it till its shape dissolved in my mind, and nothing was left but its eternal spark. I moved on to the next. Gradually, my memories turned into an endless string of shining lights, not unlike the diamond necklace that had secured our release from Rating. . . .

THE dawn came; my first dawn on the boulder. The whale of a black mountain across the abyss was still asleep, only slightly distinct from the aqua background of the skies. But then its fin became inflamed, emitting disturbing bluish redness. It was as if the mountain was the earth's distended belly, about to give birth. The tungsten thread was barely noticeable; it had not challenged the power of the night yet. Yet the darkness followed it closely; it knew that the tiny stripe represented the future. The shadow barely left the rock as the stripe turned into the sun—and changed the world.

The same with people: a barely visible trace of selfless love lights up, and we breathlessly wait for it to explode in a light that will fill us with sounds, colors, smells, clicking, songs, and the stirrings of life itself. But, like dawn, human life always begins with the color red: with blood, with the effort to tear yourself away from the dark mass of the mountain—that is, your former consciousness. It is horribly difficult and seemingly impossible. Yet all you have to do is begin the process, to make a sacrifice—start with the color of blood—and the process becomes irreversible; the sun keeps rising.

ON my second day, I overcame dizziness and fear. I no longer yearned to crawl back from the edge. Now I was possessed with the wish to throw myself down! Just what Ayushi and Gwen had done. I wanted to atone for their deaths in the same fashion. Was that the reason my destiny had landed me on this rock: to make me experience the horror of the fall and the pain of the crash?

Or, perhaps the self-preservation instinct became replaced by one of self-destruction. Or it could be something else: a desire to become one with Gwen, for example. And fear of loneliness. If we had never truly become one in life, perhaps we should become one in death?

"Perhaps," a voice said.

I shuddered at its familiarity.

Professor Schechter was lying next to me, in the same position as he had once lain next to the fireplace. His eyes were sad and mildly rebuking.

"Yuin said you were killed by my secret fear of your homosex—" I started shyly.

"That's not the whole truth." He smiled sadly. "In another life, you were my teacher, and in this one we traded places. We do it infinitely. You were attracted to me. You shouldn't have been turned off by it."

"Or, rather, I should have realized the unpleasantness of being a sex object or viewing someone as one."

"Come on"—he waved me off—"you can't fight the instinct." He rose on his elbow. "Listen, the Flood won't be such a bad thing for you. It's the only thing to put out the burning desires that would torment you if you come back to this world. How do you expect to overcome the sexual instinct? You'll return to Gwen, but you'll be drawn to all other women. Either you will torment yourself in a family or you'll end up alone like me. Stay at the *gompa*. Whether the Flood takes place or not, here your desire will be extinguished."

"No, no," I muttered. "I understand where you—I mean, where sexual instinct comes from: fear of solitude, inability to be happy alone, inability to handle your inner current of energy. But I can direct it upward; I can become both the receiver and the transmitter of the spirit."

Schechter chuckled. "I used to teach Tantra, but I never could raise this current. You won't, either: your antenna must be grounded."

"That's what a spouse is for. I will see every potential source of excitement outside our union as a bead. But, rather than tearing it off the string and sticking it into my mouth like a spoiled brat, I will study its beauty and eventually see that it's related to everything else; everything else is filled with the same ecstasy, but, when linked together, produces a million times greater voltage! You can't hold this voltage to yourself: you can't help transmitting it to the world!"

"God bless." Schechter sighed. Then he smiled again and stepped off the rock into the emptiness.

94

DAY three. My legs are stiff; my back and neck are hurting, too. Ayushi said one could not get up or move away from the edge. I cannot even get up to pee. The place is beginning to stink. But overcoming sleep remains the number one problem. You fall asleep, you fall, period. I enter the state of a lucid sleep, where sleep and reality merge. I suspect I never had it before.

Inanimate nature speaks to me. Besides the rock itself, these are my friends: a reddish stunted shrub growing out of the side of the boulder, and the ants that roam across my legs. They are my comfort, my support group: they are as alive as I am, yet they do not fear cold or animals or the fall. Or do they?

The shrub was tiny and fragile. What kind of life does it have, I mused; desperately gripping a lump of soil, afraid of the slightest gust of wind that would toss it into the abyss. Suddenly, it seemed that the shrub stirred—its antennas caught the love and care I was emitting—and instantly recoiled under the gust of wind.

I smiled at it: *Have no fear, silly.* Compared to the bush, I was huge, strong, wise—I was its God.

I reached to caress it—

"Why do you want to make love to a plant?" said the shrub, turning into Abby.

I jerked my hand away. Abby reclined, revealing a breast in the side slit of a flowery Indian robe, while stroking herself slowly.

"Why do you want to fool around with ants or baby-sit a cripple in New York?" she said. "Stay in India. You saw those young women staring at you outside the *gompa.* Slender, sinuous, with tanned flat stomachs and sturdy hips made for love. You can go teach English in a village. You'll be doing a good thing, teaching the kids. In your free time, you can write books, draw, meditate—and practice Kama Sutra with all those beauties. Why reject the pleasures God gave you?"

"Desire possesses man, and I don't want to be possessed," I said. "I have already been misled by the instinct for easy pleasure—and I had to pay for it afterwards. When you take possession of the object of your desire, you're the hunter who killed his prey. That means that, sooner or later, you'll be the prey yourself."

"Don't kid yourself." Abby turned over on her stomach and stretched with unexpected feline ease. "Spouses are each other's prey. Why not pick someone according to your taste? Even if Gwen recovers, she'll get fat and ugly, and you'll end up tired of her."

"A spiritual union does not get fat and ugly and tiresome. In marriage, you're outside the hunting framework."

Abby kneeled and brought her face close to mine. It was young, with sweet tender skin, with full moist lips, smiling at me.

"Outside the hunt lies boredom. You can keep trading in those who get fat and old; you can always get a better one. Five times out of ten, any of these Indian girls will be a better spiritual companion than Gwen, who never cared or understood things Oriental. An Indian girl will bring you physical joy, without which life is incomplete. It has been a long time since Gwen excited you—and now, she's a cripple, too. You'll have to force yourself, to deform your persona every inch of the way—why? Life must be a dance, a celebration—not a hard-labor sentence. Stay in India!"

"No, Abby." I shook my head. "You are leading me back into the maze of my habits and predilections, where only a very special partner will do. But I don't want to choose; I'm tired of the market. Choosing is a net that's thrown on top of you and prevents you from soaring; I want freedom! The unlikelier the partner, the more effectively she peels the net of your desires off you. My choice has been made—by destiny and guilt. The most horrible sin is to betray those who trust you. Or those whom life trusted you with. Do you agree—Abby?"

The shrub was trembling in the wind, its tiny leaves reaching for me. . . .

I was hungry only the first couple of days. On the third day, I began growing weak. Then came a fever. I am burning. I am no longer cold on an icy rock; if the wind is seeking shelter in my burning heart, I welcome it in and give it warmth.

I am no longer hungry. I am nurtured by Mother Earth. I drop an imaginary "tail" straight into its center, and its hot milk flows into me, up my spine, filling me with sweet shivers, with warm calmness.

My mind goes back to Gwen. Like any woman's, her features were reminiscent of the earth: her cheekbones tender and wide, her lips full, her eyes quietly sad. These were the same as the softness, beauty, and receptiveness of the earth.

I feel about the earth the same way I used to feel about Gwen: in moments of love, I would be overcome by exhausting, spasmodic tenderness and adoration of all that is feminine in the world—of the essence of motherhood and the earth. The essence that sacrifices itself to the cradle of life.

I remember making love to Gwen one night. . . . The feeling went so deep into my heart that I could not help letting out a sob. Gwen ascribed it to my orgasm, and I did not contradict her.

Now I was on the verge of tears addressed to earth—my true love and my true mother. Now I had come to realize that, as with all the children of the earth, that was my true essence: a passion for slow, deliberate motherhood, rather than for rebellious passionate magma, as Yuin claimed. Then, one should treat the earth the way a son treats his mother: with care, gentle protectiveness, respect, and patience for her advice. The latter may be nagging at times, yet it always stems from infinite love for you.

"YOU'VE been getting around and screwing up one path after another," a wheezing elderly voice said.

Ayushi was still wearing his threadbare gray robe, and he

had the same blissful grin on his face. But why did he speak so crudely?

"How else?" His eyes were fixed on the peak across the gorge. "You've screwed up your career, your family—everything. You were rising; another effort, and you would get your degree, become a professor, get tenure, a small house with a view of the mountains back in California. But you've slipped. You regressed to the chimeras of your junkie youth. If the Flood never happens, you'll end up the same bum as you were to begin with."

"What are you talking about?" I countered. "Tenure? House? Don't you see how the mountains go up and down? I've been there, done that—I know that a climb is followed by a descent. But at any point you can be on your internal peak, from which you can see both sides of the slope, the sunny and the shady one. I am barely making my way to this peak. You know one can't reach it if one is burdened by money and success. You need ropes and bindings: suffering, atonement, self-effacement, patience, empathy. I just got myself this gear. I'm only beginning to feel that a poor, obscure man is an equal of the rocks and the ground—life itself. And you're suggesting I give it up? You—my role model?"

Chortling, Ayushi slapped himself on the knee. "A teacher of wisdom must be sober and practical! What if the Flood doesn't come; what if you manage to call it off—you will never prove it! No one will notice anything. Everyone will live the way they did—everyone but you. You will be taken for a nut and kicked out of your school. The best you can count on is a few thousand dollars from a tabloid for concocting a lie about your Tibetan adventures.

"What are you bringing back with you? What have you learned? Nothing! You should have learned from Dorje: his extrasensory capacities, his knowledge of sacred mysteries and lore. You should stay here, in the *gompa*. Learn from the local monks, become a Bon teacher, and then go back. You'll be a teacher like me, and make an honorable living at a retreat."

"I have learned the openness of One," I murmured; "and it is superior to the mysteries of many."

"What's that?"

"It's an ability to see through you! You're not Ayushi! You're my fear that my life will not be complete if I do not become a guru like you. But I'm ready to accept life as if the Flood has taken place. I have not become a Bon Po expert, yet I'm perfectly happy. I have retained the main gift—life—and I learned the main thing: changing the mind. Now I can give to anyone, I can love anyone, regardless of who they are and what they possess.

"You say to be happy, I must acquire standing, be it spiritual or material. But the truth is already here: it's the ecstasy of realizing what exactly prevents one from feeling infinite love at this very moment. It is my mind, which keeps telling me lies about my separateness from everything else, about my need to acquire things. I can square off with this enemy at any time, and I can triumph—hey, where are you? You ran away!"

TOSSING my head back, I laugh, and only the skies hear me. They float by, ephemeral like my anxieties, like my past and my future—while I stay here! I don't care if it's five days till the ice starts moving. I stay put. This is it, the main event, the title fight of my life. You don't need seconds and referees and promoters. You can engage Him anytime, anywhere—you always could.

95

THE mountain across the gorge reminds me of Nagpa: the same dispassionate brown mask of a face, the same shining of the glacier as from his high brow. When I understand its speech, I'll be ready to go back to Nagpa. But my mind is not clear enough yet. There are still enough images that cause haphazard lines to run across its screen.

*   *   *

AS I observe the glacier, I wonder: why did the helicopters cut us off on the glacier when we had almost reached our destination?

By my fifth night, I know the answer. It was not the Chinese missiles that blocked our way. It was the I-to-I missiles. *I* made it! *I* ran away! *I* saved myself!

It was love that had paved our escape route. I did not break through to the top of the mountain: I broke through to another person—to Martin. How close to him I felt when I was freezing in his arms! It was in this hellish cold that my heart melted; the transparent ice that had always separated me from others broke down; and in the morning, we were rescued by the Tigers.

Then, a man does have absolute freedom! Then he really is the Master of His Destiny! He creates it with his own thought. It does not need any crutches: neither Yuin's old mantras nor Ruslanov's new computers.

A white figure in a halo of fireflies was climbing up the path. A man in a white coat: was I having a relapse of snow blindness?

"Let us assume"—Ruslanov in his medical robe stepped up on the rock and gestured to me to stay seated—"let us assume I agree with you. You don't need my machine, you don't need the ancient incantations; all you need is to realize yourself as a spirit of Oneness. But then you must be able to explain it in a scientific language that is understood in the West. For now, your explanations are jumbled and incoherent. You must sort it out, and then you will be able to lecture others, and not necessarily for money and career. In order to help others, you must speak their language. As it is . . . forgive me for being blunt, but mankind stands to gain little from your epiphanies."

"No, Doctor . . ." I peered at his robe, which was merging with the whiteness of the glacier. "You are my fear of the unknown, an attempt to rationalize everything. And you're my fear of rejection, too. But I will not explain or popularize. I'll simply live without fear, with love of One life that is contained in everything. And if this is my destiny, people around me will change, too. For real truth cannot be explained through words. Do you agree, Oleg?"

But his beard and rumpled hair were gone, and in their place the moon was shining quietly. It was a full moon, a huge yellowish circle—like the sun, except that it gave off no warmth. It was a little eerie: perhaps this was how the sun would be, no longer blinding and seething, at the End of Days preceding the Final Judgment. Perhaps the moon was just a rehearsal for the sun's demise. Then its contemplation, traditionally related to mystery and death, is a man's preparation for his posthumous travel: souls do not blink at the sun, but stream towards it, like lunatics do to the moon.

The moon and the stars are my former home; they are the lights of my hometown that I left in the dark when I embarked on my journey. When a city dweller returns, he can tell his home by the lights from afar, like the skyline of Manhattan visible from New Jersey. But if he left his home too long ago, he cannot identify the lights and merely feels a vague anxiety. This is how we look at the stars, without recognizing the abode we left long ago.

AT dawn, on day six, a cumulus cloud moved slowly over the mountain peak across from me. Similarly, my mind stirred and flowed smoothly, changing shape, dispersing, and eventually vanishing in the blue.

The sky and the mountains seem to be as dispassionate as Nagpa's silence. We feel no empathy or resentment towards them, and they don't require us to. Yet we keep asking God for His word, support, pity, intervention; then, if He fails to deliver, we rebel and call Him uncaring. But He knows what's good for us; He knows that help should come from within. Only a hard-boiled egg gets smacked with a spoon. What is alive will pick its way through. I was dead, and then He began reviving me with His blows.

What did it take to bring me here? Endless anxieties, fears, drugs, wasted money; prison, shame, exile, chases, violence, torture, deaths of friends and acquaintances; chopped flesh, smashed bones, blood and ashes . . .

Fate sees that man cannot hear his true voice, and then it pounds his eardrums with the world cacophony, so that he becomes deaf and begins hearing his inner silence. Like a sledgehammer, the mantra was pounding on my brain: *Search for me.* But in fact it was saying, *Search for yourself.* Have I found myself?

"REALLY—can you say you have reached enlightenment?" Dorje picked up the edge of his robe and settled down at my side.

His eyes were closed, and his head was intact; not a trace of blood or burns: the same gentle, calm smile I remembered.

"You should stay here, not in the *gompa,* but in a cave nearby. Make fire, drink *cha.* Forget about sutras and incantations. All you have to do is meditate till you feel you have become a Rinpoche: blessed and empty. That's what counts: not lectures, not retreats. You know there are two paths to truth: learning or suffering. You have fled them both. But if you stay here in the mountains, and contemplate about them, you will achieve enlightenment."

"I think I understood something else," I whispered without opening my mouth. "A man does not obtain spiritual energy through learning *or* suffering. It's learning *and* suffering. If he learned too much to begin with—Schechter, Ayushi, Ruslanov—then his learning must be tested by suffering. If he suffered in the beginning, like Martin, then he has to come to knowledge. If man had not tasted the apple, people would not know the Creator, and there would be no Fall or Rise. The Creator had to appear as a snake and tempt them into eating the apple. Now they will want to come back to Eden—but ragged and worn out, aware of the price of Eden in the way that only those who have gone through hell can be."

Dorje shook his head. "If you don't save yourself first, how will you save others? Enlightenment comes first, and it's the ultimate objective."

"Thanks, Dorje, but . . ." As I spoke, my heart felt squeezed by the knowledge that when I was done, I would not see him again. "I am not setting myself this objective. I had different ones before I came here: fame—saving my ass—revenge—atonement. After I met Nagpa, I chose to achieve Emptiness. But you know that every objective is a mirage, and so is enlightenment. It either comes by itself, or it doesn't come at all. To me, it must come in the outside world—through learning *and* suffering. That's my path. I don't know whether I'll reach the full light in this life; the important thing is to move and be free of the objective. Your life has taught me this, Dorje—"

I looked at the mountain facing me, and it was as if a glass pane between us broke! The mountain stirred—

The brownish rocks, shrubs, cliffs were trembling and rippling; the mountain looked like a vertical sea covered with an ornamental cloth. It was breathing, causing clouds to flow, birds to fly, the sun to shine; and for the first time, I felt I was in complete harmony with all of them. I peered into the blue dusk, and one after another, I saw tableaux, quiet and peaceful as only dreams of childhood can be. I could not see the faces, but I knew I was amid those closest to me. We were seated on Grandma's porch, in the warm, foggy evening, with birds chirping in the dark, the smoke of a distant fire wafting about, and peonies, wet and redolent with evening dew. I knew that this evening would last forever. This joy of reunion, this peace—they were paradise.

Yet paradise is merely the other side of hell. Nagpa was expecting something else from me: a center from which you can neither fall nor rise. The one that's on the other side. Therefore, I was not ready to leave the rock. Not just yet.

96

DAY seven. Dawn. The cold, the ants, the wind, the pain, the numbness, the itching—nothing matters anymore. I have merged with the boulder—no, rather, I am a whole, the transparent infinite motionlessness, with all these disturbances and torments taking place inside.

Here he comes—me, I mean—Rudra, light, ideal, blessed.

Facing me on the pillows of the fog that laps against the rock like sea waves.

"You told Dorje you were free of your objective," he says. "You betrayed your dream of Shambala."

"Potentially, the everyday world is Shambala. A creative community of people loving one another."

"But what are you prepared to do to bring it closer? The world you want to save is one of action."

"If mankind has an objective, it consists of making an effort to realize the illusory nature of its objectives. Which are set by you. You are merely my superior ego program."

"No—I am your personality, and it consists of wonderful people, dear to you. . . . Here—"

THEY lined up, suspended in front of me: the black man, Schechter, Abby, Ayushi, Ruslanov, Dorje, and many others peeking from rear rows. A crowd spun out of clouds, each smiling at me and trying to shake my hand.

"We are your persona," they said; "we are its unique aspects. Develop them, make them more individual and bright; the more attention you pay to us, the greater success and satisfaction you will achieve. Isn't this what one lives for?"

"You're not here!" I pushed away their hands. "You're the components of my mind. You're forcing me to retire into my past or my future; you're not letting me stay in the here and now—the only place where life is."

"You're a nut! Without us, you're nothing!" the crowd clamored. The front rows stepped on the rock, forcing me closer to the edge. "You'll fall without us—you'll be gone!"

"I'm your desire, your ecstasy, your pleasure," pleaded one. "I'm your powerful intellect," went another. "I'm your will aimed at achievement—"

"You're not me!" I rose to face them. "You're the heads of the hydra of mammon! A bunch of equities brokers! To some you offer crude, naked profit; to others, spiritual values of idealism! But all the investments you have made for me bottomed out! I am more than a market: I already contain everything you can offer! I am—life! I don't need you! You—are—fired!"

The crowd erupted in a groan; then, trembling, they turned into horrible monsters. Breathing fire, mouthing curses, they kept pushing me to the edge.

I must not be afraid, I told myself. They do not exist. They're just the sum of my fears, generated by my ego—the furious deities of Tibetan Bardo!

"I can see through you!" I cried out. "You're a pathetic, greedy, cowardly junta! I am the king, who out of fear surrounded myself with you and turned my realm into a police state. You have turned life into hell! But I don't need the palace guards! If I am life, I am invulnerable!"

The crowd recoiled and transformed itself into a giant yak with a human face, distorted with fear. It was my face! It was Minotaur, the monster from Ruslanov's basement.

"You're my mind!" I exclaimed, trembling as the monster advanced towards me. "You lied to me; you told me I was in charge. Now I can see through your lies!"

The beast grew still, and then, growling with fear, dashed away from the rock—straight inside the mountain. I followed him into the dark stone maze.

When I cornered him, he was wheezing and moaning: an eternally hungry, greedy, scared creature. For a moment, I felt pity; I wanted to stroke it. But I overcame the impulse; he would bite off my hand, and my head and heart would follow.

The beast sensed my hesitation. He began pleading with me. "I can be useful," he murmured; "I have always been a good friend; all I wanted was to make Rudi happy. . . . If there is no 'I,' who will be happy then?"

"There will be happiness without 'I.' Without you. You cause nothing but misery and guilt."

"The guilt will go away, and warmth and love will return. If I am not around, where will they land? By killing me, you give up the good with the bad."

"You're the only one experiencing these dichotomies. I want to realize myself. And the light of realization will drive you away. With you gone, the good and the bad will be gone, too. The mask will fall, and there will be Emptiness."

Overcoming disgust and fear, I touched his—my—face,

distorted with fear, and kissed it. "Thank you for the good things you've done. Now I release you."

WHEN I opened my eyes, I could not recognize the world. The mountains hummed; the rocks eyed me, smiling. It was not just the sounds; everything I saw was in my head. I was the bubbling brook, the howling wind, the rustling leaves, the barking dogs faraway. I used to be barred from this by the thought that this merger would erase Rudi. But now I was the World. Emptiness. God. The only thing there is.

What about personal responsibility, a voice from my past whispered.

Simple: while you're alone, you can make mistakes. But if you are It, everything that is, how can It make a mistake? Who's there to judge? There's nothing outside you. As long as you stick to your tiny place in the world, anything can unbalance you. If you're the earth, nothing can.

I planted a kiss on the boulder and stood up. I could no longer fall.

I lifted my arms to the sky and broke off a piece: blue, with snowflakes of clouds. I kissed their fragile shapes and restored it to the sky.

I came up to the very edge—and I felt I could fly. My body was set on a ray of sunshine, and the ray could lift me and carry me wherever I wished.

Now I could leave. I stuck the diary in my pocket. I no longer needed it for self-analysis. The self was gone.

Book Five

SILENCE

97

RUDI was coming down the mountain. Actually, it was not Rudi, but a pillar of light confined in a six-foot body. Nothing could hurt the pillar, nor engage it in any relationship save for receiving its love. He was not walking, or floating—he simply *was*, the way light and thought are, down the path; the mossy rocks on the way greeted him, and he greeted them back.

He was a dot; he was a circle. Everything was in him, and he was everything: the bird that passed him (the vulture who had waited in vain for his death), its feathers, the wind under them, and the sky, where all of it took place.

He was stiller than the mountains and lighter than the air at high altitude. So delightful was this sensation of lightness and freedom that he wished he could expand his body along with his conscious; that he could send his body down to the *gompa* that had come into his view below. And, barely had he thought—rather, sensed—this feeling than he saw reflections of his body rush down the slope.

Then he saw the abbot. The lama in white sneakers stood at the bottom of the ladder and eyed Rudi approaching. He was silent, but Rudi knew what his look meant.

Nagpa awaits you.

RUDI entered the cave with the same dusty ray of sunshine and dancing bits of feathers.

He put together his hands to greet Nagpa, who was seated in the corner, opened his mouth—

And he realized he could not talk.

He had turned mute, too.

If someone asked him his name, he could not tell. His speech was gone with his "I." It was redundant. All was known, all was said at the same time without words.

Then the Rinpoche had to be mute! he realized. While the teacher is young, he needs words, the way a thin reed needs holes to sound a tune. But a wide Tibetan horn does not need the holes of words; it simply bellows from the roof of the lamasery as it transmits God's breath.

Nagpa transformed in Rudi's mind from a senile old-timer to a shining saint.

Rudi knelt in front of him. Facing each other, they smiled in silence. Their mouths did not stretch, nor did their eyes blink. Neither one had any strength: one because of his old age, the other from plain physical exhaustion. They just sat in silence, letting the quietude and the immobility of their bodies do the smiling.

DO you remember why you came here?

The question landed on Rudi's conscious like light lands on the surface of water.

Yes. He who has really returned to himself must return to people. To reinforce wakefulness, one must return to those asleep. I must know the countermantra.

Listen . . .

Rudi closed his eyes. The time passed by. But the surface of his mind remained clear, reflecting nothing. He opened his eyes to make sure the lama was awake. Nagpa was still looking at him and smiling. For an instant, Rudi had an inkling of fear: he'd failed—

And then a dazzling guess, still not fully realized, but already piercing him with delight, burst in:

THE COUNTERMANTRA *IS* SILENCE!

Perhaps Yuin had failed to find the sound of the countermantra in Nagpa's mind with Ruslanov's method! There was no sound! He must have been bluffing when he bragged he could cancel his plan; he feared this irreversibility and thus sought support from his prisoner—yet he was also afraid Rudi would get to Nagpa and discover the countermantra. Hence the pursuit . . . But he did not know that the countermantra was silence.

That meant . . . Rudi had encountered the answer many times without recognizing it. Aboard the plane to Moscow, coming down from the drug Martin had injected, didn't he plead: "What are you doing to me, God?" And the answer was, "Nothing."

The answer had always been there.

The silence that follows the question was the answer.

But how was he to employ it?

According to Schechter, Creation will stop when the Creator falls silent—and nothing else! Most earthly troubles stem from attempts to counter evil with countermeasures which eventually turn to evil, too. No: one must simply refrain from doing evil. The absence of evil is the good.

Instead of the mantra, they should simply air silence. When people fail to hear what they are used to, they will be tossed back inside themselves. And the mind of the earth, which is merely a reflection of those who inhabit it, will be tossed back, too. The ice will not get its last—critical—vibration . . . and the process will be stopped.

Could it be so heavenly simple?

Wide-eyed, Rudi stared at the old man. At the same instant, it was as if a seismic shift had taken place in Nagpa's face: the mini-Himalayas of brown wrinkles came together, the black maw of his mouth fell open, the eyes squeezed—and they all began to tremble. Nagpa was laughing. . . .

THERE was no sound, yet happy humming filled the cave and the whole mountain. The lama was a clapper inside a giant bell, and the silent ringing made the world grow.

Schechter had had the same laughter, when he was leaning near the fireplace; this was the smile on the dead faces of Dorje and Ayushi. This smile, this laughter had pursued Rudy everywhere. Somewhere deep inside, he was disturbed by the inexplicability of this laughter, by the feeling that this laughter constitutes the mystery of the mantra, that to understand it is to understand life itself.

Now, the blissful smile flooded him, and laughter entered him.

Rudi laughed through his tears. All his losses and suffering flashed in front of him, as he tried to laugh his pain out of himself. He wept as he crawled across the floor, rubbing his bloody tears, wheezing, and laughing nonstop. And his laughter grew lighter with each second, until he became still at the old man's feet.

Nagpa was dead.

98

RUDI was singing without opening his mouth. He solemnly proceeded down the steps to the jeep, where Martin was waiting.

His childhood was back. Every moment, every step were awash in new sensations, new moves in new games. Like most adults, he had reconciled himself to the knowledge that his childhood was not coming back, that he was doomed to spend the rest of his days in the desert of mundane cares, where every man desperately picks at the rocky soil with a toy sandbox shovel of sex and drugs in order to dig out tiny wells of freedom. Now his childhood was back: without effort, it came back magically, whispering: I've always been there, I've always been waiting. . . .

HE had descended the mountain in the company of Gwen. They danced together down the winding path, and at every turn they were joined by more and more couples, until the whole of mankind seemed to join them in this endless dance, their throngs flooding the slopes.

We will walk on the waters of the Flood, he told himself. We shall not drown: we have severed the ties to the burden of our egos.

RIVERS was still wearing Yuin's military tunic, now clean and pressed and with an Indian flower garland over it. The bevy of giggling local girls around him added to the evidence that the detective had done some serious local canvassing.

"Motherfu—what's going on with you? Your hair—it's ablaze!"

"I have seen Emptiness, Martin."

"I bet. You don't eat for seven days, you see a lot of things. So, what does it look like?"

"What does God look like?"

Taken aback, Martin stared into space.

"DID you find out?" A sour-looking man in a white shirt and a tie called from the jeep.

"Security guy from the embassy," Martin explained quietly.

"Yes," Rudi shouted back; "but I can't tell you!"

"Why?"

"Because it's silence!" he declared enthusiastically, and then whispered to Martin, "I swear it is."

AFTER a prolonged negotiation, Rivers persuaded the embassy officer to call a helicopter to take them directly to the New York flight. Their new IDs could be delivered there, too.

The official shrugged, his expression still dour. "We can get you aboard. The FBI will meet you. Surely you know your friend here is on the Most Wanted list."

"I *was* wanted!" Rudi confirmed, bursting with joy. "But I've been found!"

The officer glanced at him in bewilderment, slammed the door shut, and picked up his portable radio.

"How about if I go back alone," Martin suggested in a whisper. "I can gather evidence by myself. I got Tune Ra, I got Larry. . . . They may throw you in jail, you know."

"Not a chance." Rudi hugged Martin. "I have already released myself from Rating. There's no going back."

THE abbot saw Rudi and Martin to the helicopter. They were about to board, when above, at the entrance to the *gompa,* Rudi saw a woman dressed in white. He froze— Margi?

The woman stepped uncertainly and stumbled, supporting herself on a monk's arm. It was Nyima. She waved farewell

and was led back to the cave. A monk adjusted her bandages. At the bottom of the hill, a group of monks carried
out two bodies wrapped in purple robes.

"Nagpa and Dorje will be cremated together," the abbot
said.

"No Bardo reading for Nagpa?"

"He who needed no mind needs no guide through its
mazes."

They fell silent, conceding the air to the roar of the helicopter's engines.

From aboard, Rudi shouted to the abbot, "Who did he
pass the mantras to?"

"Dorje. He was Nagpa's student."

"This means—" But the helicopter was already gaining
altitude.

This meant Nagpa had been passing secret mantras to his
student when both were seized by the Chinese. Perhaps
Dorje had known the countermantra all along! But he remained silent.

Of course he did—it is *silence!* Rudi thought, peering at
the mountains growing smaller in the distance. *He could not
pass it along to me: I had to gain silence myself, whether
I reached Nagpa or not.*

"Look!" Martin pointed at white smoke wafting up from
the *gompa.*

The bodies of the teacher and his student—the last two
who knew secret Bon mantras—were being cremated together. The smoke from the fire looked like a *kato,* a silk
scarf for an offering, waving good-bye to them in the helicopter—a transmission line evaporating in the sky.

99

THE sky over the Atlantic was covered with clouds: low, dense, dark gray with yellow streaks, like greasy smoke from a funeral pyre. Then, suddenly, a clearing appeared—a blue window of hope, expanded by the wind.

Soon, the barnacle-like coastline showed up.

One has to believe that a mollusk can change the ocean if it produces a perfect sound, Rudi thought. If the air is polluted with cacophony, then so is consciousness—and nature itself. The only correct sound to remove this pollution is that of silence.

ON the screen in the plane cabin, CNN ran images of blown-up buildings. Another series of terrorist attacks, the anchorman said gravely. Rudi had not seen CNN since his "debates" at Yuin's office. Now he no longer saw these disasters as chaos and spreading tumors—now it seemed like the disease's final spasm, the darkest hour before the dawn.

It's a blank screen, Yuin used to say; it's your karma that feeds you the images. But then the entire civilization was a blank screen, and it was Yuin's karma that fed the general the images of nothing but rotten garbage. Yuin was fighting his own consciousness, rather than objective reality.

Now, clumsily holding the stem of a wineglass in his calloused fingers, Rudi was deeply appreciative of civilization. His immediate past seemed like a big cloud of stench and hunger and cold: wearing the same clothes around the clock, using whatever was at hand for toilet paper, spreading grease on your face, eating half-raw meat with pieces of wool stuck in it. Civilization freed you from the quest of food and shelter and allowed you to focus on important things—on love. In order to keep civilization on an even keel, one had to balance one's own mind properly first.

EARLIER, gently stepping over the snoring Martin, a glass of Chivas in his hand, Rudi visited the bathroom, where he saw himself in the mirror: a savage, hard-skinned face with sunken eyes that seemed to belong to someone else. He looked away, feeling nothing. There was no point in studying himself in the mirror: what was around him reflected him more precisely. Earlier, dying on the windswept Himalayan plateaux, he had realized that weather, like everything else, was a mere reflection of what was inside him. He had tried to force his life to be something it was not; if remorse about these misguided efforts could end a snowstorm, it could clear up other horizons as well.

There is no earth or air, no Europe or America, Rudi thought, caressing a tiny cake of airline soap, a concentrated quest for purity; there is only Thought, whose waves lap against both the sea and the shore. Its undulations cause tsunamis and earthquakes; its plans and yearnings toss us around, hurting those around us. But a man can master this element; he can pacify his own waves and merge them with the ocean of others.

THE moment the wheels touched the ground, the sounds of Tune Ra's rave melody roared through the plane. In another hour and fifteen minutes, the announcer said excitedly, Mr. Tune Ra's last appearance this season will come to you live from DeoMorte!

"Shit," Martin muttered, awakening. "We still have to go through the bullshit with the feds at the airport."

Rudi smiled. "Why worry when we can pray? If you live in eternity, how can you be late?"

Martin groaned and gulped down the remaining Scotch.

YET no one met them at the gate.

Martin chortled. "Looks like the government, all right. The state doesn't tell the feds dick. But without papers, they'll get our asses at the passport control." He looked around. "Time to surrender. The way we look now, we'll pass for a couple of refugees from Balkan Desh. I used to know a cop who worked in that office . . . Hey, mister!" He grabbed a Customs officer by the arm. "We refugees—America, freedom, yes?"

All the blue plastic chairs in the spacious waiting room behind the passport checkpoint were taken. The tired, poor masses huddled anxiously, watching with bated breath the exchange at the front desk, where a group of agents and interpreters were holding the interviews. A burly, gum-chewing cop in a white shirt, snug against his impressive belly, guarded the exit, making sure that no seeker of American freedom could grab it without papers. His eyes met Rivers's, with a frown recorded his Chinese tunic, and moved on to Rudi's. The latter eyed the cop with a smile. The cop's face showed surprise; then his handlebar mustache trembled, and his face froze into a faint half-smile. His gaze grew distant; he seemed to be looking at Rudi, but his mind was clearly in a quiet, blissful place.

Touching Martin's knee, Rudi rose and headed for the door, his smile fixed on the cop's eyes. Holding his breath, Rivers followed.

"Motherfucker!" Martin exhaled when they had left the glass doors behind. "You picked it from Nagpa in the cave?"

Rudi glowed. "We always could see the good in one another. We just forgot about it."

HALF an hour later, their cab was hopelessly stuck in a jam downtown. Listening to Rivers's curses—he wished he had his squad car with a siren—Rudi thought how, before the seven days on the mountain, his life had been one exhausting effort to break fast out of one hopeless jam or another. Only now he was on a five-lane highway.

THEY reached DeoMorte ten minutes before the program was to go on the air. Once again, the darkness was alive with the crowd, radiating the heat of bodies pressed together and bubbling with their voices. And, as usual, the bluish smoke of grass hovered above.

No time for Buddhist stuff, Martin warned Rudi, and pro-

ceeded to kick and smash the internal organs of a couple of
hapless guards.

The backstage room was long and semidark, with arched
ceilings left over from the Catholic church that the club had
once been. Now it was furnished Tibetan-style, with low
settees and pillows, with incense wafting through the air and
quiet muttering in the corner. It was just like Johang, Rudi
thought, but for the knobs of recording equipment gleaming
in the dark along the wall.

The room seemed empty. It took Rudi a few moments
before he noticed a man seated in the back under a large
mandala embroidered with gold.

The friends approached quietly.

TUNE Ra was meditating, his eyes closed as he murmured
mantras—rather, *the* mantra. He had changed, perhaps in
the course of preparing for his departure for the ashram: his
long hair and rings were gone. He was indistinguishable
from a lama.

When they came close, he opened his eyes abruptly. Rudi
shivered: the DJ's face was drawn, and his shaven skull,
hollow cheeks, and widened eyes made him reminiscent of
Yuin.

Tune did not seem surprised.

He nodded at Martin's tunic. "The teacher shed his
clothes. He knew he was not coming into the Ark. But why
did he send you? I have already received a message on the
wind. . . ."

Something about his voice and expression, spiritual yet
arrogant, seemed painfully familiar.

"You don't recognize me?" Rudi stepped up.

With a frown, the DJ glanced at him and smiled condescendingly. "A new acolyte?"

"Yes. But not Yuin's." Rudi realized whom the DJ made
him think of: that was what Rudi himself might have looked
like when he was explaining his project to Gwen that night
at Columbia. "I changed, too—Rating will do it for you.
Remember I asked you what the mantra meant? Nothing,
you said. You thought you told me a smart lie, but in a way

it was the truth. Nothing is what your chanting will come to. Nothing means silence."

"Aha." Tune smirked. "Mara's last arrows . . . And what exactly is this silence of yours?"

"This silence means your show's canceled," Martin said. His expression showed that he welcomed a chance to cut to the chase. "You're under arrest. Get your ass—"

"The teacher said that the obscene banality of existence would be clinging to life to the very end. And what can be more obscene than a crook trying to pass himself off as a cop." Tune glanced at his watch, and, cracking his knuckles, rose to his feet. "Sorry, my man, I can't see your badge. No warrant either. Gotta go."

"I'VE got a badge for you."

Detective Tarakis, chuckling, stood behind them.

Martin was taken aback. "What are you doing here? You didn't believe—"

"Got some new evidence on this superstar here." Tarakis held up his NYPD badge.

In an instant, Tune twisted Tarakis's arm. His right knee went into Tarakis's stomach, while he kicked Martin in the groin with the left foot and, as an afterthought, kicked Rudi in the chin with his right foot.

Tune grabbed the mike and reached for the On Air button.

Martin grabbed his torso and sacked him.

With a groan, Tune started on the mantra.

"Shut him up!" Rudi cried out.

"Easier to just crack his head." Martin placed Tune in an armlock and tossed the mike aside.

Holding his stomach, Tarakis limped over to handcuff the DJ.

"What are the charges?" Tune wheezed out as Martin relaxed the lock.

"The feds will get the real stuff. For now, it's resisting arrest and distributing controlled substances." With a moan, Tarakis pulled the new perp to his feet. "You're part owner of the club. Can't breathe here for all the dope."

*   *   *

MARTIN whispered to Tarakis: "Make sure the feds don't grab Rudi while we get the evidence."

"They won't," Tarakis said mysteriously as he prodded the DJ to the exit.

"People don't want to be free!" Tune clanged his handcuffs. "Once again, they've chosen suffering."

A voice came on the intercom: "You okay, man? We're going live on the count of three. Then you're going onstage."

"Your turn, Mr. World DJ." Martin slapped Rudi on the back.

"I'm ready," Rudi said into the mike quietly and put on the headset.

"One!" went the amplified voice over the crowd. "Two! Three!"

The club came to a standstill, expecting the first note of the mantra.

BUT Rudi was silent. Silence filled the airwaves.

The only sound was that of the blood circulating through his ears. The crowd remained standing. For the first time, they were discovering the source of music inside, rather than outside: the humming of the common genes, the oratorio of the cells of the universe, the white noise of Being that dissolved all the borders between them.

IOO

SHE was walking down the hall. She was wearing a hospital robe, and the walk was not really hers, crooked and limping. A woman in white was supporting her arm.

Rudi recognized her right away and froze, struck by a sense of déjà vu. Then he ran to meet her, and the floor felt soft and treacherous, like snow on the mountain slope.

"Gwen!"

The nurse turned back first.

"Varya?!"

THE Russian girl's face, happy and amazed at the same time; Martin's frown; the severe faces of other nurses—all of these vanished. Once again, just like in Nagpa's cave, he lost his voice. Too excited to breathe, he was looking in Gwen's eyes—the velvety black shells with a tiny pearl of a stye in one of them. He peered at the night sky through binoculars, but, instead of isolated stars, he saw nothing but solid shining.

"You've lost weight," she said quietly.

"I dropped what I did not need." His voice was throaty and stuttering.

"Did you find what you were looking for?"

"Yes. I found what I had fled from."

She reached for him, and stumbled. He caught her in his arms, and, once again, froze as he felt her cast through the pajamas. His entire being was crashing into smithereens of unbearable pain and happiness.

AT her bedside, he held her hand, white and thin. She was too weak to talk, and all he heard was Varya's voice, coming to him through a sea of static, as if he were calling from Lhasa. Gwen closed her eyes, and it was only the light pressure of her fingers that told him she heard him. This touch, ever so light, was like a hand on his throat, sending a hot wave through his chest and up to his eyes.

ON the night when Rudi dashed to the lab after Ruslanov's call, Varya went out for a walk, too nervous to sleep. That saved her life.

She saw a group of men pouring out of a black jeep outside their building. Moments after they entered, the lights went on in their apartment.

She ran off and called a man whose telephone number she knew by heart.

"He used to work for my dad, so I was in love with him—just like with Rudi," she said simply as she adjusted Gwen's blanket.

Igor was a student of Ruslanov's who had put the lab secrets to commercial use, and later helped Yuin break up Nagpa's secrets.

But here were the workings of a mysterious Russian soul. Although Varya did not know what was happening, she sensed the worst, and the fear in her voice triggered an inexplicable reversal in Igor's conscience. He hopped into his car and drove to pick Varya up. He found out that her adoptive parents were dead, "the Yank" was on the lam— and, as he comforted Varya, he fell in love with her all over again.

Igor grabbed Varya—and flew with her to America.

IN New York, they went looking for Martin, whom Varya knew to be a friend of Ruslanov's. But Martin was already gone, they were told by his partner, Tarakis. Amazingly, hours of investigating Rudi had failed to accomplish what a few minutes with a pretty Russian girl, disconsolate with grief, did. Tarakis had come out an ardent believer in Ruslanov's theories.

Igor obtained permission to conduct experiments at a clinic in New Jersey. His first priority was to write suggestions for Gwen, fresh out of her coma but still immobile, and for Tarakis's ulcer and depression.

The suggestions worked, which finally convinced Tarakis of Rudi's innocence and set him on Tune Ra's trail.

Gwen was improving, too. Although she was still largely unconscious, her subconscious was receptive to the suggestions that reached her through headphones. When she finally regained her senses, it was regarded a miracle; her case was to be presented at a scientific conference. Soon, she was able to talk, and she immediately told the police that Rudi was innocent.

GWEN was already asleep, lulled by Varya's melodic voice, but Rudi could not let go of her wrist.

Martin had to tap him on the shoulder. "We've got to go see Larry. You'll have time to get mushy later."

*   *   *

NOTHING seemed to have changed in Schechter Junior's lab: piles of diagrams and tables on the floor, plastic globes and items of clothing scattered around, and a sink filled with dishes. Apparently, Larry had spent the last few weeks indoors, preparing for the Flood.

He seemed unsurprised to see them.

"The ice stress is waning!" he exclaimed the moment he saw them, and went back to peer into the computer screen. "Looks like the Flood has been canceled, my dear student! The chaos theory works: one day the universe is all ice and fire, the next day it's butter and cheese!"

"It's not chaos," Rudi said calmly. "It's the mantra."

LARRY listened to their story impatiently, spilling the coffee he offered them, and lighting up cigarettes off unfinished ones. Finally he stuck one in his coffee cup and cried out:

"Of course it is silence! I could have guessed! Counterphase! It's the basic strength of materials!" He went through a pile, looking for a diagram. "If you stop at the elastic limit and start reducing the pressure, the material will revert to the original condition, minus plastic deformities."

"True," Rudi said, smiling. "This material is the consciousness of mankind. But it will become different at the end."

"You're sure about that?" Martin winced.

"One bead can speak for all the beads."

"You know," Larry said shyly, "I went over some of my father's lectures. Even tried meditating. I couldn't get into a trance, of course—all sorts of thoughts got into my head—though some of them were quite funny—"

Rudi caught his breath. Larry painfully resembled his father as he peered over the pages on the floor.

"See, the switch of the poles is necessary and fair. Africa will grow cold, Alaska will be the new Riviera. . . . Continents go through reincarnations as well, and the earth will exist until each of them has undergone the same conditions as others did."

"Yuin would agree," Rudi remarked. "But he who can live the lives of others inside himself does not need a change in poles. Perfect compassion puts an end to suffering."

"Enough talk." Martin scooped up a pile of printouts. "You can go on philosophizing at the FBI as you give testimony. Keep in mind that we're all witnesses."

"We have never been anything more than that," Rudi said. "We just forgot about it and deemed ourselves judges."

EPILOGUE

ON a February day, cold and brittle like a dawn in the mountains, Rudi was waiting for Gwen outside Columbia University's Lowe Library. He wondered about the normalcy their lives had acquired in the year since he came back. He was working on his doctorate; Gwen was working on her degree, too, and working at a publishing house, where Rudi's Himalayan diary was about to come out.

Gwen left the building and descended the steps, supporting herself with a cane. Rudi ran up the stairs to help her. Since she'd become pregnant, he'd worried about her nonstop.

"We won't be able to dance here again," she said, nodding down the steps. "At least, not for quite a while. Are you getting tired of walking me?"

"You're the one who's walking me. It's harder to overcome your own self than a staircase—or a mountain."

When they reached the campus exit, she held on to the wrought-iron gate to rest. "This is where you asked me who was singing the mantra," she recalled. "By the way, the editor asked me to find out: what was the argument that Yuin wanted to hear from you?"

"I don't know. Perhaps this: His motivation consisted in decoding the meaning, and the final result would be perceiving the author's persona."

"Too wordy for one black button."

"Actually, the question about the argument came not from Yuin, but from my Minotaur—whom I killed. Then, what was left was . . . silence. Perhaps that's the black button. Then the argument *was* the countermantra! And that's why Yuin did not pronounce the argument when he was dying. And he was right: the argument was in the diary—the lacunae. What he expected of me was *conscious silence*. That was the black button that would cancel his plans. He was afraid of this absurd silence that would destroy all mental constructs. He wanted to hear it from someone else *like* him—that was me."

Gwen looked at him closely. "Was or is?"

Rudi pondered. "Yuin lived in time," he said finally. "Which has a beginning and an end, a Flood and a Renaissance—a round dial. Nagpa was in the center of the circle, where there's no Flood, no beginning or end. That's where I wanted to be."

"Life has time. It also has good and evil."

"Life is God. In Him—I mean, Him or Her—there's no time, no good or evil. Suffering and pleasure are experienced only by our ego—our mind. Only mind is tied by its karma. But it changes; it's not real. Real, clear consciousness is beyond changes, beyond karma, beyond good and evil. It is an echo of silence. Neither good nor bad. It is Yahweh—the Being."

IN Riverside Park, Gwen sat on a bench and opened her notebook to write some things down. The editor was trying to make the book more commercial, but Rudi was completely immersed in his doctoral thesis, where, among other things, he drew parallels between Judaism and Hinayana.

Gwen was more than a little worried about her husband's indifference to the publication: his grant was not large, and the little money they had made from their magazine stories was gone. Now there was a child coming. . . .

The doctors told her that the hip would heal soon and have no effect on childbirth and that the embryo was developing normally. Both the change in her husband and the unexpectedness of the good fortune that befell her ("a fortunate fall," she joked) still elicited quiet amazement in her. Yet she could not help being worried about her health—money—the future. No matter what, the old Rudi was not quite dead; he was still hoping to bluff his way through problems and was not paying quite enough attention to the same Mother Earth about whom he waxed poetic in his diary. She told him that perhaps he should implement the Judaic part of his doctorate and treat the Mother—things practical, that is—with proper devotion. He joked her off.

"The editor wants this to be authentic," she told him. "You need to check all the Tibetan names. You mix them up with Sanskrit ones, which are no longer being used in Tibet, he said. He knows: he edited the memoir of the Dalai Lama's masseur."

"The names get in the way." Rudi smiled. "Tell him to delete them all."

She shook her head. "He also wants to know how you intend to finish the book. The diary stops on that meditation rock."

"I don't know." He shrugged. "We already know: there can be no end. One thing I understood in Tibet: the best things—like the end of a snowstorm—happen by themselves. You can't cause a miracle. Any plan is violence committed by the part towards the whole."

She sighed. "He wants less philosophy—and more details about our, well, personal life."

He understood her pause. "You should write your own book. It will be more interesting than mine."

"Yeah, right. You had adventures. I was in a coma."

"You will write what you saw in your dreams. What you told me."

She fell silent, as if retreating into herself. Then she re-surfaced and consulted her notebook. "The beads that Dorje turned into a diamond necklace—did he do that through hypnosis or transmutation? It's not clear—"

"Both!" Rudi locked his hands together. "You can explain it by means of suggestion, aimed not just at the people around you, but at the beads as well. He forced the bone beads to believe that they were diamonds; and so they became! That is, he forced this belief on one bead. I remember him kissing it and holding it to his forehead. His love made the bead remember that it was made of the same substance as he; that it was unrealized God. Dorje did not breathe his energy into it, but he inspired it with this thought. And the bead made an evolutionary leap by becoming harder and shinier. That's why the bones of the saints don't rot!"

"Déjà vu." Gwen poked at a chestnut with her stick. "Looks like a bead, too. This is the same alley where you strolled with the professor, right? He said something about chestnuts, didn't he?"

"Yes. If one rises above itself—that is, immerses into itself to the end—it will transfigure the rest. It's Indra's necklace: one reflects all, all reflect one. Same with mankind: it is enough that one person returns to his true nature, to God-Emptiness, for all the other beads to begin to change. If we become the denizens of Shambala in New York, this city will gradually become a Shambala."

"With all the spokes that hold my bones together, maybe I'm really a bead that God first dropped and then put on a string." Gwen lifted her sleeve to stroke the professor's beads. Rudi had given her the beads as a present when she left the hospital. "But for me, they're the beads of Virgin Mary. I remain a Christian."

"What's the difference?"

"Buddhism has no place for the love of Christ."

"Christ is an attribute of Emptiness: its love."

THEY strolled along the Hudson, with Gwen pausing to rest from time to time.

"Is this where you wanted to jump when Tarakis interrogated you?" She nodded at the brownish water lapping at the bank.

"I was impatient. There's no getting away from it."

She instinctively touched her stomach. "Are you saying that the moment when the ice did not move was just a pause? Was it just *a few moments of silence* before apocalypse? The Flood can happen at any time, right?"

"But it will not flood our consciousness—nor the baby's." He stroked her stomach. "All it means is that we are diving in one place and resurfacing at a different one. Whether we'll be happy there depends on our minds. Which we can change at any time, even an instant before the Flood. It's really a beautiful notion, this Ice Sword of Damocles:

it means we love every instant without trying to cling to it."

"Then let those in Judea flee for the mountains," she quoted. "Perhaps we should flee in advance—at least for the sake of our child?"

Gwen thought of Varya, with whom she had developed a sisterly relationship. Igor had found a job in Colorado, and he and Varya had settled in a huge ranch house not far from Ayushi's old ashram. Varya could not get enough of the area; she called it "God-saved," and was happy she would be bringing up her future children there. She was pregnant, too, and had already decided to call the baby Oleg, after Ruslanov, about whom she often cried. Gwen comforted her and rejoiced over their happiness, yet sometimes was ashamed to feel a tinge of envy: the supposedly impractical Russians—according to the novels she had studied—had turned out to be far more practical-minded than her own family.

"That was Yuin's plan," Rudi said, taking her mind off her anxieties. "And you know how he ended up. No, we won't flee. There is no division between this world and the next one; the world is one. Wherever we and our children are, we are always in heaven—or never and nowhere."

Gwen sighed. By accident, she tore off an orange thread, one of many that held the beads together, and tossed it into the water. "All right, Father. Let's give ourselves to the flow. Don't look at me like that: you'll always be a missionary—not a scientist. What about this?" She held up the orange threads. "Does it stand for something, too?"

"Maybe the beginning of the new cycle—the new generation." He put his arms around her and whispered in her ear, "If you want to save yourself in the mountains, we can do that. I get the rest of the advance, and we go to Tibet. Do you remember I told you there was a place where I actually saw you? Where the young sherpa vanished? With the scent of the ocean?"

He was interrupted by the ringing of the phone in Gwen's pocket.

She listened. "For you. The Devil's Works Department."

*   *   *

IT was Martin, now in charge of the FBI's psy-ops section. "Listen, if you want to go back to the Snowland, I can offer you a bargain of a lifetime. Uncle Sam will pay all expenses."

"How did you know?" Rudi murmured. "Are you bugging me?"

"Message on the wind, old buddy. Come on over. We got a little problem here."

Pensively, Rudi pushed the End button and returned the phone to Gwen.

"What's going on? Are you going somewhere?"

He told her.

"Oh, God." After a pause, she shrugged. "Sure—it's your world, with mountains and tents. You're a nomad."

He embraced her again. "Every nomad dreams of a tent. You are my tent in the empty plateau. We'll go together."

AS they strolled in the bright spring sun, Rudi glanced at the silhouettes of their shadows. For a moment, they looked like a stocky Yuin and a lama leaning on a cane.

Yuin and Nagpa—they, too, are part of our family, he thought. Motion and rest. Sound and silence. Escaping to freedom and accepting one's lot wherever you are. Rage and tenderness. Laughter and compassion. Hello and good-bye. Always at the same time. Never an *or*. Always an *and*.

Dmitry Radyshevsky is the former New York bureau chief of the *Moscow News,* and the author of *Moscow Undercover Special,* a bestseller in his native Russia. He currently lives in Israel.